SHADOWS OF THE SWORD

✛

"CONTROLLING THE SWORD" by Kristine Kathryn Rusch: The ancestral sword drew generations of children to their destiny—but forever cursed all who were unworthy of its touch.

✛

"LASSORIO" by Eric Lustbader: The sullen warlord Lassorio ruled a dark, diminished Camelot—until the night a snow fox led him to a place of magic, horror...and love.

✛

"THE GOD-SWORD" by Diana L. Paxson: Centuries before the time of Arthur, a Swordbearer and his Druid lover must join the battle for the soul of ancient Britannia.

✛

"SILVER, STONE, AND STEEL" by Judith Tarr: Joseph of Arimathea carried a Mystery to the world's end—and discovered his place in an eternal dream of wizards, gods, goddesses, and blood.

✛

"SWORD PRACTICE" by Jody Lynn Nye: The young boy-king must discover: Does Arthur rule the sword—or does Excalibur rule the king?

✛

"GOLDIE, LOX, AND THE THREE EXCALIBEARERS" by Esther M. Friesner: What're *you* starin' at? Even Merlin's *verklempt* when the destined Swordbearer for the age turns out to be Brooklyn's Lady of the Lox—teen deli waitress Goldie Berman! *Who knew?*

✛

EXCALIBUR

EDITED BY
RICHARD GILLIAM, MARTIN H. GREENBERG,
AND **EDWARD E. KRAMER**

ASPECT

WARNER BOOKS

A Time Warner Company

⬤ Warner Books, Inc., 1271 Avenue of the Americas, New York, NY 10020

Aspect is a trademark of Warner Books, Inc.

Printed in the United States of America

First Printing: May 1995

10 9 8 7 6 5 4 3 2 1

Library of Congress Cataloging-in-Publication Data

Excalibur / edited by Richard Gilliam, Martin H. Greenberg, and Edward E. Kramer.
    p. cm.
  ISBN 0-446-67084-7
  1. Arthurian romances—Adaptations. 2. Knights and knighthood—Fiction. 3. Historical fiction, American. 4. Fantastic fiction, American. 5. Arthur, King—Fiction. I. Gilliam, Richard. II. Greenberg, Martin Harry. III. Kramer, Edward E.
PS648.A78E95 1995
813'.087660837—dc20   94-24139
                                                   CIP

Cover illustration by Paul Youll
Cover lettering by Carl Dellacroce
Cover design by Don Puckey
Book design by H. Roberts

Contents

The Question of the Sword

JANE YOLEN

Answer: Excalibur.
What is the question?

We could argue steel, the weight
of the blade, the iron strips
tempered in water, in wine, in blood,
in fire, in the hammering
in the dark, brooding smithies.

We could argue wars, the weight
of souls, the confluence of river sides
where waves wap in waters wan,
where hands rise up above the mere
to snatch victory in the silver light.

But I'd rather argue a man's own weight,
the thrust of my loins, the thickened blade,
the straight-edge of permission,
my quillion thighs

for bringing life,
for the ending of it:
blade, strip, steel,
and the pattern of the wave.

The God-Sword

DIANA L. PAXSON

hey rode out across the moor just as dusk was falling, thirteen men, sitting their tough little ponies as easily as they had when they served with the Sarmatian Numeri, the best auxiliary cavalry Britannia could field. Every man of them had put in his twenty years with the Legions before retiring to the vicus below the fort at Bremetennacum. And yet, thought Hamytz-sar as he moved into the center of the formation, though he had been born and bred here, he did not belong to this land.

With him the line of the Sword-bearers who had accompanied the Iazyges warriors that the Romans had settled in Britannia came to an end. The last of Hamytz's sons had died in Gallia as rival generals battled for the imperial diadem. He felt the baldric that held the familiar weight of the Sword across his back slip, and hitched it forward. Who would carry it when his arm failed? Who would call the spirits when his voice was still? Or would it matter? Would anything matter if Rome's might failed and the wild tribes came flooding in?

They breasted the rise, and for a moment the priest could

see the lay of the land—dim, heather-clad undulations of hillside with trees springing up wherever there was a little protection from the wind. Low clouds were rolling in from the western sea; there would likely be rain by morning. That would not matter; these men whose ancestors had roamed the steppes had a homing sense as acute as that of their ponies. They did not even need to see the stars. Hamytz looked up—in the north country one was always most conscious of the great sweep of the sky—this evening it was strewn with banners of fading flame like a dead battlefield.

Nor would the Painted People be bothered by a little rain, he thought then. They had never accepted the barrier that the emperor Hadrian had thrown across the North to stop their raiding, and now that the Legions had been ordered back across the Narrow Sea, only the veterans, settled on farmsteads near the forts where once they had served, stood between them and the rich lands of the South. Once Britannia had lain secure beneath the peace of Rome, but Rome herself was beleaguered. Without men to man it, the Wall was no more than an inconvenience. Still, things had been quiet for the past moon. There was no reason, Hamytz told himself sternly, to think it might be this night that they would come.

The Dragon pennant fluttered on its pole, gold thread glinting in the last of the light, then sagged again as the riders plunged down a winding watercourse, out of the wind. The ponies' hooves rang on stone; the bones of earth were very near the surface here. Hamytz straightened, a familiar tension beginning to build within him, and it seemed to him that the Sword grew heavier, as if it were already beginning to draw down power.

The pace quickened. The ponies knew that soon they would be able to graze on the dry grass in the hollow. The cliff face above it was a featureless blur in the half-light. Hamytz could barely make out the humped shape of the offering stone.

Uryzmag, in the lead, gave a soft command. As one the horses came to a halt in a semicircle. Hamytz dismounted, wincing a little as his joints complained, and his horse was led away. Ruddy light glinted suddenly as torches were lit and set into the ground. He heard an unhappy bleating as the bound goat was lifted from Arvgad's saddle and laid down.

Silence fell, and after a moment Hamytz realized they were all watching him. He unpinned his cloak and laid it aside. Beneath it, like the rest of them, he wore a warshirt made in the traditional way with overlapping scales carved from the hooves of mares. And like theirs, his spangenhelm was worn with service and lovingly burnished. But fixed to its crest was a wolf's tail, to which were fastened amulets in the shapes of spearheads and tiny swords that chimed and clattered as he moved.

The other men grouped themselves around him. With fingers grown stiff from the damp air Hamytz fumbled with the firepot and blew on the coal within until it glowed. A pinch from the bag of sacred herbs sent sweet smoke swirling past him. He took a deep breath and felt his perceptions begin to alter, simultaneously more detached from ordinary things and more profoundly aware. His knuckle joints no longer hurt, but he could hear each separate breath from the men around him, and the cry of an owl above the crag, and more faintly, the voice of the boy as he quieted the grazing mares.

He could feel, as vividly as he sensed any of the other warriors, the presence of the Sword.

He picked up the pot of smoking herbs and moved around the circle, letting each man wash his hands in the purifying smoke and breathe it in. The dull drumming of lance-butts striking the earth in unison started behind him, and the men began chanting as they did before battle. Hamytz took a deep breath, feeling the familiar shift in his spirit.

Now he scarcely needed the torchlight, for each shrub and stone had its own glow. He could feel the power of the wolf that was the totem of his god rising within him, and the spirit of the red dragon that flew from their standard, answering, seeing it not as a wyrm but as his own people pictured it, with clawed legs, and wings.

He set down the pot and stood, bowed legs braced, facing the altar stone.

"I am Hamytz son of Hurtzast," he cried. "Servant of Batradz like my fathers before me, from generation to generation, since first we rode the Sea of Grass. I have fought many battles, my arm has struck down many—"

"It is the voice of the god we would hear, battle priest." Uryzmag interrupted him. "Bring forth the Sword that we may pray to him!"

"The Sword!" other voices echoed. "Show us the Sword!"

Hamytz nodded—it was always hard, in the first ecstatic rush as the power rose in him, to remember why he was here. He took a deep breath, and his skin pebbled in response to the energy around him. As he moved toward the rock formation below the crag, the Sword grew heavier; he staggered as he reached the stones. There was power there, too, from the blood that had been poured over them. With feet braced firmly, the priest reached behind his left shoulder and gripped the hilt, muscles still mighty after four decades under arms flexing as he drew it free.

He could feel it quiver in his hand, hot and cold at once. His pent breath came out in a grunt as the weapon wheeled upward, lightnings dancing around the circle as torchlight flashed from the blade. For a moment Hamytz savored its perfect balance. It would cleave flesh as easily as it cut the air; it trembled, lusting to smite the foe. But Hamytz had had many years to master the spurt of battle-fury that came when he drew that blade. It could be used, but not by him. The priest was its custodian only. Someday, legend told, a king who was worthy to wield it would be born.

The cleft was a black wound in the flat surface of the offering stone. Hamytz swung the blade downward, inserting it with the secret twist that would lock the blade in place, and felt the shock throughout his body as the power in the Sword was earthed in the rock below.

For a moment he swayed, then he stepped back, staring. Surely more than torchlight blazed from that bright blade!

"Behold the Sword of War!" he cried. "God-steel, star-steel, cast flaming down from heaven to bury itself in earth's womb. Spell-steel, forged by Kurdalagon, master of Chalybes' magic, sorcerer-smiths of our ancient homeland. Neither breaking nor bending, neither rusting nor tarnished, this immortal blade we honor!"

He bowed and from a dozen throats came a wordless ululation of praise. Uryzmag stood closest, holding the goat. Once drawn, the blade must be blooded. Usually, the sacrifice was some small animal, though there were stories that in time of great need the Iazyges had sometimes offered it the blood of men.

The hairs lifted on Hamytz's neck.

"Bright One, we call you—" he said hoarsely. "Behold, your weapon is waiting. Come down now and bless your sons, for the land is troubled and we have need!"

If possible, the Sword seemed to shine even more brightly, but the god was not yet present—Hamytz had not expected it. With an odd dancing step he began to move sunwise around the stone, directing a portion of his awareness to keep him steady on the rocky ground. When first he served the god, he had been easily distracted, but increasingly, as he grew older, the problem when the god-power took him was to retain contact with the ordinary world.

"Old wolf, gray wolf, I call you—" he whispered, "leader of wolves and power that binds them. Battle-craft you teach us, and the will to wield it. Come to us, hear us, come to us now!"

Heat pulsed in his solar plexus and he gasped, fighting for control. To give way to trance was unmanly. "Great Dragon, ruler of the skies, fly to us. Your word is justice; your roar brings victory! Come to us—" He could not finish, but the others took up the refrain. "You are the center," he whispered, "the axis of the world, the linchpin of heaven—"

Hamytz had ceased to move. Unwilled, his body was stiffening, his arms rising. Panic shuddered through him—or was it desire? The god-power had never been so strong before. But it was the Sword that must be its channel. To be possessed by this ecstasy was the way of the kam, not the warrior.

"Batradz!" Hamytz cried, his body arching in invocation. Power answered like a bolt from heaven. To his altered sight the Sword blazed as the god-power flared through it into the earth, and then, like lightning after thunder, the force surged back through his feet and up his spine, blasting all resistance, bearing his spirit away.

Hamytz was not aware that he had fallen, or that the spears were continuing the rhythm as he lay twitching on the ground. Now the crag and the stone and the men who cried out their petitions to the god were the dream. Ahead lay a radiance beyond description, and as that light touched him, he laughed for joy. In its midst stood an armored figure. The Sword-priest fell to his knees.

"*Mighty One . . .*" His heart spoke. "*Strengthen your people. The wild tribes are coming. Our young warriors have been taken and only old men remain to protect their families.*"

"*Once* you *were the wild tribes . . .*" answered a voice that seemed to come from all around him. "*This was their land before you came. . . .*"

"*But if not here, then where shall we find a home? Is a painted barbarian chieftain to inherit your sword?*"

"*Fool!*" Hamytz quailed as the brightness billowed crimson. "*You seek to douse your hearth when your thatch is on fire. Get you back to the Middle World, for your enemies are upon you! Save yourself, or there will be nothing to leave!"*

Power pulsed outward, and Hamytz was swept away.

He was falling, hurtling downward, whirling helplessly into the void. There was an eternity, it seemed, of fire and darkness before the world began to make sense to him again. Sound returned first, even before sensation. There were shouts, and someone was groaning. Hamytz tried to make out words.

"Ho, Caradawc, this one's dead already—" The voice spoke British with the harsh accent of Alba. Hamytz was distantly aware that someone had kicked him, but he was not yet sufficiently back into his body to feel pain.

"Search him—he might be hiding gold—"

"Not me. He's god-struck! The dead be worse than the living, with his kind!"

From farther off came shouting and the clash of spears. Perhaps he *was* dead, thought Hamytz dizzily. But if he were a spirit, he should be able to *see* . . .

"I'll take his sword, then—the one that's standing there!"

Awareness whirled back in a sudden torrent of fear. Hamytz smelled smoke, and the sweet stink of blood, and the damp tang of approaching rain.

"Caradawc, do not!" the first man cried. " 'Tis some outlander witchery!"

"But a fine blade—" A clap of thunder interrupted his words, followed by a burst of shouting.

"By Taranis! They rally! Come away, come away!"

Hamytz heard hoofbeats and knew that at least one of the Iazyges had made it back to the horses. His people were no use afoot, but they rode like centaurs. Stones scattered as the pony went by, then came a meaty thunk and a cry.

"Cynwal, Cynwal!" cried the man who had wanted the Sword, followed by a torrent of profanity as the hoofbeats approached again. "Ye murdering scum—'tis my brother ye've spitted there. But I'll return!" he cried, "for the sword an' his blood-price, so I will!"

The hoofbeats grew louder, but the running feet were swifter still. Struggling to come fully into his body, Hamytz heard both fade. His dizziness increased, but his eyelids were fluttering. With a convulsive twist he found himself suddenly upright, eyes wide. There were bodies all around him—men of the Painted People stripped for battle, their naked limbs tattooed in blue, and his own comrades, lying like fallen dragons in their shirts of scales. Farther off he could sense a moving blur of horses, and in the sky beyond them a lurid light that must come from the burning roofs of Bremetennacum.

It had come, then, the great breaking of the Wall that they had feared. He had seen enough burning towns in his time to judge from the brightness of that glow how little would survive of his home. For a moment longer he stared, and felt on his brow the first stinging drops of rain. Then his body, outraged by the violence with which his spirit had been returned to it, revolted. Hamytz felt pain drive like a hammer through his skull, and knew no more.

"Ach, now, be you still. 'Tis a fair knock those wolves must have given you to lay such a strong man low. You'll need rest—"

The words were in the British tongue, but the voice was light, with a lilt like birdsong, and the hands that went with it soft as they stroked the hair back from his brow. Hamytz sighed, trying to reconcile his last, anguished, memories with the warm darkness in which he was lying now.

"Not . . . a blow. . . ." he croaked painfully, fighting to remember the words, then coughed.

"Do you say so? But men often forget what led up to a crack on the skull," the woman replied. "You were half-drowned and half-frozen, anyhow, and you should be glad of the warmth of Rhiannon's fire."

"Rhiannon . . ." Hamytz struggled to open his eyes. A flicker from the hearth showed him the slope of a thatched roof and a circular, whitewashed wall. A great many bags and bundles seemed to be hanging from the long poles that peaked above him: his nostrils flared at the sharp scents of drying herbs. But mostly it was the sturdy shape of the woman that claimed his attention, the firelight behind her kindling sparks of flame in the masses of her hair.

"Rhiannon merch Gutuator—" she replied, a little defiantly, and when he did not react, laughed. "You be no man of this country, I think, not to have heard of the Druid's daughter. Nor even a Briton, by your tongue and your gear. Be you a christened man?"

Slowly he shook his head. "I am a man of the Iazyges—I served with the Legions and came home to Bremetennacum when my time was done."

He heard the quick intake of her breath. "I thought perhaps you had been in the fighting, but you had crawled some ways when I found you."

Crawled . . . Dimly he remembered a storm, and slipping in the mud of the road. He had not even run away—he had crawled like a worm. The woman's voice seemed to come from a distance.

"The ravens were busy over the hill behind you, but I went no farther. For the dead I could do nothing—better to spend my strength for a living man."

"And what of the vicus?" he forced himself to ask.

Slowly she shook her head. "That was a great burning. But no refugees have come from the town. Unless the Alban wolves took slaves, I do not think that any survived. I am sorry. Did you lose family?"

"There were none of my blood left." He coughed, trying to ease the ache in his chest. "And none of my people now. I am alone."

"As I am alone. . . ." It seemed to Hamytz he heard her whisper, but suddenly a fit of shivering took him, and he could not be sure. In another moment he felt warm again, too warm. He tried to push his covers away.

There was a soft exclamation as she touched his brow. "The fever—I feared it! But do you drink this and you will be better—I will not lose you too!"

A horn cup was set to his lips and Hamytz drank instinctively, grimacing as the bitter stuff went down. He found himself wondering who else she had lost. But sleep overcame him before he could ask.

In his delirium Hamytz dreamed. He was climbing the mountain of the gods, moving as easily as a boy. A part of him knew this was because the cord that held spirit to body had become very thin, but that no longer mattered. He sought the light like a warrior coming home after a long campaign, eager to enjoy his rest and the fruits of victory.

But when he came to the peak, the god was sitting with his back turned. Hamytz hesitated. Finally the silence stretched beyond his bearing.

"Lord, I have served you! I have fought long and hard, and cared for your people. Will you not welcome me?"

There was a long silence, and then a whisper so faint he could not tell if it came from the god or from the depths of his own soul.

"You ran away. Where is the Sword with which I entrusted you?"

Anguish swept Hamytz's spirit, sudden and devastating. It was true! He had lost control of his spirit and been unable to defend himself. He was a warrior no longer. "In the hand of an enemy . . . we were taken by surprise! There was nothing I could do!"

"You lie—" came the implacable answer. "The Sword

stands still where you set it. It has not yet been defiled. But each hour it stays unguarded increases the danger. In a righteous cause it will bring victory, but disaster if used for greed or gain. Any power may be turned to evil if misused, and mine above all. It is not your honor only that will be lost if the Sword is taken, but the peace of the world."

Hamytz recoiled, but the men of his line had been bred to bravery—even the courage to defy the gods. "What peace does the world have now?" he cried. "My sons are dead in a senseless war, my people scattered. There is nothing for the Sword to guard—the children of Batradz are no more!"

"Think you that ye are my only children?" The Voice rang out through all the worlds. "Have you no care for this land that has nourished you, or the generations that will come after? Shall they live as wolves, or worse—for my hounds are honest beasts that live by their own laws—shall they devour each other because a weapon of destruction has been loosed upon the world?"

"Then destroy it!" Hamytz exclaimed. "Send down a bolt of lightning to melt it to a lump once more!"

"By men it was made to carry my power; by men it must be controlled. Live, son of Hurtzast! Until you have seen the Sword to safety, your task is not done!"

Hamytz sought for words to plead—he had done his best and he was weary—the god could not wish him to go back again! But already the sky was darkening. Thunder boomed; the air around the god glowed livid as a dying fire. In the gloom the figure of the god loomed suddenly monstrous. Hamytz recoiled. No human soul, however courageous, could stand before the Face he sensed the god was wearing now. As that terrible figure began to turn, he fled once more.

"The Sword!" Hamytz's own voice brought him back to trembling awareness. He struggled to sit, but could not resist the soft hands that pressed him back against the sleeping furs.

"Be still now—" came a woman's voice. Roxana? But no—the words were British, and his wife had died years ago. He blinked and saw a face worn with lack of sleep, though good bones shaped the skin. Memory began to return. He licked dry lips, forcing himself to think in the native tongue.

"You are . . . Rhiannon."

"Indeed—" she answered, an unexpected beauty lighting her strong features as she smiled. "And who is it I have been nursing for three nights and three days?"

"I am Hamytz son of Hurtzast . . . I was . . . a priest of our god."

"A man of the old wisdom among the Horse People?" Her smile deepened. "Then you are doubly welcome here. My father used to tell how our own tribes dwelt in the land of the Scyths, long and long ago. Perhaps we come of ancient kin."

He stared at her. For six generations the Iazyges had lived among the British they protected, with them but never of them, too concerned with maintaining their own identity to wonder what wisdom might be found in their new home. Certainly it had never occurred to him that the British themselves might once have been newcomers here. Any kinship between them would be ancient indeed, but he found the thought oddly comforting.

He started to tell her so, and began to cough again. But this time the stuff that had stopped his lungs came up easily, and though the paroxysms were violent, when they ended, he breathed more freely than he had in days.

"I will bring you food now," she said when he lay back at last. "The worst is over. Now you need strength to heal."

Hamytz rested with eyes closed, listening to the woman as she moved about the hearth. *I will get well, but for what?* he wondered. *I am a warrior no longer—* He shivered a little, remembering, *I ran away. . . .*

He ate the food the woman brought to him, but though he was no longer in pain, he slept badly, haunted by memories.

The next morning Rhiannon helped him outside to sit in the thin autumn sunlight. It was only then that Hamytz realized how isolated she was. The house was built in the old British style, round, with a thatched roof. It nestled in the lee of a hillside with a view down the long valley. If he stood, he could just see the pale line of road leading north to the Wall, but there were no other habitations in sight, and no people—only the white sheep grazing the hillside and the hawks that circled against the pale sky.

"Have you no other family? No kin?" he asked her that evening when they sat beside the fire. Rhiannon shook her head.

"My parents came here from the Summer Country, in the South. The Christian priests would not have my father live in the town," she answered, "and the people were afraid to seek him openly, though they valued his knowledge of the old ways. This place is far enough away so the Romans could ignore us, but close enough that men who needed a judgment according to the ancient laws, or women who wanted my mother to brew up a medicine for some ill, could come. I was the only one of their children that lived, and now they are both gone, so I, like you, am alone."

"But you are young—you should have a man and babes of your own."

"Not so young that I would trade my freedom for the sake of a lad's bright smile." Rhiannon pushed back her hair and bent to stir the gruel. "I would perish within walls. And what need have I of such safeguards? The northerners fear my curses and our own folk swear by my spells."

Hamytz looked, and indeed there was a thread or two of

silver in her burnished hair. But to him she seemed little more than a child. He sighed.

"Then you have no need of any protection I might offer you. As soon as I can travel, I will be gone."

She looked up at him swiftly, and he saw her face go first red, then pale. "What are you saying? You can hardly walk to the door!" she cried, and then, "Did you think I wished to be rid of you?" She reached out to him, and the touch of her hand sent a tingling through his flesh that reminded him oddly of the Sword.

"You cannot afford to keep me forever—" He tried to smile. "I have always earned my own bread. My home is gone, but in times like these there is always work for a fighting man."

He could see that she doubted him, but he schooled his face to give nothing away. She was right of course—he might put up a good front, but there was no virtue left in him. He had let the trance take him; he had run away. If he survived long enough to find a new place, the first time his strength was tested, he would fall. And the sooner the better, he thought then, but not here, not where Rhiannon could see that her labors had been wasted.

"Is that what you will do, truly?" she asked. The dark fires of her hair hid her face as she bent to stir the pot; he could not tell if she were mocking him. "When you raved with fever, it seemed there was some task that weighed on your mind. *The Sword of God . . .*" she said in his own tongue. "Often you cried out those words. What do they mean?"

Hamytz stared at her. The Iazyges never spoke of their Hallows to outsiders, but there were none of his blood left to know, and Rhiannon was of the Wisefolk of her own tribe.

"The Sword of God. My glory," he said finally, "—and my shame. It is the sacred sword through which the power of the god whom the Romans call Mars came down to us. I was its guardian."

"And what became of it?"

He gestured toward the hills. "It still stands yonder, thrust into the stone where the Painted People came upon us as we called the god."

Rhiannon's eyes widened. "Did they take it?"

"I do not know—" Hamytz grimaced. "My lord sent his lightnings, but I was helpless. I do not know."

"You must reclaim it!" she exclaimed. "If it is as you say, in the wrong hands it could do great destruction. Do your people leave the Hallows lying about to be misused by the unwise? I assure you it is not so among my own!"

Hamytz groaned, his hands coming up to cover his face as if to shut out her words. "It is true—it is true, and I have betrayed my trust. Earth will hold the Sword for a time, and the spells upon the sheath can keep it quiet, but only deep waters could hide it forever. It is a Chalybes blade, forged by forgotten magic in the land from which we came."

"Calib . . ." she echoed, and he was too weary to correct her. "When you are stronger"—she looked up at him—"we will fetch it from your shrine, and if you are still unable to care for it, we will find a deep tarn in which to sink it from the sight of men."

"Unworthy. . . ." That was the word she had been too kind to say. Or perhaps, he thought numbly, it should have been "afraid."

As the moon of harvest drew on, Hamytz continued to mourn his lost honor. But increasingly, as time passed, his body was reasserting its will to live. He walked farther each day and ate more, began to busy himself making small repairs about the place and to help with the sheep. In other times he would have been too proud to serve a woman, or even to live so close to one who was not his wife or kin. But he was not a warrior anymore. During the day, activity kept him from brooding, but he dreaded the hours of darkness when he lay rigid, fighting sleep, or thrashed in the grip of evil dreams.

On a night when the wind whispered in the thatching and the wild geese lamented the turning of the year, Hamytz dreamed that he was alone on a desolate moor. Wolves howled behind him, and he struggled to go more quickly. If only he had some way to defend himself! But at the thought it seemed to him he heard laughter. *"You had a weapon, but you threw it away! Son of Hurtzast, where is the Sword?"*

Hamytz turned, seeking his tormentor. Something touched him and he lashed out, hit soft flesh and heard a cry—

—and woke, shaking, to see in the glow of the banked coals a woman sprawling on the floor.

"Rhiannon!" he swore, thrusting his covers aside, grabbing her. "I did not know it was you—I must teach you how to wake a sleeping warrior—" He was babbling, he knew, to cover terror. When she gasped and stirred, his relief was so intense that his knees weakened and he dropped back to the bed with the girl still in his arms.

She drew a shuddering breath, and some of his fear eased. "Are you hurt?"

"I'll do well . . . enough . . . when I get back my wind!"

"Why did you wake me? Is something wrong?" he asked then.

"You were moaning. . . ." Rhiannon frowned up at him, and he looked away.

"A nightmare—" he said shortly. "I am sorry I disturbed you. It will not happen again." He started to release her, suddenly very much aware that he was naked, and she clad in only a shift, but she clutched at him.

"I will stay with you," Rhiannon said then, "and keep the bad dreams away."

He stiffened, startled into looking back at her. "That is not a very good idea," he said carefully. "You need your sleep, child."

"I am a grown woman, Hamytz-kam, and rest is not what I need."

He took a deep breath, and began to tremble as he caught the flowery scent of the oils she combed into her hair. His flesh was telling him that indeed she was a woman, warm and solid in his arms, and that he had lain too long alone. But of course it was impossible.

"Rhiannon, I had a son your age," he said harshly. "I am an old man, used up. I am no good to you."

"I am not your daughter, and there was strength enough in your arm to knock me across the room. A man's seed is good so long as he lives. Lie with me, Hamytz, and I will give you new kin." She caught his hand in her own and carried it to her breast, and the touch was like the lightning of the god.

"I am not worthy—" he groaned, but she covered his mouth with her hand.

"Surely that is for me to decide!" Her strong fingers lingered a moment on his lips, then flickered lightly across the wiry hair on his chest and downward, where his treacherous flesh was already awakening. He knew he should stop, but he could no more resist her than he had the god.

Smiling, the woman sank back upon the bed, and as she opened herself to receive him, Hamytz discovered that some manhood remained to him after all.

Dawn found them still entwined. Hamytz opened his eyes and blinked in amazement. He had not slept so deeply in years.

At his movement, Rhiannon stirred and smiled. "How is it with you?"

Hamytz grunted ruefully. "You should know. You have bewitched me, woman. I have not performed so vigorously since I was twenty winters old!" Even now he could not say for sure which of them had conquered. She had seduced him, and yet he remembered how he had made her cry out as she lay panting in his arms. There was something in that notion of mutual conquest and surrender that teased at his memory. Then Rhiannon laughed aloud, and the thought fled. He had never noticed how her face lit when she was amused, but then he had not given her much to laugh about, until now.

"Well, it is fitting, for you are a Druid," she said then.

At that, the laughter left him. "Not anymore. You made me live when I was dying, and you have made me a man again. But to restore my spirit . . . is a task for the god."

Rhiannon frowned and sat up to face him. "Because of the Sword? Then go back and retrieve it. Do you think that all I wanted of you was your body? I have enough of my father's wisdom to know it is no use to heal the flesh when the spirit is wounded still. Until you do your duty, you will never be whole."

It was true. And until now, that knowledge had filled him with despair. But her embrace had healed him thus far—that now he had the courage to try to redeem his trust, even if the Sword rebelled at his impious touch and the god-power struck him down.

"Why did your people come to the North?" Rhiannon slowed, looking back at him. They had set out for the shrine as soon as the morning chores were done, and the brightness of the sky and the crisp tang of the air seemed to mark it a god-blessed day.

Hamytz, who had dropped back the better to admire the free-swinging grace of her stride, smiled wryly and quickened his pace to come up with her. It was almost worth having to go afoot to watch her walking, but there would be other times. He felt himself as foolish as a boy with his first love, but since last night, every touch, every look had been a revelation. Yesterday, perhaps, he would have given her a short answer, but now, after all she had given him, Hamytz wanted to make it a worthy tale.

"Not by our own choice, as I was told. There had been bad winters on the Sea of Grass; all the tribes were moving, and the Iazyges, though fierce fighters, were few. We moved south—like them—" he gestured upward, where a late group of wild geese were sketching a straggling line across the sky. "And came down at last to the plain of the Danuvius, seeking a new home in the Empire. But there was no room."

For a moment then, Hamytz had a sense of himself and his people and the flying geese as a unity. For men the cycles of migration might be less regular, but everyone moved, just the same. Even the wild tribes that they fought obeyed the same law. Rhiannon moved closer, waiting for him to continue.

"We could fight no longer. Our king made treaty with the great emperor, Marcus Aurelius, to divide our warriors among the Legions," he went on. "Fifty-five hundred were sent here to Britannia with their wives and families to serve as numeri with the Sixth Valeria Victrix at Bremetennacum. The prefect was a man called Lucius Artorius Castus, a great commander. My people honored him, and when, at the end of their terms of service, those first warriors of the numeri became citizens, many took his name. In the tribe I am the son of Hurtzast, but I was listed as Hamicus Artorius Sarmaticus on the Legionnary roll."

"And so your family has lived here for two centuries?" Rhiannon asked. "That is longer than mine!"

"Some of the men married local girls, and after a time they sent men of the Roxolani, who were a related tribe, to join us. But I am of the true line of Urs-barag, bred from the days when we roamed the Sea of Grass to serve the Sword."

"But not to wield it?" she asked, eyeing him curiously.

"The god wields it—" Hamytz answered, "or a man when the god is in him—a king when he rides to defend his people. And it has been long since the Iazyges had a king. . . ."

"Or the Britons either—" Rhiannon echoed him. "But there is never any lack of enemies!"

Hamytz nodded. There was a saying, among his people, that sundered kinfolk made the bitterest foes, and the tribes who dwelt beyond the Wall had never forgiven those of the South for going under the yoke of Rome. For a few moments they went on in silence, then his foot turned on a loose stone and he lurched against her.

"Are you hurt?" Rhiannon reached out to support him, and Hamytz pulled her into his arms.

"Only my feet—" He grinned when he had finished kissing her. "My folk set a child on his first pony while he is still toddling. I am not used to walking so far."

"Well, we are nearly there—" She pointed. "The place where I found you is just over that rise, and somewhere beyond that is your shrine."

Hamytz squinted against the sun. Ahead, long slopes covered with bracken the color of dried blood ran down from a weathered outcropping of gray stone. He was used to approaching from the northward, but he recognized, even from behind, the cliffs below which he had left the sword.

Though Rhiannon still stood within the circle of his arms, he could feel the joy draining out of him. "Listen—when I take the Sword, I do not know what may happen," he said soberly. "I want you to stand well away."

"Can it be touched by a woman?"

"In the past, when all the men were at war, it was sometimes guarded by the wife of the chieftain, though she did not call the god," he answered. He let go of her and began to walk again.

The trail here was pocked with old hoofprints, but no horse had come this way since the last rain. Still, there was something—his gaze fixed suddenly on a raven, flapping upward to settle in a stunted oak tree. Other black blots already weighted the branches. Hamytz frowned. If there were still pickings left from the fight, why were the birds in the tree, and if not, why were they here at all?

The trail curved abruptly around some rocks and suddenly he was looking down into the hollow. He thrust Rhiannon behind him and stepped back into the shadow of the stone, old instincts awakening as he scanned the ground. There was a short, indrawn breath behind him as the woman saw the bodies, but they were no threat anymore. Indeed, there seemed to be no danger at all. The Sword stood where he had left it, its immortal steel gleaming in the afternoon sun. Except for the stirring of the grasses in the wind, nothing moved.

"We should bury the bones—" Rhiannon started past him, but Hamytz held her.

"Stay here," he said in a low voice. "We can worry about them when I have the Sword."

He could feel her resistance, but her father had trained her well and she stayed put as Hamytz started down the hill.

He took a deep breath, and let it out slowly, his spirit opening to awareness of the hidden forces in the hollow with a rush that dizzied him. Pain and anger pulsed in uneasy confusion as the spirits of the unburied dead became aware of his presence. Rhiannon was right—they would have to be given the proper rites and set free. But more strongly than either, Hamytz sensed the brooding power of the blade.

He shuddered, wondering how a moon spent in such surroundings had affected it. He would have to purify it when he got it home—in that moment it hardly struck him as odd that he should so swiftly have learned to think of Rhiannon's house in those terms.

"Bright One . . . Holy One . . ." he muttered. "It is your priest who stands before you, returning to do your will. Let me take your Sword back into my keeping, and forgive the weakness that kept me from doing so before—" He waited a moment, listening, and his ears began to ring at the increasing pressure in the air. He had feared the god might have departed; now Hamytz was afraid because He was here.

But there was nothing to be gained by waiting. He set his feet and reached to grasp the hilt, and gasped as all the pain the bloody earth had absorbed shocked upward. But pain no longer mattered. He leaned against the blade till it curved as no mortal weapon could without breaking, twisted to release the springy steel, and pulled it free.

There was no cloud in the sky, but he heard thunder, or perhaps it was the clamor of his own heart as the power of the Sword flared through every vein. With a wordless shout he swung it high, and the blade leaped in his hand like a wild thing. The spirit in it had always been strong, but now it was all he could do to hold on. If he could get it sheathed, it might calm—he staggered, calling on the god to help him get it away from the offering stone.

"Hold!"

Hamytz stared, shock for a moment overwhelming all other powers. As if the Sword had brought life back to all the scattered bodies, the hollow was suddenly full of armed men. But they were all warriors of the Painted People, brandishing spears. The man in the lead was big, red-bearded, his hair hacked off in mourning.

They were hidden here, some part of his mind that was still thinking observed. *That is why the ravens flew into the trees. It is the one called Caradawc, returning as he promised, for the Sword.* And then, *He did not know the trick to draw it, but I have done it for him. . . .*

"My thanks to you, old man. I was fearing to break the blade. But I will take it now." Caradawc strode forward.

"That you will not—" Hamytz found his voice again. "But come a little closer, and the Sword will take *you!*" The weapon danced in his hand, hungering. He laughed, feeling that force linked to his own will, neither possessed nor possessing, but united, as he and Rhiannon had been not so long ago.

The Alban looked at him more closely, and stopped short, staring. "I know you—It is dead you were, lying beside my brother. Do you have a cauldron to revive the dead, then, or is it a ghost standing here?"

"If you come closer," Hamytz grinned mirthlessly, "you will learn—"

Caradawc eyed him thoughtfully, perhaps seeing from Hamytz's stance that, dead or living, here was a fighting man.

"Maybe so," he said, lifting his hand, "but I know a surer way."

A thrumming behind him was Hamytz's only warning. He never saw the warrior who cast the spear, but only a blur in the air. Because he was turning, it slashed through his left shoulder instead of piercing his back, spinning him. The second spear missed entirely, but the third man, taking more time, aimed true. Hamytz saw death coming, but the shock of the blow to his shoulder held him and he could not move. The spear caught him in the solar plexus and slammed him backward against the stones.

Even before the pain hit him, Hamytz knew this blow was mortal. But he was still on his feet, pinned against the cliff face, still able to meet Caradawc's widening eyes.

"Are you not dead yet? We will break you, then! You cannot keep the Sword from me now!"

"Do you think so?" whispered Hamytz. He had brought no sacrifice to feed the Sword before he sheathed it, but now there was blood aplenty, dripping from the gash in his shoulder, welling through his tunic around the shaft of the spear. He lifted the Sword crosswise and laid the blade against his belly, turned it and repeated the act, crimsoning the bright steel.

Shock and blood loss were beginning to affect his vision. He saw his enemy grow dark and bright with each pulse, and the world was spinning, but the stone against his back was solid, and the wildness in the Sword had become a steady blaze of power.

"You cannot take it—" he said harshly. "Without the will of the god and its guardian no man shall ever hold this blade."

"What is to prevent me?" asked Caradawc, but his voice held less assurance now.

"Lord—" Hamytz whispered in his own tongue, lifting the Sword, "take back your own. . . ."

"Do not fear," the answer came, *"the Sword is in My hand, and so are you."*

A shudder ran through Hamytz's body, and his vision blurred. *This is death,* he thought, but he was still standing, still holding the Sword. And because he was beyond all pride, and because of what he had learned from Rhiannon, his mind was able to relinquish control of his body without fear as the god entered in.

He took a step forward, the spearshaft bobbing from his belly, and Caradawc gasped. Hamytz could feel the weight and the movement, but he did not decide his body's actions, and he did not feel its pain.

"Go—" a great voice boomed through him. "Fight your own battles on your own land. There is only death for you here!" Ever so slowly, Hamytz's arm lowered, until the tip of the Sword hovered a hand's breadth from Caradawc's breast, and stayed there, perfectly steady, while the high color drained from the Alban's ruddy cheeks.

"Get the chieftain away—" whispered one of the others, "or that thing will have not only our lives but our souls!" He darted forward and jerked his leader backward, and Caradawc, eyes dilated, did not try to pull away.

"That is well . . ." said the same great voice. "Now begone, and pray you never face Me upon a battlefield. . . ."

To Hamytz they were all shadows, wavering figures that diminished until they became one with the shadows of horses, and both grew smaller and smaller as they ran away. He felt no triumph, and he sensed only sadness from the mighty Presence that filled his body. It was over. Only one task remained. He lifted the Sword over his shoulder, set its tip to the mouth of the sheath strapped to his back with the precision of long practice, and thrust it home.

And as the spells worked into the leather began to mute the weapon's power, the force that had filled Hamytz's body gently withdrew. Pain, for a little while, remained at bay, but the strength was flowing out of him. He went down first upon one knee, and then to the other, and then, in a gradual relaxation, collapsed onto his side with the spearshaft resting on the ground.

Awareness retreated inward. He was a boy again in his first battle, shrieking a battle cry; he was dancing with the other men to celebrate the birth of his son; he was riding escort to an emperor. . . . It had been a good life, he thought in wonder, and a good ending. He would be able to face his forefathers without shame after all.

A long time after, it seemed, he felt soft hands stroking the hair back from his brow.

"Hamytz, can you hear?"

The voice was Rhiannon's, and he struggled to open his eyes. "I am sorry—" Surprising, how hard it was to speak, "you wasted all your care."

"You gave me joy, and perhaps something more, if I have correctly judged the moon." Something warm and wet touched his cheek—her tears.

He drew a careful breath. "Take the Sword. Guard it. If you bear a child, teach him—or her—to keep it for the king that is to be. But if there is no one . . . cast it into the sea. . . ." For a moment the only sound was his labored breathing. There was so much he wanted to say to her, but he knew he would not have the strength for much more. Footfalls echoed within his awareness as the wolf that was his totem came to bear him away.

"I will remember," Rhiannon said steadily.

"That is well. Now, pull out the spear—"

"If I pull it out, you will die. . . ."

"I hope so," his lips twisted in an attempt to smile. "Better quick than slow. If you love me, do it now—" he added as she stayed still.

Rhiannon caught her breath on a sob and, bending suddenly, kissed his brow. Perhaps he should have said that he loved her, he thought then. But she must know that. He had entrusted more than his life into her care.

He felt the first curling clutch of pain as she set her hands upon the shaft, and then the white blaze of agony as she pulled the spearhead free. He saw Rhiannon's pale face above the bloody spear, and then, as awareness whirled away, other faces—a girl with russet hair and a face like his dead son's, and others, and finally a boy with fair hair and the eyes of a king.

He will come, then . . . Hamytz thought dimly. *I have not failed.*

"You have done well," said the god.

Hooves drummed in the earth, or perhaps it was only the final, convulsive beating of his heart as the last of his blood spurted onto the ground. There was a brightness beyond him. Hamytz turned toward it. His flesh quivered once, then was still, but his blood fed the earth of Britannia as it had fed the Sword.

Lassorio

Eric Lustbader

ne hundred years after the death of Arthur, the King, England lay in ruins. The glory that was Camelot was vanished, replaced by painful memories and bitter rivalries. Camelot itself was now merely a castle sold off by the monarchy to pay old and mounting debts. It was inhabited by a particularly loathsome warlord whose reputation for cruelty was surpassed only by his penchant for killing. Some said it was just revenge for the betrayals visited upon Arthur during his reign by those dearest to him.

The new king was a weakling, surrounded by corrupt ministers and advisors who were cleverly and systematically plundering the wealth of the country and the power devolved upon them.

As for Avalon, the once and present home of Arthur, the King, it had moved progressively farther and farther into the protective mists beyond Lake Gallion where, it was still whispered during harvest festivals when superstition blossomed like primroses, Viviane, the high priestess of Avalon, the Lady of the Lake, had taken possession of Arthur's magical sword, Excalibur. But this story, and others like it, were widely regarded as folk tales and nothing more. Avalon, more ancient than Stonehenge and more magical, had by this time receded so far into the mists of Time, it had passed beyond mere memory. The weak and wizened mage Merlin, who some said had engineered with sorcery Arthur's rise to power, had retired with his sister and sometime lover, Morgaine, beyond the mists. He had had his fill of the world of man, of deceit and treachery. Besides, it was whispered, he was slowly and painfully dying of the poison administered to him by his sister's favored son, Mordred.

One hundred years after Arthur, the King, had been borne upon his ebon-draped barge across Lake Gallion to Avalon was not a time of legend. Or of magic. Whether this was tragedy or freedom was hotly debated at All Hallows and other festivals, when the Druidic gods were trotted out by rote and petitioned to grant bountiful crops.

Jonathan Charles Lassorio, a warlord with a penchant for placing the heads of his enemies upon pikes outside his war-tent or his residence, took possession of the castle Camelot one hundred years to the day that Arthur, the King, had shed his mortal coil. The more superstitious folk of Glastonbury shire found that significant and they began their heated debates all over again.

The warlord Lassorio had once been married to a fair-haired lady with skin as pale as milk and eyes the color of the winter sky reflected in ice. It was widely told that he had murdered her because she had not provided him with the brood of male heirs he had desired. In fact, at the time Lassorio took possession of the castle Camelot, he was without issue.

Lassorio was born and bred for war. In the company of his father, an enormous and intimidating Celt with an almost elemental personality, he had made his first kill at twelve, felling a buck in full flight. Even at that age Lassorio was strong enough to pull the gut string of his father's longbow to its limit.

Less than a year later, he had killed his first man.

Lassorio's father took him into battle, having fashioned for him a suit of armor to his specifications. He taught his son all he knew of warfare and combat, which was considerable. What Lassorio knew of politics he had picked up on his own.

He found the shedding of blood a holy pursuit. While he felt nothing kneeling in the chill and drafty stone church of his home shire, his blood sang in the height of battle. In this manner he won for himself fame, riches, an army to give even the king pause and, at last, real property.

Thus he came to the castle Camelot, taking possession of it and all the lands around it for one hundred and fifty hectares. When he was not at war, Lassorio was an inveterate hunter. This he did on his own. Most on his staff said it was because he was a lout who, by and large, eschewed people, who saw no use for them save as bloodsport. But, in fact, it recalled the halcyon days of his youth when he and his father would roam the wild forests tracking spoor of the most dangerous animals with just bows-and-arrows across their backs and knives for skinning sheathed at their hips.

He slipped from the castle in the hour before dawn when all the world was asleep and dreaming. Alone, he traversed the plowed and planted farmland, skirting the town itself, and plunged headlong into the thickets of the forest whose far edge abutted the misty shore of Lake Gallion. And there he would wander for days at a time while those inside the castle lived their lives in relief of the absence of his incarcerating presence.

On one such hunting expedition in the last week of the year, Lassorio was overcome by a fierce snowstorm. He felt the pressure dropping perhaps an hour before the snow came. The sky was pewter-white and low, the clouds so massed, they were without definition. Lassorio, sniffing the chill air, turned the collar of his leather coat up against the nape of his neck as a sole concession to the change in the weather, and continued tracking the spoor he had run across at first-light.

The paw-prints were those of a snow-fox, the largest he

had ever seen. The sight had set his blood to boiling. He had never before killed a snow-fox. He had, in fact, only come across the prints of one other, when he had been with his father in winter, but they had lost it after three days of intense tracking and physical adversity. In the end, Lassorio's father had stumbled descending a steep, rock scree and, falling head over heels, had fractured his leg.

Lassorio would never forget the sight of his father lying white-faced, staring at the bones protruding through skin and leggings. Lassorio had been obliged to drape his father over his shoulder and carry him back home. This had taken five days and by that time it was too late. The corruption of the flesh had turned so serious that the leg had to be cut off. Lassorio could not sleep that night. The screams of his father echoed through the cavernous castle. He had sat up alone, huddled in the darkness, while his mother did the surgeon's bidding, attending her husband. Apparently, the excruciating pruning could not halt the corruption and within a week Lassorio's father was dead.

Now, deep in the Glastonbury forest, Lassorio picked up his pace, loping between the trees, over tangled roots and tiny copses of sprouting mushrooms. He knew that the coming snow would obliterate the spoor and he was determined to discover the snow-fox's lair before that happened. Ever in his mind was the image of his father's pain and helplessness, and his own horror at the sight of both.

The spoor took him ever westward, toward the edge of the lake, which he had heard spoken of many times but had yet to visit himself. War had occupied him fully and richly; the running of his domain he left to others.

By the telltale signs of the spoor, he knew he was drawing closer to the snow-fox. By the time the snow came, he was certain he was within the animal's territory. He lifted his head to the lowering sky and cursed aloud.

No! he thought. *I am so close!*

But the veils of snow seeping through the pine boughs only thickened, and an arctic wind howled through the forest, blowing the flakes in every direction. Even the master hunter Lassorio was at last forced to seek shelter. He came upon a small thatch-and-stone cottage by the side of the lake. He had not known he was this close to Gallion, but in the foul weather he could see nothing but an expanse of gray mist, embroidered with veils of white snow. *It is nothing,* he thought. *Just another lake.*

It was getting much colder, and cursing his luck, Lassorio tramped to the door of the cottage and, putting his heavy fist to the door, pounded for entry.

When the door opened, he saw an old man with a long white beard and curious eyes the color of emeralds.

"Yes?" the old man said. Then, as Lassorio stamped his feet in the cold like a dray horse, the old man spied the hunting bow and arrow-filled quiver strung across his back. "Ah, a hunter caught in the storm." He beckoned with a liver-spotted hand. "Come in, come in, sir."

He does not know who I am, Lassorio thought as he crossed the threshold. *All the better.*

It was warm in the cottage. A fire burned in the stone hearth, and the delicious smell of stew emanated from a black iron pot suspended over the flames. Lassorio looked around, found the interior surprisingly spartan: just a narrow bunk, a rough plank table and two chairs, a worn rug on the flagstone floor, shelves of an open pantry and not much else. It reminded him of war; a soldier's kit: spare, orderly and easily transportable. And yet, there was an indefinable aspect that gave the impression the old man had been here for decades.

"Sit down, sir," the old man said, bustling about. "I have warm stout for you." He handed over a battered metal tankard. "Homemade." When he grinned, his yellow teeth gleamed like ivory. "I am called Gwydion. How may I address you, sir hunter?"

"Jonathan," Lassorio said, surprising himself. "Just call me Jonathan."

"A fine name," Gwydion said. "Strong and proud."

But no one had called Lassorio by the Christian name given him by his father since his father's death. Even Lassorio's wife had called him Charles. Until this moment, he had thought Jonathan buried in the casket with his father. Something had had to take the place of his ruined leg. Lassorio could not bear the thought of his father winging heavenward maimed.

The two men drank together, and as they talked, as the tankards were refilled again and again, Lassorio felt a profound sense of freedom and release. With Gwydion he did not have to be the fierce warlord, the liege lord of the Glastonbury fiefdom. He could shed the mantle of blood and power he had spent almost all his life constructing. Until this moment, he had had no idea he might want to do that, or that his solitary forest forays were an attempt to do just that.

"Tell me, Jonathan, what do you hunt for in this evil weather?" Gwydion asked. "Even the most fanatic hunter knows the time to remain by family and hearth and drink strong autumn mead."

"I am used to winter hunting," Lassorio said. "I was bred to it by my father. As for family, I have none, which is just as well for the likes of me."

Gwydion, refilling his tankard, gave him a quizzical look. "Why, every young man such as yourself has need of a family, of love and solace, joy and caring."

"Family is nothing more than a burden," Lassorio said. "You care for someone and then she dies. Where is the use in that?"

Gwydion put down the pitcher of stout, went to the window, clouded with ice and snow. "When I was a young man, not much older than you are, I loved a woman. She did not die, but she betrayed me. And loving me still, she betrayed me again. How could this be? I thought. Until, as a much older man, I realized that there are all kinds of loves. She had a vision of the future that was her first love, overriding all others. I was the only man for her; we two were a whole. And yet she chose to betray me." He turned to look at Lassorio, his emerald eyes flashing as they must have done when he was young. "And yet, I love her still. I would not have given up my time with her for anything. Do you understand, young Jonathan? Love has as a major component pain. This is inevitable, necessary, even. Because it is only through the pain that we come to recognize love's true worth."

The wind howled through the forest, sweeping across the lake. Already, there were pockets of ice extending out from the shore and, deep below the surface, fish hung motionless, sleeping until spring.

Gwydion quit his post at the window and crossed the room. He gripped Lassorio's shoulder with surprising strength. "How did you lose her, Jonathan?"

This question had been asked of Lassorio many times, and perhaps his stony silence had played its part in giving rise to the rumors of murder. Lassorio glanced at Gwydion but found only sympathy in those emerald eyes. The human touch loosened a tongue long held in check.

"She was the love of my life," Lassorio said in a whisper. "We met when she was but fifteen and fell in love instantly." He put his head down. "The sun was always in her eyes. No two people had ever loved one another more. She knew I wanted a son, an heir to teach as, once, my father had taught me. And with every passing month that she remained barren, her sorrow grew. I tried to reassure her, to tell her our love was enough, but she saw through me. You are right, Gwydion, in what you say about love. I loved her deeply and most truly, but it was not enough. I wanted more; I wanted a son and in her heart she knew it. It did not make her love me less, but she ached to make me happy, and at last she came to me, her face glowing, and told me she was with child.

"It was a most difficult pregnancy. She was ill from the first, but she bore it well, knowing what happy issue would result. I was away at war for much of the early months and so knew nothing of the increasing difficulties she was having, for her letters spoke of nothing but love and happiness.

"Imagine my shock when I returned home to discover she had been abed for a fortnight. The physician could do nothing for her, so, at her request, I sent for an herbalist. She spent eighteen hours with my wife, at the end of which time she emerged from our chambers to inform me that there were grave complications. She told me that I could save either my wife or the baby but not both. I asked her if she could divine the sex of the baby and she told me it was male. She also said that if my wife survived, she would never be able to bear children.

"She had put a sword through my heart. I would not have told my wife, but the herbalist had already done so. My wife begged me to save the child. 'It is our only hope,' she said.

" 'How do you mean?' I said, shocked. 'I cannot live without you.'

" 'But if I survive, the baby will die, and then you will never forgive me. Our love will forever be poisoned and all that we have had will be destroyed.'

" 'No, no,' I said, kneeling beside the bed. 'We will survive, you and I. We must. I will make it so.'

"But she merely smiled down at me and, placing her warm hand against my cheek, said, 'I have no doubt that you will try. But I know you, just as I know how it will end. The baby is the answer to our prayers. It must survive.'

" 'No!' I shouted. 'I forbid such talk! I cannot survive without you.'

" 'But, darling, you must see that I *will* survive. You will see me every day in the baby.'

"She continued in this manner every day as she got progressively worse and the baby came closer to being born. But I would not give in. Then the night came when she screamed. I told her I would summon the physician, but she stayed me. 'He cannot help me now,' she said through her gasps of pain. 'Summon the herbalist.'

"I did as she bade me, telling myself that I did not understand her meaning. But when the woman came and examined my wife, she told me that the time had come. 'You must choose, sir, now,' she told me. 'Otherwise they both will perish.'

"She pressed the herb potion into my hands and I threw her from the room, tending to my wife myself." Lassorio put his head in his hands. "I am a warrior by profession, Gwydion. I have seen atrocities and suffering on the battlefield that would curl your hair. But, my God, I had never seen a person suffer as my wife was suffering. Hour after hour, I held her hand and wiped her brow and helped her make ready for the baby's coming, while she screamed and cried and begged me to administer the potion that would enable the baby's birth and would ensure her death."

He lifted his head, looking into the old man's eyes. "But I was selfish, Gwydion. I loved her but I wanted more. I wanted her and I wanted my son, even though I had been told I could not have both. I clung to hope, to my selfishness, her agony engulfing me, until the baby started to come and I thought that it was going to be all right, the physician and the herbalist were wrong. I would have my wife *and* my son."

Lassorio rose. He felt as if he had been in battle for three days straight. All the muscles of his body ached and his head throbbed. He stood at the window, looking out over the lake, seeing only the past in the swirling snow. When he spoke again, his voice was cracked and hoarse.

"But, in the end, they were right and I was wrong. Terribly, fatally wrong. My wife and my son were entangled. They would not give each other up, and so each drowned in the other's fluid."

Behind him, Gwydion put down his tankard. "And now what do you think?"

"I think I murdered my wife and my son," Lassorio said. There, it was out. At last.

"And so now you choose to continue to murder rather than face what you have done."

Lassorio rested his head against the windowpane, the cold lancing through him. "Murder?"

"You are no hunter, I will warrant," the old man said. "When was the last time you slew an animal solely for sustenance? No, you kill for the sport of it. To take a life."

"It is what I do, what I know."

"Learn something else," Gwydion said with some disgust. "Before your soul is withered beyond repair."

"I have no soul," Lassorio said, staring out at the lake where, it was said, Excalibur lay entombed. "I buried it along with my wife and child, my future."

"You have made your own future," Gwydion said. "You have no one else to blame for that." He warmed his hands by the fire as he used a long wooden spoon to stir the stew. "Tell me, what is it you hunt on this coldest day of winter?"

"The snow-fox," Lassorio said.

"No," the old man said. "What you hunt is your own soul. And with each kill you damage it further."

Lassorio watched the wind in the thick boughs of the firs. "Living life alone on the shore of Gallion has made you something of a philosopher, old man."

"I would caution you not to hunt the snow-fox," Gwydion said. "Especially at this time of year. The first weeks of the new year are the time for kits. The snow-foxes are heavy with life now."

Lassorio was about to reply when he saw movement at the corner of his eye. Immediately, he turned his head, his hunter's instinct aroused, and he saw the snow-fox. He dropped his tankard, lunged for his bow and quiver. "I thank you for your hospitality, Gwydion," he said as he opened the door.

"Where are you going?" the old man said. "It is nearly dusk. You will freeze."

"I will be back," Lassorio said, "when my hunt is done."

The snow had reached the tops of his ankles and he loped along in easy strides. Through the falling snow he could make out the paw prints as he followed the snow-fox. As he went, he notched an arrow. He could see the animal bounding through the trees just at the shoreline, weaving in and out. It was a magnificent creature, very large, but all Lassorio could see was his father's face twisted in pain, and the ruined, bloody bones protruding through his shredded legging.

Keeping the snow-fox in sight, he held his bow at an angle, drew it back until he heard the tension singing in the string like the storm winds through the pines. As the snow-fox paused for a moment to scrape at something beneath the crusty surface of the snow, Lassorio let fly the arrow.

The snow-fox leaped into the air as the arrow pierced it, but instead of dropping to the ground, it took off through the trees. It was easy to follow its bloody trail. Lassorio blew snow from his face as he went, drawing out another arrow and notching it.

The snow-fox veered abruptly to its left, inexplicably leaving the cover of the trees, heading out onto the ice of the lake. Lassorio followed it, but he lost time testing the thickness of the ice, and aiming became problematic at this distance because the wind scudding across the lake was blowing snow into his face. He went on, keeping the snow-fox in sight, following the blood. Soon, he thought, he would not need another arrow, the beast would bleed to death.

But Lassorio was a hunter and he had no wish to inflict such torture on any creature, so he picked up his pace and, when he was within range, struck the snow-fox with the second arrow. Now the animal collapsed onto the ice and, in a frenzy of the kill, Lassorio hurried toward it, his mind ringing with his father's screams.

There it lay, its white fur stained with blood. Its magnificent head, the muzzle buried in its bloody belly, was really quite beautiful. It had run him an admirable race. Its preserved head and skin would hang proudly in the castle Camelot. He went toward it, but stopped. He saw that it had clawed open its own belly. It was a female and, as Gwydion had predicted, pregnant. Three tiny kits lay on the ice beside their mother. Two were dead, but one was huddling against her fur, trying to suckle.

He picked it up by the scruff of its neck. It was an ugly mewling thing, but so pitiful. He placed it inside his coat and tunic where it would be warm against his breast. He had his knife out to skin the mother when he heard a sharp crack like the report of lightning close at hand. Then his world canted over and he was plunged into the dark, icy waters of the lake.

Down and down he sank while he tried his best to rise. Shock and the extreme cold half-paralyzed him so that his arms waved ineffectually and his legs dangled uselessly.

Into darkness he slid until all he could hear was his own heartbeat and the air rushing out of his lungs. He looked up, but now he could not even see the chunks of ice that had given way beneath his weight. He blinked once, lowered his gaze to a dark shape drifting by. He reached out, touched the fletched feathers on two arrows protruding from the snow-fox. Its tail brushed the back of his hand, then it was gone, whirled away from him by a swift current.

Still he slid downward as if pulled by another such current. He knew he would die within minutes, the utter cold sucking the life from him even before the water entered his lungs and drowned him. He thought of his father's agonized death, his dead wife and son, and Gwydion's warning not to hunt the snow-fox.

What you hunt is your own soul.

He thought of the snow-fox, as dead as his own soul, and the lives he had robbed over the years. Now he was certain that he sank because his soul—what was left of it—was weighted down by death. Each and every murder he had committed rose from his depths like the bubbles streaming from his closed lips to suffocate him.

This was his end now. He found that he could accept that, an end to his torment and guilt, an end to the obsessive hunt. Besides, the babble of the past, the ghosts that haunted him, were finally growing dim and still. A strange kind of peace began to settle over him.

Then pain bloomed in his chest and he started awake. It came again, a sharp nipping and squirming. The snow-fox kit! Sunk deeply in the ice floe of his past sins, he had forgotten all about it. Now he felt it scratching and biting him in its desperation to live. It wanted to live even if he no longer did.

Life! Even the word seemed alien to him, as if spoken in his father's native Celt instead of the civilized Saxon English. He looked at the snow-fox kit through the lens of the water and it no longer seemed ugly. He could already discern in its tiny face its mother's regal beauty. He wanted the kit to live, he knew that.

And, looking down past the small squirming body, he saw a pale light the color of a winter's sky reflected in ice. The light was like a column, like tendrils of weed twining upward to meet him. As he sank, he passed into this column of light and the pressure on his lungs became bearable again. If he did not begin to breathe, he was at least not drowning. And the intense cold seemed to abate so that a modicum of feeling began to creep from his extremities toward his chest, abdomen and brain.

Lassorio, astonished, reached the base of the column of light and found beneath him a woman's face. This face was not drowned, nor was it, strictly speaking, alive. It just was. And as he looked, the woman's mouth opened and out of it rose a longsword with runes engraved along the entire length of its blade. The hilt, guard and butt were fashioned of gold, in a simple but eternal pattern. Without thinking, he knew that this was Excalibur, Arthur, the King's, weapon, the sword with which he had united a war-torn country, the sword of Avalon.

"Here is the sword of Mysteries," the woman said in his mind. *"Once it lay in stone, once it took more than mortal man to wield it. That time of giants is gone. But the sword remains to be wielded as it may. Unlike all other weapons, it is a sword of life. Speak not death's name in its presence."*

And, again, without thinking, Lassorio reached down to grasp it as it rose to him hilt first. As he did so, the woman vanished. He heard a terrible roaring in his ears, the world became a blur before his eyes, and his stomach felt as if he had been turned on his head, hung by his heels, then abruptly cut down.

When next he opened his eyes, he found himself lying on the shore of Lake Gallion. Mist rose all around him, but at least the snow had ceased to fall. He rose, thinking he had had a dream, but he was wet and shivering. His bow and quiver of arrows were missing, and Excalibur, the sword of Avalon, lay like a cross in the snow.

Not a pace away, the snow-fox kit lay drenched and panting but still alive. Lassorio picked it up. It was so weak that it could not lift its head and it shivered horribly. Holding on to Excalibur, he stumbled away, trying to find Gwydion's cottage, but the master hunter Lassorio had lost his way, and exhaustion and darkness obliged him to give up.

All through the night, he sat curled beneath the snow-laden firs. While owls hooted in the boughs, flapping sturdy wings, he cared for the kit. Keeping it warm, feeding it water, melted snow he had warmed in the palm of his hand. He could not feel the tips of his fingers nor the soles of his feet, but he cared more about the kit than for himself.

He kept the kit close to his ear, heartened in the blackness by the tiny sounds of its breathing. Against his will, he dozed off once or twice, only to start awake, his heart beating like a hammer, listening for each breath the kit took. Between the boughs, he could see the stars and, since he felt nothing when he knelt in Christian churches, he prayed to the myriad points of light that as a child had fascinated him. Words failed him, but he prayed nonetheless, a mute litany of feeling.

At what point the tiny snow-fox gave up its last breath he could not say. Perhaps he had dozed off again. In any case, there came a time when he no longer heard that little engine sighing, when the shivering stopped and the body lay cold and lifeless in his hands.

"Ah, God, what have I done!" And Lassorio wept as he had not been able to do when his father died, or when he had buried his own stillborn son. He wept as he had alone and un-attended at the side of his wife's grave.

Placing the tiny corpse in the snow, he scrabbled for his skinning knife, but it, too, was gone, lost, no doubt, beneath the ice-encrusted surface of the lake. So he took up Excalibur, mighty sword of Arthur, the King, the uniter of Britain, and drove it point first into the snow at the base of the fir. He worked like a madman, chipping away at the ice and rock-hard earth until he had made a deep grave. Into this, he placed the kit, weeping still, and used the sword's point to cover the body. Then, the sword across his knees, he sat with his back against the fir and stared out at the lake, at Avalon, hidden in the mists.

He must have fallen asleep, for when he awoke, it was near midnight, judging by the polestar. He was still staring into the mists rising off the icy lake, but now he discerned movement there, and he rose, peering out. Starlight illuminated a figure coming toward him from out of the mists. At first, he thought it was the woman out of whose mouth he had pulled the sword—Viviane, high priestess of Avalon, the Lady of the Lake. But then, as she came closer, he found he stared into a face whose every feature had been graven in his mind.

As he watched, astounded, he saw the milky skin, the corn-silk hair, the eyes the color of a winter's sky reflected in ice.

It was his wife, come back to him!

Unlike all other weapons, it is a sword of life, the woman had said of Excalibur. And here was his beloved, returned from the dead.

She held out her arms to him as she stepped upon the shore, and Lassorio ran to her, picked her up, held her tight and swung her around in silent triumph. Beneath the fir tree, he kissed her hard on the lips and said, "Dearest, I can scarcely believe that you have come back to me."

"Hold me, Charles," his wife said. "I have been away such a long time."

"But now you are back," he whispered, softly stroking her hair. "That is all that matters."

"I love you so," she sighed as she melted in his arms.

He took her, having had neither his wife nor any woman for a great time, and plunged inside her. He felt whole again, his guilt expunged, all his sorrows washed away in the great cataclysm they made together. Safe and warm in her arms, he drifted into a deep and dreamless sleep, and did not awake until it was already light and the winter birds were calling to one another across the icy expanse of the lake.

He rolled over, ready to say good morning to his beloved, but she was gone. In her place lay curled and breathing lightly a large snow-fox, which stared at him out of bright blue eyes.

The next day, Lassorio helped the snow-fox deliver four kits, all of which were born healthy and hungry. When he was done, he drew Excalibur from the icy ground into which he had thrust it. It felt light as a feather. How easy it would be, he thought, to strap on the sword, take it back with him to Camelot. With its magic he could, no doubt, reclaim the throne that had been Arthur's, could quite possibly even reunite all of England. Once this might have been his fate, but that Lassorio no longer existed. Perhaps he had discovered what Arthur, Mordred and even the wizard Merlin had not: the true healing nature of the sword's power.

He left the snow-fox there beneath the fir tree with her babies suckling at her teats and went down the slippery bank to the lake. Fog, lying low like a tapestry of water spiders, shrouded Gallion. He stood for a long time while the dew dripped dolefully from the trees and the world around him slowly vanished. What he expected he had no idea.

Perhaps he slipped into a trance, for it seemed to him now that he heard the far-off tolling of a bell. Its tone was so ethereal, so exquisite, he was certain that it came from no man-made carillon, that it could emanate only from Avalon itself, lost in fog and time across Gallion's expanse.

As if this were a signal, he raised the sword high over his head, pointing the tip into the fog. The tolling continued to reverberate across the lake, building in intensity until it filled up the day as the burning sun does in high summer.

And then, as he watched, a dark form appeared from out of the fog. As it glided toward him, he began to recognize its outline. A black barge was being poled across Gallion, a vessel, he had absolutely no doubt, that had originated in Avalon. He half expected to see Arthur, tall and stately and fierce, the King somehow resurrected if only for this sorcerous moment. But now that the barge was closer, he recognized the figure standing at its prow: it was Gwydion.

With his flowing beard, his fierce crow's eyes and his black robes, Lassorio recognized him for who he really was.

"I knew you were destined for the Sword, hunter," Merlin said. His voice, coming across the water, possessed an eerie echo. "Now you can continue Arthur's work. England sorely needs another man of firm hand and iron resolve."

Lassorio shook his head. "For me, the magic has already been worked."

"But Excalibur can bring you everything. Do you not understand its power?"

"Oh, I understand it perfectly." And so saying, Lassorio headed out into the lake. He held the sword carefully by its blade, and when he was close enough to the black barge the water was circling his chest. "This no longer belongs to me," he said, handing it hilt first to the magician. "It belongs to the ages."

Merlin frowned. "But you are part of the scheme, hunter."

"Whose scheme, magician, yours or mine? This man who stands before you has been purged of his taste for war, intrigue and suffering."

Merlin was silent a long while before he nodded. "I see that even after all these years magic still retains its facility for wonderment." He smiled and lifted his hand, and the barge began to back away into the gathering fog. "Go with God, Sir Lassorio," he whispered.

The black water, purling around Lassorio's chest, had lost its chill. He bent down, dipped his head beneath the tiny wavelets set up by the barge's departure. Curiously, the tolling of the Avalon bell was clearer beneath the lake, but when he raised his head, water streaming down his face and neck, even the echoes, caught by the fog, had vanished.

There was no sign that Merlin or the barge had ever existed. He turned, heading back to shore. His step was light, despite his exhaustion and the weight of his sodden clothes. And why not? He was eager to return to the castle Camelot, which for the first time since he had taken possession of it, seemed to him like home.

For My Father,
Who Told Me Stories of The Ancient Kings of England
Straight From His Own Head.

Controlling the Sword

KRISTINE KATHRYN RUSCH

e preferred the bayonet. A musket shot poorly at best and was likely to blow up in a man's face. A knife could be knocked free. But a bayonet garroted the enemy well, surprising a man at arm's length and not giving him time to recover.

But weapons debates were moot now. Nicholas spent his days in the family estates near Kent, hiding from the *ton* with its debutantes searching for husbands and randy widows expecting satisfaction. To them he was a hero. They looked at the poorly healed scar on his cheek, and saw not the edge of a blood-spattered knife that came too close to the eye, but the romantic mark of an untamed rake. They touched his empty right sleeve, pinned to his shoulder, with admiration, wanting the story. But he could not tell a green girl about the heat in Salamanca, the blood lust in the eyes of the Frenchman who slit him from shoulder to wrist, and the awful infection that made his arm swell and ache until the bone surgeons decided to hack it off.

After three nights of witty repartee, he could take no more. He had been in hiding ever since.

He spent his evenings alone in the library, a fire in the hearth, a glass of port clutched in his left fist. He had not realized what a luxury it had been to sit before a fire, a glass of port in one hand, a good cigar in the other—an enjoyment in which he would never again partake. The books around him had been his father's, Romances and Grand Adventures, monographs from the colonies, and Histories of everything from the house and family to the Far and Mysterious East. Once he might have read, but these days he did not. He stared into the orange flames burning black against the stone face of the hearth or the two swords crossed beneath his father's portrait, their red tassels dangling on the dust-covered marble mantle.

The swords frightened him.

At night he would dream that he would hear them clatter against the flagstone before the hearth. Once he had run down the stairs expecting to see them lying on the floor, dripping with blood, but the library had been as he left it, his empty glass beside the chair and the cherry-red embers still giving off a bit of warmth.

The carriage that pulled into the yard was black with a dray horse, obviously hired. Nicholas watched from the large windows in the hall as the young boy opened the door, then hesitated before stepping down alone.

The boy was slight, his hair dark. As he turned, Nicholas gasped. No doubt. This was his brother's child.

Not that there had been a doubt before. The letter from the solicitor had arrived almost a month earlier carrying copies of the boy's birth records. Richard Adam Lucien Worth, heir apparent to the family fortune. Nicholas would act as guardian until the lad reached his majority.

Nicholas sighed. He went to the door, which Simms the butler had already opened, and stood behind it, sinister lord of the manor. Simms was warmer: he hurried down the stairs to help the boy. The cabbie merely waited until the baggage had been removed from the back, then clucked to the horse and drove away, leaving the boy standing in the dust. The bags were two, patched and poor, certainly not befitting a lord's son.

A lord's son. Until a month before, Nicholas had thought he had inherited the family estate.

The boy stared at the house, his thin mouth open. He had Randolph's face not the face of the man known throughout London for his way with the ladies, but the older brother Nicholas remembered, the one who hesitated before he acted, lest he incur their father's wrath.

The house, with its wide turrets and branching wings, probably did look imposing to a boy raised on the Scottish moors. His mother had fled to her family upon discovering Randolph's indiscretions. But her parents had died some years back, and she had followed them with an ague. Neighbors contacted Randolph's solicitors when they found the boy living alone.

Nicholas hadn't even known Randolph was married.

Simms reached the boy and immediately picked up his cases. The wind caught most of the conversation, but Nicholas could catch the deferential tone in Simms's voice, the way he gently said, "Young Master." Nicholas nodded. Good. The boy would need someone gentle. Nicholas certainly wouldn't be it.

As they walked up the stairs, the boy kept glancing back at Simms, as if he expected the older man to drop the cases. The boy's breeches were torn and his hair needed trimming. The wind brought with it the scent of little-boy sweat—he needed a scrubbing, had probably not had one since his mother died, if then. When the boy saw Nicholas, he stopped, his eyes growing darker, just as Randolph's would have.

"Me lord uncle." The boy's voice had a touch of the Scottish burr.

The title and the deference rankled. Nicholas didn't want

the boy here. He wanted to be left alone, with his meager fires, his one arm and his port. "You're to call me Nick," he said, "after the very devil himself."

Then he spun on one booted foot and stalked to the library, slamming the door behind him.

Simms and Pratt, the housekeeper, had managed to keep the boy away from him for three whole days. On the fourth, Nicholas trotted down the stairs just after noon, his head thick and achy with the drink he had imbibed the night before. He had planned to go to the stables, to work Midnight, but the idea of sitting astride the big black stallion, reins caught in only one hand, was ridiculous. An entire bottle of port had not drowned the image.

Still, he wore his riding boots and coat, and carried his short whip. Perhaps after a bit of nuncheon he would have the courage to mount a horse—any horse—one-handed.

As he passed the library, he saw the boy, standing before the cold hearth, staring up at the crossed swords. The boy didn't hear Nicholas approach. This time the lad looked not like Randolph but like Nicholas himself a lifetime ago, when he thought the swords a symbol of his future as a warrior.

" 'Tis said your great-great-great—ah, I don't know how many greats—grandfather used those swords against Cromwell."

The boy jumped at the sound of Nicholas's voice, and turned, his body snapping to attention.

Nicholas put his left hand behind his back. He wasn't sure what had possessed him to speak to the boy. "The old man was named Richard, which is, I believe, your given name."

"Me mother called me Dickie," the boy said.

"Here in England," Nicholas said, "we shall call you Richard."

The boy licked his lips. " 'Taint a boy's name," he said, his voice small.

The desire behind the protest was not lost on Nicholas. "Perhaps you're right. 'Tis too formal for a boy. But Dickie has no dignity. When we sup tonight, you shall tell me which of your given names you prefer to use."

The boy's tongue appeared again, over the tops of his lips. They were chapped. "You want ter sup together?"

"Tonight," Nicholas said, and bowed once, a slight acknowledgment of his rudeness. The boy looked horribly lonely. And why wouldn't he be? In a strange country, in a strange home, with a man who in a fit of pique had compared himself to the devil?

"Them swords," the boy said. "Ya ever use them?"

Nicholas permitted himself a wry smile. "Once," he said. "When I was a boy."

"Could ya learn me ter use them?" The boy was stiffly formal, his hands clasped behind his back in an unconscious imitation of Nicholas.

"I was right-handed," Nicholas said. "I doubt I could show you anything." He slapped his whip against his boots. "Dinner. Seven sharp."

Then he went to the stables to see if he could mount Midnight.

He had been little older than the boy the afternoon he had tried the sword. He had moved one of the stools close to the hearth, and stood on the top. The mantel—kept highly polished in those days—stabbed him in the chest. He had to stand on his toes to reach the hilt of the top sword. He yanked it up and back from its perch. The sword weighed twice as much as he expected. It nearly dislodged his father's portrait. He swung it down to save the art, and lost his balance in the process.

The fall seemed interminable. His right arm, his sword

arm, led the way, and the sword hit first, its clang echoing through the great room. He landed on his back, which knocked the air out of him. The hilt jabbed into the soft skin beside his spine. Pain shot up and through him, making him gasp.

Footsteps echoed in the outer hall, but he couldn't pick himself up, couldn't force himself to stand and hide his misdeed. Collins, his father's man, arrived first, and stopped at the door, his wig askew, his heavy features flushed with exertion.

"Lord, young man," he said. "You done it now. You damned yourself, 'tis what you've done."

"Don't fill his head with such nonsense." His father pushed past Collins. His blouse was loose and his graying hair untied and flowing over his shoulders. His breeches were newly cleaned and in one hand he held a matching great coat. He had been about to go out. "What have you done, boy?"

Nicholas was still gasping for air. No words emerged. He rolled off the hilt and onto his side. Each movement brought him agony. Collins stooped beside him, and pried the hilt from his right hand. " 'Tis doomed you are," he said. "You'll be a cripple for the rest of your days."

The pain was enough that Nicholas believed him. He might never stand again.

" 'Tis a silly superstition," his father said, "and I'll not have you speak to him of it." He took the sword from Collins and rehung it beneath the portrait without benefit of the stool. "I told you not to touch anything in this room, lad."

"Aye." Nicholas's voice wheezed out of him. Slowly the air was coming back. Cool air touched his bare skin as Collins lifted up his shirt.

"He has a nasty bruise, milord. I think we should send for the doctor."

Nicholas hated the doctor, a man with dirty fingers and a stained coat. "No," he said, sitting up. "I'll be all right."

"Leave us," his father said to Collins.

"As you wish, sir." Collins stood and bowed. He left the room.

His father put a hand behind Nicholas and helped him to his feet. The movement was painful, but not unbearably so, now that his wind was returning.

"What did he mean, 'crippled'?"

His father gave him an odd look, as if for the first time he were seeing his son as a man. "A wives' tale," he finally said. " 'Tis scratched into the hilt in Latin: 'He who cannot control the sword is forever at its mercy.' My father couldn't wield it properly, and later lost his leg in fighting the insurrection in the colonies. There was an uncle who played with the swords and lost a finger. The stories go like that. The superstitious always look for ways to explain misfortune."

Nicholas nodded. The pain in his back ran up and down his spine. He longed for a chair and a cold compress over his eyes. "Are you going to punish me, sir?" he asked, wanting this meeting to end.

"I think your accident was punishment enough," his father said. "Just remember: This room is not a place for little boys."

He had wrestled with the horse and lost. When he came down the stairs for supper, every inch of his body ached. His man had had to clean straw from his hair, and scrub blood from his chin from the time he had bitten his lower lip. He wanted nothing more than a long, quiet evening with a lot of port to drown the humiliation from memory.

The boy was already at the table, in what had once been Randolph's spot, to the left of the master of the house. Head bent, hands clasped in his lap, the boy appeared smaller than he was.

"Heads up, lad," Nicholas snapped. "This is a meal, not a church."

"Sorry, sir." The boy brought his head up, his longish hair falling into his eyes. He brushed it away with one hand.

Nicholas leaned on his left hand as he eased himself into the chair. Each movement made him ache. He was like a child, unused to the saddle. He would be limping for days.

A door banged in the kitchen, then Simms emerged, carrying a silver tureen. Apparently he and Mrs. Pratt had decided to go all out for this meal. Simms set the tureen down and began ladling out the soup. The broth had a savory odor, and Nicholas's stomach rumbled.

The boy gulped, and bobbed his head, once. "I've made up me mind, sir," he said.

"Yes?" Nicholas watched as Simms set the soup bowl in front of him. Beef, potatoes and carrots floated in the thin brown broth. He didn't care what the boy had decided. He merely wanted to end the meal and get on with the evening.

"Adam, sir. Do ya think they'll find it manly enough here in England?"

Simms set broth in front of the boy. Nicholas blinked at him for a moment, confused. Then he remembered the conversation from the afternoon. The boy was choosing his name. He nearly said that anything was better than Dickie, but the boy's hopeful look stopped him. "I daresay they'll think it first-rate."

The boy—Adam now—flushed with pleasure. He dug into his soup, clutching his spoon in his fist and shoveling food in his face like a boy in an orphans' home.

"Adam, did your mother teach you to eat like that?"

Adam froze. "Nay, sir. She said a lad should eat slow ter enjoy the meal."

Nicholas nodded. He wished he could dig through the food as Adam had done. "Do as she taught you," he said. Then he rubbed his remaining hand on his breeches and picked up his own spoon. Eating left-handed still felt awkward to him, and he had never before done it in front of another. His hand shook as he brought it to his lips.

"Did ya kill him?"

Nicholas swallowed the rich soup, and frowned. He set his spoon down. "Kill whom?"

"The man what done it ter ya. Took yer arm."

Nicholas felt the heat rise in his cheeks. No one had ever asked him a direct question about his injury. Not even the girls of the *ton*. They had hinted, but never once asked. "Aye," Nicholas said. It was difficult to get the words past his lips. "I stuck him with my bayonet."

And the man had screamed before he fell, one more body on top of a pile of bodies in all that smoky heat. Nicholas's last act with his right arm. He had fainted himself, moments after that.

"Good," the lad said. "Then yer a hero, like they say."

Nicholas's appetite had fled. He swallowed, somehow feeling it important to speak. "No, lad. Killing another man does not make me a hero."

"But ya made it through one of the bloodiest battles of the war."

Nicholas picked up his spoon. He had to eat. He made himself dip the spoon in the broth. "Aye," he said. "And sometimes I wish I hadn't."

That night, he dreamed an old dream, one he first had in Spain. He was feverish, lying on a cot in the heat, men screaming around him. Flies buzzed around his face, and the tent smelled of rotting flesh. His arm hurt so badly that each touch sent him into agony.

The bone surgeon stood over him, his uniform covered with blood. "We have to take the arm."

"No." Nicholas's throat was parched and the words were little more than a whisper.

Then Collins came up behind the surgeon, the sword in his work-roughened hands. " 'Tis because of the accident, young man," Collins said. "If you'd not taken the sword, you'd keep the arm."

"Superstition!" His father's voice boomed over the screaming men. "My son cannot control the weapon. He deserves to die."

"Take the arm," Collins said. " 'Tis the boy's fate. He'll live, leastways."

Nicholas made himself sit up. The darkness was oppressive. He could still feel the heat from the dream. The stench of rotting flesh and too many bodies packed too close together remained in his nostrils. But he felt the bed linens beneath him, and saw the familiar shapes of his armoire, fireplace and chair outlined in the thin moonlight streaming through the window.

With the back of his hand, he wiped the sweat off his brow, then put his head on his knees.

"Marriage is easy in Scotland, you know."

The muscles in Nicholas's back tensed. He had heard Randolph's voice. But that was impossible. He brought his head up. The moonlight outlined his brother, sitting in the chair that had been empty a moment before. Randolph was relaxed, an elbow leaning on the chair back, and his left ankle resting on his right knee. Typical Randolph, all fluidity and ease.

"The girl was pretty, and Father wanted an heir." Randolph grinned, as if they were having a conversation over dinner. "When she told me she was pregnant, I wed her and brought her back here. All seemed fine, until her eighth month, when she caught me with Lady Alexander *in flagrante dilecto.* The girl fled, against the doctor's advice, and since we never heard, we assumed the child had died."

It was a dream. It had to be. Randolph was dead. Nicholas sat cross-legged. "You lost your soul somewhere, Dolph. 'Twas not the way to treat your wife and child."

Randolph shrugged. "We never said the banns. She wasn't landed. Father said we could get it annulled, if it ever really existed."

Nicholas rubbed his hand over his eyes. The movement made him feel wide awake. "Strange thing to come back from the grave to tell me, Dolph. I care less about your sham of a marriage than you did."

"I think not, Brother," Randolph said. "There is no marriage on record. You could cut the boy if you like."

A chill ran down Nicholas's spine, as if Randolph had run his dead fingers along Nicholas's skin. "I have no intention of denying the boy his inheritance."

Randolph stood. As he turned, the moonlight reflected off his white shirt, revealing a small, bloody hole near his heart. "Don't lie to me, Nicky. 'Tis why you try to drown yourself in drink, to hide the anger you feel at losing the title yet again. This time to a boy."

" 'Tis not why I'm angry!" The words exploded from Nicholas with a force that he hadn't known he had. "I am angry at you, Dolph. You died while I was gutting Frenchmen for Wellington. You died in a duel you didn't have to fight, protecting some woman's nonexistent honor—"

"Actually," Randolph said, leaning against the wall, arms crossed over the hole in his chest, "I died protecting my own nonexistent honor."

Nicholas was shaking. He had lied to himself so effectively, he hadn't realized there was anger beneath the drink. "I came home half a man to find I had nothing to come home to. No family, no one who cared so much as a whit that I survived."

Randolph shrugged. "You came home to all this. Without the boy, you could be lord here."

"I have none of your ambitions," Nicholas said. "I have my own income and no need for the estate."

Randolph bowed, slightly, in mockery. "Then I had no

need to come here. Forgive me, dear brother. As usual, I have misunderstood you."

Nicholas placed his hand behind him to brace himself on the bed. His outburst had left him shaken. " 'Twas a senseless way to die," he said.

" 'Twas a senseless way to live." Randolph's voice had an unusual seriousness. He ran a hand through his hair, and then grinned. "You needn't worry, Nicky. This will be my only trip. No sense in the neighbors thinking the manse is haunted."

"They wouldn't think of ghosts, Dolph," Nicholas said. "They would merely use it as confirmation of my growing insanity."

But by the time he finished the sentence, the moonlight illuminated a bare patch of wall and an empty chair. Nicholas took in a deep breath. He was still shaking, and he hadn't moved, but Randolph was gone.

The dreams were over. Nicholas was awake for the rest of the night.

The next morning, he left his chamber early and went to the stables. He took out the gentlest horse, a mare his father had purchased for guests, and dismissed the grooms. Then he worked at mounting, concentrating each time on retaining his balance. Over the year of his illness and recovery, he had lost much strength. The problem was not really the loss of his arm but the loss of strength in his body. What had once been effortless now took a great deal of concentration and energy. He mounted on the second try, and controlled the reins with his left, letting the mare set the pace while he relearned how to ride.

He returned to the house at noon, planning to change before nuncheon. As he passed the library, he noted Adam, staring at the swords. The boy stood in the same position he had used the day before: hands clasped behind his back, head up, shoulders back, and brow furrowed as if in concentration.

Nicholas tucked the quirt in his boot and went into the library. " 'Tis truly not a room for boys," he said, hearing his father's voice speak through his own.

Adam looked around sharply, as if he hadn't realized that Nicholas was there. "I'm sorry, sir," he said.

Nicholas glanced at the swords. They gleamed. Mrs. Pratt kept them cleaned, just like she kept the portrait free of dust. Only the mantel seemed to escape her careful attention. "The swords fascinated me as a boy," he said.

"And me da?"

Something in the boy's tone made Nicholas turn. The boy had bit his lower lip in anticipation of Nicholas's response.

Nicholas chose his words carefully. "Swords were not your father's weapons."

"But I thought ya took one each. Ter Spain." The boy's face reddened as he spoke. His small body was rigid as a soldier's before a general.

"To Spain?" Nicholas frowned. The boy thought his father had fought with Wellington. *Yer a hero, then.* The boy knew nothing of Randolph, nor of his death. "Nay. The blades we use now tip the ends of rifles. I daresay your father was good with a gun."

But not good enough. Or quick enough.

You could cut the boy if you like.

"A gun?" the boy asked, as if guns lacked romance.

"Aye," Nicholas said. The air felt fragile between them. The wrong word would shatter the moment.

Adam returned his gaze to the swords. "Me ma did na talk about him, 'cept ter say I got the look of him."

"In your face," Nicholas said. "You have the look of him as a boy in your face."

Adam's body tensed. "He were a good man, right, sir? I asked Father John, and he said he did na know."

Your father drank too much and cared nothing for you. He made no provisions for you, and probably would have turned you away had he lived. Nicholas licked his lips. One couldn't say such things to a child. It was hard enough growing up with a real father—a taciturn man who only noticed when a boy did something wrong. Growing up alone in a strange home had to be twenty times more difficult.

"Your father," Nicholas said slowly, "was the best man he knew how to be."

The boy whirled, beaming. "I knew it. The old missus next door, she said 'twere a crime the way he treated his family. But she did na know him. Ya knew him."

"Once," Nicholas said. A lump had risen in his throat. He had to swallow hard to make it go away. He had been fifteen when he left the house, and already Randolph was lost to him. His big brother had become a man more interested in the gay festivities of the *ton* than in the political realities of England. Perhaps the ghostly Randolph had been right; perhaps Nicholas had been angry. But it had been the anger of a second son who thought the eldest was squandering the family name. Since, Nicholas had made his own name, and had learned that such things were rarely important.

"Once?" the boy repeated. "Then she was right?"

The joy had fled from the boy's expression. Randolph had never had a face that mobile. Nicholas felt the loss. He hadn't realized how much he had basked in the warmth of the boy's emotion. "Ah, lad," he said. "Men are not saints, no matter how much you want them to be."

And because he could no longer stand to field the boy's questions, Nicholas turned and quickly climbed the stairs.

That night, long after the rest of the house fell asleep, Nicholas sat in the library and stared into the flames. He held a glass of port in his left hand—the same glass that he had poured when he arrived. The port no longer eased the ache or prevented the dreams, and he was tired of waking with a muzzy head and a sour taste in his mouth.

He stared at the swords. Superstition. Yet here he was, crippled for the rest of his life, just as Collins had said. Perhaps if he took the swords down successfully . . .

He shook his head. The thought was silly. Even if he removed the swords, he would still miss an arm. He would always and forever retain a physical memory of that field in Salamanca.

You could cut the boy.

Rich, landed and powerful. And still unable to hold a glass of port in one hand and a cigar in the other. He had his commission and his income from his mother's home near London. More than enough for a man who lived as he did.

A man who for another ten years had to raise a boy not his own.

And me da?

Lad, your da was no better than the rest of us. Nicholas stood, leaving the port on the table, and headed up to bed. As he passed the swords, he touched the tassels lightly with his good hand. A shiver ran up his back.

He who cannot control the sword is forever at its mercy.

Aye. 'Twas truth in that.

The next morning, Nicholas was up at dawn. He took Midnight on a canter through the property, noting that the servants had kept it up despite his neglect. He would go over the books in the afternoon, making certain all were well paid. He and the stallion returned lathered. The groomsmen offered to take the horse from him, but Nicholas did the work instead. He needed to stretch his muscles, and he needed to learn to take care of himself with a single hand.

He finished mid-morning, and paused outside the stables to take a deep lungful of air. He hadn't seen this time of day in weeks, perhaps months. The sunlight cast everything in gold and gave the grounds a freshness they lacked by midday. He stood for a moment, basking in it, then went inside.

As he passed the library, a movement caught his eye. He went to the door, his soldiering instincts making him move quietly. Adam had pulled a stool over to the mantel—the same stool Nicholas had used years before—only Adam had his back to the door. He leaned across, the edge of the mantel pressing against his chest, as he reached for the hilt of the nearest sword.

Nicholas tried to speak, but the words stopped in his throat. If the boy did not try this time, he would try later. Nicholas remembered that much of his childhood. Instead, he positioned himself only a few feet away from the boy, close enough to use his body to break the boy's fall.

Adam grabbed the hilt and eased the sword off its perch. Its weight unbalanced him and he swayed. Nicholas took a step inward. His heart knocked against his chest. A remembered pain ran up his back, but still he waited.

Adam gripped the top of the mantel with his left hand and steadied himself, the sword pointing downward.

It was nearly as long as the boy. Adam held his place and swung the sword at an imaginary enemy. The sword made a whoosh in the air. He stopped quickly, the back of his clothes suddenly drenched in sweat.

Nicholas swallowed. He had been holding his breath. Something inside him felt envy at the boy's prowess. Perhaps if he had had such strength, perhaps then, he would not be standing here, like this.

Adam took his other hand off the mantel and swayed precariously. He braced his right wrist with his left hand and tried to return the sword to its place. But its weight was too much for him to lift above his head, and he started to tilt to the side.

Immediately, Nicholas was beside him. He put his arm around Adam's waist, holding the boy in place. The boy was warm and too thin. Nicholas could feel the knobs of the boy's spine through his shirt.

"Lor', sir," the boy said. His voice was breathless. "Ya scared me."

Then they were even. Nicholas steadied the boy, then took the sword from the boy's grasp. The sword was lighter than he remembered, with a more elegant feel than a bayonet. With a simple movement, he returned the sword to its place above the mantel. Then he helped the boy down.

The boy's face was crimson. He kept his head bowed, hunching his shoulders forward as if he expected to get hit. Nicholas returned the stool to its place.

" 'Tis sorry I am, sir," Adam said. "I should na have touched it."

What have you done? I told you not to touch anything in this room, lad.

Nicholas's father's words nearly escaped his lips. But Nicholas stopped them. He had wanted his father to hold him, to reassure him about the bruise that would plague him for nearly two weeks. His father had said nothing more.

The accident is punishment enough.

"You may do as you wish," Nicholas said. He swallowed the fear and anger that were threatening to overtake him. "You are lord of this place, after all."

The boy's eyes widened. He had clearly never thought in such terms.

"But," Nicholas said. "I am your guardian, and I think it might be wise if you listen to me."

The boy bit his chapped lips. "I will na touch them again, sir."

Nicholas crouched in front of the boy, seeing for the first time the fatigue lines beneath the boy's eyes, the hollows in the boy's cheeks, the sores on the inside edge of the boy's lips. Although the boy now lived in rich circumstances, he still had no one to care for him. "The swords fascinate you, don't they, boy?"

Adam nodded. His wide eyes stared at Nicholas's face.

"England has no use for swordsmen," Nicholas said.

"I do na wish ter be a soldier, sir," the boy said, his flush growing even deeper. "Beg pardon."

Adam beneath bodies on the fields of Salamanca: flies swarming overhead, the sun beating down with an intensity foreign to England. The boy flailed with his right hand, trying to get someone's attention, but he did not call for help.

Nicholas swallowed. "No offense taken," he said.

The boy took a deep, slow breath, as if he were trying to calm himself.

"If I can find someone to teach you, would you like to learn the sword?"

The boy exhaled. His eyes watered. He blinked rapidly, and averted his gaze. "Do ya think I could?"

"Aye," Nicholas said. "As long as you take other lessons. We'll teach you to speak the King's English and find you a tutor so that you can attend Cambridge when the time comes."

Adam nodded, willing to agree to anything, it seemed, as long as he could touch the sword.

"Go now, and tell Simms we need an early nuncheon. I'm hungry, aren't you?"

"Aye, sir." The boy fled as if the hounds of hell pursued him. Nicholas stood and surveyed the swords. Clean, and polished, shining in the daylight, they still had a menace to them.

The boy would learn to control them. And he would learn the history of their use. Weapons did not cripple. Men did.

Perhaps, in time, Adam would understand that.

Perhaps, in time, others would understand as well.

Perhaps a man would no longer need a favorite weapon, and the bloody fields would become a distant memory.

Nicholas stared at the swords, as he had when he was a boy.

One could only dream.

Surgeon's Steel

DIANA GABALDON

t was near evening; the sun sank invisibly, staining the fog with a dull and sullen orange. The evening wind off the river was rising, lifting the fog from the ground and sending it scudding in billows and swirls.

Clouds of black-powder smoke lay heavy in the hollows, lifting more slowly than the lighter shreds of mist, and lending a suitable stink of brimstone to a scene that was—if not hellish—at least bloody eerie.

Here and there a space would suddenly be cleared, like a curtain pulled back to show the aftermath of battle. Small, dark figures moved in the distance, darting and stooping, stopping suddenly, heads uplifted like baboons keeping watch for a leopard. Camp followers; the wives and whores of the soldiers, come like crows to scavenge the dead.

Children, too. Under a bush, a boy of nine or ten straddled the body of a red-coated soldier, smashing at the face with a heavy rock. I stopped, paralyzed at the sight, and saw the boy reach into the gaping, bloodied mouth and wrench out a tooth.

He slipped the bloody prize into a bag that hung by his side, groped farther, tugging, and finding no more teeth loose, picked up his rock in a businesslike way and went back to work.

I felt bile rise in my throat, and hurried on, swallowing. I was no stranger to war, to death and wounds. But I had never been so near a battle before; I had never before come on a battlefield where the dead and wounded still lay, before the ministrations of medics and burial details.

There were calls for help, and occasional moans or screams, ringing disembodied out of the mist, reminding me uncomfortably of Jamie's story of the *tannasg*, the doomed spirits of the glen. Like the hero of that story, I didn't stop to heed their call, but pressed on, stumbling over small rises, slipping on damp grass.

I had seen photographs of the great battlefields, from the American Civil War to the beaches of Normandy. This was nothing like that—no churned earth, no heaps of tangled limbs. It was still, save for the noises of the scattered wounded and the voices of those calling, like me, for a missing friend or husband.

Shattered trees lay toppled by artillery; in this light, I might have thought the bodies turned into logs themselves, dark shapes lying long in the grass—save for the fact that some of them still moved. Here and there, a form stirred feebly, victim of war's sorcery, struggling against the enchantment of death.

I paused and shouted into the mist, calling his name. I heard answering calls, but none in his voice. Ahead of me lay a young man, arms outflung, a look of blank astonishment on his face, blood pooled round his upper body like a great halo. His lower half lay six feet away. I walked between the pieces, keeping my skirts close, nostrils pinched tight against the thick, iron smell of blood.

The light was fading now, but I saw Jamie as soon as I came over the edge of the next rise. He was lying on his face in the hollow, one arm flung out, the other curled beneath him. The shoulders of his dark blue coat were nearly black with damp, and his legs thrown wide, booted heels askew.

The breath caught in my throat, and I ran down the slope toward him, heedless of grass clumps, mud, and brambles. As I got close, though, I saw a scuttling figure dart out from behind a nearby bush and dash toward him. It fell to its knees beside him and, without hesitation, grasped his hair and yanked his head to one side. Something glinted in the figure's hand, bright even in the dull light.

"Stop!" I shouted. "Drop it, you bastard!"

Startled, the figure looked up as I flung myself over the last yards of space. Narrow red-rimmed eyes glared up at me out of a round face streaked with soot and grime.

"Get off!" she snarled. "I found 'im first!" It was a knife in her hand; she made little jabbing motions at me, in an effort to drive me away.

I was too furious—and too afraid for Jamie—to be scared for myself.

"Let go of him! Touch him and I'll kill you!" I said. My fists were clenched, and I must have looked as though I meant it, for the woman flinched back, loosing her hold on Jamie's hair.

"He's mine," she said, thrusting her chin pugnaciously at me. "Go find yourself another."

Another form slipped out of the mist and materialized by her side. It was the boy I had seen earlier, filthy and scruffy as the woman herself. He had no knife, but clutched a crude metal strip, cut from a canteen. The edge of it was dark, with rust or blood.

He glared at me. "He's ours, Mum said! Get on wi' yer! Scat!"

Not waiting to see whether I would or not, he flung a leg

over Jamie's back, sat on him, and began to grope in the side pockets of his coat.

" 'E's still alive, Mum," he advised. "I can feel 'is 'eart beatin'. Best slit his throat quick; I don't think 'e's bad hurt."

I grabbed the boy by the collar and jerked him off Jamie's body, making him drop his weapon. He squealed and flailed at me with arms and elbows, but I kneed him in the rump, hard enough to jar his backbone, then got my elbow locked about his neck in a stranglehold, his skinny wrist vised in my other hand.

"Leave him go!" The woman's eyes narrowed like a weasel's, and her eyeteeth shone in a snarl.

I didn't dare take my eyes away from the woman's long enough to look at Jamie. I could see him, though, at the edge of my vision, head turned to one side, his neck gleaming white, exposed and vulnerable.

"Stand up and step back," I said, "or I'll choke him to death, I swear I will!"

She crouched over Jamie's body, knife in hand, as she measured me, trying to make up her mind whether I meant it. I did.

The boy struggled and twisted in my grasp, his feet hammering against my shins. He was small for his age, and thin as a stick, but strong nonetheless; it was like wrestling an eel. I tightened my hold on his neck; he gurgled and quit struggling. His hair was thick with rancid grease and dirt, the smell of it rank in my nostrils.

Slowly, the woman stood up. She was much smaller than I, and scrawny with it—bony wrists stuck out of the ragged sleeves. I couldn't guess her age—under the filth and the puffiness of malnutrition, she might have been anything from twenty to fifty.

"My man lies yonder, dead on the ground," she said, jerking her head at the fog behind her. " 'E hadn't nothing but his musket, and the sergeant'll take that back."

Her eyes slid toward the distant wood, where the British troops had retreated. "I'll find a man soon, but I've children to feed in the meantime—two besides the boy." She licked her lips, and a coaxing note entered her voice. "You're alone; you can manage better than we can. Let me have this one—there's more over there." She pointed with her chin, toward the slope behind me, where the rebel dead and wounded lay.

My grasp must have loosened slightly as I listened, for the boy, who had hung quiescent in my grasp, made a sudden lunge and burst free, diving over Jamie's body to roll at his mother's feet.

He got up beside her, watching me with rat's eyes, beady-bright and watchful. He bent and groped about in the grass, coming up with the makeshift dagger.

"Hold 'er off, Mum," he said, his voice raspy from the choking. "I'll take 'im."

From the corner of my eye, I had caught the gleam of metal, half-buried in the grass.

"Wait!" I said, and took a step back. "Don't kill him. Don't." A step to the side, another back. "I'll go, I'll let you have him, but . . ." I lunged to the side, and got my hand on the cold metal hilt.

I had picked up Jamie's sword before. It had been made for him, larger and heavier than the usual. It must have weighed ten pounds, at least, but I didn't notice.

I snatched it up and swung it in a two-handed arc that ripped the air and left the metal ringing in my hands.

Mother and son jumped back, identical looks of ludicrous surprise on their round, grimy faces.

"Get away!" I said.

Her mouth opened, but she didn't say anything.

"I'm sorry for your man," I said. "But my man lies here.

Get away, I said!" I raised the sword, and the woman stepped back hastily, dragging the boy by the arm.

She turned and went, muttering curses at me over her shoulder, but I paid no attention to what she said. The boy's eyes stayed fixed on me as he went, dark coals in the dim light. He would know me again—and I him.

They vanished in the mist, and I lowered the sword, which suddenly weighed too much to hold. I dropped it on the grass, and fell to my knees beside Jamie.

My own heart was pounding in my ears and my hands shaking with reaction as I groped for the pulse in his neck. I turned his head, and could see it, throbbing steadily just below his jaw.

"Thank God!" I whispered to myself. "Oh, thank God!"

I ran my hands over him quickly, searching for injury before I moved him. I didn't think the scavengers would come back; I could hear the voices of a group of men, distant on the ridge behind me—a rebel detail coming to fetch the wounded.

There was a large knot on his brow, already turning purple. Nothing else that I could see. The boy had been right, I thought, with gratitude; he wasn't badly hurt. Then I rolled him onto his back, and saw his hand.

Highlanders were accustomed to fight with sword in one hand, targe in the other, the small leather shield used to deflect an opponent's blow. He hadn't had a targe.

The blade had struck him between the third and fourth fingers of his right hand, and sliced through the hand itself, a deep, ugly wound that split his palm and the body of his hand, halfway to the wrist.

Despite the horrid look of the wound, there wasn't much blood; the hand had been curled under him, his weight acting as a pressure bandage. The front of his shirt was smeared with red, deeply stained over his heart. I ripped open his shirt and felt inside, to be sure that the blood was from his hand, but it

was. His chest was cool and damp from the grass, but un-
scathed, his nipples shrunken and stiff with chill.

"That . . . tickles," he said, in a drowsy voice. He pawed
awkwardly at his chest with his left hand, trying to brush my
hand away.

"Sorry," I said, repressing the urge to laugh with the joy of
seeing him alive and conscious. I got an arm behind his shoulders and helped him to sit up. He looked drunk, with one eye
swollen half-shut and grass in his hair. He acted drunk, too,
swaying alarmingly from side to side.

"How do you feel?" I asked.

"Sick," he said succinctly. He leaned to the side and threw
up.

I eased him back on the grass and wiped his mouth, then
set about bandaging his hand.

"Someone will be here soon," I assured him. "We'll get
you back to the wagon, and I can take care of this."

"Mmphm." He grunted slightly as I pulled the bandage
tight. "What happened?"

"What happened?" I stopped what I was doing and stared
at him. "*You're* asking *me?*"

"What happened in the battle? I mean," he said patiently,
regarding me with his one good eye. "I know what happened
to me—roughly," he added, wincing as he touched his forehead.

"Yes, roughly," I said rudely. "You got yourself chopped
like a butchered hog, and your head half caved in. Being a sod-
ding bloody hero again, that's what happened to you!"

"I wasna—" he began, but I interrupted, my relief over
seeing him alive being rapidly succeeded by rage.

"You didn't have to go! You *shouldn't* have gone! Stick to
the writing and the printing, you said. You weren't going to
fight unless you had to, you said. Well, you *didn't* have to, but

you did it anyway, you vainglorious, pigheaded, grandstanding Scot!"

"Grandstanding?" he inquired.

"You know just what I mean, because it's just what you did! You might have been killed!"

"Aye," he agreed ruefully. "I thought I was, when the dragoon came down on me. I screeched and scairt his horse, though," he added more cheerfully. "It reared up and got me in the face with its knee."

"Don't change the subject!" I snapped.

"Is the subject not that I'm not killed?" he asked, trying to raise one brow and failing, with another wince.

"No! The subject is your stupidity, your bloody, selfish stubbornness!"

"Oh, that."

"Yes, that! You—you—oaf! How dare you do that to me? You think I haven't got anything better to do with my life than trot around after you, sticking pieces back on?" I was frankly shrieking at him by this time.

To my increased fury, he grinned at me, his expression made the more rakish by the half-closed eye.

"Ye'd have been a good fishwife, Sassenach," he observed. "Ye've the tongue for it."

"You shut up, you fucking bloody—"

"They'll hear you," he said mildly with a wave toward the party of Continental soldiers making their way down the slope toward us.

"I don't care who hears me! If you weren't already hurt, I'd—I'd—"

"Be careful, Sassenach," he said, still grinning. "Ye dinna want to knock off any more pieces; ye'll only have to stick them back on, aye?"

"Don't bloody tempt me," I said through my teeth, with a glance at the sword I had dropped.

He saw it and reached for it, but couldn't quite manage. With an explosive snort, I leaned across his body and grabbed the hilt. I heard a shout from the men coming down the hill, and turned to wave at them.

"Anyone hearing ye just now would likely think ye didna care for me owermuch, Sassenach," he said behind me.

I turned to look down at him. The impudent grin was gone, but he was still smiling.

"Ye've the tongue of a venomous shrew," he said, "but you're a bonnie wee swordsman, Sassenach."

My mouth opened, but the words that had been so abundant a moment before had all evaporated like the rising mist. The sword felt cold and heavy in my hand.

"I'll tell ye later why," he said softly, and laid his good hand on my arm. "But for now, *a nighean donn*—thank ye for my life."

I closed my mouth. The men had nearly reached us, rustling through the grass, their exclamations and chatter drowning out the ever-fainter moans of the wounded.

"You're welcome," I said.

"Hamburger," I said, under my breath, but not far enough under. He raised an eyebrow at me.

"Chopped meat," I elaborated, and the eyebrow fell.

"Oh, aye, it is. Stopped a swordstroke wi' my hand. Too bad I didna have a targe; I could have turned the stroke, easy."

"Right." I swallowed. It wasn't the worst injury I'd seen, by a long shot, but it still made me slightly sick. The tip of his fourth finger had been sheared off cleanly, at an angle just below the nail. The stroke had sliced a strip of flesh from the inside of the finger, and ripped down between the third and fourth fingers, splitting his hand halfway to the wrist.

"You must have caught it near the hilt," I said, trying for

calm. "Or it would have taken off the outside half of your hand."

"Mmphm." The hand didn't move as I prodded and poked, but there was sweat on his upper lip, and he couldn't keep back a brief grunt of pain.

"Sorry," I murmured automatically.

"It's all right," he said, just as automatically. He closed his eyes, then opened them.

"Take it off," he said suddenly.

"What?" I drew back and looked at him, startled.

He nodded at his hand.

"The finger. Take it off, Sassenach."

"I can't do that!" Even as I spoke, though, I knew that he was right. Aside from the injuries to the finger itself, the tendon was badly damaged; the chances of his ever being able to move the finger, let alone move it without pain, were infinitesimal.

"It's done me little good in the last twenty years," he said, looking at the mangled stump dispassionately, "and likely to do no better now. I've broken the damn thing half a dozen times, from its sticking out like it does. If ye take it off, it wilna trouble me any more, at least."

I wanted to argue, but I knew he was right. Besides, there was no time; wounded men were beginning to drift up the slope toward the wagon. The men were militia, not regular army; if there was a regiment near, there might be a surgeon with them, but I was closer.

"Once a frigging hero, always a frigging hero," I muttered under my breath. I thrust a wad of lint into Jamie's bloody palm and wrapped a linen bandage swiftly around the hand. "Yes, I'll have to take it off, but later. Hold still."

"Ouch," he said mildly. "I did say I wasna a hero."

"If you aren't, it isn't for lack of trying," I said, yanking the linen knot tight with my teeth. "There, that will have to do for now; I'll see to it when I have time." I grabbed the wrapped hand and plunged it into the small basin of alcohol and water.

He went white as the alcohol seeped through the cloth and struck raw flesh. He inhaled sharply through his teeth, but didn't say anything more. I pointed peremptorily at the blanket I had spread on the ground, and he lay back obediently, curling up under the shelter of the wagon, bandaged fist cradled against his breast.

I rose from my knees, but hesitated for a moment. Then I knelt again and hastily kissed the back of his neck, brushing aside the queue of his hair, matted with half-dried mud and dead leaves. I could just see the curve of his cheek; it tightened briefly as he smiled, and then relaxed.

Word had spread that the hospital wagon was there; there was already a straggling group of walking wounded awaiting attention, and I could see small groups making their way up the slope, men carrying or half-dragging their injured companions. It was going to be a busy evening.

I missed Marsali and Young Ian badly. Colonel Everett had promised me two assistants, but God knew where the Colonel was at the moment. I took a moment to survey the gathering crowd, and picked out a young man who had just deposited a wounded friend beneath a tree.

"You," I said, tugging on his sleeve. "Are you afraid of blood?"

He looked momentarily startled, then grinned at me through a mask of mud and powder-smoke. He was about my height, broad-shouldered and stocky, with a face that might have been called cherubic had it been less filthy.

"Only if it's mine, ma'am, and so far it ain't, Lord be praised."

"Then come with me," I said, smiling back. "You're now a triage aide."

"Say what? Hey, Harry!" he yelled to his friend. "I been

promoted. Tell your momma next time you write, Lester done amounted to something, after all!" He swaggered after me, still grinning.

The grin rapidly faded into a look of frowning absorption, as I led him quickly among the wounded, pointing out degrees of severity.

"Men pouring blood are the first priority," I told him. I thrust an armful of linen bandages and a sack of lint into his hands. "Give them these—tell their friends to press the lint hard on the wounds or put a tourniquet round the limb above the wound. You know what a tourniquet is?"

"Oh, yes, ma'am," he assured me. "Put one on, too, when a panther clawed up my cousin Jess, down to Caroline County."

"Good. Don't spend time doing it yourself here unless you have to, though—let their friends do it. Now, broken bones can wait a bit—put them over there under that big beech tree. Head injuries and internal injuries that aren't bleeding, back there, by the chestnut tree, if they can be moved. If not, I'll go to them." I pointed behind me, then turned in a half-circle, surveying the ground.

"If you see a couple of whole men, send them up to put up the hospital tent; it's to go in that flattish spot, there. And then a couple more, to dig a latrine trench . . . over there, I think."

"Yes, sir! Ma'am, I mean!" Lester bobbed his head and took a firm grip on his sack of lint. "I be right after it, ma'am. Though I wouldn't worry none about the latrines for a while," he added. "Most of these boys already done had the shit scairt out of 'em." He grinned and bobbed once more, then set out on his rounds.

He was right; the faint stink of feces hung in the air, as it always did on battlefields, a low note amid the pungencies of blood and smoke.

With Lester sorting the wounded, I settled down to the work of repair, with my medicine box, suture bag, and bowl of alcohol set on the wagon's tailboard and a keg of alcohol for the patients to sit on—provided they could sit.

The worst of the casualties were bayonet wounds; luckily there had been no grapeshot, and the men hit by cannonballs were long past the point where I could help them. As I worked, I listened with half an ear to the conversation of the men awaiting attention.

"Wasn't that the damnedest thing ye ever saw? How many o' the buggers were there?" one man was asking his neighbor.

"Damn if I know," his friend replied, shaking his head. "For a space there, ever'thing I saw was red, and nothin' but. Then a cannon went off right close, and I didn't see nothin' but smoke for a good long time." He rubbed at his face; tears from watering eyes had made long streaks in the black soot that covered him from chest to forehead.

I glanced back at the wagon, but couldn't see under it. I hoped shock and fatigue had enabled Jamie to sleep, in spite of his hand, but I doubted it.

Despite the fact that nearly everyone near me was wounded in some fashion, their spirits were high and the general mood was one of exuberant relief and exultation. Farther down the hill, in the mists near the river, I could hear whoops and shouts of victory, and the undisciplined racket of fifes and drums, rattling and screeching in random exhilaration.

Among the noise, a nearer voice called out; a uniformed officer, on a bay horse.

"Anybody seen that big, redheaded bastard who broke the charge?"

There was a murmur and a general looking-around, but no one answered. The horseman dismounted and, wrapping his reins over a branch, made his way through the throng of wounded toward me.

"Whoever he is, I tell you, he's got balls the size of ten-pound shot," remarked the man whose cheek I was stitching.

"And a head of the same consistency," I murmured.

"Eh?" He glanced sideways at me in bewilderment.

"Nothing," I said. "Hold still just a moment longer; I'm nearly done."

It was nearly dawn before I came back to the tent where he lay. I lifted the flap quietly so as not to disturb Jamie, but he was already awake, lying curled on his side facing the flap, head resting on a folded blanket.

He smiled faintly when he saw me.

"A hard night, Sassenach?" he asked, his voice slightly hoarse from cold air and disuse. Mist seeped under the edge of the flap, tinted yellow by the lantern light.

"I've had worse." I smoothed the hair off his face, looking him over carefully. He was pale, but not clammy. His face was drawn with pain, but his skin was cool to the touch—no trace of fever. "You haven't slept, have you? How do you feel?"

"A bit scairt," he said. "And a bit sick. But better now you're here." He gave me a one-sided grimace that was almost a smile.

I put a hand under his jaw, fingers pressed against the pulse in his neck. His heart bumped steadily under my fingertips, and I shivered briefly, remembering the woman in the field.

"You're chilled, Sassenach," he said, feeling it. "And tired, too. Go and sleep, aye? I'll do a bit longer."

I *was* tired. The adrenaline of the battle and the night's work in the surgeon's tent was fading fast; fatigue was creeping down my spine and loosening my joints. But I had a good idea of what the hours of waiting had cost him already.

"It won't take long," I reassured him. "And it will be better to have it over. Then you can sleep easy."

He nodded, though he didn't look noticeably reassured. I unfolded the small worktable I had carried in from the operating tent, and set it up in easy reach. Then I took out the precious bottle of laudanum, and poured an inch of the dark, odorous liquid into a cup.

"Sip it slowly," I said, putting it into his right hand. I began to lay out the instruments I would need, making sure that everything lay orderly and to hand. I had thought of asking Lester to come and assist me, but he had been asleep on his feet, swaying drunkenly under the dim lanterns in the operating tent, and I had sent him off to find a blanket and a spot by the fire.

A small scalpel, freshly sharpened. The jar of alcohol, with the wet ligatures coiled inside like a nest of tiny vipers, each toothed with a small, curved needle. Another, with the waxed dry ligatures for arterial compression. A bouquet of probes, their ends soaking in alcohol. Forceps. Long-handled retractors. The hooked tenaculum, for catching the ends of severed arteries.

The surgical scissors with their short, curved blades, and the handles shaped to fit my grasp, made to my order by the silversmith, Stephen Moray. Or almost to my order. I had insisted that the scissors be as plain as possible, to make them easy to clean and disinfect. Stephen had obliged with a chaste and elegant design, but had not been able to resist one small flourish— one handle boasted a hooklike extension against which I could brace my little finger in order to exert more force, and this extrusion formed a smooth, lithe curve, flowering at the tip into a slender rosebud, against a spray of leaves. The contrast between the heavy, vicious blades at one end and this delicate conceit at the other always made me smile when I lifted the scissors from their case.

Strips of cotton gauze and heavy linen, pads of lint, adhesive plasters stained red with the dragon's-blood juice that made them sticky. An open bowl of alcohol for disinfection as I worked, and the jars of cinchona bark, mashed garlic paste, and yarrow for dressing.

"There we are," I said with satisfaction, checking the array one last time. Everything must be ready, since I was working by myself; if I forgot something, no one would be at hand to fetch it for me.

"It seems a great deal o' preparation, for one measly finger," Jamie observed behind me.

I swung around to find him leaning on one elbow, watching, the cup of laudanum undrunk in his hand.

"Could ye not just whack it off wi' a wee knife and seal the wound with hot iron, like the regimental surgeons do?"

"I could, yes," I said dryly. "But fortunately I don't have to; we have enough time to do the job properly. That's why I made you wait."

"Mmphm." He surveyed the row of gleaming instruments without enthusiasm, and it was clear that he would much rather have had the business over and done with as quickly as possible. I realized that to him this looked like slow and ritualized torture, rather than sophisticated surgery.

"I mean to leave you with a working hand," I told him firmly. "No infection, no suppurating stump, no clumsy mutilation, and—God willing—no pain, once it heals."

His eyebrows went up at that. He had never mentioned it, but I was well aware that his right hand and its troublesome fourth finger had caused him intermittent pain for years, ever since it had been crushed at Wentworth Prison, when he was held prisoner there in the days before the Stuart Rising.

"A bargain's a bargain," I said with a nod at the cup in his hand. "Drink it."

He lifted the cup and poked a long nose reluctantly over the rim, nostrils twitching at the sickly-sweet scent. He let the dark liquid touch the end of his tongue and made a face.

"It will make me sick."

"It will make you sleep."

"It gives me terrible dreams."

"As long as you don't chase rabbits in your sleep, it won't matter," I assured him. He laughed despite himself, but had one final try.

"It tastes like the stuff ye scrape out of horses' hooves."

"And when was the last time you licked a horse's hoof?" I demanded, hands on my hips. I gave him a medium-intensity glare, suitable for the intimidation of petty bureaucrats and low-level army officials.

He sighed.

"Ye mean it, aye?"

"I do."

"All right, then." With a reproachful look of long-suffering resignation, he threw back his head and tossed the contents of the cup down in one gulp.

A convulsive shudder racked him, and he made small choking noises.

"I did say to sip it," I observed mildly. "Vomit, and I'll make you lick it up off the floor."

Given the scuffled dirt and trampled grass underfoot, this was plainly an idle threat, but he pressed his lips and eyes tight shut, and lay back on the pillow, breathing heavily and swallowing convulsively every few seconds. I brought up a low stool and sat down by the camp-bed to wait.

"How do you feel?" I asked a few minutes later.

"Dizzy," he replied. He cracked one eye open and viewed me through the narrow blue slit, then groaned and closed it. "As if I'm falling off a cliff. It's a verra unpleasant sensation, Sassenach."

"Try to think of something else for a minute," I suggested. "Something pleasant, to take your mind off it."

His brow furrowed for a moment, then relaxed.

"Stand up a moment, will ye?" he said. I obligingly stood, wondering what he wanted. He opened his eyes, reached out with his good hand and took a firm grip of my buttock.

"There," he said. "That's the best thing I can think of. Having a good hold on your arse always makes me feel steady."

I laughed, and moved a few inches closer to him, so his forehead pressed against my thighs.

"Well, it's a portable remedy, at least."

He closed his eyes then and held on tight, breathing slowly and deeply. The harsh lines of pain and exhaustion in his face began to soften as the drug took effect.

"Jamie," I said softly, after a minute. "I'm sorry about it."

He opened his eyes, looked upward, and smiled, giving me a slight squeeze.

"Aye, well," he said. His pupils had begun to shrink; his eyes were sea-deep and fathomless, as though he looked into a great distance.

"Tell me, Sassenach," he said a moment later. "If someone stood a man before ye, and told ye that if ye were to cut off your finger, the man would live, and if ye did not, he would die—would ye do it?"

"I don't know," I said, slightly startled. "If that was the choice, and no doubt about it, and he was a good man . . . yes, I suppose I would. I wouldn't like it a bit, though," I added practically, and his mouth curved in a smile.

"No," he said. His expression was growing soft and dreamy. "Did ye know," he said after a moment, "a colonel came to see me, whilst ye were at work wi' the wounded? Colonel Johnson; Micah Johnson, his name was."

"No; what did he say?"

His grip on my bottom was beginning to slacken; I put my own hand over his, to hold it in place.

"It was his company—in the fight. Part of Morgan's Riflemen, and the rest of the regiment just over the hill, in the path of the British. If the charge had gone through, they'd ha' lost the company surely, he said, and God knows what might have become o' the rest." His soft Highland burr was growing broader, his eyes fixed on my skirt.

"So you saved them," I said gently. "How many men are there in a company?"

"Fifty," he said. "Though they wouldna all have been killed, I dinna suppose." His hand slipped; he caught it and took a fresh grip, chuckling slightly. I could feel his breath through my skirt, warm on my thigh.

"I was thinking it was like the Bible, aye?"

"Yes?" I pressed his hand against the curve of my hip, keeping it in place.

"That bit where Abraham is bargaining wi' the Lord for the Cities of the Plain. 'Wilt thou not destroy the city,'" he quoted, "'for the sake of fifty just men?' And then Abraham does Him down, a bit at a time, from fifty to forty, and then to thirty, and twenty and ten."

His eyes were half-closed, and his voice peaceful and unconcerned.

"I didna have time to inquire into the moral state of any o' the men in that company. But ye'd think there might be ten just men among them—good men?"

"I'm sure there are." His hand was heavy, his arm gone nearly limp.

"Or five. Or even one. One would be enough."

"I'm sure there's one."

"The apple-faced laddie that helped ye wi' the wounded—he's one?"

"Yes, he's one."

He sighed deeply, his eyes nearly shut.

"Tell him I dinna grudge him the finger, then," he said.

I held his good hand tightly for a minute. He was breathing slowly and deeply, his mouth gone slack in utter relaxation. I rolled him gently onto his back and laid the hand across his chest.

"Bloody man," I whispered. "I knew you'd make me cry."

*   *   *

The camp outside lay quiet, in the last moments of slumber before the rising sun should stir the men to movement. I could hear the occasional call of a picket, and the murmur of conversation as two foragers passed close by my tent, bound for the woods to hunt. The campfires outside had burned to embers, but I had three lanterns, arranged to cast light without shadow.

I laid a thin square of soft pine across my lap as a working surface. Jamie lay facedown on the camp-bed, head turned toward me so I could keep an eye on his color. He was solidly asleep; his breath came slow and he didn't flinch when I pressed the sharp tip of a probe against the back of his hand. All ready.

The hand was swollen, puffy and discolored, the sword-wound a thick, black line against the sun-gold skin..I closed my eyes for a moment, holding his wrist, counting his pulse. *One-and-two-and-three-and-four . . .*

I never prayed consciously when preparing for surgery, but I did look for something—something I could not describe, but always recognized, a certain quietness of soul, the detachment of mind in which I could balance on that knife-edge between ruthlessness and compassion, at once engaged in utmost intimacy with the body under my hands; capable of destroying what I touched in the name of healing.

One-and-two-and-three-and-four . . .

I realized with a start that my own heartbeat had slowed; the pulse in my fingertip matched that in Jamie's wrist, beat for beat, slow and strong. If I was waiting for a sign, I supposed that would do. *Ready, steady, go,* I thought, and picked up the scalpel.

A short horizontal incision over the fourth and fifth knuckles, then down, cutting the skin nearly to the wrist. I undermined the skin carefully with the scissors' tips, then pinned back the loose flap of skin with one of the long steel probes, digging it into the soft wood of the board.

I had a small bulb-atomizer, filled with a solution of distilled water and alcohol; sterility being impossible, I used this to lay a fine mist over the operating field and wash away the first welling of blood. Not too much; the vasoconstrictor I had given him was working, but the effect wouldn't last long.

I gently nudged apart the muscle fibers—those that were still whole—to expose the bone and its overlying tendon, gleaming silver among the vivid colors of the body. The sword had cut the tendon nearly through, an inch above the carpal bones. I severed the few remaining fibers, and the hand twitched disconcertingly in reflex. I bit my lip, but it was all right; aside from the hand, he hadn't moved. He felt different; his flesh had more life than that of a man under ether or Pentothal. He was not anesthetized, but only drugged into stupor; the feel of his flesh was resilient, not the pliant flaccidity I had been accustomed to in my days at the hospital in my own time. Still, it was a far cry—and an immeasurable relief—from the live and panicked convulsions that I had felt under my hands in the surgeon's tent.

I brushed the cut tendon aside with the forceps. There was the deep branch of the ulnar nerve, a delicate thread of white myelin, with its tiny branches spreading into invisibility, deep in the tissues. Good, it was far enough toward the fifth finger that I could work without damage to the main nerve trunk.

You never knew; textbook illustrations were one thing, but the first thing any surgeon learned was that bodies were unnervingly unique; a stomach would be roughly where you expected it to be, but the nerves and blood vessels that supplied it might be anywhere in the general vicinity, and quite possibly varying in shape and number as well.

But now I knew the secrets of this hand. I could see the engineering of it, the structures that gave it form and movement. There was the beautiful strong arch of the third metacarpal, and the delicacy of the web of blood vessels that supplied it. Blood welled, slow and vivid: deep red in the tiny pool of the open field, brilliant scarlet where it stained the chopped bone; a dark and royal blue in the tiny vein that pulsed below the joint, a crusty black at the edge of the original wound, where it had clotted.

I had known, without asking myself how, that the fourth metacarpal was shattered; the joint of the fourth finger that lay within the hand. It was; the blade had struck near the proximal end, splintering the head of the tiny bone near the center of the hand.

I would take that, too, then; the free chunks of bone would have to be removed in any case, to prevent them irritating the adjoining tissues. Removing the finger from the metacarpal joint would let the third and fifth fingers lie close together, in effect narrowing the hand and eliminating the awkward gap that would be left by the missing finger.

I pulled hard on the mangled finger, to open the articular space between the joints, then used the tip of the scalpel to sever the ligament. The cartilages separated with a tiny but audible *pop!* and Jamie jerked and groaned, his hand twisting in my grasp.

"Hush," I whispered to him, holding tight. "Hush, it's all right. I'm here, it's all right."

I could do nothing for the boys dying on the field, but here, for him, I could offer magic, and know the spell would hold. He heard me, deep in troubled opium dreams; he frowned and muttered something unintelligible, then sighed deeply and relaxed, his wrist going once more limp under my hand.

Somewhere near at hand, a rooster crowed, and I glanced at the wall of the tent. It was noticeably lighter, and a faint dawn wind drifted through the slit behind me, cool on the back of my neck.

Detach the underlying muscle with as little damage as

could be managed. Tie off the small digital artery and two other vessels that seemed large enough to bother with, sever the last few fibers and shreds of skin that held the finger, then lift it free, the dangling metacarpal surprisingly white and naked, like a rat's tail.

It was a clean, neat job, but I felt a brief sense of sadness as I set the mangled piece of flesh aside. I had a fleeting vision of him holding Alexander, newly born, counting the tiny fingers and toes, delight and wonder on his face. His father had counted his fingers, too.

"It's all right," I whispered, as much to myself as to him. "It's all right. It will heal."

The rest was quick. Forceps to pluck out the tiny pieces of shattered bone. I debrided the wound as best I could, removing bits of grass and dirt, even a tiny swatch of fabric that had been driven into the flesh. Then no more than a matter of cleaning the ragged edge of the wound, snipping a small excess of skin, and suturing the incisions. A paste of garlic and white-oak leaves, mixed with alcohol and spread thickly over the hand, a padding of lint and gauze, and a tight bandage of linen and adhesive plasters, to reduce the swelling and encourage the third and fifth fingers to draw close together.

The sun was nearly up; the lantern overhead seemed dim and feeble. My eyes were burning from the close work and the smoke of fires. There were voices outside; the voices of officers, moving among the men, rousing them to face the day—and the enemy?

I laid Jamie's hand on the cot, near his face. He was pale, but not excessively so, and his lips were a pale rosy color, not blue. I dropped the instruments into a bucket of alcohol and water, suddenly too tired to clean them properly. I wrapped the discarded finger in a linen bandage, not quite sure what to do with it, and left it on the table.

"Rise and shine! Rise and shine!" came the sergeants'

rhythmic cry from outside, punctuated by witty variations and crude responses from reluctant risers.

I didn't bother to undress; if there was fighting today, I would be roused soon enough. Not Jamie, though. I had nothing to worry about; no matter what happened, he wouldn't fight today.

I unpinned my hair, and shook it down over my shoulders, sighing with relief at its looseness. Then I lay down on the cot beside him, close against him. He lay on his stomach; I could see the small, muscular swell of his buttocks, smooth under the blanket that covered him. On impulse, I laid my hand on his rump and squeezed.

"Sweet dreams," I said, and let the tiredness take me.

Prayer of the Knight of the Sword

NANCY HOLDER

Sister, where hast thou been?

n Glastonbury they gathered, veiled by the mist: the four exquisite queens of this Earth, this Air, this Fire, this Water. This England. In their glittering robes of gold, silver, ruby, and sapphire, they stood with their arms around each other and watched the old man plodding his way to the mount. He was very, very old; he was wizened and feeble. Yet within his breast beat a great and holy heart, and in his head he carried a staff. His name was Joseph, and he was near death.

They wept for him, and they hoped for England.

The sky was hushed and gray; he did not see them as his worn feet found the way; he paused often to catch his breath and wipe his brow. She of the Air cooled his cheeks with kisses; She of the Earth lay upon the path to make it smoother; She of the Fire caressed him with warming rays; and She of the Water opened her arms and caused a spring to form, at the which he knelt to take a cooling drink.

"Praise be to God," Joseph said, crossing himself, and the four queens smiled tenderly. Then he continued on. The route was steep and there were no trees. He leaned more heavily on his staff, using it to steady himself as his legs shuddered and wobbled.

"But a little more," whispered the Queen of the Air, and the sisters clasped hands and wished for him his youth again, though it was not theirs to give.

He struggled on, and at last he reached the top. Wheezing, he looked down at the rude village of Glastonbury. A wind gusted his white hair and beard, and his eyes filled with emotion. The sisters knew that though he was a stranger here, he had grown to care for the harsh people who were now rising from their slumbers to tend to their flocks, their children, their homes.

"As I have tended to your souls," he whispered. He leaned on his staff. It sank a few inches into the moist soil. "Here will I build a church. The first church of Our Lord in this land. I will share with you stories of life everlasting."

The Queen of the Earth sighed. She murmured to the others, "Sisters, it is time."

And as they gathered around the old man, roots shot from the base of the staff; and at its head, leaves grew, and thorns and branches, rich and new and living. The old man cried out; he grabbed his chest and tumbled to the ground.

"Not yet, not yet," he rasped. "My work . . ."

And as the sun rose, the four queens threw off their veils and encircled him, North, South, East, West.

"Wha—what? Who are you, angels?" he managed as he held his chest.

"Rest, Arimathea," said the Queen of Fire. She touched his chest. "We'll take you now to a place of saints."

And as they traveled with the bier back down the mount and toward the water, the staff grew and grew, and became a thorn bush.

And She of the Fecund Valleys cut it down and brought forth metal.

And She of the Wind and Clouds blew the flames that forged the metal.

And She of the Red Fires gave the metal shape.

And She of the Still and Raging Depths cooled it.

Sister, where hast thou been?

The walls were breached.

Thousands and tens of thousands poured into the Holy City, shrieking the Berserker howls of their forefathers. Like madmen they raged over the walls, over the palms and stones, and no Infidel was safe—no Moslem man, no Jewish child, no woman of any heresy. To the sword, to the cleansing blade! Thousands slain, and tens of thousands: the streets of Jerusalem ran with the blood even of those who had paid for safe passage with gold and jewels, and fair daughters. Now the Holy Crusaders cut them all down, and burned the mosque around those they had promised to spare. Butchery most foul, betrayal most unchristian.

Geoffrey de Troyes staggered through the carnage and wept. His hands were stained with red, though he had not touched a single unbeliever with his sword. Blood and gore covered his black tunic with its white cross of Jesus the Christ and dripped onto his sollerets. He fell once, twice, as the sky foamed black with smoke and desperate pleas: *For the love of your god, for the love of your mothers.*

"We're routing them!" A tonsured youth clapped Geoffrey on the back. The young man's face was smeared with blood and soot; his eyes were wild in the mask of crimson and black. "Jerusalem is free at last!"

Geoffrey said nothing. The youth dashed away and plunged his sword into the side of a mongrel dog. It yelped piteously, raising its front left paw as if to stop the vicious boy.

Its head tilted upward, fell back, and then the creature crumpled to the ground.

"You swine!" Geoffrey shouted. The boy laughed over his shoulder and raced on, in search of other sport.

Geoffrey fell to his knees and folded his hands over his breast. This was because of that lance, that damned—

No, he must not blaspheme. The priests had proclaimed it genuine. It was the very Lance that had pierced the side of Our Sovereign Lord. A holy relic, a sign that God was on their side. That the armies of Christendom must prevail over the hordes of the East.

When they found it, wedged in the cleft of a rock in the valley where once the damned had sacrificed to Baal, it raised the spirits of the Crusaders, who had been so downtrodden and downhearted, and reminded them of their holy purpose. They became the Lord's own anointed, soldiers of the cross; they became avenging angels. They swooped down upon the unsuspecting multitudes and they—

—they—

Geoffrey vomited. He could not be one of them. He could not be here. He had thought to be a hero, a martyr for the Lord's Own cause. Not a murderer, not a barbarian savage. This was not what he was; he had wanted to be a hero, though that reeked of the sin of pride.

The smallest of sins committed this day.

"Oh, my God, my God, we have forsaken thee," he murmured, crossing himself. "Verily, verily, we are become thine enemies." He was ashamed, and terrified. The sky was a smoking conflagration of scarlet and ebony; he could see the wrath of God raining down on them, His hands full of thunderbolts, His eyes burning with righteous fury.

Geoffrey trembled. Fires soared and shot into the air, higher than the raging Dome of the Rock, than the walls of the ancient city. To his right, the Mount of Olives smoked; small fires licked the bases of some of the trees. They had come to save the Holy City, but it seemed their fate was to destroy it.

"In the name of the Lance!" The booming voice of Richard, his liege, rose over the shrieks and the crackling and the crashing. Geoffrey tried to follow the voice, running toward the west through the smoke. A woman jumped in front of him and fell onto her knees and then onto her side. She held her bloody hands toward him in supplication, then uttered a cry of terror as Geoffrey fell beside her, clasping her fingers against his chest.

"My sister," he whispered, though she was not his sister, not in Christ at any rate. "Alas, woman."

Her lips moved; she whispered something; she pleaded. He imagined her asking for water, or clemency. For him to spare her life and carry her to a safe haven. Without thinking, he picked her up and staggered forward. He had no idea where to take her. There was no security in Jerusalem, neither for Crusader nor for heathen.

Tears and sweat streamed down his face. Smoke clouded his way. Warriors rushed past, some merely jostling him, others rudely pushing him into the stone walls. His armor was heavy, the woman, though light, a burden. She was coughing and hiding herself with her veils. Her legs were round and firm, the curve of her breast but inches from his fingers. Though the men here took several wives, he and his fellows had taken vows of chastity that many, to his shame, were breaking that day. Vows of poverty long ago forgotten as they had looted their way to the Holy City.

The only vow they had honored was that of obedience, and that in all probability because Richard was a brutal master who brooked not the slightest variation from his edicts. He had told his warriors to spare no unbeliever, no man, no woman, no child. Geoffrey was committing a grievous fault; he should be fighting this woman's kinsmen, not attempting to save one insignificant female.

Her veil fell away, but he couldn't see her face. He felt the soft fabric tattering against his hand. She turned her head and whimpered against his chest. She sounded very young. Geoffrey himself was sixteen.

He had never had a woman.

She murmured in the heathen language. He had no words, not a single one, though some of the others had taught him how to say, "How much? Too much!" and thought it a great joke. Now he wanted to ask her which way? Where were her kinsmen? Where was her family? But all he could do was ignore her weeping and concentrate, and pray to God for mercy for them both.

He carried her out under rows of smoldering arches and narrow, dark alleyways. She seemed to have fainted, or else she was dying. He said to her, "Hold, woman," and he realized it was the first time he truly thought of her as a woman, even as a human being. Urgency grew within his breast; he must find someone who spoke her language, and make an attempt to bring her to Christ, and thus to save her. It would be small recompense for all that he had done.

But what he had done, he had done for the sake of Him Who had died for the sins of the world. Had he not?

He stumbled, perplexed, exhausted, fearful for her life and for his own. Images of home flashed through his mind: his simple village of cottages and huts; and Joseph's Tower on the mount above, the flowering thorn bush that grew up the sides of the tower like lush ivy. The flowers on Midsummer's Eve, roses and lavender and larkspur. Oh, the beauty of it, the perfection.

England, his land, his love . . .

He shook his head. Was it for England that he must murder women? Or for the Pope? Or for the exaltation of his lord?

It was a lie, an abomination, and he was a fool and a devil if he obeyed Richard's edicts any longer.

"England," he whispered, calling to her. The woman stirred. His conceit: He would call her England until he had reason to call her some other name: Both, he felt, were in peril; both needed saving.

Both required miracles.

And then, through the smoke, verily, a miracle indeed: in the valley below, the white tent of the Lance, white-and-black banners flapping in the hot winds, rose like a desert mirage before his desperate eyes. It was surrounded by a throng of guards in full battle armor. They gleamed magnificently in the fiery light, like angels. He could never hope to get past them.

And She of the Air caused the wind to blow.

And She of the Fire caused the firestorms to rage smoke on the wind.

And She of the Water caused all the earthen jars to crack, and the waters to run down the streets and make the stone slick.

And She of the Earth caused the world to shake, so that the knights fell to their knees.

And in the confusion Geoffrey rolled through the flaps of the tent, and the woman flew sprawling out of his embrace. In a crack of thunder, the world went black.

When he awoke, he heard the woman coughing. She said something that sounded very like "Milord?" Reaching for her, he found nothing but the earth.

And then he saw a brilliant, shining light at the far side of the tent. It was like a flame, hot and golden, and in the center of it a long object floated. The Lance!

He got to his feet and stumbled toward it, his hands before him like one walking in his sleep. He heard nothing but a strange rumbling; and then he heard sweet, dulcet voices, as if from the throats of princesses.

Geoffrey crossed himself. "Holy Mother," he whispered. The long object . . . it was not a lance. It was a sword, of bronze and silver and gold; it was heavily engraved and encrusted with jewels at the hilt. A miracle, or a trick? Had his lord lied to them all? Were they fighting merely for treasure?

The light gleamed; it seemed to take a shape. The shape of . . . He squinted hard. His lips parted.

Of a holy woman, veiled and crowned with roses, standing upon a serpent. He whispered her name:

Britannia, Mother. Gaia, Mother.

She was tall, and braids of golden hair hung down like ropes. Her robes were white and blue, and red and brown. She opened her hands and the sweet sounds of women's voices emanated from her, and sang his name: *Geoffrey.*

"My lady, my queen." He knelt and crossed his hands over his chest, and bowed his head. "My liege."

England.

Her ivory hand grabbed the sword from the light. He held his breath. The sword came down on his right shoulder, though he felt it not; and down on his left. He closed his eyes.

"Rise, our knight."

When he opened his eyes, four queens stood before him, all of equal loveliness. One was cloaked in blue, and one in white; and one in red, and one in amber. They hovered above the ground, and their hands were clasped. Their faces were filled with entreaty.

In his hands he held the sword. He gasped from its weight; it was as if his muscles were torn from the bone as he fought to keep from lowering it to the dirt. Its gleam fascinated him: he looked at the glow and saw:

"Oh, my England," he whispered. The verdant valleys, the

clear streams, the clear, cloudless skies. His heart filled. "Oh, yes."

Then the glow shifted, slanted and dimmed; and he saw:

The poverty of the serfs: children, starving, and women dead in childbirth. Men under the lash while the nobles dined in fine, rush-strewed castles. And like a wounded creature, the land rising like a dragon and shrieking in sore pain:

England

"Ah, no. No." It couldn't be. That was not the truth of his beloved country.

"Aye." The voices were firm. And they showed him more: peasants struggling to pay taxes, old men dying in the mud. On the cold, harsh wind, the wailing and keening of thousands, the laughter of very, very few.

An old man struggling up a hill.

A young man, and . . .

joy,

relief,

prosperity,

salvation.

"What are you telling me?" Geoffrey whispered. "What am I seeing?"

As one person, the queens stretched out one hand and pointed beyond him. "Look." Their voices were truly angelic.

He turned, and gave a shout of surprise.

Near the entrance of the tent, his own body lay beside that of the woman. He looked down at himself, at his blood-smeared fingers as they gripped the sword.

"Am I dead?" he whispered, his voice shaking. "Is this . . . is this heaven?" Although he was sure it could not be.

"Yet shall you live. Until you reach England, and help save her. For there we serve a Cause beyond religions, and you shall be our Champion."

As they spoke, blood dripped from his hand, and slid in

gouts onto the blade; and the drops formed a word, and the word was

EXCALIBUR.

"Take you this sword, and take it home. For we have searched, and none in England are worthy of it for the nonce. But in your hand it will be safe, until one is born whose time will come. And until that time, Geoffrey de Troyes, shall you live."

He took a breath, and told himself that if he were still breathing, he must yet live. But the form on the floor spoke otherwise; he said, "The woman?"

They smiled as one. "The mother of a king." And in that moment his heart was smitten with love for her, and he knew he would adore and protect her though it cost him his life.

He wandered home, and it took years. And when the moon and stars were in their places, She of the Air blew the sails of his ship; and She of the Water made his way gentle; and She of the Earth cleared the forests for him; and She of the Fire kept warm his hope, and the life of the woman, until they reach the British shore. Geoffrey knelt and kissed the sand, and the woman stood waiting and watching, holding the sword with both her hands, for it was too heavy for her.

Through spring, summer, winter, and fall, they made their way to Glastonbury. Geoffrey and the woman never aged; they remained young and strong. And as they reached the village, she whispered, "A wizard named Merlin will make a bridge of dragon's breath, and a knight will come to me, Geoffrey, but it will not be you. His name will be Uther, and he will be a king."

He knew it, and was sad; for he loved her beyond all reasoning. But he was the Knight of the Sword, and her protector; and her safety was his charge and sacred duty.

"He will get on you in turn a king, the greatest king," he answered, and though his heart was sore, he rejoiced, for it would be his king, the King of England. And if truth be spoken, he loved England even more than he loved the maid.

To Glastonbury, in the snow: around them, the people starved; they begged alms, they abased themselves. The woman, shocked, wept that she had nothing to give them, but Geoffrey loved them and blessed them, murmuring, "In time, my lady, you shall give them everything."

To Glastonbury.

And within his breast beat a great and holy heart, and in his hand he carried the Sword.

Sister, where hast thou been?

Geoffrey worked his way up the path to Joseph's Tower, his left hand plunging into the thorn bush for purchase; his sword hand ever full. The sky was hushed and gray as his feet found the way. She of the Air cooled his cheeks with kisses; She of the Earth lay upon the path to make it smoother; She of the Fire caressed him with warming rays; and She of the Water opened her arms and caused a spring to form, at the which he knelt to take a cooling drink.

"Praise be to God," Geoffrey said, crossing himself, and his companion smiled tenderly.

Then he reached the top of the mount, and the base of the tower. The wild thorn bush had overtaken the citadel. The village below had fallen into ruin.

A large rock stood beside the portcullis, and at the sight of it, Geoffrey burst into tears of sorrow and relief.

"My lady, go you within," he whispered.

They regarded each other, they who had traveled for years

together. She said, "My name is Igraine." She kissed him once, full and hot on the lips; and his loins stirred.

Then she withdrew.

The sky was black, and rumbled with thunder. The last clouds over England, Geoffrey prayed. And he became aware that he was not alone.

"I knew that you were with us, always," he whispered.

The four sisters revealed themselves. "Hail, Knight," they sang in their lovely voices. They gathered round him, and put their hands each on his—so gentle, so strong!—and drove the sword down into the stone.

From the tower Igraine cried out once, as Geoffrey sank to the ground.

Sister, where hast thou been?

To Avalon, to Avalon:

In the forest they gathered, hidden by the shadows. Below them, the tourney was laid out, banners of red and blue flying above the lists, and the knights clashed and battled in their shining armor while nobles in ermine and peasants in rough weaving looked on.

"Anon, he comes," whispered She of the Water, and the others looked upon the young, beardless man in the white hawberk blazoned with a black dragon, and moved back to give him room.

" 'Zounds," he cursed. He pulled off his *chapel-de-fer* and raked his hair in a gesture of distress. "How on earth could I forget Kay's sword?"

She of the Fire cast sunbeams on the stone. In its cleft, the sword of gold and silver, sapphire and ruby sparkled in the golden light. As the youth gave a cry and ran toward it, a circle of light illuminated his head like a crown, and the sisters took one exultant breath together. The wind stirred the leaves where they stood; and for a moment it seemed the boy could see them. That would not have been surprising, given who and what he was.

"Praise be to the Holy Mother!" he cried, and grabbed the sword easily as She of the Earth released it from her breast. It was too heavy for him, and it crashed against the rock as he strained to hold it with both hands. The clang resounded through the forest, startling the creatures that lived there; an owl shot from the boughs of an oak; a trio of deer scattered into deeper shadows.

And to *Joseph*, whispered Earth, Air, Fire, Water. *For the soul of England.*

And to Arthur, for its honor.

But most of all, to Geoffrey de Troyes, for its heart.

"Arthur, what the devil are you about!" shouted a man below, at the tourney yard.

"Kay! Kay!" Arthur called. "Kay, I've got you a new sword! A better one!"

And as he ran down the embankment, half-carrying, half-dragging the immense blade, the astonished throngs began to gather; cries rose up and nobles and peasants fell to their knees.

"A miracle from God!" someone shouted. And the boy stood bewildered, the sun a crown on his head, the sword wavering in his untried hands.

And he was a king over all the realm; and his knights were knights of truth, justice, and mercy. Their quests were noble and their hearts, pure—

—for the most.

Then he was old; and as he stood by the ruined Tower and watched the sky fill with flame and cries, he wept; for his reign was at an end, and he had not protected his Holy Lady, Britannia, as he had been charged. His honor, not hers, had come first. The quest for the Grail a bargaining with God, that He should make him and his people great.

Arthur was feared, but he was not loved.

His tears were bitter as gall, red as blood; he wanted to die and he sensed that soon he would.

Sister, where has thou been?

In armor of gold, Geoffrey waited with white-robed Joseph on the banks of the island as the bier of the King drew near; and She of the Earth, and She of the Air, and She of the Fire watched over Arthur.

Joseph lifted him up, and Geoffrey knelt and pledged his fealty.

And She of the Water swam with the Sword,

the Lance,

the Staff,

and sank beneath the water and baptized it anew, with hope, and reverence, and love:

Closer, anon, ever closer to the dream

of England, blessed England.

As Geoffrey led the way to the Mother, blessed Lady Mother, who waited on the banks with tears and open arms: Britannia, Gaia, Igraine.

"But for you, it would not be," she said to Geoffrey.

"No, lady," he whispered, "but for Joseph, and King Arthur."

"Humble to the last," she rejoined. "And made meek by love. And that is why you were—and are—our Knight of the Sword. Why you are our Hope. And why you shall never perish."

Their voices raised, the four queens gathered round him—

North, South, East, and West; Earth, Air, Fire, and Water.
Faith, Hope, Charity, but the greatest of these—

Sister, where has thou been?

With our Brother.
Searching for heroes, our loves, our own. Not holy seers or
courageous kings, but true men of the heart. For only those who
love can save England,
and the world

Find them, Excalibur!
Oh, dear Caliburn.
Wake them, and move them.
Cupid's arrow is a sword.

The Prayer of the Knight, the love song, amen.

Echoes of the One Sword

T. WINTER-DAMON

I.

Whence came the One Sword blade?
From the Land of the Living.
From the Land of the Happy Dead.
From Fairyland, Beyond the Lake.

Whence came the King Sword blade?
From Avalon where it was forged.

II.

Who brought forth the One Sword, King Sword?
Why, Lugh Lamfada, Lugh of the Long Arm,
Three magickal gifts from Fairyland brought forth.

Boat of Mananan, Son of the Sea God—
Boat knowing all a man's thoughts,
Would travel where e'er he wished.

Horse of Mananan, Son of Lir—
Horse claimed could travel anywhere
O'er land and o'er the blue chain of sea.

Most wondrous of all Mananan's treasures—
Sword hight *Fragarach,*
Sword hight the Answerer,
Sword could cut through any mail.

III.

Fairy sword of Fergus, *Calad cholg,*
Blade hight Hard Dinter, two-handed swung
In battle, slashing circles shining
Bright the arch of seven colors slicing,
Sweeping down whole ranks of foemen,
Reaping blood harvest with each fell stroke
Of mighty Fergus's Rainbow Sword.

IV.

Caliburn the One Sword named by
Oxford cleric, bishop of St. Asaph,
Regum chronicler, Geoffrey of Monmouth.
Yes, selfsame Caliburn *Morte's* Malory
Translates as signifying Cut-Steel.
The One Sword the Welsh hight *caladvwlch*—
Precious stones glitter at haft and hilt.

V.

The One Sword, Once and Forever King's Sword,
Some say the sword of stone and anvil six times
Pulled. Sword of Liege Might Transference,
Lady of the Lake's blessing gift-sword,
Bringer of justice, symbol of all the Lord's good.

VI.

Mighty the One Sword, yet mightier its scabbard,
Merlin spake to Arthur of its secret lore-worth—
Scabbard worth ten of the King Sword, "For while
You keep bladesheath upon the Sun Lord's person,
Liegeship shall lose no blood, despite how sore struck,
How grievous Your darkling enemies may strive to wound."

VII.

Whence came the King Sword blade and scabbard?
From the Isle of Immortality—
From the Isle of Appletrees, of course!
From the Isle of Enchantress Morgan.
From the Isle of Promise, in the Land of Summer—
From Avalon where they were forged of dreams.

Whence came the One Sword blade and scabbard?
From Fairyland, Beyond the Lake.

Grass Dancer

OWL GOINGBACK

harlie's coming.

Roger Thunder Horse poked his head above the sandbags and sighted along the barrel of his M-16 rifle. He focused his attention at the forest beyond the perimeter wire, searching for a line too straight, an angle that didn't belong, something out of the ordinary. He knew the enemy was out there. Somewhere. Everything was just too damn quiet. Too still. Like the calm before a storm. Things always got that way right before they got hit. Even the tiny green treefrogs had hushed their shrill cries. Like Roger, they also waited.

The men of 3rd Battalion 26 Marines, K Company, knew what it was like to engage the enemy, and to face death. Their tiny outpost, stationed on top of a mountain known to them only as Hill 861, came under rocket and mortar attack nearly every night. Located in the province of Quang Tri, Hill 861 was just below the Demilitarized Zone, near the border of Laos, in the godforsaken country of Vietnam.

Two miles southeast of Hill 861 was the Khe Sanh Combat

Base, home for a little over six thousand U.S. and South Vietnamese soldiers. Khe Sanh was a regular city compared to Hill 861. The base had an airstrip, twenty-four howitzers and half a dozen tanks. A couple of miles south of the base was the village it was named for. Several other U.S. Marine outposts were scattered around the base, in an effort to keep the North Vietnamese from moving south across the border.

Neither the combat base nor the surrounding outposts had much of a deterring effect upon the North Vietnamese. Intelligence reports compiled during the past two months showed that Charlie was moving massive amounts of troops and firepower below the DMZ in preparation for something big. North Vietnamese Army divisions 325 C, 324 and 370, along with a regiment of the 304th—an elite home guard from Hanoi—were already entrenched in the area, with more units moving in every day. According to the latest estimates, there were somewhere between thirty and forty thousand North Vietnamese Army regulars in the surrounding countryside, compared with an allied force totaling less than seven thousand men.

Early yesterday morning, Company I from Hill 881 had made contact with a battalion of North Vietnamese Army regulars dug in between Hill 881 South and Hill 881 North. The tropical forest covering the mountains was so thick, they hadn't seen the enemy until they were right on top of them. Twenty marines were killed, and another thirty wounded, in the first two minutes of the firefight.

Less than an hour after the ambush, an NVA defector had appeared at the Khe Sanh airstrip waving a white flag. The defector, a 1st Lt. La Than Tonc, informed the base commander that North Vietnamese troops were preparing to overrun the base in an effort to sweep across two northern provinces to seize the city of Hue.

Charlie's coming.

Hearing the news, Roger and his fellow marines had dug

their trenches deeper, added more sandbags to the bunkers, and reinforced the perimeter with additional claymore mines, triple coils of barbed wire, German razor tape and trip flares. They had done all they could do to protect themselves. Now it was just a matter of waiting to be hit.

The waiting was the hardest part. To pass the time, most of them played cards, smoked pot, sang or shot rats. There were a lot of rats in the bunkers and trenches of Hill 861. A few, usually the new guys, would stare at the jungle for hours until they developed a blank look in their eyes known as the thousand-yard stare.

Roger wiped a hand across his face. He watched the sun as it slowly sank behind the hills to the west. Darkness was coming, and with it would come the enemy. Shadows already gathered in the valley below. To the south, a haze of bluish smoke marked the location of the village of Khe Sanh—or what was left of it. The Viet Cong had attacked Khe Sanh earlier in the day. They didn't like it that the villagers were friendly toward the Americans, trading fresh vegetables for canned rations, cigarettes and candy.

He had seen what the VC did to civilians who were friendly to Americans. Children with their limbs hacked off. Women with their vaginas cut out. Old people gut-shot and left to die. In the six months he had been in Vietnam, Roger had seen enough horrors to last him a lifetime. Maybe two.

Six months. Six months till I can get out of this hell hole. Six months till I can go home.

Going home was all he ever thought about. Day and night. Night and day. The war had lost all meaning for him. He no longer cared who won. Survival was the only thing that mattered anymore. He was just putting in his time, keeping his head down, trying not to get shot before he rotated out.

Less than a year had passed since he left the Kiowa Reservation in Oklahoma, but it seemed like a lifetime. He longed for the wide-open spaces where a man could feel the wind on his face and sleep under the stars without worrying about mortar attacks or snipers. He missed driving into town on a Saturday night to catch a movie. He missed ice-cream cones. But most of all he missed his aunt, Ruth, and his brother, Jimmy. He still remembered how upset they had been when he told them he was leaving.

"What's that?" Jimmy had asked as Roger entered the kitchen. He'd noticed the envelope in Roger's shirt pocket. Aunt Ruth turned away from the stove, where she was cooking scrambled eggs and sausages.

"Bad news?" she had asked, eyeing the envelope suspiciously. Aunt Ruth may have been well into her sixties, but she was still as sharp as ever. She didn't miss much. Roger had hoped to wait until after breakfast before discussing the contents of the letter, but he'd just have to go ahead and break the news to them.

"I'm afraid it is, Aunt Ruth," Roger said, standing beside Jimmy. "It's from Washington. I've been drafted."

Aunt Ruth put a hand on the counter to steady herself. She recovered quickly and grabbed a towel to wipe her hands off.

"Here, let me see that." She crossed the room and held her hand out. Roger handed her the envelope. Aunt Ruth read the letter twice before giving it back to him.

"So, what are you going to do?" she asked.

Roger shrugged. "What else can I do? It's not like I have a choice."

"There's always a choice to any situation." She walked back to the stove to stir her eggs. "You could go to Canada till the war's over."

Roger thought about it a moment, then shook his head. "No, that would be running away. People would say I was a coward then. I wouldn't be able to call myself a warrior, or much of a man for that matter. No, Aunt Ruth, I can't run."

She turned and looked at him, a sadness in her eyes. He really didn't have a choice. A lot of young men were moving to Canada to avoid the draft, but they weren't Indians. Roger was full-blooded Kiowa. In his veins flowed the blood of his ancestors. The blood of warriors. If he ran, he would bring disgrace on the entire tribe.

"When do you leave?" she asked.

"I have to report for my physical first thing Monday morning."

"Do you have to go away?" Jimmy asked, tears forming.

"Yeah, I have to," Roger said, squatting down beside his brother's wheelchair.

Jimmy, who was eleven, suffered from a painful spinal disease that curved his backbone and made it nearly impossible for him to walk. If nothing else, the military would provide a steady paycheck. With enough money, they might be able to find a doctor who could fix Jimmy's back. Ever since their parents had been killed in a car wreck, and they had moved in with their Aunt Ruth, there was barely enough money to buy food, let alone pay expensive doctor bills.

Roger stood up. "I almost forgot. I've got a favor to ask."

He crossed the kitchen and walked back into his bedroom. When he returned, he carried his dance regalia, which consisted of buckskin leggings, moccasins, a ribbon shirt, porcupine hair roach, bells, dance stick and fan, and an eagle-feather bustle.

"I need you to take care of this stuff until I get back," Roger said as he laid the regalia in Jimmy's lap.

Jimmy started to protest, but changed his mind and remained silent. He knew what an important responsibility he was being given. An honor. Not only was Roger one of the best traditional dancers in the state, but the forty-three golden eagle feathers used in the regalia had been passed down for generations, from one Thunder Horse to the next. Roger had used thirty-six feathers to make the bustle and the other seven for the fan.

Jimmy ran his fingers gently over the feather bustle. "It makes my hand tingle."

Roger smiled. "It's supposed to. That bustle is a medicine piece. What you're feeling is its power . . . its energy. Not only are those eagle feathers sacred, they're medicine feathers. The spirits of your ancestors are in those feathers, Jimmy. I guess a little bit of my spirit is in them too. They'll protect you while I'm gone, keep you safe till I get back."

Jimmy looked down at the bustle, then back up. "What if you don't come back?"

"Then the regalia is yours, all of it," Roger said, a sadness coming over him. It would be the first time he and Jimmy had ever been apart.

"You know I can't dance," Jimmy said.

Roger laid his hand on Jimmy's shoulder. "You can do anything you put your mind to. Anything at all."

He turned away and went back into his room to pack. Vietnam was a long way away.

Whump!

The first mortar shell landed about fifty yards away. Dirt and rocks rained down like tiny hailstones all around him.

Whump! Whump! Whump!

Three more rounds landed in the same area as the North Vietnamese walked a line of fire from east to west.

"Incoming!" someone yelled, but by then everyone already knew they were under attack.

Roger hunched lower and searched for something to shoot at. The sun was down and night had come. The shadows along the perimeter were as deep as those in the valley below. He thought he saw movement along the fence line but couldn't be sure. A few seconds later someone set off a trip flare.

The flare streaked into the sky and exploded, splattering the area into a metallic brilliance as it drifted gently in the air, swinging slowly back and forth. Roger saw several dozen men in black clothing, VC guerrillas, scurry along the fence line. As the flare revealed their position, the VC opened fire with machine guns and rifles. Roger returned fire.

Charlie's here.

Slapping a fresh clip into his M 16, Roger hit the bolt release and chambered a round. He held his breath to steady his hands and squeezed off a short burst. There seemed to be no end to the number of enemy soldiers swarming up the hill. A company of NVA regulars, about two hundred strong, had joined the VC at the fence. Using bamboo ladders, they had already breached the outer perimeter in two places. Those in the lead used satchel charges to clear a path through the claymores. Once past the minefield, there were only two more fences between them and the base.

The area between the fences was lit up like a carnival as explosions, flares and tracer rounds split the night. The noise was a deafening blend of detonations, shots, screams and curses. From somewhere near the outer perimeter a bugle sounded, its shrill notes like that of a wailing demon. Roger would have loved to throttle the neck of the person blowing it, for each piercing note caused his flesh to crawl.

As Roger raised up to fire off another burst, he felt a hand upon his left shoulder. He turned and saw 1st Lt. Chris McGee standing next to him.

"I wouldn't poke your head up too far," the lieutenant warned. Roger looked up and saw a stream of blue-green tracer rounds pass like fireflies above his head. The North Vietnamese had opened up on their position with a heavy machine gun. Roger nodded and hunkered lower in the trench.

Lt. McGee, an artillery officer, kneeled down and placed a radio on the ground before him.

"What happened to your radio operator?" Roger asked. He had to yell to be heard.

"He took a round between the eyes," McGee yelled back. He picked up the radio's receiver and called the artillery unit at Khe Sanh.

"Oh-eight to Marine Artillery Jacksonville. We have enemy troops inside the wire. Request H and E shells, fire number five."

"Jacksonville to Oh-eight," came the reply. "What kind of fuses?"

McGee looked at Roger, who shrugged. He thumbed the button to talk. "Oh, hell, mixed quick and delay, I guess."

"Roger, Oh-eight." The radio hissed.

Twenty seconds later, Roger ducked as a single artillery shell whistled over their heads, sounding as loud as a freight train roaring through a narrow canyon. The shell exploded just beyond the outer fence. Two more quickly followed.

McGee thumbed the receiver again and shouted above the noise. "Oh-eight to Jacksonville. Mixed shells H and E, and WP. Air burst twenty meters. Keep it working up and down the road." He turned to Roger and motioned for him to take cover.

Roger dove to the bottom of the trench as a salvo of artillery shells sailed over their position. The shells, both high explosive and white phosphorous, detonated along the edge of the forest. Night became day and the earth trembled as burning phosphorous and white-hot steel slammed into the ground. Trees exploded, bushes burned, and soldiers were ripped apart, their screams of agony drowned out by the shells bursting above their heads. Roger stood up and watched as NVA soldiers endured the hellfire of the howitzers.

But though the artillery shells rained death down upon them, the North Vietnamese hadn't been stopped. Nor had they given up. As those in the front died, others crawled forward to take their place. Like an army of spiders, they kept coming.

"Out of my way!" someone yelled.

Roger leaped to the side as James Smith—Smitty to everyone—slid into the trench. Smitty, a muscular black man from southern Alabama, was a machine gunner in the same squad as Roger. Back in the States he had been an amateur boxer. In Vietnam he was a professional killer. Pushing between the lieutenant and Roger, Smitty rested the barrel of his M-60 machine gun on the stack of sandbags in front of him.

"I figured you could use some help, Geronimo," he said as he fed an ammo belt into the gun.

"Hell, the lieutenant and I were planning on winning this war by ourselves," Roger answered.

Smitty grinned, cocked the M-60, aimed, and commenced killing the enemy. Roger turned his attention back toward the fence line and proceeded to do the same.

Jimmy Thunder Horse sat up with a start, his heart pounding. At first he wasn't sure where he was, the darkness was so complete. But gradually his eyes adjusted and he could make out the familiar shapes in his bedroom. The nightstand beside his bed. His dresser. His desk. He listened carefully and was further reassured that all was well by the gentle snoring of Aunt Ruth from down the hall.

"Just a dream," he whispered. "It was just a bad dream."

Bad dream nothing. He had just had the worst nightmare of his life. Jimmy had been in a deep forest, fleeing from something he couldn't see. Though it was nighttime, the sky was lit with explosions of colors. Red. Yellow. White. Like the Fourth of July. He wasn't alone. Dead things ran with him. Half-naked men with no arms, or parts of their faces missing, lumbered along beside him. He tried to outrun them, but the ground was slick with blood. He slipped and fell and the men were upon him. All of them had the same face. They were all Roger.

Jimmy leaned over and turned on the lamp on his nightstand. His hands still shook as he opened the nightstand's drawer and took out a stack of letters. The letters, fifteen in all, were from Roger. He opened the first envelope and removed a photograph.

The picture of Roger had been taken a little over two months ago. He was standing on top of a building made out of sandbags. There were similar buildings in the background, with narrow trenches between them. Roger wore green fatigue pants and dusty combat boots. He was shirtless, which showed how thin he'd become in the last six months. Around his neck hung a pair of dog tags and his medicine pouch. In his right hand he held an M-16. In his left he held a dead rat. Roger was smiling in the picture.

Jimmy had stared at the picture for hours, studying every little detail of it. Maybe, he thought, if he stared at the photograph long enough, he could make Roger climb out of it and come home. The letter that came with it portrayed a different side of the war than what was shown on the evening news. Roger talked about humorous things, like rat races, mud football and burning shit on latrine duty. For the life of him, Jimmy could not understand what was so funny about burning shit.

All of the letters Roger sent to Jimmy were lighthearted. But there were others, sent to Aunt Ruth, that told a different story about Vietnam. Jimmy wasn't supposed to have seen the letters, but he found them in the kitchen closet, tucked behind his aunt's jar of sassafras roots. The letters spoke of horrors unimaginable to an eleven-year-old boy. They told about firefights and land mines, body counts and mutilations. One thing for sure, despite how cheerful he seemed in the letters he sent to Jimmy, Roger was scared. He had sent extra money home in his last letter to Aunt Ruth, with a request that it be used to purchase a special prayer song at the next powwow.

He put the letters back, threw off his covers and swung his legs over the side of the bed. He lowered himself carefully into his wheelchair and rolled across the room to the far wall. Roger's dance bustle hung from a nail on the wall, low enough that Jimmy could take it down whenever he wanted. He slipped the bustle off the nail and laid it in his lap.

His hand tingled as he gently touched the eagle feathers. The bustle had lost none of its power. As he stroked the feathers, an image of Roger came to mind. Jimmy saw his brother step proudly as he entered the dance arena during the grand entrance, his face painted, his head held high. He saw him challenge the other dancers in the sneak-up dance, dropping to one knee to search for the enemy's trail, only to rise again to charge the drum. Roger never missed a beat when he danced, never failed to turn toward the drum when an honoring beat sounded. People always said that Roger's medicine was strong, that the Great Spirit came upon him when he danced.

A tear ran down Jimmy's cheek. It fell upon one of the eagle feathers. Jimmy quickly wiped it off. "Please, Roger, come home. Come home and dance for me."

Everything went white. The blast was so bright, it left its image etched on the inside of Roger's eyelids. The heat singed his hair and the force knocked him to the bottom of the trench.

Artillery round. Didn't hear it coming. Was it ours, or one of theirs?

He sat up and shook his head to clear his vision, but his left eye refused to clear. Wiping a hand across his face, he discovered that he had been wounded. Roger stared in disbelief at the blood smeared on his palm.

Further examination with his fingertips showed the wound to be a minor one. A small cut ran across his forehead, directly above his left eyebrow. At the most, it might require a couple of stitches to mend.

He was lucky. The artillery round had come close to being a direct hit. Fortunately, his flak jacket and helmet had taken most of the shrapnel. Roger started to get back up when he noticed Lt. McGee lying in the bottom of the trench with him.

Roger felt for a pulse in McGee's neck, but his fingers slipped into a bloody gash. He fumbled a pack of matches out of his shirt pocket and lit one. The tiny flame showed that the artillery blast had ripped away the right side of McGee's neck and a good portion of his face. Roger shuddered and extinguished the match.

He pushed himself away from Lt. McGee's body and stood up. Smitty still fired away with his M-60, apparently unaware they'd even been hit. But as Roger stepped beside him, he noticed that Smitty operated the gun with his left hand. His right arm hung useless at his side. Bone showed where shrapnel had torn away the upper third of Smitty's bicep.

"Hell of a blast, eh, Chief?" Smitty grinned.

"Jesus!" Roger said. He took off his belt and tied it around Smitty's right arm to stop the flow of blood. "You stupid idiot. You want to bleed to death?"

"Don't much matter one way or another," Smitty answered. "We're all gonna die anyway." He nodded toward the fence line. Roger looked, and felt his stomach knot in terror.

The North Vietnamese had already reached the last barricade. In a few seconds they would be over it and down in the trenches. There were hundreds of them. Too many to fight.

"We've got to get out of here!" Roger grabbed Smitty by his shirt and tried to pull him back.

"Ain't going nowhere," Smitty said, tearing free from Roger's grasp. He turned back to his M-60 and fired away.

"We're going hand-to-hand. You can't fight with that arm!"

Smitty ignored him.

"You'll be killed!" Roger shouted as he scrambled along the trench to take up a new position farther back. He wasn't sure if Smitty heard him. Seconds later, a grenade exploded where the big man stood. Roger turned away and didn't look back.

As he hurried along the trench, Roger realized that there was nowhere to run. The North Vietnamese had broken through the defenses and were about to overrun the base. Everywhere he looked, he saw the enemy. In the trenches along the south side of the base, the marines had thrown away their guns and fought with bayonets and knives.

Movement to his left caught his attention. Roger turned and saw a VC toss a satchel charge into a bunker. Before the VC could get clear of the blast, Roger cut him in half with a burst of automatic fire. No sooner had he killed the Viet Cong than two NVA regulars jumped into the trench in front of him, weapons firing.

He threw himself to the ground. The deadly spray of bullets kicked up dirt all around him. Roger shot back. One soldier went down, the top of his head blown off. The other, though wounded, continued to fire his weapon.

Roger rolled to his right to get out of the way. A pain ripped through his left thigh.

I'm hit!

He emptied his clip into the enemy soldier, skimming the bullets along the ground. He tried to stand up, but his leg crumpled beneath him like an accordion.

Get up! Get up! Get up!

Though Roger's brain screamed the command, his body refused to listen. He looked at his left leg and saw that he had taken several rounds in the thigh. Blood spurted from the wound.

Oh, God. He hit an artery.

Roger knew he would bleed to death if he didn't get medical attention right away. He would put a tourniquet on his leg, but he had used his belt to put one on Smitty's arm. Unless . . .

He pushed himself up on his elbows and looked around. His M-16 was only a few feet away from him. The rifle was equipped with a sling that could be used as a tourniquet.

Got to get to it. It's my only chance.

He gritted his teeth, rolled over on his stomach and crawled toward the rifle. He only had a few feet to crawl, but it seemed like a mile. His body broke out in a cold sweat as pain shot through his left leg. He stopped and took several deep breaths.

Come on. Come on. You can do it.

Roger reached out and grabbed the M-16 and dragged it to him. He unhooked the sling and tied it tight around his leg. The effort made him dizzy and it was all he could do to keep from passing out. He had just gotten the tourniquet tied when he heard voices approaching him. They were not speaking English.

Panic flared through him. He fumbled to get the empty clip out of the magazine and replace it with a full one. As he slipped a full clip into the rifle, three North Vietnamese soldiers came around a corner ahead of him. All three were armed with AK-47s. Seeing Roger, they raised their weapons and fired. Roger did the same. It was a good day to die.

Pain danced down Jimmy's spine as he pulled himself out of the wheelchair. He held onto the car door for support and used the outside rearview mirror to look at his face. Aunt Ruth had braided his hair for him before they left the house, tying a hawk feather to the left braid. His request had surprised her, for he had never bothered to fix his hair for a powwow before.

With a steady hand, he drew a line across his cheeks with a stick of red greasepaint. A line of black went just below the red.

When they arrived at the fairgrounds, Jimmy had waited until after his aunt went to speak with the head singer before returning to the car. He had left the back door unlocked so he wouldn't have to ask her for the key. She hadn't noticed the items hidden beneath the blanket on the back floorboard.

The leggings and breechcloth had been a pain to put on by himself, but he finally managed to get everything tied in place. The leggings were too long and had to be pinned up, and he had to stuff the moccasins with newspaper to keep them from falling off his feet. The ribbon shirt went on easily, though it was two sizes too big, and the porcupine hair roach was only cocked a little to the left. He also had to struggle to get the bells on, but he was able to bend over far enough to tie them just above his calves. Wiping his fingers off on a paper napkin, Jimmy reached into the car for the final piece of regalia.

He leaned his weight against the car door and tied the leather thongs around his waist. Once they were tied, he adjusted the bustle so that it hung in the small of his back. He had to hurry. It was almost time. He could hear the arena announcer call for everyone's attention. Aunt Ruth would be with the announcer. In her purse was the letter that had arrived at the house the day before.

Jimmy double-checked to make sure the bustle was secure. Satisfied, he picked up the eagle-feather fan and dance stick in his right hand. He held his breath as he let go of the door long enough to slip a crutch off the backseat and under his left arm. A crutch was sheer agony to use, but this was one time when a wheelchair just wouldn't do. Closing the car door, he made his way slowly toward the arena.

The crowd around the arena stood, many with their heads bowed. Jimmy moved carefully so as not to make his bells jingle too loudly. He didn't want to be noticed. Not yet anyway.

The drum was set up in the center of the dance arena. A dozen or so singers sat around it on folding metal chairs. Jimmy noticed that several of the singers held their hands in front of their eyes, as if to hold back tears, as they listened to what was being said. The arena announcer stood and faced the audience, his left arm around Aunt Ruth's waist. His voice echoed across the fairgrounds as he spoke into the microphone.

"Roger Thunder Horse was known by many of you. He was a fine young man, a skilled dancer, a loving son, nephew and brother. When the government called on Roger, he didn't run away, like a lot of young men have done. He went to serve his country, the best he could, in that far-off place called Vietnam.

"A month ago Roger wrote to his aunt, Ruth, telling her how bad things were over there. He wanted her to ask the drum to sing a special song for him so that he might come home safely. Roger sent Ruth some money to lay on the drum to pay for the song, which she did.

"Well, this is the first powwow since Roger's letter and the drum was going to sing that song for him." The announcer paused and swallowed hard, trying to control the quiver in his voice.

"Yesterday, Ruth got a letter from the United States Government. Roger Thunder Horse died in combat while defending his base from the Viet Cong."

A heavy silence fell over the grounds.

"At this time the drum asks that you remain standing as we sing a special veteran's song for Roger Thunder Horse. We also sing it for all the young men and women still serving ·their country in Vietnam. May they come home safely."

The head singer struck the drum with his drumstick. His voice lifted in song. The other men seated around the drum joined in.

As the song began, the head man dancer moved away from

the bench to lead the dance. The other dancers—those who were veterans—waited until he passed where they stood and then followed him. The head lady dancer took Ruth by the arm and led her around the arena so that she, too, could dance to honor her nephew.

Jimmy pushed his way through the crowd and positioned himself at the eastern entrance to the arena. The regalia he wore had belonged to one of the finest dancers in the state. Wearing the regalia was one way of paying tribute to Roger's memory. Dancing in it was another.

As the head man dancer passed in front of where he stood, Jimmy took an agonizing step forward. He stepped again, leaned his weight on the crutch, rolled his hips, and dragged his back leg. He bit his lower lip to keep from crying out in pain. He would not cry out. His brother had been a warrior. He would be one too.

As he moved out into the arena, Jimmy saw an image of Roger in his mind—proud, dancing like the wind—and knew that his brother's spirit went with him. A few more steps brought him into plain view of everyone.

One of the singers looked up and saw him, a surprised expression on his face. He nudged the singer seated next to him, who also looked up. Just then the head singer—a large, powerful man named Henry Strong Bear—spotted Jimmy in the arena. Henry smiled, raised his drumstick high into the air and struck the drum a powerful blow.

The drum, like a heartbeat—God's heartbeat—echoed across the land. The vibrations entered Jimmy, filled him. For the first time he felt what Roger had felt, knew what it was like to dance. The feeling took his breath, made tears roll down his face. He threw his head back and yelled. The other dancers yelled, too, answering his war cry.

Jimmy threw his crutch away in anger. He expected to fall,

but didn't. If anything, as he shuffled along, his steps grew stronger.

He turned his head and moved his body, imitating the movements he had seen Roger do so many times before. He screamed again, in pain this time, as the bones in his spine straightened and realigned themselves. The drum sounded an honoring beat. Jimmy turned toward it and raised his eagle fan high.

Louder beat the drum. Louder sang the singers. Their voices lifted up to the heavens. Jimmy's body burned like it was on fire, but he felt strength and flexibility he had never known before. He twisted and turned, lifted his legs high, and brought his foot down with each beat of the drum. He circled the dance arena once. Twice. Three times. As he did, a strange and wonderful thing happened.

Where Jimmy stepped on the bare earth, grass suddenly appeared. The tiny blades of grass sprouted from the ground and grew several inches in a single heartbeat. They appeared in the shape of a footprint, but quickly spread to form a thick carpet of green.

The other dancers stopped and stared in amazement at what was happening beneath Jimmy's feet. A hush fell over the spectators as they, too, noticed. Some pointed. Others prayed. And then the crowd cheered as they realized that what they were witnessing could only be a miracle.

Jimmy danced faster. Gone was the pain that had crippled his body. His back straight, his head held proud, he danced like no one had ever seen before. And with each step he took, more grass sprang up. Thick. Green. Alive. The arena, once bare dirt, was soon covered with grass. New life to replace the life that was lost.

The song changed from a veteran's song to a sneak-up dance. Jimmy dropped to one knee and shielded his eyes, searching for an imaginary enemy as he had often seen Roger do. He shook his bustle and rolled his shoulders, rising to charge the drum when the tempo picked up.

Singers from the audience ran to join those already in the arena. Leaping over benches and folding chairs, they raced each other to the drum. Thirty. Forty. Maybe even fifty. They stood eight rows deep. Their voices echoed across the fairgrounds.

And in the arena, Jimmy danced alone. Sweat poured off his tiny body as he twisted and turned. He saw neither the singers nor those who watched him. He saw only Roger.

Basked in a brilliant white light, Jimmy's brother danced beside him in full regalia. Roger smiled as he challenged him, tried to outdo him, pushed him to dance even harder. Together they circled the arena. Side by side they danced the war dances, the sneak-ups and the crow hop. Together they moved. Side by side. As one.

The songs finally came to an end. The last drumbeat fell. Jimmy stopped and closed his eyes. He felt the pounding of his heart, and the wetness of tears on his cheeks. He didn't want to open his eyes again, afraid of what he would see, but knew he had to. Finally, he opened his eyes and looked up. He was alone. Roger was gone.

" 'Bye, Roger. I love you."

He turned and saw the singers by the drum, and the crowd outside the arena. He also saw the blades of grass stirring gently in the wind and knew that something special had happened. Last, he looked down at his legs and realized that not only had he walked, he had danced.

Jimmy's body trembled as he lifted his face toward the sky and said a prayer of thanks. As he finished his prayer, someone touched his arm. He turned. Aunt Ruth stood beside him.

"Are you okay?" she asked. She wiped the tears from his cheeks with a damp handkerchief. She had also been crying.

Jimmy nodded. He took a deep breath and swallowed, choking back a sob. He didn't want Aunt Ruth to see him cry.

Crying was for children. He was the man of the house now. He had to be a warrior, like his brother.

"He was here, you know," Jimmy said. "Roger. He danced with me. Did you see him?"

Ruth nodded. "Yes, Jimmy, I saw him. We all saw him. He was in the wind . . . in the grass."

She looked into his eyes, and smiled. "And he was in you, Jimmy. I saw Roger's spirit in you when you danced. In your movements, in the way you held your head. They were the same. His spirit will be with you always. . . ."

"It's in the regalia," Jimmy whispered. "His spirit is in the bustle."

"Not just in the bustle," Ruth corrected. She placed her hand on his chest. "Roger's spirit is here. In your heart. It will always be here. Forever."

She took Jimmy's hand and led him slowly out of the arena. The dancing was over for now. Behind them the grass continued to grow.

All We Know of Heaven

PETER CROWTHER

dam sat with the rest of the fifth grade on the grass outside Forest Plains School. The greensward ran down from the school entrance to Sycamore Drive, where a high, metal fence separated the children from the sidewalk. Momentarily oblivious of the other children and squinting his eyes at the sun's glare, reflected off the windows of the Forest Plains General Hospital diagonally opposite, he looked up the street to the corner of Sycamore and Main.

Still squinting, and now holding his hand above his eyes as though he were saluting, Adam watched a man cross by the intersection and jog the last few steps to get out of the way of a car, which had slowed down anyway to turn from Main onto Sycamore. The man waved to the car, smiling. The man in the car waved back, also smiling.

Adam felt the warmth of the smiles. It was as strong as the May sunshine. Even stronger. Thinking about it, maybe that was the warmth he most missed at home: smiles.

He turned back to see Mrs. Stewart come out of the

school holding a book. A movement by his side caused him to turn in time to see Jimmy Jorgensson finger a thick booger out of his left nostril and casually wipe his hand on the grass. "Save some for lunch, Jimmy," Mrs. Stewart trilled as she moved her chair around so that it faced the group. The assembled children tittered. She missed nothing.

Chrissie Clemmons, sitting cross-legged in front of them, leaned back and whispered, "That's another piece of brain you'll never use, JJ."

Adam smiled.

Jimmy gave Chrissie a Bronx cheer, just like Adam had seen his father do at the ball game, only without the volume. Chrissie stuck out a tongue reddened by eating raspberry candies and leaned forward again.

"Okay, class," Mrs. Stewart announced, "let's settle down now." She took her seat and smoothed out her skirt.

Brian Macready had once told a small group of wide-eyed would-be playboys that he'd seen up that skirt once, all the way to Mrs. Stewart's pubes. "I tell you," he'd said conspiratorially, "the lady wears no pants." They'd been in fourth grade then and Adam had taken every opportunity to check out the facts.

Face it: It was his duty.

He had dropped pencils, math books, erasers and all manner of other objects just to get a glimpse of the fabled thatch. But no luck. Just a missed recess for continued clumsiness—he'd been trying for almost an entire week. It had been a timely reminder of the benefits of subtlety and, although he remained vigilant, Adam learned to pick his opportunities only when they actually presented themselves.

But since then, whenever Mrs. Stewart crossed her legs or lifted one leg as she bent down to pick up something from the floor, Adam turned away.

The reason was that Mrs. Stewart was a mother.

Okay, so Barnaby Stewart was only six years old—"That's

just one step up from an erection," the worldly Chrissie Clemmons had confided to Adam and several others one day behind the gym—but some things just weren't done. And Adam sure wouldn't like anybody trying to get a flash of his mother's private parts. No sir! Particularly with his mom in the hospital and all defenseless. In fact, he might just have to haul off and smack them in the face it he ever caught somebody doing it. Which is just the way he always felt when he went with his father to visit her and they were interrupted by some doctor who wanted to check her over.

Check her over.

It always sounded so ominous. And, hand-in-hand with his sad-faced father, Adam would schlep out of his mother's room while the doctor pulled the screens around the bed and went to work. But doing *what?*

Adam felt his cheeks go red as he imagined the doctor lifting his mother's white gown. *"Hmm, nice bush, Mrs. Showell. Now, if you have no objections, I'd just like to—"*

Adam shook the thought out of his head. The comment would have been a waste of time, anyway. His mother never objected to anything anymore.

In fact, she never *did* anything anymore.

Adam reached out and pulled a few blades of grass, scrunched them up in his hand and looked up. Mrs. Stewart was holding up a book for everyone to see.

" . . . of our finest writers," she was saying.

He read the book's title. Boy, was it long. *The Acts of King Arthur and His Noble Knights: From the Winchester Manuscripts of Thomas Mallory.*

"That's not a title, it's a sentence—a life one!" Felipe Stroymaur hissed behind his hand with a snigger. Felipe kind of had the image of himself as a comedian and there was no doubt that, at least to the ten-going-on-eleven-year-old inmates of Forest Plains School's fifth grade, he'd be following in the footsteps of Eddie Murphy and Steve Martin. Even Mrs. Stewart had to laugh at him sometimes, though she usually tried to do it without anyone noticing. Everyone did, of course.

"Felipe, you are *so* precocious," Mrs. Stewart droned.

"Thank you, ma'am," he replied, and there was another round of sniggers.

"Life sentence."

Those were the words that the doctor had used to Adam's father last week when they had made their usual weekend visit to the hospital. Adam only went down there on Saturday and Sunday afternoons. His father would have him wear his best pants and a shirt and they would drive down to the hospital and sit by his mom for an hour or so.

During the entire visit, John Showell would hold his wife's hand and just stare at her. Or he would stare at the stack of screens and dials on the table by her side, watching the little green lines and digital displays give out an occasional blip every few seconds.

Adam had not been with his mom and dad when the delivery truck had sideswiped their car, but there were times—dark times when the lights were out and he could hear his father walking the night floors, drinking coffee and smoking cigarettes—that he almost wished that he had. He would get out of bed every now and again and go into his father's room and watch him sitting on his mom's side of the bed, whispering to her photograph.

"John Steinbeck was born in Salinas, California, in nineteen hundred and two," Mrs. Stewart said, in a tone designed to create amazement. "And he was awarded the Nobel Prize for Literature in 1962. Anyone know what that is?"

Nobody did, apparently.

"The Nobel Prize . . ."

As Mrs. Stewart explained, Adam stared at the book's cover.

It showed a gray, armor-suited knight on horseback, reining back and waving his sword. His horse wore what looked like a green-and-brown patchwork quilt, all the way from the tip of its tail to the point of its nose. The lines on the knight's helmet made him look brave—even the horse looked brave. Adam wondered what it must have been like to be a knight in the days of King Arthur.

He glanced around at the other children and saw that they were settling down, becoming engrossed. Mrs. Stewart was reading from the book.

" ' . . . a great block of marble, and in the marble was set a steel anvil in which a sword was driven. In letters of gold was written: WHOEVER PULLS THIS SWORD FROM THIS STONE AND ANVIL IS KING OF ALL ENGLAND BY RIGHT OF BIRTH.' " Her voice had assumed a booming resonance as she read from the inscription. Now she lowered the volume again and, with a slight breeze blowing through her hair, she leaned forward to the children.

" 'The people were amazed,' " Mrs. Stewart continued, " 'and carried the news of the miracle to the Archbishop, who said, *Go back into the church and pray to God. And let no man touch the sword until High Mass is sung.* And this they did, but when the service was over, all the lords went to look at the stone and the sword, and some tried to draw out the blade, but no one could move it.

" '*The man is not here who will draw this sword,* said the Archbishop, *but do not doubt that God will make him known.*' "

Mrs. Stewart paused while she pulled back a piece of hair that had blown over her eyes. Adam watched her, open-mouthed. The words from the book had triggered off a memory.

"No one could move it."

When Mrs. Stewart resumed her place in the tale of King Arthur and the sword, Excalibur, Adam was not listening. Instead, he was thinking back to the first time that he and his father had visited the hospital. It was something he had replayed in his mind many times over the months that he and his father had been living alone.

John Showell had still been limping badly, even though it was already a month since the accident. And he wore a bandage and a large pad over his right eye, where his face had collided with the back of Angela Showell's head. Then she had rebounded into the window on her own side of the car just in time to take the impact as the truck's back end smashed into them. The Showell family car, an eleven-year-old Dodge sedan, had mounted the curb halfway along Beech Street and taken down the telephone pole. The Dodge's wheel arch had pushed back through the engine block, snaking the pedal-stems off the floor like gunshots. At the time, John Showell's feet had been pressing on those pedals and, even now, almost eight months since the accident, he walked with difficulty.

But John Showell had got off lightly compared with his wife.

Adam's dad hadn't allowed Adam to visit the hospital at first because Angela Showell's face had been so badly hurt. But finally the day came and Adam dressed his best, taking particular care with his appearance. He even bought a small bunch of bluebonnets—with his own allowance—from Wild Things over on Main Street. The owner, Geoff Macavoy, whose son, Danny, was also in fifth grade, knew all about the accident and he didn't want to take Adam's money. But Adam had insisted.

Sitting on the grass, with Mrs. Stewart's voice droning pleasantly in the background, Adam remembered Mr. Macavoy's eyes and how they looked so shiny.

Later that first afternoon, Adam had walked into Forest Plains General Hospital with his silent father, listening to the sound of their shoes clacking on the polished floors. They had gone through the large, automatic glass doors, past a large, circular reception desk and along a long corridor to the elevators. His father, who now seemed to carry a fug of cigarette smoke with him wherever he went, had pressed the button and waited, hands in his pants pockets. Adam had been surprised that his father had taken no flowers himself, nor even any candies.

The elevator had arrived with a *ting* and they got in. Adam's father had pressed "4" and leaned against the back of the elevator car. The doors had closed with a *shusssh*, and Adam had felt the initial jerking movement of the car as it started up. But then there had seemed not to be any motion at all. He had supposed it was so they could carry really sick people around in there without spilling things.

The *ting* of the elevator arriving on the fourth floor had seemed much quieter than when Adam had been standing waiting for it to arrive. The doors had slid open to reveal a tin sign tacked to the wall corner. The sign read:

WARD 14

INTENSIVE CARE

In an increasingly rare show of physical contact, John Showell had placed his arm around Adam's shoulder and, with a couple of pats, guided him out of the elevator, through a small wooden-slatted swing gate to the Ward 14 reception desk. A young nurse, who actually seemed to be not much older than the girls in his year, had smiled warmly at Adam and made a big deal out of admiring his bluebonnets. Adam had remained silent throughout the ordeal.

He had watched his father sign his name in a book on the counter and then followed him through two full-length swinging doors, which actually overlapped at the middle.

Halfway along the small corridor on the other side of the doors, Adam's father had stopped, just in front of an open door, and visibly straightened himself up. Then he had said,

"Come on, Adam, let's see how your mom's doing today, huh!" And they had walked into the room.

What had he been expecting?

Throughout many of the lonely nights that followed that first visit, Adam tried to picture what he had been expecting—hoping?—to find. Whatever it had been, it was not what he discovered when he walked into the small room that Sunday afternoon, when the first fall of leaves from the trees was already making the sidewalks along Main Street slushy and the winter snows were building up across the Canadian border.

An imposter.

Someone was trying to plant an imposter in his family.

There, stretched out on a metal cot, its frail arms attached by wires and tubes to a host of blinking and dripping objects, was an emaciated husk of humankind. He had blinked, first at the absurdity of anyone trying to make him believe that this was his mom . . . and then he had blinked again, wetly this time, at the realization that it was.

The figure's mouth was slightly open, its cheekbones drawn and languid. The eyes were closed tightly, sleeping perhaps, though there was no movement beneath them. Adam realized that whatever dreams his mother dreamed now—if, indeed, she dreamed at all—were lonely landscapes of fractured memories, missed opportunities and failed intentions.

On her cheek was a long Band-Aid. On her head was a taped wire which led to a stacked bank of what looked like hi-fi equipment, each box showing digital displays and traveling blip-lines: a second wire, attached to a pad on Angela Showell's left forearm, also ran into the equipment. Adam watched them blip, thinking that this was the only way his mom could talk to him now.

But the biggest, meanest-looking wire of all was a large-diameter tube that ran from a separate machine standing beside the bed into his mom's throat. Adam reached toward it, unthinking, and heard a voice say, "No!" sharply. He turned to his side and suddenly saw that they were not alone as he had first presumed. There was a woman in here. She rose to her feet from a chair at the side of the room, a folded copy of *Life* magazine in her hand, and smiled at him. It was a practiced smile.

"No one can move that, young man," she said.

He looked around and saw his father's glassy eyes watching him. Then he dropped the neat bundle of bluebonnets onto his mother's unmoving feet and ran to him. They cried together.

"No one can move that."

"Adam?"

He blinked and looked around. The other kids were watching him. He cleared his throat and tried to smile. "Yes, ma'am," he said, recovering his composure.

"Are you with us, Adam? You wanting your lunch, is that it?"

"No . . . I mean, yes. Yes, ma'am, I'm with you."

"Good. I'm pleased to hear it." And in that split second when the rest of the class were turning their own faces away from him, Mrs. Stewart slipped Adam a gentle smile—*"It's okay, Adam, I know what you're going through"*—and then spoke to the whole group. "So—anybody—what is the message we get from the story of King Arthur and Excalibur?"

A hand went up near the front.

"Yes, Sally," Mrs. Stewart said.

"Does it mean that it's good to be strong?"

Mrs. Stewart smiled and nodded. "Well, yes, it does, Sally. But the strength it talks about isn't simply physical strength— like Arnold Schwarzenegger—" She held up her right arm and flexed the muscle, scowled at it and shrugged. Everyone laughed as she returned the arm to her lap. "It means a strength of purpose, too," she added. "It means . . . " She searched for the words. "It means that if your cause is good, then you will prevail."

" 'Prevail'?"

Mrs. Stewart leaned forward and rubbed a tousled blond head. "I'm sorry, Andy. 'Prevail' means 'to win' . . . 'to succeed' . . . 'to be—' "

The lunch bell sounded its clamor across the grass, and a ripple of movement began at the edges of the gathering, working its way to the middle. Within what seemed to be only a few seconds, the grass cleared of bodies and books and a tide of color swept noisily toward the school buildings and the waiting cafeteria.

Only Adam and a smiling Mrs. Stewart remained.

Adam gathered his books and walked over to her and she smiled at him warmly. "Hi, Adam."

He nodded.

"You like that story?"

He nodded again.

"Yeah, me too. It's a doozy." Mrs. Stewart ran a hand through her hair, the way Adam's mother used to do, and picked up her file of papers from the grass. "You going in to eat lunch?"

"I guess," Adam said.

"Mmm-hmm," said Mrs. Stewart, nodding. "Something you wanted to ask me maybe?"

Adam shifted his weight from foot to foot. "What were you going to say?"

"Pardon me?"

"At the end, there. You were going to say something. 'To *be* something,' you started to say." He took a breath. "To be *what*?"

The teacher frowned and tried to think, then shrugged. "Oh, to be something . . . yes! I think I was going to say 'to be victorious.' "

Adam nodded.

"Is that what you meant?"

"I guess so, but just 'To be' is enough."

And he ran to the buildings leaving behind Mrs. Stewart with a puzzled expression on her face.

That night, after he had returned from his regular evening visit to the hospital, Adam's father sat with Bob Wissan, a friend from around the block, and talked. Bob was a doctor.

Adam had been sent upstairs to get ready for bed, but he sat cross-legged in the shadows of the upstairs landing, leaning against the banisters, listening.

"What can I tell you?" Bob said, his voice sounding sad.

"Don't speak too loud," Adam's father said.

"Oh, yes, sorry."

Adam could hear coffee percolating. The sound was so much a part of his mother's home, her own activities, that, just for a second, Adam thought that maybe it had all been a big joke . . . a dream or something. That he could stand up and walk downstairs for his mom to pick him up and spin him around, while the smell of fresh coffee wafted through the house with the sound of her laughter and all of their collective happiness. But he knew that that wasn't to be. He listened.

"Just give it to me straight is all I ask, Bob."

"I've given it to you straight." Bob Wissan paused. "Angela isn't going to be coming home, Jack," he said. "Not tomorrow, not next week, not even next year."

"You're saying there's no chance at all?"

There was no response to that, or none that Adam could hear.

"But she's still breathing! And they told me—"

"Well, okay, yeah . . . there's a chance. One chance in a million that Angela will recover. But, I'm telling you—*me, I'm* telling you—it won't happen.

"It's the machine that breathes for her . . . through the endotracheal tube that they inserted: it's not Angela breathing, it's the machine. The tube goes all the way down her throat and into her lung. It inflates and deflates her lung—which is what you and I do by ourselves—and monitors the gases in her body. It's a mechanical procedure, nothing more."

Adam heard glasses clink and then a muffled "No thanks, Jack."

"And that's not all, Jack," Bob Wissan continued. "She has muscle relaxants, which are designed to keep her from fighting the breathing apparatus; analgesics to keep her free from pain; hypnotics to keep her sedated—"

"Jesus Chr—"

"No, hear me out, Jack. She has drips to her subclavian vein, which take samples and provide parenteral feeding; a monitor stuck into her main artery to measure the oxygen and carbon dioxide content of the blood and to make sure the mixture of gases is correct; and an ECG to check on her heart."

Another clink.

"She's gone, Jack. Let her rest."

Adam heard a sob.

"Let her rest."

"I—I can't. God help me, I can't." John Showell sobbed. "That's like . . . that's like asking me to mourn her while she's still alive!"

Adam crept along the floor to his bedroom.

Much later, in the security of his bed, in the confines of his room, Adam clasped his hands behind his head and stared into the nighttime sky through his window. His heart was beating fast. It was now or never.

He slipped from the bed and pulled on his clothes.

As the library clock struck midnight, Adam was running through darkened back gardens, heading for Main Street. He felt like a knight on horseback, riding to rescue the fair maiden.

Adam figured that there seemed to be so many patron saints for so many things, maybe there might be one for ten-year-old boys with a mission. And, sure enough, things seemed to be going his way.

The people on the main reception desk were busy talking as he casually walked by.

The corridor to the elevators was deserted.

And, when he reached them, both of the elevators were standing open-doored . . . just like they were waiting for him. He stopped inside the one on the right and pressed the button for the fourth floor. The elevator doors closed, hissing ominously.

When the doors opened again, Adam half expected to see a doctor waiting for him . . . or his father, his pajama pants on underneath his topcoat, drumming his fingers against his leg. But there was nobody. Silence reigned.

He tiptoed out onto the corridor and stepped over the swing gate. Just as he was preparing to move forward, a nurse walked out of his mom's room, stood for a second and checked her watch. She was facing a blank wall. If she turned to her left, she would walk farther down the corridor to more rooms and a group of desks. If she turned to her right, she would come face-to-face with Adam. He waited. Which way would she choose?

The nurse rubbed her face with both hands and turned left. Adam opened his mouth wide, so that his sigh of relief would be silent, and moved forward . . . into his mom's room.

The light was on but muted. It came from two wall lights, one on the wall facing the bed and the other above the chair to the right of where he stood. On the chair was a copy of *Time* magazine. It had Clint Eastwood on the cover.

The figure on the bed looked the same as it had always looked, and Adam felt a pang of guilt that he could ever have doubted that it was his mother. Her face was the same, if thinner, and her hair was just as golden and tousled. Adam wanted to speak to her, but he knew that he did not have the time. He pushed the door closed behind him so that they could be alone, him and his mother.

With the steady drone of daytime hospital noises finished for the day, Adam could hear his mother breathing. But no, the sound was not coming from the bed—although his mother's frail chest moved gently, up and down, up and down—but from the stack of hi-fi equipment at its side. Something in one of the boxes creaked and sighed . . . *creak . . . sigh . . . creak . . .*

He dropped to his knees and scuffled along the floor to the array of wires that led from one piece of equipment to another. It was darker down here, and he had trouble finding where everything was. But soon he saw the wall socket.

He lay down on the floor so that he was in a position to see the digital displays and the blip-lines, and reached his hand out until it touched the plug. He looked up at the displays and pressed the switch.

The displays disappeared.

Adam waited to hear alarms.

There was nothing.

He shuffled back, taking great care not to disturb anything that might fall over, and stood up.

Creak . . . sigh . . . creak . . . sigh . . .

Adam's blood ran cold, as though someone had poured icy water down his back.

He looked in horror at the equipment. The displays were still out. What had gone wrong?

He knelt down beside the boxes and listened.

It was the one on the floor, the big one, that the creaking and sighing noises were coming from. He moved back and stared at the box. Switches and tiny panels covered the face.

He lay down on his stomach and looked around the back of the box. There was no wire coming from it. No wire leading to the wall socket.

Creak . . . sigh . . . creak . . . sigh . . . Outside in the corridor footsteps sounded.

Adam rolled over soundlessly beneath his mother's bed.

The footsteps grew louder until they were right outside the door. And then they started to fade. Adam waited until he could no longer hear them and then pulled himself out from under the bed. As he reached his hand up, he touched his mom's arm. He pulled his hand back, staring at his fingers, twitching them as though he had just inadvertently dipped them into a jar of acid. He shuffled out into the light and got to his feet.

Looking down at his mother, Adam watched the almost imperceptible movements of her chest beneath the bedclothes. It matched the sounds of the machine beside her.

He moved over to the bed and sat on its side, next to her. This time, he took her hand from where it lay on her stomach, and held it in his own. It felt warm. He bent over and sniffed. It smelled of hospital . . . of drugs and medications, of machinery and wiring. It smelled of many things, but it did not smell of his mother.

He turned and glanced at the door, biting his lip nervously, then looked back at her face. It was just the same as it had always been, and yet . . . and yet it was different. She was there but not there. It was the face of the woman who had looked after him all of his life . . . and the face of a woman he didn't know at all.

"She's gone, Jack. Let her rest."

The words of Bob Wissan echoed through his head. He saw them like words on a class board, shimmering, fading. And then Mrs. Stewart's face appeared.

"The strength isn't simple physical strength—like Arnold Schwarzenegger . . ."

He leaned closer and whispered, "Mom? Mom . . . are you there, Mom?"

"*. . . asking me to mourn her while she's still alive.*"

Adam moved one of his hands away from his mother's hand and looked at it. It was shaking.

"*If your cause is good, then you will prevail.*"

Still holding his mother's hand tightly in his left hand, Adam reached out his right hand toward her throat. It was no longer shaking. Then he took hold of the thick tube, staring wide-eyed at his fingers as they folded around the wide cuff just above the thick patch on Angela Showell's neck.

"'*And Arthur grasped the sword by its handle,*' he heard Mrs. Stewart say, '*and easily and fiercely drew it from the anvil and the stone. . . .*'"

He braced himself and pulled.

The tube offered no resistance and withdrew itself from his mother's neck with an ease that almost made Adam fall from the bed, his foot narrowly missing a small, white pan of strange instruments. Adam checked the door for any sign that somebody had heard and then turned back to the bed.

The end of the tube had not come free.

"*The tube goes all the way down her throat and into her lung,*" Bob Wissan had said.

Adam moved away from the bed, now holding the tube with both hands.

He closed his eyes and kept pulling.

Arm over arm he seemed to pull until, at last, the tube came free, squirming across the floor, its end wet and shiny. As he watched, it came to a rest and blew a small bubble, which suddenly popped.

Creak . . . sigh . . . creak . . . sigh . . .

The machine was still breathing.

Adam dropped the tube and walked carefully to the bed.

His mom's chest no longer moved. Now she was truly still.

He sat beside her again and held her hand for a minute or

so. Then he held it to his face before resting it gently across her stomach.

As he looked at her face, Adam thought he saw the faintest ripple of movement . . . a shadow, passing across her features and drifting away.

Although she did not look any different from the way she had looked only minutes earlier, there was now a peace about Adam's mother. And as he made to leave the room, Adam realized that what he was looking at on the narrow hospital cot was little more than a photograph. An image of something that had once been . . . the briefest record of a moment passed. But memories—*real* memories—were the priceless and insubstantial things that you carried in your head, not disposable bits of card containing chemical magic and mystical likenesses.

Creak . . . sigh . . . creak . . . sigh . . . said the machine, only now its voice sounded lonely.

Adam rose to his feet and left the room, satisfied that it was now completely empty.

Minutes later, he was running through the early-morning darkness, the bravest of all the knights of old, resplendent in tunic and color, strong of will and truth, and accomplished of purpose . . . breathing in the faint perfume of night-scented stocks and the promise of summer.

Going home.

Parting is all we know of heaven,
And all we need of hell.

—Emily Dickinson (1830–1886)

Passing

CHARLES DE LINT

Great God! I'd rather be
A pagan suckled in a creed outworn;
So might I, standing on this pleasant lea,
Have glimpses that would make me less forlorn.

—William Wordsworth,
from "The World Is Too Much
with Us"

— 1 —

he sword lies on the grass beside me, not so much a physical presence as an enchantment. I don't know how else to describe it. It's too big to be real. I can't imagine anyone being able to hold it comfortably, little say wield it. Looking at it is like looking through water, as though I'm lying at the bottom of a lake and everything's slightly in motion, edges blurring. I can see the dark metal of the sword's pommel and cross guard, the impossible length of the blade itself that seems to swallow the moonlight, the thong wrapped round and round the grip, its leather worn smooth and shiny in places.

I can almost believe it's alive.

Whenever I study it, time gets swallowed up. I lose snatches of the night, ten minutes, fifteen minutes, time I don't have to spare. I have to be finished before dawn. With an effort, I pull my gaze away and pick up the shovel once more. Hallowed ground. I don't know how deep the grave should be. Four feet? Six feet? I'm just going to keep digging until I feel I've got it right.

—— 2 ——

Lucy Grey was a columnist and feature writer for *The New-ford Sun*, which was how she first found herself involved with the city's gay community. Her editor, enamored with the most recent upsurge of interest in gay chic and all things androgynous, sent her down to the girl bars on Gracie Street to write an op-ed piece that grew into a Sunday feature. Steadfastly heterosexual in terms of who she'd actually sleep with, Lucy discovered she was gay in spirit, if not in practice. Sick of being harassed by guys, she could relax in the gay clubs, stepping it out and flirting with the other girls on the dance floor and never having to worry about how to go home alone at the end of the night.

Her new girlpals seemed to understand and she didn't think anybody considered her a tease until one night, sitting in a cubical of a washroom in Neon Sister, she overheard herself being discussed by two women who'd come in to touch up their makeup. They were unaware of her presence.

"I don't know," one of them said. "There's something about her that doesn't ring true. It's like after that piece she did in *The Sun*, now she's researching a book—looking at us from the inside, but not really one of us."

"Who, Lucy?" the other said.

Lucy recognized her friend Traci's voice. It was Traci who befriended her the first night she hit Gracie Street and guided her through the club scene.

"Of course Lucy. She's all-look-but-don't-touch."

"Sounds more to me like you're miffed because she won't sleep with you."

"She doesn't sleep with anybody."

"So?"

"So she's like an emotional tourist, passing through. You know what happens when the straights start hanging out in one of our clubs."

It becomes a straight club, Lucy thought, having heard it all before. The difference, this time, was that the accusation was being directed at her and she wasn't so sure that it was unfair. She wasn't here just because she preferred the company of women, but to avoid men. It wasn't that she disliked men, but that her intimacy with them never seemed to go beyond the bedroom. She was neither bisexual, nor experimenting. She was simply confused and taking refuge in a club scene where she could still have a social life.

"You're reading way too much into this," Traci said. "It's not like she's seriously coming on to anyone. It's just innocent flirting—everybody does it."

"So you don't want a piece of what she's got?"

Traci laughed. "I'd set up house with her in a minute." Sitting in the cubicle, Lucy found herself blushing furiously, especially when Traci added, "Long-term."

"What you're setting yourself up for is a broken heart."

"I don't think so," Traci said. "I try to keep everything in perspective. If she just wants to be friends, that's okay with me. And I kind of like her the way she is: social, but celibate."

That was a description Lucy embraced wholeheartedly after that night because it seemed to perfectly sum up who she was.

Until she met Nina.

—— 3 ——

It all starts out innocently enough. Nina shows up at the North Star one night, looking just as sweet and lost as Traci said I did the first time she saw me on Gracie Street, trying to work up the nerve to go into one of the clubs. She has her hair cut above her ears like Sadie Benning and she's wearing combat boots with her black jeans and white T-shirt, but she looks like a femme, and a shy one at that, so I take her under my wing.

Turns out she's married, but it's on the rocks. Maybe. There's no real intimacy in their relationship—tell me about it.

Thinks her husband's getting some on the side, but she can't swear to it. She's not sure what she's doing here, she just wants a night out, but she doesn't want to play the usual games in the straight bars, so she comes here, but now that she's here, she's not sure what she's doing here.

I tell her to relax. We dance some. We have a few drinks. By the time she goes home, she's flushing prettily and most of the shadows I saw haunting the backs of her eyes are gone.

We start to hang out together. In the clubs. Have lunch, dinner once. Not dates. We're just girlpals, except after a few weeks I find myself thinking about her all the time, fixating on her. Not jealous. Not wondering where she is, or who she's with. Just conversations we had running through my mind. Her face a familiar visitor to my mind's eye. Her trim body.

Is this how it starts? I wonder. There's no definition to what's growing inside me, no, I used to like men, now I'm infatuated with a woman. It's just this swelling desire to be with her. To touch her. To bask in her smile. To know she's thinking of me.

One night I'm driving her home and I don't know how it happens, but we pull up in front of her apartment building and I'm leaning toward her and then our heads come together, our lips, our tongues. It's like kissing a guy, only everything's softer. Sweeter, somehow. We're wrapped up against each other, hands fumbling, I'm caressing her hair, her neck, her shoulder—until suddenly she pulls away, breathless, like me, a surprised look of desire in her eyes, like me, but there's something else there, too. Not shame. No, it felt too good. But confusion, yes. And uncertainty, for sure.

"I'm sorry," I say. I know she's been passing, just like me. Gay in spirit. We've talked about it. Lots of times.

"Don't be," she says. "It felt nice."

I don't say anything. I'm on pins and needles, not understanding the intensity of these feelings I have for her, for another woman, not wanting to scare her off, but knowing I want more. "Nice" doesn't even begin to describe how it felt to me.

Nina sighs. "It's just . . . confusing."

This I understand.

"But it feels wrong?" I ask.

She nods. "Only not for the reason you're probably thinking. It's just . . . if I was sure Martin was cheating on me . . . that our marriage was over . . . I think it would be different. I wouldn't feel like *I* was betraying him. I could do whatever I wanted, couldn't I?"

"Do you still love him?"

"I don't know," Nina says. "If he's cheating on me again, the way I think he is . . . " She gives me a lost look that makes me want to just take her in my arms once more, but I stay on my own side of the front seat. "Maybe," she says in this small voice, her eyes so big and hopeful, "maybe you could find out for me . . . for us. . . ."

"What? Like follow him?"

Nina shakes her head. "No. I was thinking more like . . . you could try to seduce him. Then we'd *know*."

I don't like the way this is going at all, but there's a promise in Nina's eyes now, a promise that if I do this thing for her, she'll be mine. Not just for one night, but forever.

"You wouldn't actually have to *do* anything," she says. "You know, like sleep with him. We'd only have to take it far enough to see if he's cheating on me."

"I don't know," I tell her, doubt in my voice, but I can already feel myself giving in.

She nods slowly. "I guess it's a pretty stupid idea," she says. She looks away, embarrassed. "God. I can't believe I even asked you to do something like that."

She leans forward and gives me a quick kiss, then draws back and starts to get out of the car.

"Wait a minute," I say, catching hold of her arm. She lets

me tug her back into the car. "I didn't say I wouldn't do it. It's just . . . we'd need a good plan, wouldn't we? I mean, where would I even meet him in the first place?"

So we start to talk about it, and before I know it, we've got the plan. She tells me where he goes after work for a drink on Fridays. We figure it'll be best if she goes away somewhere for the weekend. We work everything out, sitting there in the front seat of my car, arms around each other. We kiss again before she finally leaves, a long, deep kiss that has my head swimming, my body aching to be naked against hers. I don't even consider second thoughts until I wake up alone in my own apartment the next morning and begin to realize what I've gotten myself into.

I remember the last thing she said before she got out of the car.

"If he *is* cheating on me . . . and he takes you to our apartment, could you do something for me before you leave?"

"What's that?"

"There's a sword hanging on the wall over the mantle. Could you take it with you back to your place?"

"A sword."

She nodded. "Because if it's over, I'm not ever going back to that place. I won't ever want to see him again. But . . . " She gave me a look that melted my heart. "The sword's the only thing I'd want to take away with me. It used to belong to my mother, you see. . . ."

I lie there in bed thinking about it until I have to get up to have a pee. When I'm washing my face at the basin, I study my reflection looking back at me, water dripping from her cheeks.

"Lucy," I say to her. "What have we gotten ourselves into this time?"

— 4 —

It was a quiet night at Neon Sister, but it was still early, going on to eleven. Lucy saw Traci sitting by herself in one of the booths beside the dance floor. She was easy to spot with her shoulder-length dreadlocks, her coffee-colored skin accentuated by the white of her T-shirt. Lucy waited a moment to make sure Traci was alone, then crossed the dance floor and slid into the booth beside her. She ordered a drink from the waitress, but wasn't in the mood to do more than sip from it after it arrived. There was always something about being in Traci's calm, dark eyed presence that made Lucy want to open up to her. She didn't know what it was that usually stopped her, but tonight it wasn't there.

"I'm not really gay, you know," she said when the small talk between them died.

Traci smiled. "I know."

"You do?"

Traci nodded. "But you're not sure you're straight, either. You don't know who you are, do you?"

"I guess. Except now I'm starting to think maybe I am gay."

"Has this got something to do with Nina?"

"Is it that obvious?"

"We've all been there before, Lucy."

Lucy sighed. "So I think I'm ready to, you know, to find out who I really am, but I don't think Nina is."

"Welcome to that club as well."

Lucy took another sip of her drink and looked out at the dance floor. An hour had passed and the club was starting to fill up. She brought her gaze back to Traci.

"Were you ever in love with a guy?" she asked.

Traci hesitated for a moment, then gave a reluctant nod. "A long time ago."

"Does it feel any different—I mean, with a woman?"

"You mean inside?"

Lucy nodded.

"It doesn't feel different," Traci confirmed. She studied

Lucy, her dark gaze more solemn than usual, before going on. "Straights always think its hard for us to come out—to the world—but it's harder to come out to ourselves. Not because there's anything wrong with what we are, but because we're made to feel it's wrong. I used to think that with the strides in gay rights over the past few years, it wouldn't be like that anymore, but society still feeds us so much garbage that nothing much seems to have changed. You know what kept going around and around in my head when I was trying to figure myself out?"

Lucy shook her head.

"That old *The Children's Hour* with Shirley MacLaine from the sixties—the one where she finds out she's a lesbian and she kills herself. I was so ashamed of how I felt. Ashamed and confused."

"I don't feel ashamed," Lucy said.

"But you do feel confused."

Lucy nodded. "I don't know what to do."

"Well, here's my two cents: Don't be in a rush to work it out. Be honest—to yourself as well as to Nina—but take it slow."

"And if I lose her?"

"Then it was never meant to be." Traci gave her a wry smile. "Pretty lame, huh? But there's always a grain of truth—even in populist crap like that. You wanna dance?"

Lucy thought about the night she'd overheard Traci and another woman discussing her in the washroom, thought about what Traci had said about her, thought about what she herself was feeling for Nina. Didn't matter the combination of genders, she realized. Some things just didn't change. She gave Traci a smile.

"Sure," she said.

It was a slow dance. She and Traci had danced together many times before, but it felt different tonight. Tonight Lucy couldn't stop focusing on the fact that it was a woman's body moving so closely to hers, a woman's arms around her. But then ever since kissing Nina last night, everything had felt different.

"Gay or straight," Traci said, her voice soft in Lucy's ear, "the hurt feels the same."

Lucy nodded, then let her head rest against Traci's once more. They were comforting each other, Lucy realized, but while Traci was offering more, the dance was all that Lucy had to give.

—— 5 ——

So I go ahead and do it. I meet Martin in Huxley's, that yuppie bar across from Fitzhenry Park, and I flirt outrageously with him. Picking him up is so easy, I wish there was a prize for it. I'd collect big-time.

By the time we've had dinner, I've got enough on him to take back to Nina, but I'm curious now, about him, about where they live, and I can't seem to break it off. Next thing I know, I'm in their apartment, the same one I sat outside of a few nights ago, necking with his wife in the front seat of my car. Now I'm here with him, sitting on their couch, watching him make us drinks at the wet bar in the corner of the living room.

He comes back with a drink in each hand and gives me one. We toast each other, take a sip. This is seriously good brandy. I like it. I like him, too—not a man-woman kind of thing, but he seems like a nice guy. Except he cheats on his wife—whom I'm trying to get into my own bed. It's time to go, I realize. Way past time to go. But then he floors me.

"So when did you meet Nina?" he asks.

I look at him, unable to hide my surprise. "How did you—" I break off before I get in too deep and take a steadying breath to try to regain my composure. It's not easy with that pale blue gaze of his wryly regarding me. Earlier, it reminded me of

Traci, kind of solemn and funny, all at the same time, like hers, but now there's something unpleasant sitting in back of it—the same place the hurt sat in Nina's eyes the night I first met her.

"She's sent other people to get the sword, you know."

I've been trying to avoid looking at it all night, but now I can't stop my gaze from going to it. I remember thinking how big it was when I first stepped into the living room and stole a glance at it. No way it was going to fit into my handbag. I'd given up on the idea of walking out with it pretty quick.

"What story did she tell you?" Martin went on. "That it belonged to her grandmother and it's the only thing she's got left to remind her of the old bag?"

Not grandmother, I think. Mother. But I don't say anything. One of the things I've learned working on the paper: If you can keep quiet, nine out of ten times the person you're with will feel obliged to fill the silence. You'd be surprised the kind of things they'll tell you.

"Or did she tell you about the family curse," he asks, "and how the sword has to be sheathed for it to end?"

I still say nothing.

"Or did she tell you the truth?"

This time he plays the waiting game until I finally ask, "So what is the truth?"

"Well, it's all subjective, isn't it?"

There's an undercurrent of weirdness happening here that tells me it's really time to go now. I take a good swig of the brandy to fortify myself, then pick up my jacket and slip it on.

"I don't mean to sound so vague," he says before I get up. "It's just that, no matter what she's told you, it's only a piece of the truth. That's what I mean about it all being subjective."

I find myself nodding. What he's saying is something I learned my first week at the paper: There's no one thing called truth; just one's individual take on it.

"We're not married," he says.

"Uh-huh. It's kind of late for that line, isn't it?"

"No, you don't get it. She's not even human. She's this . . . this *thing*."

His gaze shifts to the sword above the mantle, then returns to mine. I realize the unpleasant thing I see sitting in the back of his eyes is fear.

"What are you saying?" I ask.

"She really is under a curse, except it's nothing like what she probably told you."

"She didn't say anything about a curse—except for being married to you."

"The way things look," Martin says, "I deserve that. But we're really not married. I don't have a hold over her. It's the other way around. She scares the shit out of me."

I shake my head. Considering the size of him and the size of her, I find that hard to believe.

"I met her a few years ago," he explains. "At a party. I made her a promise, that I'd help her break the curse that's on her, but I didn't. I broke my promise and she's been haunting me ever since."

Curses. Haunting. It's like he's trying to tell me Nina's a ghost. I'm beginning to wish that I'd just let it play out in the restaurant and gone on to my own place. By myself. Too late for that now. He's still sitting there, looking at me all expectantly, and I have to admit that while I think it's all a load of crock, I can't seem to check my curiosity. It's a bad habit I bring home from the office. It's probably why I applied for the job in the first place.

"So what's this curse?" I ask.

"She's trapped in the shape of that sword," he says, pointing to the mantle.

"Oh, please."

Nina passing as gay I can buy—I've been doing it myself. But passing as human as well?

"Look. I know what it sounds like. But it's true. She promised me a year of companionship—good company, great sex, whatever I wanted—but at the end of that year I had to fulfill my part of the bargain, and I couldn't go through with it."

"Which was?"

The only thing I'm really interested in now is how far he'll take all of this.

"The sword once had a scabbard," Martin says. "When it was sheathed, she could stay in human form. But the scabbard got lost or stolen or something—there was something enchanted about it as well. It kept its bearer free from all hurt and harm. Anyway, the way things are now, she can only be human for short bits of time before she has to return into the sword."

I give him a noncommittal "Uh-huh."

"The bargain I made," he says, "was that I'd sheathe the sword for her at the end of the year, but I couldn't do it."

"Why not?"

"Because I have to sheathe it in myself."

I sit up straighter. "What? You mean impale yourself on it—a kind of *seppuku* like the samurai used to do in Japan?"

He doesn't answer me, but goes on instead. "See, for the curse to be broken, I have to believe that it'll work while I do it. And I have to want to do it—you know, be a willing sacrifice. I can't do either."

I look at him, I read his fear, and realize that he really believes all of this.

"So why don't you just get rid of the sword?" I ask, which seems reasonable enough to me.

"I'm scared to. I don't know what'll happen to me if I do."

I think of Nina. I think of this big guy being scared of her and I have to shake my head.

"So . . . has Nina threatened you?"

He shakes his head. "No, she just stands there by the mantle, or at the foot of my bed, and looks at me. Haunts me. She won't talk to me anymore, she doesn't do anything but stare at me. It's driving me crazy."

Well, something sure is, I want to say. Instead I consider the sword, hanging up there on the wall. I try to imagine Nina's—what? Spirit? Essence?—trapped in that long length of blade. I can't even work up the pretense of belief.

"So give it to me," I say.

He blinks in confusion, then shakes his head again. "No, I can't do that. Something horrible will happen to me if I do."

"I don't think so," I tell him. "Nina specifically asked me to take the sword with me when I left. You say she's sent other people to get it. Doesn't it seem obvious that all she wants is the sword? Give it to me and we'll all be out of your life. Nina. The sword. Me." *Your sanity,* I add to myself, *though maybe a good shrink can help you get some of it back.*

"I . . . "

He looks from me to the sword, torn. Then he comes to a decision. He gets up and fetches a blanket, wraps the sword in it and hands it to me.

"Look," I say, staggering a little under its weight. "What you really should do is—"

"Just go," he tells me.

He doesn't physically throw me out, but it's close. Truth is, he looks so freaked about what he's doing that I'm happy to put as much distance as I can between us. I end up hauling the sword down to the street to where I parked my car. It won't fit in the trunk, so I put it on the back seat. I look up at the window of the apartment above me. Martin's turned all the lights off.

It's weird, I think, sliding into the driver's seat. He seemed so normal when I first picked him up in Huxley's, but then he turned out to be loopier than anyone I've ever met on this side of the Zebrowski Institute's doors. It just goes to show you. No wonder Nina wanted to leave him.

I stop at that thought, the car still in neutral. Except that wasn't why she said she wanted to leave him. I look up at the darkened apartment again, this time through my windshield. Though now that I think about it, if I were in her position, I probably wouldn't want to tell the truth about why I was leaving my husband either.

I shake my head. What a mess. Putting the car into gear, I drive myself home. I have a column due for the Monday paper and I don't know what it's going to be about yet. Still I know this much. It won't be about swords.

—6—

Nina really was out of town, so Lucy couldn't call her. "I don't want to lie to him," she'd told Lucy. "That'd make me just as bad as he is." What about Nina's lying to her? Lucy wondered, but she knew she was willing to give Nina the benefit of the doubt, seeing how nuts her husband was. Besides, even if Nina wasn't out of town, the only number Lucy had for her was the same as Martin's—she'd looked his up as she was making herself a coffee on Saturday morning.

She'd left the sword where she'd dropped it last night—wrapped in its blanket on the floor in her hallway, right beside the front door—and hadn't looked at it since. Didn't want to look at it. It wasn't that she believed any of Martin's very weird story about the sword and Nina, so much as that something about the weapon gave her the creeps. No, that wasn't quite right. It was more that thinking about it made her feel odd—as though the air had grown thicker, or the hardwood floor had gone slightly spongy underfoot. Better not to think of it.

Saturday, she did some grocery shopping, but she stayed in with a video on Saturday night. Sunday afternoon, she went into the office and worked on Monday's column—deciding to do a piece on cheap sources for fashion accessories. She finished it quickly and then spent a couple of hours trying to straighten out the mess on her desk without making any real noticeable progress. It was the story of her life. Sunday night, Nina called.

As soon as she recognized Nina's voice, Lucy looked down the hall to where the sword still lay and thought of what Martin had told her.

"I've got the sword," she said without any preamble. "It's here at my place. Do you want to come by to pick it up?"

"And take it where?" Nina asked. "Back to Martin's and my apartment?"

"Oh. I never thought of that. I guess you need to find a place to live first."

She hesitated a moment, but before she could offer her own couch as a temporary measure, Nina was talking again.

"I can't believe he just gave it to you," she said. "Did he give you a hard time? Was . . . seducing him . . . was it horrible?"

"It didn't go that far."

"But still," Nina said. "It couldn't have been pleasant."

"More like strange."

"Strange how?"

Was there a new note in Nina's voice? Lucy wondered. A hint of—what? Tension?

"Well, he hit on me just like you said he would," she said. "He picked me up at Huxley's after work, took me out for dinner and then back to"— she almost said "his" —"your place."

"I guess I'm not surprised."

"Anyway, as soon as we got to the apartment, almost the first thing he asked me was when I'd met you. Nina, he told me you guys were never married. He told me all kinds of weird things."

There was a moment's silence on the line, then Nina asked, "Did you believe him?"

"The stuff he was telling me was so crazy that I don't know what to believe," Lucy said. "But I want to believe you."

"I'll tell you everything," Nina said. "But not now. I've just got a few things to do and then I'll come see you."

Lucy could tell that Nina was about to hang up.

"What sort of things?" she asked, just to keep Nina on the line.

Nina laughed. "Oh, you know. I just have to straighten my affairs, say good-bye to Martin, that kind of thing."

Lucy found herself remembering Martin's fear. Crazy as he was, the fear had been real. Why he should be scared of Nina, Lucy couldn't begin to imagine, but he had been afraid.

"Listen," she said, "you're not going to—"

"I have to run," Nina broke in. "I'll call you soon."

"—do anything crazy," Lucy finished.

But she was talking to a dead line.

Lucy stared at the phone for a moment before she finally cradled the receiver. A nervous prickle crept up her spine and the air seemed to thicken. She turned to look at the sword again. It was still where she'd left it, wrapped in Martin's blanket, lying on the floor.

There's no such thing as enchanted swords, she told herself. She knew that. But ever since leaving Martin's place last night, there'd been a niggling little doubt in the back of her mind, a kind of "What if?" that she hadn't been able to completely ignore, or refute with logic. She couldn't shake the feeling that *something* was about to happen and whatever it was connected to the sword and Martin. And to Nina.

She stood up quickly and fetched her car keys from the coffee table. Maybe it was stupid, worrying the way she was, but she had to know. Had to be sure that the boundaries of what could be and what could not still existed as they always had. She left so quickly, she was still buttoning up her jacket when she reached the street.

It took her fifteen minutes to get to the apartment where Nina and Martin lived. She parked at the curb across from the building and studied their place on the third floor. The windows were all dark. There was no one on the street except for a man at the far end of the block who was poking through a garbage can with a stick.

Lucy sat there for five minutes before she reluctantly pulled away. She cruised slowly through the neighborhood, looking for Nina's familiar trim figure. Eventually the only thing left to do was drive back to her own apartment and wait for Nina to call. She sat up in bed with the telephone on the quilt beside her leg, trying to read because she knew she wouldn't be able to sleep. After a while she phoned Traci, nervous the whole time that Nina was trying to get through while she was tying up the line. She told Traci everything, but it made no more sense to Traci than it did to her.

"Weird," Traci said at last.

"Am I blowing this way out of proportion?" Lucy wanted to know.

She could almost feel Traci's smile across the telephone line.

"Well, it is a bit much," Traci said. "All this business with the sword and Nina. But I've always been one to trust my intuition. If you feel there's something weird going on, then I'm willing to bet that there is—something on a more logical level than curses and hauntings, mind you."

"So what do I do?"

Traci sighed. "Just what you're doing: wait. What else can you do?"

"I know. It's just . . ."

"You want some company?" Traci asked.

What Lucy wanted was Nina. She wanted to know that Martin had nothing to fear from her, that Nina wasn't about to do something that was going to get her into serious trouble. But Traci couldn't help her with any of that.

"No," she told her friend. "I'll be okay."

"Call me tomorrow."

"I will."

Finally she drifted off with the lights on, sitting up against the headboard, the book still open on her lap. She dreamed that the sword lay on the other side of the bed, talking to her in a low, murmuring voice that could have belonged to anybody. When she woke, she couldn't remember what it had told her.

—— 7 ——

By nine o'clock, Monday morning, I'm a mess. Punchy from the weird dreams and getting so little sleep. Sick with worry. Nina still hasn't called and I'm thinking the worst. It kind of surprises me that the worst I imagine isn't that she's done something to Martin, but that she doesn't want to see me anymore.

I'm already late for work. I consider phoning in sick, but I know I can't stay at home—I'm already bouncing off the walls—so I go in to the office. I know I can check my machine for messages from there and at least I'll be able to find something to keep me busy.

I have this habit of going over the police reports file when I first get in. It's kind of a gruesome practice, reading the list of break-ins, robberies, rapes and the like that occurred the night before, but I can't seem to shake it. It's not even my beat; I usually get assigned the soft stories. I think maybe the reason I do it is that it's a way of validating that, okay, so the city's going down the tubes, but I'm still safe. I'm safe. The people I know and love are safe. This kind of horrible thing goes on, but it doesn't really touch me. It's fueled by the same impulse that makes us all slow down at accidents and follow the news. Sometimes I think we don't so much want to be informed as have our own security validated.

This morning there's a report of an apparent suicide on a street that sounds familiar. They don't give the victim's name, but the street's all I need. Shit. It's Martin. It says, Caucasian male did a jump from his third-story apartment window, but I know it's Martin. The coroner's still waiting for the autopsy report; the cops are pretty much ruling out foul play. But I know better, don't I? Martin himself told me what'd happen if he got rid of the sword and he looked so terrified when I left his place Friday night.

But I still can't believe it of Nina. I can't believe all this crap he told me about her and the sword.

I've only been away from home for thirty-five minutes, but I immediately close the file and phone my apartment to check for messages. Nothing. Same as ten minutes ago—I called when I first got here.

There's nothing all day.

I try to stick it out, but in the end I have to leave work early. I start for home, but wind up driving by the apartment—looking for Nina, I tell myself, but of course she wouldn't be there, hanging around on the pavement where Martin hit. I know why I'm really doing this. Morbid curiosity. I look up at the windows, third floor. One of them's been boarded up.

I go home. Shower. Change. Then I hit the bars on Gracie Street, looking for Nina. The North Star. Neon Sister. Girljock. Skirts. No sign of her. I start to check out the hard-core places, the jack-and-jill-off scenes and clubs where the rougher trade hangs out. Still nothing. The last place I go into, this blond leatherette in a black push-up bra and hot pants smiles at me. I start to smile back, but then she makes a V with her fingers and flicks her tongue through them. I escape back up the stairs that let me into the place. I'm not sure what I am anymore—gay, straight, what—but one thing I know is I'm still not into casual sex.

Once outside, I lean against the front of the building, feeling just as lost as I did the night Traci took me under her wing. I don't know what to do anymore, where to turn. I start to look for a pay phone—I figure I can at least check my answering machine again—when someone grabs me by the arm. I yelp and pull free, but when I turn around, it's Nina I find standing there beside me—not the blond from the club I just left.

"Sorry," she says. "I didn't mean to make you jump like that."

She's smiling, but I can see she really means it. She leans forward and gives me a kiss on the lips. I don't know what to do, what to think. I'm so glad to see her, but so scared she had something to do with Martin's death. Not magic mumbo jumbo, nothing like that. Just plain she couldn't take the shit from him anymore and it all got out of hand.

"Martin's dead," I say.

"I know. I was there."

My breath catches in my throat. "You . . . you didn't . . . ?"

I can't get it out, but she knows what I'm asking. She shakes her head. Taking my arm, she leads me off down the street.

"I think we have to talk," she tells me.

She leads me to my car, but I don't feel like I'm in any condition to drive. I start to go to the passenger's side.

"I can't drive," Nina tells me.

Right. So we sit there in my car, parked just off Gracie Street, looking out the windshield, not saying anything, not touching each other, just sitting there.

"What did he tell you about me?" Nina asks finally.

I look at her. Her face isn't much more than a silhouette in the illumination thrown by the street lights outside. After a few moments, I clear my throat and start to talk, finishing with, "Is it true?"

"Mostly."

I don't know what to say. I want to think she's crazy, but there's nothing about her that I associate with craziness.

"Where did you go after you called me?" I ask instead.

Nina hesitates, then says, "To the lake. To talk to my sister."

"Your sister?"

I hadn't stopped to think of it before, but of course she'd have family. We all do. But then Nina pulls that piece of normal all out of shape as well.

"She's one of the Ladies of the Lake," she says. "Bound to her sword, just like me. Just like all of us."

It's my turn to hesitate. Do I really want to feed this fantasy? But then I ask, "How many are you?"

"Seven of us—for seven swords. My oldest sister is bound to the one you'd know best: Excalibur."

I really have to struggle with what I'm hearing. I'd laugh, except Nina's so damn serious.

"But," I say. "When you're talking about a Lady of the Lake . . . you mean like in Tennyson? King Arthur and all that stuff?"

Nina nods. "The stories are pretty close, but they miss a lot."

I take a deep breath. "Okay. But that's in England. What would your sister be doing here? What are you doing here?"

"All lakes are aspects of the First Lake," Nina says. "Just as all forests remember the First Forest."

I can only look blankly at her.

Nina sighs. "As all men and women remember First Man and First Woman. And the fall from grace."

"You mean in Eden?"

Nina shakes her head. "Grace is what gives this world its

worth, but there are always those who would steal it away, for the simple act of doing so. Grace shames a graceless people, so they strike out at it. Remember Martin told you about the scabbards that once protected our swords?"

"I guess. . . ."

"They had healing properties, and when men realized that, they took the scabbards and broke them up, eliminating a little more of their grace and healing properties with each piece they took. That's why I'm in my present predicament. Of the seven of us, only two still have their swords, kept safe in their scabbards. Three more still retain ownership of their swords. Nita—my sister—and I don't have even that. With our swords unsheathed, we've lost most of our freedom. We're bound into the metal for longer and longer periods of time. A time will come, I suppose, when we'll be trapped in the metal forever."

She studies me for a long moment, then sighs again. "You don't believe any of this, do you?"

I'm honest with her. "It's hard."

"Of course. It's easy to forget marvels when your whole life you're taught to ignore them."

"It's just—"

"Lucy," Nina says. "I'll make the same bargain with you that I made with Martin. I'll stay with you for a year, but then you must hold up your side."

I shake my head. I don't even have to think about it.

"But you wanted to sleep with me," Nina says. "You wanted my love."

"But not like this. Not bargaining for it like it's some kind of commodity. That's not love."

Nina looks away. "I see," she says, her gaze locked on something I can't see.

"Tell me what you'd want me to do," I say.

Nina's attention returns to me. "There's no point. You don't believe."

"Tell me anyway."

"You must take the sword inside yourself. You must do it willingly. And you must believe that by doing so, you are freeing me."

"I just stick it into myself?"

"Something like that," Nina says. "It would be clearer if you believed."

"And what would happen to me?" I ask. "Would I die?"

"We all die, sooner or later."

"I know that," I say impatiently. "But would I die from doing this?"

Nina shakes her head. "No. But you'd be changed."

"Changed how?"

"I don't know. It's—" She hesitates, then plunges quickly on. "I've never heard of it being done before."

"Oh."

We look some more out the windshield. The street we're on is pretty empty, cars parked, but not much traffic, vehicular or pedestrian. Over on Gracie we can see the nightlife's still going strong. I want to ask her, Why didn't you tell me the truth before? but I already know. I don't believe her now, so what difference would having heard it a few days earlier have made?

"Did you love Martin?" I ask instead. "I mean, at first."

"I'm not sure what love is."

I guess nobody really is, I think. Is what I'm feeling for Nina love? This feeling that's still swelling inside me, under the confusion and jumpiness—is it love? People die for love. It happens. But surely they *know* when they make the sacrifice?

"I really didn't kill him," she tells me. "I went to the apartment—I'm not sure why or what I meant to do—and let myself in. When he saw me, he went crazy. He looked terrified. When I took a step closer, he threw himself out the window—straight through the glass and all. He didn't say anything and he didn't give me a chance to speak either."

"He told me he was scared."

Nina nods. "But I don't know why. He had no reason to be scared of me. If I hadn't harmed him in the two years since he failed to keep his side of our bargain, why should he think that I'd hurt him now?"

I have no answer to that. Only Martin could explain it, but he'd taken the secret with him on his three-story plunge to the pavement below his window.

"I should go," Nina says then, but she makes no move to open the door.

"What about the sword?" I ask.

She turns to me. My eyes are adjusted enough to the vagaries of the lighting to see the expression on her face, but I can't figure it out. Sadness? My own feelings returned? Fear? Maybe a mix of the three.

"Would you do this for me?" she asks. "Would you bury the sword—in hallowed ground?"

"You mean like a churchyard?"

She shakes her head. "It will need an older hallowing than that. There is a place where the river meets the lake."

I know where she's talking about. The City Commission keeps the lawns perfectly groomed around there, but there's this one spot right on the lake shore where a stand of old pines has been left to make a little wild acre. The trees there haven't been touched since the city was first founded, back in the 1700s.

"Bury the sword there," she tells me. "Tonight. Before the sun rises."

I nod. "What'll happen to you?"

"Nita says it would let me sleep. Forever." She smiles, but it doesn't touch her eyes. "Or at least until someone digs it up again, I suppose."

"I . . . I'd do this other thing," I say, "but I'm too scared."

She nods, understanding. "And you don't believe."

She says it without recrimination. And she doesn't say anything at all about love, about how to make the sacrifice willingly, I'd have to really love her. And she's right. I don't believe. And if I love her, I don't love her enough.

She leans across the seat and gives me a kiss. I remember the last time she did this. There was so much promise. In her kiss. In her eyes. Now she's only saying good-bye. I want to talk to her. I want to explain it all over again. But I just let her go. Out of the car. Down the street. Out of my life.

There's a huge emptiness inside me after she's gone. Maybe what hurts the most is the knowledge I hold that I can't let go—that I love her, but I don't love her enough. She asked too much of me, I tell myself, but I'm not sure if it's something I really believe or if I'm only trying to convince myself that it's true to try to make myself feel better. It doesn't work.

I drive home to get the sword. I unwrap it, there in my hall, and hold it in my hands, trying to get some sense of Nina from it. But it's just metal. Eventually I wrap it up again and take it down to my car. I get a shovel from the toolshed behind the building. It belongs to the guy who lives on the ground floor, but I don't think he'll miss it. I'll have it back before he even knows it's gone.

And that's how I get here, digging a grave for a sword in hallowed ground. I can hear the lake against the shore, the wind sighing in the pines above. I can't hear the city at all, though it's all around me. Hallowed ground—hallowed by something older than what I was taught about in Sunday school, I guess. Truth is, I turned into an agnostic since those long-ago innocent days. I was just a girl then, didn't even know about sapphic impulses, little say think I might be feeling them.

It's easier to dig in among the roots of these pines than I would have thought possible, but it still takes me a long time to get the grave dug. I keep stopping to listen to the wind and the sound of the lake, the waves lapping against the shore. I keep stopping to look at the sword, and the minutes leak away in little fugue states. I don't know where my mind goes. I just suddenly find myself blinking beside the grave, gaze locked on the long length of that sword. Thinking of Nina. Wanting to find the necessary belief and love to let me fill the emptiness I feel inside.

Finally it's getting on to the dawn. The grave's about four feet deep. It's enough. I'm just putting things off now. It's all so crazy—I *know* it's crazy—but I can't help but feel that it really is Nina I'm getting ready to lay in the hole and cover over with dirt.

I consider wrapping the sword back up again, but the blanket was Martin's and somehow it doesn't feel right. I pick the sword up and cradle it for a moment, as though I'm holding a child, a cold and still child with only one long limb. I touch the blade with a fingertip. It's not particularly sharp. I study the tip of the blade in the moonlight. You'd have to really throw yourself on it for it to pierce the skin and impale you.

I think maybe Nina's craziness is contagious. I find myself wishing I loved Nina enough to have done this thing for her, to believe, to trust, to be brave—crazy as it all is. I find myself sitting up, with the sword tip lying on my knees. I open my blouse and prop the sword up, lay the tip against my skin, between my breasts, just to see how it feels. I find myself leaning forward, putting pressure on the tip, looking down at where the metal presses against my skin.

I feel as though I've slipped into an altered state of consciousness. I look down to where the sword meets my skin and the point's gone, it's inside me, an inch, two inches. I don't feel anything. There's no pain. There's no blood. There's only this impossible moment like a miracle where the sword's slipping inside me, more and more of its length, the harder I push against it. I'm bent almost double now and still it keeps going inside me, inch after inch. It doesn't come out my back, it's just being swallowed by my body. Finally I reach out with my hands, close my fingers around each side of the hilt, and push it up inside me, all the rest of the way.

And pass out.

— **8** —

When I come to, the air's lighter. I can't see the sun yet, but I can feel its light seeping through the trees. I can still hear the lake and the wind in the pines above me, but I can hear the traffic from the city, too.

I sit up. I look at the grave and the shovel. I look at the blanket. I look for the sword, but it's gone. I lift my hands to my chest and feel the skin between my breasts. I remember the sword sliding into my chest last night, but the memory feels like a hallucinatory experience.

No, I tell myself. Believe. I hear Nina's voice in my mind, hear her telling me, *"It's easy to forget marvels when your whole life you're taught to ignore them,"* and tell myself, *Don't invalidate a miracle because you've been taught they're not real. Trust yourself. Trust the experience. And Nina. Trust Nina.*

But she's not here. My body might have swallowed the sword, impossibly sheathing the long length of its metal in my flesh, but she's not here.

My fingers feel a bump on my skin and I look down to see I've got a new birthmark, equidistant from each of my breasts. It looks like a cross. Or a sword, standing on its point. . . .

I feel so calm. It seems as though I should be either freaking out completely or delirious with wonder and awe, but there's only the calm. I sit there for a long time, running my finger across the bump of my new birthmark, then finally I button up my blouse. I fill the grave—this goes a lot quicker than digging it did—and cover up the raw dirt with pine needles. I

wrap the shovel in my blanket and walk back to where I parked
my car on Battersfield Road.

— 9 —

Traci has to know the whole story, of course, so I tell her
everything. I don't know how much she believes, but crazy as it
all sounds, she believes that I believe, and that's enough for her.
I'm afraid of getting involved with her at first—afraid that I'm
turning to her on the rebound from what I never quite had
with Nina but certainly felt for her. But it doesn't work that
way. Or if I am rebounding, it's in the right direction.

I remember Nina telling me that I'd be changed if I—I
guess absorbed the sword is the best way to put it—but that she
didn't know how. I do now. It's not a big thing. My world hasn't
changed—though I guess my view of it has to some degree.
What's happened is that I'm more decisive. I've taken control
of my life. I'm not drifting anymore—either in my personal life
or on the job. I don't go for the safe, soft stories anymore. One
person can't do a whole lot about all the injustice in the world,
but I'm making damn sure that people hear about it. That we
all do what we can about it. I'm not looking for a Pulitzer; I
just want to make sure that I leave things a little better behind
me when I go.

Six months or so after Traci and I start living together, she
turns to me one night and asks me why it didn't disappoint me
that Nina never came back to me after I did what she asked.

"It's because I remember what she told me in that dream I
had the night Martin died," I explain. "You know, when I
dreamed the sword was lying on the bed beside me and talking
to me? I didn't remember when I woke, but it came back to me
a few days after I got back from the pine grove."

Traci gives me a poke with her finger. "So aren't you going
to tell me?" she says when I've fallen silent.

I smile. "She said that if she was freed, she might not be

able to come back. That really being human, instead of passing for one, might mean that she'd be starting her life all over again as an infant and she wouldn't remember what had gone before."

Now it's Traci's turn to fall silent. "Is that why you want us to have a kid?" she asks finally.

With modern medicine, anything's possible, right? Or at least something as basic as artificial insemination.

"I like to think she's waiting for us to get it together," I say.

"So you're planning on a girl."

"Feels right to me."

Traci reaches over and tracks the contour of my sword birthmark with a finger. "Think she'll have one of these?"

"Does it matter?" I ask.

"Doesn't matter at all," Traci says. She rolls over to embrace me. "And I guess it means we don't have to worry about what to name her either."

I snuggle in close. I love finally knowing who I am; loving and being loved for who I am. I just hope that wherever and whenever Nina is reborn, she'll be as lucky as I feel I am.

Nights of the Round Table

LAWRENCE SCHIMEL

Over dinner he wished he would disappear,
whisked away by magic to anywhere he could not hear
his parents fight.
He hoped he might,
like Merlin,
find himself deaf and mute within
a Whitethorn Wood.
But he could
not escape the round kitchen table;
unable
to eat,
yet forbidden to leave his seat
until he'd cleaned his plate.
He dreamed of happy families as his parents fought and ate.
Afterwards, he went up to his room and wept
until he slept.

Their life was constant war:
cursing, shouting, a slammed door.

Innocent dinner prattle
invariably turned into a battle.

On his birthday
they
called a cease
fire. Peace,
until his mother sallied forth into the den
to confront her husband once again.
They argued where to take him for dinner.
Soon, his mother reemerged, the winner.
He ordered a Shirley Temple at
the restaurant. "Think you're old enough to drink that?"
his father asked him
when the drink arrived, a blue plastic sword hooked over its rim.
"Don't say that. You'll ruin his birthday night."
Already they had begun to fight.
He swirled the cherry in his drink, feeling very alone.
"Who pulls this sword from stone
and anvil," he thought,
trying not to listen as his parents fought,
"by sign and right of birth is king of all England."
He lifted the garnish in his hand
and tugged the cherry from the plastic sword.
It did not end their discord;
the restaurant table was square.
The cherry plunked back into his drink, loosing the tiny air
bubbles on the bottom of the glass.
It reminded him of a summer's day at camp when en masse
his bunk went down to the lake to jump
into the water from a rope tied to a tree. Standing on a stump
on the shore
he saw a glint of metal, like the flash of ore
in a miner's pan.

He waded into the water for a closer look and, breaking the ban,
swam out towards the girls'
camp on the other side. Diving deep, as if he searched for
    pearls,
he found the source of the glinting light:
an open blade of a Swiss Army Knife held tight
in the hand of a blond-haired
girl. Although he was scared,
he could not help
watching the way her hair curled about her like strands of kelp
reaching for the surface.
Her face
seemed so serene.
He could not tell if the keen
blade were meant to cut her free
from the rocks she
was tied to, or to slit her wrist.

He stabbed at the lemon twist
of his mother's diet Coke.
His father pulled out a pack of Lucky's and began to smoke.
His mother glared and looked about to
object, but didn't get the chance. His father asked him, "What do
you want for your birthday?" He laid the sword atop
his plate and said, "I only want the fighting to stop."

Here There Be Dragons?

MARION ZIMMER BRADLEY

hen Lythande entered the town, it looked eerie. Pale light from a waning moon spread a thin, cold radiance over the snow that covered the deserted streets of the town. In accord with her usual custom, Lythande first looked about for an inn or tavern, where she could, for the price of a pot of beer, which she never drank, listen to all the gossip and see if anyone in the village had need of the services of a mercenary magician.

There was but one inn, and it looked run-down. A weak and yellowish lamplight spilled out the window. A bare handful of people were huddled around an ancient dark wooden bar. Lythande looked around to orient herself, and closed her eyes, not really believing what she saw. The population seemed all to have been taken from an ancient engraving in a text on witchcraft she had once seen. Men, women and even a few children all had about them some faint family likeness, something vaguely deformed; yet, looking a little more closely, she saw no physical deformity. She wondered then if they suffered some spiritual deformity.

Oh, this was absurd; what was a spiritual deformity any-how—or was there any such thing?

Well, it would make more sense to go inside rather than standing out here in the cold gawking and having neurotic notions about them.

Lythande hoisted her backpack and the case of light wood covered in colored embroidered wool, which contained her harp. She shoved the door open. A blast of heat smote her in the face and smelled of burned meat and the acrid odor of stale beer. Lythande had been hungry; but on smelling the meat in this inn, she felt suddenly that the very thought of food was revolting.

She stepped up to the bar and asked quietly for a pot of beer. The barman set a large mug before her. He was an odd little gnome of a man with queerly pointed ears, who looked, Lythande thought, more like the village idiot than a barkeeper of any sort.

"Come far today, stranger?" he asked her in a gritty voice.

"Far enough," Lythande answered politely.

"Stranger, be you a magician?" asked the queer little gnome of a man. "And do you take commissions at a reasonable price?"

"I am, and I do," Lythande observed. "But what would you consider a reasonable price? And how can I tell you a price unless I first know the scope of the job?"

He leaned over and drew a curtain that hung, she thought, over a window to the street outside. But as he drew it aside, Lythande stared—for it led not to the outside but to a view of a flight of steps that came out on a sunlit landscape out of doors; there were large expanses of sunlit summer trees and long green meadows where there should be nothing but snow.

"Just to go out yonder and see what's there. Le'me tell you another magician asked thirty silvers—and so I hung that curtain up. An'I can always just draw it closed. It won't bother us if'n we don't bother it none."

Lythande felt like laughing. This was not an attitude toward magic she had encountered before—and she would have sworn that she had seen and heard them all. But she only asked soberly, "What would you consider a fair price?"

"Mebbe three silvers, just to walk outside an' see something that probably ain't there?" he said sharply with an unpleasant smile.

"There may be monsters or something worse at the top of those steps," Lythande said carefully. "What if I must come down even faster than I went up? Will I have any time to come back here and collect enough silvers to do away with some mighty ogre?"

For, she thought, the world behind those stairs might be anywhere—but the only place it was certainly *not* was outside in the snowy street.

The little gnome behind the bar said, "You can leave that there harp; I'll take care of it an' your pack too."

Lythande regarded him with something less than perfect trust. "I never leave my harp. And what if I need something from the pack? I could as easily leave the Blue Star from my brow."

She looked at the stairs again. They were quite narrow, and it would be difficult to handle the harp while climbing them. And it was possible she would need both hands free for defense or spell casting.

She rummaged in the pack and took out her book of spells. "This at least I carry with me." She placed the harp and pack together in an out-of-the-way spot behind the bar and whispered a few words over them. In answer, a faint blue light glowed around them. "The rest you may keep for me; if I do not return, some member of my Order will claim pack and harp and remove the spell that guards them."

"As you wish, Sir Sorcerer," Bat-ears said respectfully, edging away from her belongings. "Is it likely that you will not return? Have you had any premonitions? Can you arrange to send me a message from the Other Side? Maybe what's good on the stock market?"

"What kind of ghoul are you?" Lythande asked in disgust.

"No offense meant," Bat-ears answered. "But you magicians—all that bosh about the afterlife, but nothing really useful, like never knowin' what's good on the stock market, or what will win at the racecourse. . . . You magicians give me a pain."

I wonder if any of you know what you give me, Lythande thought, but aloud she made only a vague murmur, which could be taken to mean almost anything.

She thrust the spell book into the pocket of the breeches under her mage-robe, went toward the window and heaved it open. It opened on a flight of stairs. Not really giving herself time to think, she set her foot upon the lowest step of the stairs and went up.

There were more stairs than there looked to be, and the sky was growing darker as she climbed them. Halfway along the flight of stairs, she felt a curious disorientation, no longer sure she was climbing; might she not, rather, have been descending?

Abruptly the stairs came to an end, and Lythande came to a stop with an unpleasant jolt. It was fully dark now, and Lythande could see only a little way through the thick darkness. She came to a stop and looked around, wanting to assess this strange country somewhere above and behind the inn. Behind her, the stairs seemed to disappear into a thick mist.

If I turned around now and went down the stairs, would I wind up in that same bar? she wondered. She would not bet on it; or even that she *could,* now, return to the firelit interior of the inn. At least not by simply turning round and heading back the way she had come, whether it be up or down. By the prickling of the Blue Star on her forehead, she knew that powerful magic was somewhere in the darkness around her.

She felt within her pockets. Her hand came out clutching a little carved-wood crucifix that she had been given a few years ago by a wandering priest. Now she began to wonder whether this powerful talisman kept her from seeing something very evil.

What was it the priest had said? "You shall know the truth, and the truth shall make you free." Yes, that was it.

She held up the crucifix and said, "Symbol of truth, show me the truth!" All at once, as if a veil had been snatched from her eyes, a burning metallic sun turned the landscape an evil-looking sulfurous yellow. She put the crucifix carefully back into her pocket, but the landscape didn't change.

She thought she should return to the inn, now that she had seen what was here; go back and tell them what lay beyond their window. But would they do anything, or would they simply thank her, draw the curtain and let it stay there, out of sight and out of mind? And if she did, would she violate her Magician's Oath to fight the forces of evil wherever they should be found?

She stepped forward into the burning sunlight, which felt terribly hot on her face. She felt like turning about, and bolting back up—or was it down?—the stairs.

But she did not. She told herself that she had seen no evil yet; all that she knew for certain was that there was magic here. She could not be sure it was evil, however horrible the land looked around here. But her vows bound her not to turn her back on evil without at least doing her uttermost to fight it.

Was she even equipped to fight it? She had left her harp with the barman, and more than once the sound of her harp alone had been sufficient to drive some evil away. Well, it was no good thinking about it; for better or for worse, she had come into this place without her harp, essentially unarmed, and without any magical weapon she must face it.

Face what? So far she had only seen the wicked color of an alien sun. Maybe she would see nothing else.

Although that sun, she told herself, seemed evil enough. But what was so evil about an alien sun and a sulfur-colored landscape? Was it only that they were different? In some ways it might almost be considered weirdly beautiful.

But that concept was too much for her. Her mind so revolted at the thought of calling that lurid landscape *beautiful* that she thought she would vomit. With a fierce effort she controlled herself and brought her rebellious stomach to order. She drew herself fiercely upright and forced herself to go a bit farther into the burning alien landscape.

After a few steps she turned about, seeking the stairs where she had entered. There was no sign of them, nor of any door or exit.

So, she told herself, *there may be no return—at least not now.*

No! Against that, her mind rebelled. *I cannot stay here. There must be a way back; anything else is completely unthinkable.* Yet she knew the unthinkable might well become fact, and wanting it to be different would not make any difference at all. So she must put all her ingenuity to the business of return. She must above all remember where the stairway had been located and hope that sooner or later she would have a chance to go up it again, even if it must be at a dead run being pursued by whatever evil was there.

She sighed, and started in the direction of the magic she could feel nearby. Then there was a roaring sound in that direction; it sounded like some beast, but no normal beast she could think of.

What could it be? Maybe she had traveled not only in space but in time as well. And she had had no psychic warnings of any magical beast either. The magic she *could* feel did not feel animal in nature.

But were her sudden fears of a magical beast some form of warning? Magic sometimes worked that way. Somewhere in the distance, there was a burning glow accompanied by that same dreadful roaring. Lythande thought that if the stairway had still been there, she would have run up—or down—it at once. Maybe that was why it was no longer there. Above all she must keep track of where it had been, in case there was a danger somewhere here that she could escape only by taking to her heels.

That roaring continued coming in her direction; and the prickling of the Blue Star told her that she was approaching the magic she felt. For defense she had a magical dagger and a non-magical dagger; but she suddenly felt she could have used a sword. She had never carried a sword in her life, and wondered why she was suddenly thinking of one.

The answer was not far to seek. A little path led through the trees, and at the very edge of the road stood a stone about waist high on which was standing another round stone. It was engraved in low relief with a carving of a strange, long-necked beast. And driven into the stone halfway to the hilt was a long sword.

She stared at it in disbelief. She knew of such things from old ballads—there were at least a dozen that she herself knew and sang about swords stuck into stone. But she had never expected to see one. Even to a magician, such things did not happen, and yet, unless she wished to deny the evidence of her own eyes, there it unmistakably was.

The animal carved into the stone was very strange. She had never seen anything like it, not in a menagerie or an exhibit of exotic beasts, not even in a display of magical beasts kept by a magician who had a roc and a camelopard. Yet the evidence of her own eyes was undeniable. And she had been wishing for a sword. But she had not expected her wishes to receive an answer so quickly.

At that very moment she heard through the bushes a terrible roaring sound, and saw the bushes swaying and jerking as if something very large were crashing through the plentiful underbrush. She jerked the sword free of the great stone, hardly noticing that she was doing it, and ran. If she was to see this strange beast in the flesh, she was in no hurry to validate her fears. Not even to reassure herself about her own sanity.

Now she caught a glimpse of a long, snakelike neck, unusually high, of a curious leathery green. It had large reptilian eyes that looked almost as if they were on long, insectoid stalks. The eyes swiveled, and Lythande had the uncanny feeling that they were searching for her in the underbrush.

Then the beast's eyes found hers, and it both stopped in its tracks and stared at her. Lythande stared back. She was not eager to try out her new sword against anything so large or fierce. But, she wondered, did she have a choice?

She held the sword upright before her. By tradition, swords such as this had special powers. What did this one do?

As if the sword were talking to her, she heard a voice in her head. *By what right do you assume you are meant to do anything about this creature? You came into its world, not it into yours. It is big and terrifying; but if you let it alone, it will let you alone. This is not your fight.*

Lythande considered that. Somehow she was sure that the barkeeper had wanted her to kill this creature, for all his talk of just going to see what was there. But this creature was not evil—which was more than she could be sure of the barkeeper and his fellow villagers.

They did not pay me to kill or dispose of a dragon—or whatever this is. They very specifically paid me to go into the world behind their window and see what was there. Just to see it, not to do anything about it. I made it clear that for what they offered to pay I would but go and look if anything was there. That was the bargain, and I have kept it.

So Lythande should do nothing now, but go back at once and tell her story. But in order to do that, she must remember where the stairs were located. Could she find them even now?

She still stared into the beast's eyes, not daring to look away. But now the beast turned away from her, starting off along a side path. It sighed, growled and breathed out fire, igniting the underbrush and presumably cooking whatever small animals might be in there.

By the light of the burning forest, Lythande turned about and ran toward where she had last seen the stairs. She almost tumbled down them and with great relief slid through the window into the bar.

The little barkeep with bat-ears looked up and said, "So, Sir Magician, back again? What did you find on the other side of those stairs?" He looked at the sword, still in her hand.

Lythande felt her skin crawl, and the Blue Star on her forehead flashed brightly. The sword picked up the light and reflected it back at her. There was evil around her here; she knew that as surely as if the sword had shouted it out so that the whole room could hear.

She forced herself to reply calmly while trying to think of what to do next. "A dragon, or some strange beast, breathing fire. It was setting the woods on fire."

He looked perturbed. "And did you kill it?"

"No," said Lythande. "I did not; for three silvers I agreed to go into that land and see what was there, not to kill anything. For killing, my price is substantially higher."

"Oh," said Bat-ears. "I believed your Magician's Oath bound you to destroy evil wherever you found it."

It does, Lythande thought. *Does it require me to kill all of you?* Aloud she said only, "And so you believed you could get me to kill the beast for you without payment? By what right do you expect me to destroy an innocent beast blamelessly going about on its own affairs and harming no one? It is only doing what all creatures do, looking for its food."

"But it will burn the woods up, breathing fire!"

"They are not my woods; if it wants to burn them, whoever owns the woods may go and kill it, or pay someone to do so. I am a magician, not an exterminator. The beast does not menace anything of mine." *But what am I to do with you?*

As Lythande considered the question, she heard a crackling noise behind the curtain, which the barkeeper had drawn again after she came through the window. Sniffing unobtrusively, she smelled smoke. Behind her, she realized, a great fire was breaking out. *It must have spread from the dragon in the woods,* she thought. *Those stairs were wood, after all. So I don't have to do anything about these people; the gods are doing it already.*

She bent quickly and picked up her pack and the case with her harp, extinguishing the blue glow as she did so, and slung them over her shoulder. She went into the street. She would rather walk all night than stay anywhere near these people, even if the inn were not about to catch on fire.

She turned her back on the inn and walked quickly away. Suddenly the inn buckled and, with a great explosion, erupted skyward. *They should not have grudged me a lawful fee,* she thought, *but at least I got a good sword out of it.* She stowed the sword carefully in her pack, then continued to walk. Maybe she could reach the next town before the moon set or it began snowing again.

Goldie, Lox, and the Three Excalibearers

Esther M. Friesner

t was a slow day at Berman's Kosher Deli (Samuel Berman, prop.), a day for taking inventory of pickles and kraut cuke by cuke and strand by strand. Outside, the cold war raged, Krushchev pounded his shoe and promised all America a paid-up ideological burial, but inside all was peace and herring. A warm breath of pastrami-scented air wafted over the establishment every time Mr. Berman opened the steam table, and the only thing that got pounded was the pickup bell, summoning the attention of the lone waitress—Mr. B's niece—whenever an order was ready to go.

There was only one customer in the dining room that day—that nice old man from Nostrand Avenue, the one with the long white beard and the funny hat, the one who always ordered a lox-and-onion omelet, then pointed at it and declared, "*That's* what's wrong with the government! Feh!" before devouring it. But then, slow days are when most things have time to happen.

Goldie Berman watched her uncle count the row of hanging salamis for the third time. She sighed and looked out the front window, longing for freedom. Even if she didn't have to stay and help in the store, where would she go? Uncle Sammy made what he called "a decent living," but it didn't yield a decent allowance for his pretty niece. He didn't begrudge her the money, he just didn't have it. Every spare penny went into Goldie's college fund.

Maybe I should tell him I don't wanna go to college, Goldie thought. And in the same thought banished the very idea. Aunt Marsha would bust a blood vessel. She was the maiden sister of Goldie's late mama—the one all the other smugly married females in the family whispered about at Cousins' Club meetings, the one they spoke to and smiled at too sweetly, so that it would take a blind and deaf woman not to understand how deeply, how deliciously they pitied her singleness.

She was also college educated, and she loudly maintained the importance of a girl getting her college degree. She did this with a zeal born of defensiveness and the desire for self-vindication. She also threatened to bust a blood vessel with astonishing regularity, particularly when her intentions were thwarted. No one knew whether this was something she'd picked up at college or not.

Goldie didn't want to think about Aunt Marsha's insistence that she devote herself to her studies, or Uncle Sammy's cheerful refusal to think of her as any older than nine, or the other relatives' tiresome habit of referring to her as "Poor-Goldie-Selma-and-Max's-girl-they-should-rest-in-peace." Somewhere out there—beyond the plate-glass window with its golden-edged lettering, beyond the bustle of Flatbush Avenue, beyond a neighborhood that voted for Adlai Stevenson with a single-minded idealism unseen since the days of the ILGWU formation or the Children's Crusade—somewhere there was something more waiting for Goldie Berman.

And if she couldn't find out what it was, there was always

Long Island. She turned and leaned back against the sparkling display case and let her mind wander through realms unknown.

Actually, realms known: A young man named Nathan Krantz, to be exact, sophomore at Brooklyn College and premed into the bargain. (A parlay like that could spell a ticket to Great Neck, eventually, and a tract house where the furniture would glitter more brightly than the kitchen floor, mainly because you couldn't put a plastic slipcover over a kitchen floor.) Nathan Krantz was, as they say, smitten. He was always hanging around Goldie or the deli or both. Not a bad catch for a mere junior at Midwood High, if Goldie did say so herself. Which she did. Goldie was not one to hide her light under a bushel, especially not in Uncle Sammy's establishment, where all the bushels were loaded with garlic dills.

So it was only natural that she became so abstracted by reveries of a future that did not smell like stuffed derma that she did not notice the tall, dark lady who entered, took a seat in the dining room and waited in vain for service.

Morgan le Fay was not the sort of person to be kept waiting long.

"Did you not hear me, wench?" The dark woman's eyes flashed fire. "I told you, fetch me food and drink at once, lest your life pay the forfeit."

"Yeah, yeah, yeah." Goldie woke reluctantly from dreams of becoming Mrs. Doctor Krantz. (A boy doesn't take a girl to see every Elvis movie ever made when he hates The King but she doesn't unless his intentions are honorable, right?) "Keep-ya shirt on, lady. I only got two hands." With a toss of her blond head, she slipped behind the counter and pretended to take a deep interest in reading the entrails of a whitefish.

A shadow fell over the girl and the tiny gold-and-white corpse. "None defies black Morgan, save at peril of their lives," the silk-gowned apparition hissed. She raised her arms, clad in shimmering waves of midnight blue spiderwebbed with silver brocade. Stark white hands curved like a raptor's talons above Goldie's head as the enraged enchantress's blood-red lips began to writhe over a litany of curses in an alien tongue.

"Goldie, go wait on the lady," Uncle Sammy said mildly.

"Awright, awright awready!" Goldie stalked out from behind the counter and back to the table that Morgan had abandoned. "Whuddummeye, a slave or something?" She thrust one neatly manicured hand into the pocket of her bright yellow apron and pulled out an order pad. "So whadaya want?" she asked, sighing as if the little pad and the well-gnawed pencil stub were the weight of the world.

The lady drifted slowly back to her table and settled down. "I do not frighten you, wench?" she asked, head cocked to one side as if that view of Goldie might reveal some hidden mystery.

"We got some very nice cawnbeef today, you should try it." Goldie ignored the question as artlessly as she had earlier ignored the questioner. "Or you want maybe a nice piece of brisket? It's Uncle Sam—it's one of our specialties." (Goldie believed that referring to her employer by his familiar name was unprofessional and also likely to cheat her out of tips.) "Also the soup doojoor today is lima bean and barley. So whadaya want?"

"You," the lady cried, and grasped the younger woman's wrists. There was a flare of pale green light, an eruption of snowy smoke, and the women vanished from the deli.

Although, of course, from Goldie's point of view, it was the deli that vanished. She didn't like that at all. Ever since that fateful day three years ago when Uncle Sammy had appeared on her doorstep out of nowhere to inform her that her parents had died in a car crash (a freak sleet storm in Teaneck, he claimed), he had as good as adopted her. The deli was her second home.

In Goldie Berman's veins ran the blood of generations of nice Jewish girls who had just gotten their houses in order when one or another of the menfolk would arrive to announce that the Cossacks (or the Crusaders, or the Teutonic Knights, or any of a wide selection of overfed, underbrained bullyboys) were en route. In other words, drop the *kashe varnishkes* and grab your valise: Move it or lose it. It was therefore understandable that in view of all of those unscheduled but vital hasty departures in her race-memory, Goldie hated any less-than-necessary bailouts from her beloved hearth.

Even if the hearth did smell like pastrami.

"Awright, what is this?" she demanded, looking around at a landscape bleaker and more desolate than a month-old noodle *kugel*. The women stood in the midst of a blasted plain under a sky heavy with a pall of stormclouds. Winks and wormlets of levin-light crawled in the belly of the heavens. Thunder rumbled like the passage of the deadcart laden with corpses over a pavement cobbled from skulls.

Goldie glanced up. "Gee, looks like rain."

"Let the storm break!" Morgan cried, flinging her head back to laugh at the lowering sky. "Let the very floodgates of heaven open and send their torrents roaring over me! I fear them not! I dare them all! I defy them!"

Goldie pursed her lips. "Yeah, I guess you're right. It really don't look much like rain." She regarded her blank order pad, sucked on the end of her pencil, and repeated, "So whadaya want?"

No bolt of raw celestial power could have left the dark-robed woman more thoroughly thunderstruck. "Wench, do you mean to say that you still do not tremble? I have snatched you from the bosom of your family, whisked you by all the power of my arcane spells into the very realm of death, the vastness of Annwn, and still you stand there, unperturbed?"

Goldie raised her bright green eyes. "Mnyeh," she said with a shrug. "What can I say? In the deli business, you meet all kinds. That's what Uncle Sa—Mr. Berman always says, anyhow.

Up until now, I woonta believed him. But you know what, lady? Customer or no, I gotta say this: You're a mental case."

A hot wind blew from nowhere into nothing, billowing the huge sleeves of the older woman's robes. "You dare to call Morgan a *mental case*?" she hissed.

"I dunno. Who's this Morgan?"

"*I* am Morgan!" The words rolled out more majestically than any peal of thunder.

Goldie was from Brooklyn, even if her parents had tried to raise her in New Jersey. Majestic cut no ice in Flatbush.

"Yeah? How come you got a guy's name, huh?" Goldie asked.

"Morgan-is-not-a-guy's-name," the lady replied between clenched teeth.

"Coulda fooled me." Goldie looked off to where a stand of black hemlocks broke the monotony of the barren, rocky vista. "I went to joonya high with a guy named Morgan Hershkovitz, and if anyone woulda told him Morgan *wasn't* a guy's name, he'd'a made'm wisht they was dead, mainly by killing 'em."

"Impertinent creature, I am Morgan le Fay, sorceress and queen!"

"Oh, well, *Fay*—! Fay I can understand. I got a Cousin Fay down in Miami. Pleaseta meetcha, Fay. I'm Gwendoline Berman, but everyone calls me Goldie." She offered the Queen of Air and Darkness her hand.

Morgan threw back her head and shrieked. Rage had about as little effect as majesty on Goldie.

"Hunh! Whadaya think, I got cooties?" She made a big deal of wiping the scorned hand of friendship on her apron before retreating to her order-taking pose. "So you want some soup doojoor to go with that conniption fit or what?"

"Fool, do you still refuse to know me?" Balefire leaped from the lady's upturned palms, spouting into the form of a fiery dragon whose tail lashed out across the rumbling sky and whose jaws gaped wide to swallow one small, blond figure in a cheap rayon dress from Korvette's and a cheaper waitress's apron. "I am mistress of the unholy powers. To serve my evil ends, I coupled with my own half brother, Arthur, once and future king of all Britain! From that sin-steeped begetting I brought forth Modred, imp and traitor, who by his lust toppled the glimmering dream of Camelot and by his greed for power dealt his sire a mortal wound. And when the news was brought to me, do you know what I did?"

Goldie shrugged again. "Search me."

"I *laughed*! Aye, in the very teeth of the destruction my womb had brought forth, I laughed."

"You know who makes me laugh?" Goldie confided. "Danny Kaye."

Morgan le Fay ground her hands together slowly, as if there were a certain white neck between them. The dragon gave her a perplexed look before dissolving in a shower of sparks. "Your laughter is of no interest to me, girl. Your name is of no interest. I came seeking you as I might have come seeking many another—not for who you are but for what you might be."

"Oh, *reeeeeeally*?" Had the Pentagon but known, Goldie Berman's command of sarcasm was a greater secret weapon than ever the Bomb would be. "And what, pray, might I be then?"

Morgan's black eyes fixed themselves upon Goldie hungrily. "You are the one foretold, the maiden, the vessel, the heir to all the powers of the lost lady, Vivian, Nimue, the guardian of the holy blade, the keeper of the sword's great mystery. Aye, by the spear and the cauldron, you are *she*!"

Goldie listened. A snort escaped Goldie's delicate nostrils. It was followed by a second snort, and a third. Then the floodgates (of giggles, not of heaven) opened wide and sent torrents of helpless laughter washing over Morgan le Fay.

"Are you *quite* through?" the dark queen demanded, icicles dropping from her lips.

Goldie could only bob her head and struggle to hold back more laughter. "Oh, lady, are you ever a card!" she cried. She laughed so hard that she had to hubble over to a boulder, holding her midriff the while, and sit down until the fit left her.

Morgan gestured and a second boulder floated over to set itself down at a comfortable distance from the first. The Queen of Air and Darkness settled herself on her rocky throne, crossed her legs, reached into her sorceress's gown and pulled out a pack of Pall Malls. She lit one with the tip of her tongue and took a long drag. The smoke leaving her lungs traced strange runes on the air.

"Fine," she said levelly to empty space. "Good. Have it your way, Merlin. I tried. Pity knows, I tried."

There came a shudder and a shake of the landscape, and Berman's Kosher Deli bloomed where once the wasteland of Annwn had sprawled. Goldie found herself sitting in one of the dining-room chairs at a table with the dark lady and the funny old man from Nostrand Avenue.

"I'm glad to hear you finally agree with me, Morgan," he said affably. "All that empty showmanship, for what? The direct approach is always the best."

"I *used* the direct approach." Morgan sulked.

"Direct for a lass of our lost Britain, perhaps. For this charming girl—" He smiled at Goldie and shrugged. "Go figure!"

"I begya pardon," Goldie remarked, unsure of what all this was about. She was fairly certain it involved her in one way or another, but she had certain grave doubts on a number of vital points, such as the true identity of her erstwhile lox-and-onions customer and whether or not all this flitting in and out of the deli was going to ruin her hair. "I don't believe I've had the pleasure." Her rising inflection betrayed her doubts as to whether it *would* be a pleasure at all.

"How do you do, my dear?" the old man said, offering her his hand across the remnants of his omelet. He had an accent just like Cary Grant's. "We are so glad you've decided to accept the quest."

"Hanh?" said Goldie.

Merlin gave Morgan a sideways glance. "You didn't get around to telling her?"

"You try telling her anything," Morgan spat. "I have a headache."

"Oh, come now, such a fuss! It's quite simple, really." The old man poured himself another glass full of soda from the big bottle of Dr. Brown's Cel-Ray on the table.

Goldie leaned forward, a nervous feeling in the pit of her stomach. Every time her chemistry teacher, Mr. Venable, said *It's quite simple, really,* about anything, she wound up getting a D on the next quiz.

"You see, dear child," the gray-haired gentleman continued, "it's the Law of Mythopoeic Conservation at work. Every few centuries or so, give or take a decade, a certain crisis-point is reached among the sustaining legends of the world. Some centuries are more crisis-prone than others, I'll admit. There was that nasty fellow a while back—the German creature—who tried to initiate the Siegfried agenda much too far before its proper time. You saw where that got him."

"It didn't get him where he shoulda been got soon enough," Goldie snarled. She wasn't following more than one word out of a dozen, but no one needed to explain to her about "the German creature." If it wouldn't have been for the health codes, she might have spat on the floor at any reference to the abominated monster.

The old man beamed at this sudden show of comprehension. "Ahhh, then you *are* aware of the danger such untimely twiddlings with legend can be! In some few cases, only the twiddler is destroyed, but in most, alas, he manages to take out quite a goodly chunk of innocent people's lives too." He sipped his soda. "That is why we make heroes."

"So do we," Goldie said. "Unc—Mr. Berman makes a nice hero with turkey and lettuce and—"

"What did I tell you?" Morgan le Fay puffed another stream of smoke at the ceiling, enjoying Merlin's abrupt discomfiture.

The wizard screwed up both his determination and his mouth. "Madam," he informed the sorceress, "I did not single-handedly engineer the careers of so many worldwide heroic archetypes by happenstance. Nor shall I allow one mortal girl's obtuseness to stand in the way of all that you and I both hold sacred, never mind if it be from different sides of the fence and for different reasons."

"Go ahead." Morgan gestured idly with her cigarette. "You've convinced me that you're the hottest thing since sliced brimstone. Now convince her."

"Convince me what?" Goldie asked suspiciously. In her short life, most convincings had been aimed at making her buy something she didn't need or take off articles of clothing she did not wish to shed at the moment and in that particular company.

Merlin folded his hands on the tabletop. He gazed at Goldie with a look that reeked of sincerity and harmless-little-old-man deceit. "My dear, I have been remiss. Perhaps it were better if I began at the beginning."

"Okay," Goldie drawled, still regarding him askance. She cast one all-encompassing glance about the dining room to see if any fresh clientele had entered, but these two odd ducks were it as far as the deli's current custom went. She had no convenient excuse to get herself gone.

"For starters, what do you know of the tale of King Arthur and his knights?"

Goldie's shrug was getting a thorough workout, so often and so eloquently had she used it this day. "Some," she said. "I think maybe we musta read some about him in English class. Only English comes right after lunch and I always get sleepy then. He was this king of England, right? And he pulled this sword outa this stone and he got married and there was all these knights in shining armor riding around on white horses, killing dragons and rescuing damsels in distress and stuff like that. And then I think it all stopped when they started having history instead."

Merlin's fingertips began to drum. Morgan snickered. "Basic," he said. "Crude and basic, but in essence correct, my dear. For which rudimentary scholarship on your part I am, I assure you, deeply grateful."

Morgan nudged him sharply. "You lost her again," she said, indicating the placid glaze that had drifted over Goldie's eyes when the wizard spoke.

Merlin cleared his throat loudly and tapped Goldie's hand. The girl jumped in her seat and glowered at him. "Hey! All you get to buy around here's a sandwich, okay?"

"No offense meant, child," the graybeard said. His teeth were commencing to grind together, much as Morgan's had when she first confronted Goldie. "What I am *trying* to tell you is that we need your help."

"Yeah? Whaffor?"

"For this." He gestured, and a mighty sword revealed itself between the Cel-Ray and the little aluminum dish of pickles that Mr. Berman always served his customers, *gratis.*

Goldie gasped. Who wouldn't? It was a sword straight out of legend and into delicatessen. Two hands were needed to clasp the hilt of that blade and raise it on high. So was a good, strong back.

"Wow," said Goldie. "Some pigsticker, you should pardon my French."

Morgan groaned. She ground out her first cigarette on the back of her hand and lit up another.

"So that's what you want I should help you with?" Goldie went on. "Okay, how? You wanna maybe know a good place to get it sharpened up? Unc—Mr. Berman always has Morris the scissors-grinder man take care of the carving knives every Tuesday. Maybe you know Morris? He's got a funny-looking little car, kind of an old jalopy, with this grinding wheel in the back. He does nice work. You could do worse."

"Excalibur's edge was honed and whetted on the beaks of immortal eagles whose wingspan darkened the sun when the world was in its infancy," Morgan intoned. "Excalibur's blade was forged in the fires of Annwn's blackest heart, cooled in the mystic waters of the holy cauldron, whose power it is to raise the dead. When Excalibur's edge grows dull, then shall the sun itself grow dim, the moon run red with blood, and the all-devouring sea lay waste the trembling plowland. Excalibur is the sword of heroes, the steel of song, the blade of prophecy, and you would have us place it in the care and keeping of *Morris*?"

"Oh." Goldie nodded. "Gee, too bad. I bet Uncle Sammy—I mean Mr. Berm—Oh, who *cares* who knows he's my uncle! I bet he coulda gotcha a nice discount."

There was no gauging the volume of Morgan's shriek. It was not like the Queen of Air and Darkness to lose her composure so readily or so frequently. Merlin knew this from long familiarity with the lady. Therefore was Goldie made all the more wonderful in his eyes, and all the more worthy of the great responsibility he was about to bestow upon her.

"My child," he said, "we thank you for your kindness. If you care enough about Excalibur to express concern that its blade be kept keenest, we have not mistaken the choice. You are the one."

"I am the one what?" Goldie wanted to know (quite reasonably).

"You are the one who shall guard the blade against the coming of the king."

"Huh?" said Goldie.

"That did it." Morgan slammed her fist on the table. "That's enough. I concede. I'm convinced. No one could be that thick about all this by accident. The girl has obviously been tampered with."

"I have not!" Goldie's indignation burned hot and high. "I never let Nathan get to second base, even! *Tampered* with! I like *that*, I gotta tellya!"

"Morgan, don't be ridiculous," Merlin replied, his words dry as stale pumpernickel. "The girl is untouched by our great enemy, as well as by any other man."

"Nathan respects a lady." Goldie gave a *so-there* sniff and pursed her lips at Morgan, who merely snarled.

"Believe that if you will," the dark queen replied. "And I will believe the evidence of my eyes and ears. Elezamwel the Enchanter is a subtle foe. For years untold and centuries past counting he has desired to possess the powers of this fey-forged blade." Here she gestured dramatically at the sword still lying beside the pickles. "Yet great though the evil strength of his vile sorceries be, the sword itself stands girt with virtue against him so long as it remains either in the wardship of one of its three natural guardians—Merlin, myself, or the Lady—else bestowed upon its rightful lord and master, the once and future king!"

By this time, Morgan was on her feet. She had whipped herself up into a nice family-sized frenzy. If truth be told, there are some people who are never happy unless they are grandstanding, although they will deny this to the death. Still they persist in viewing the world as one epic opera after another, ignoring the fact that between the acts there are more than a few sitcoms and hemorrhoid-remedy commercials.

Therefore, when Morgan finished saying her say—or ranting her rant—and struck a pose more suitable to a stained-glass window than to the dining-room section of Berman's Kosher Deli, Goldie got the giggles once more. In hindsight, it was not the wisest or the kindest thing she might have done.

"What...is...so...funny...*now?*" Morgan demanded, each word escaping her lips through thorns and fire.

Goldie pressed her knuckles to her mouth and tried to smother her unfortunate mirth. She made a hash of it. "I'm— I'm sorry, lady, but you—you look just like my aunt, Yetta, when she found out Cousin Julie went and married an Irish girl!"

"And what is wrong with being Irish?" Morgan demanded. "Merlin and I are of the elder blood, the blood that flows hot and bright in the veins of the *Sidhe,* who are themselves the descendants of the Tuatha de Danann, the old gods and heroes of Ireland."

"Any of them tries to marry a Berman and you'll find out what's wrong with it," Goldie replied.

Morgan smoldered with a rage that cast a ruddy glow on her cheeks from within. Merlin scrambled out of his seat and stepped between the ladies before the Queen of Air and Darkness could spontaneously combust.

"Please, child, you will learn far more, far quicker if you permit us to speak uninterrupted." He stooped to pat Goldie's hand like an affectionate grandfather.

Goldie yanked it away. "Explain whatcha want, only don't touch the merchandise," she instructed him.

"Very well." Merlin passed his hand over the pickle dish. At once the cukes began to shimmer with an unearthly radiance before melting into a rippling sea of verdant light. As the wizard spoke, his words were transformed to vision on the briny surface. "The sword Excalibur was given to King Arthur by the Lady of the Lake. Some name her Vivian, some Nimue, and some besmirch her honored name with accusations of treachery against myself." Here the vision showed a lovely woman, clad all in white samite, holding open the trunk of an oak tree while a doddering, besotted Merlin stumbled inside. "This is, of course, sheer fabrication." The wizard's keen eyes met Goldie's.

"And a very nice piece of fabrication, too," Goldie agreed, eyeing the Lady's gown. "Only she shoulda wore a slip with it. You can see her whole business, if you don't mind my saying so."

"Uh, yes. Quite." Merlin lost himself for an instant, but recovered quickly. "After the battle of Camlann, where Arthur slew Modred and was in turn most desperately wounded by his bastard son—"

"That's my boy," Morgan purred.

"—he commanded his faithful knight, Sir Bedivere, to convey him to the shores of the selfsame lake whence he had received Excalibur at the Lady's hand. Sir Bedivere took the blade and heard his lord order him to cast it back into the waters. Twice did Sir Bedivere attempt the feat, and twice did he find himself unable to do it. The sword was too fair, too fine— thought he—to merit a watery grave."

Goldie gazed into the pickle dish. She saw Sir Bedivere take Arthur's sword and go to the lake shore, only to stand there helpless for a time before hiding the sword in the reeds, returning to kneel at his lord's side and whispering something in the king's ear.

"What's he saying?" Goldie asked.

"He is telling Arthur that he has done what he was commanded to do. Now see where Arthur asks him what he saw when he threw the sword back into the lake!"

"What's to see?" Goldie found herself unable to take her eyes from the tableau before them. "It goes splash."

"So Sir Bedivere said." Merlin smiled. "And by that very saying, King Arthur knew that his friend was lying. Still Bedivere persisted in his lie a second time, for Excalibur was in truth a sword of wonders. A second time the good knight could not bring himself to throw the blade into the waters, a second time he lied to his king, and again Arthur knew it by Bedivere's reply to the question: 'And what happened when you threw the sword into the lake?' "

"Gee, some dumb bunny, that Bedivere," Goldie opined. "If it'd been me, I'd'a made up another story."

"Vivian is rolling in her grave," Morgan muttered, and ate her still-burning cigarette.

"Oh, hush," Merlin told the sorceress-queen. "Vivian doesn't even *have* a grave. If there was anything left of her by the time the fish had their fill, it's been covered over with a lot of silt by now."

Goldie tugged at Merlin's sleeve. "So then what?" she wanted to know. "Bedivere fibs twice and then what happens? Arthur decides he better go do it himself or what?"

Merlin favored the girl with a well-satisfied look of approval. "Ah, there is hope for you yet, child, if you take an interest in the tale. Whether or not the evil Elezamwel has succeeded in working his wiles upon you, the mettle of your spirit remains at heart untouched. That is good. Very well, hark to the tale's end: The third time, Sir Bedivere determined to carry out his lord's last request, and so he did. He stood on the lake shore and flung the blade away from him with all his might. The sword Excalibur flew from his grasp, out across the waters and—"

"Splash," Goldie suggested.

"No," Merlin corrected her. "Just when it looked as if *splash* was inevitable, an arm clad all in white samite thrust itself from the lake, seized the sword by its hilt, brandished it thrice above the waters, and drew it back down into the depths of the lake forever." He bowed his head, the tale told.

Goldie rested her chin on one fist. "They don't make forever like they used to," she said, poking the sword's hilt with her pencil stub. "At least it didn't rust up too bad, under the lake and all. That is one stupid place to keep a sword, you know? This Lady of the Lake musta been nine kindsa retard, if you ask me."

"What we ask you," Merlin said, "is to show us just how few kinds of retard you are."

"Huh?"

The wizard gestured, and all at once Goldie found herself divested of pencil, pad, apron and rayon dress. Instead she was clad neck to ankles in a gown of white samite. This time, Merlin had also provided a slip.

It was not enough for Goldie.

"What's the big idea?" she shrilled, leaping up from the table. "Uncle Sammy! Uncle Sammy, call the cops! This old geezer swiped my clothes!"

Samuel Berman looked up at long last from his inventory. His countenance grew stern, his broad, blue-shadowed face contorted into a dull scowl. He wiped his hands on his apron and came out from behind the counter. "What are you buncha *meshugennehs* doing to my Goldie?" he rumbled.

Goldie ran and clung to him, using his wide body like a shield. "They're nuts, Uncle Sammy!" she cried. "Be careful, the old guy's got a sword."

"We mean no harm." Merlin rose from his place, hands extended palm upward in the conventional gesture of peace. "We have merely come here to give the child her inheritance."

"What inheritance?" Mr. Berman demanded. "When her parents—they should rest in peace—were taken from her three years ago, she got all the inheritance that was coming to her. Mostly, nothing."

"You fat fool, we do not speak of such trifles as mortal goods and chattels." Morgan spoke with supreme disdain, looking down her nose at the deli man. "She is the chosen one, the heir to all the estate of the lost Lady Vivian. Hers is now the keeping of the sword Excalibur, now and unto the hour of her death."

"Hanh?" said Mr. Berman.

"Clearly this response must be an inherited characteristic," Merlin remarked aside to his colleague.

And for once, Morgan giggled.

Something strange came over Goldie then. Perhaps it was the way in which Merlin spoke to Morgan as if there was no one else present—or at least no one else worth noticing. Perhaps it was Morgan's unfailing attitude of snobbery and condescension. There was no selfless humor in her attack of the titters, merely evidence that she found Goldie and all things touching her to be laughable, trifling, like the antics of a half-trained pup.

Or perhaps it was just the fact that white samite looks very pretty, even sopping wet, but it makes some people itch like the dickens, slip or no slip. Whichever it was, it got under Goldie's skin something fierce, and once under, it kindled up a royal rage.

"The *nerve* of you!" Goldie came out from behind her uncle's body, fists ready for a fight, eyes ablaze with battle-fury. "You come inta a person's place of business and just 'cause you buy a lousy lunch plate and maybe a glassa Cel-Ray, you think you own the joint and we're some kinda dummies? Well, lemme tell you, you don't and we're not!"

She strode over to Morgan le Fay, wagging an admonishing finger boldly in the face of the Queen of Air and Darkness. "You think I don't know what you birds are after? Ha! Maybe I don't do so well in Mr. Venable's class, but that doesn't mean I'm slow on the uptake. You've got this sword, right? And it's gotta be kept safe for whoever's the hero doojoor. If he's got it, everything's swell. If he don't got it, you've gotta hold on to it for him until he shows up. Am I right or am I right?"

"You are right and in danger of losing that finger," Morgan growled.

Before the dark lady could react, Goldie's wagging finger leaped for her throat, accompanied by its four brethren. Seizing Morgan by the neck of her robe, Goldie yanked her forward and repeated, "Am I right?"

"You're . . . right," Morgan breathed, struck all of a heap by the girl's unlooked-for audacity.

Satisfied, Goldie let Morgan drop. "That's not all I'm right about, I bet. I bet you had this friend who hung out under this lake holding on to this sword. You two were just the lookouts, but she got to handle the goods. Only she died and now you need someone to step in for her. I'm it. How'm I doing?"

Merlin clasped his hands, an expression of purest joy on his aged face. "By all the blessed powers, she understands! Ah, I *knew* she would. I knew she was the one. For a time I feared, for I sensed an emanation of evil hovering nigh her, but in the end I knew that she would—"

"I quit," said Goldie. She folded her arms, sat down at the table with the sword, and drank what was left of the Cel-Ray straight from the bottle.

"You what?" Merlin and Morgan asked in harmony.

Goldie set down the bottle with a heavy clunk. "I quit. Acshally I can't quit, 'cause I didn't take the job. And I won't. Getcherselfs another girl."

"You can't quit!" Merlin gasped.

"Watch me," Goldie replied calmly. "Just you gimme back my old dress and we'll call it square, okay?" She scratched her arms vigorously through the white samite.

"But—but you are *she*!" This time it was Morgan's turn. "For years we have searched for you. There can be no other. Merlin and I may guard the blade, but not forever. Nor is it ever ours to bestow. The time of the hero is at hand! The king returns! In this darkest of dark hours, when mortals have unleashed the black winds of fire that can reduce all earth to one vast Annwn, his spirit *must* come among you again! If he comes not, there will be nothing to stand between you and your own doom."

"And if he comes, but does not receive the blade from your hands, he will be as helpless as you to stave off the horrors that shall be unleashed," Merlin added solemnly.

Goldie leaned back in her chair. A little of the fire went out of her eyes. She was, as she claimed, not exactly slow on the up-take. She had grown up in the shadow of the Bomb and she made the connection. Her eyes drifted toward the sword. "Don't look much like a fallout shelter to me," she commented.

"You'd be surprised," Merlin said softly.

She regarded him with a wonderful look of comprehension. Her smile was neither bold nor sassy, but serene. "Yeah," she said. "I bet I would." She reached for the hilt of the sword.

"Stop!" Mr. Berman seized her wrist in a grip that had immobilized whole roast turkeys awaiting the knife. "You know what you're getting yourself into, Goldie?"

"I think so, Uncle Sammy. I take the sword and I hold on to it until some guy comes along who—" She hesitated. "I don't gotta wait on the bottom of a lake, do I?" she asked Merlin.

"Not unless you insist, my dear," the wizard replied, eyes twinkling.

"Oh. Okay. That's a load offa my mind." She rose to her feet and grasped the sword, lifting it with one hand as if it weighed no more than a quarter-pound order of potato salad.

"It is accomplished." Morgan closed her eyes, making a strange symbol with her fingers. "Guard it tenderly. Now that the sword Excalibur is once more in the keeping of its Lady, it shall not pass to another without her blessing and consent." She opened her eyes and pressed Goldie's free hand to her brow.

"Choose well the one to whom you entrust this blade, for to him you grant a great, mighty and awesome power." And she vanished.

"Choose well," Merlin echoed. "Him to whom you give the blade by word or by deed shall be the making or the destruction of mankind. Promise me that you will be worthy of this trust."

"Okey-dokey," said Goldie. She crooked her little finger and kissed it. "Pinky swear."

"In your fair hands and upon your soul be it, then." His hands danced through the air and he was transformed, gowned in the full regalia of a master wizard. He gestured again and clouds of blue smoke rose up to engulf him.

"Oops."

The smoke disappeared, but not the wizard. Merlin fumbled with a small brown leather purse at his belt. "Almost forgot," he explained sheepishly, putting down several dollar bills beside his plate and adding an extra for the tip. "Superb service, my dear," he said, and this time vanished without benefit of the smoke effect.

"Hoo boy," said Mr. Berman, wiping his brow. "This one I don't believe. Oh, well, they're gone. I got work to do." He waddled back toward the counter, muttering to himself.

Goldie stood where she was, still clad all in white samite, still holding the sword. She stared at the blade, but marvel of marvels, it was not the stare of one who has been smacked in the forehead with a speeding volleyball. No, this stare contained little or no bewilderment and much quiet wonder. The sword was not a stranger; it was instead like some long-lost friend Goldie never knew she'd had until now.

And then Uncle Sammy called, "Goldie! You think you're gonna wait on the customers like that? Go in the back, put on my old raincoat, go home and get into something decent, it's a shame if the neighbors was to see you."

"Yes, Uncle Sammy," Goldie responded automatically. She was still looking at the sword. She headed for the back room, bearing the bright steel before her like a torch to light the way. Excalibur's blade shimmered with a radiance that had nothing to do with the overhead fluorescent lighting. Gazing upon such glory, Goldie felt as if she could follow that sweet brilliance any-where, even to the bottom of a lake. Although she found Mr. Berman's raincoat, she could not bring herself to set the sword down even for the instant required to slip her arms through the sleeves. She ended by going through a modified juggling act, shifting the sword hand-to-hand, and managed to get the coat on awkwardly at best. She was just on her way out the front door, sword still in hand, when all of a sudden—

"Goldie!"

She stopped short and turned. She had never heard her uncle speak to her in such harsh tones before. "Where do you think you're going?"

"I'm just going home, like you said."

"Like that you go?"

"I put on the raincoat."

"Who's talking from raincoats? You go blind now or what? The *sword*, Goldie!" Mr. Berman slammed a midget salami down on the cutting board to emphasize his words. "You can't go out on the streets of Brooklyn with a piece of hardware like that. What are people gonna think, hah?"

"That it's a king-sized switchblade, maybe?" Goldie tried to charm her uncle. It had always worked before.

"Nobody likes a *weisenheimer*." To borrow freely from Queen Victoria, Uncle Sammy was not amused.

"So whadaya want I should do with it?" Goldie asked, searching her uncle's face and the cold cuts for an answer. "Stick it under my coat? Put it in a brown paper bag? What?"

Mr. Berman merely folded his arms and frowned at her.

Now Goldie truly was at a loss. "Uncle Sammy, I gotta

take it with me. You heard what they said. I gotta take care of it. I promised."

Mr. Berman remained immovable.

"What, we don't got a bag big enough back there?"

Mr. Berman unfolded his arms and drummed his fingers on the thick wooden cutting board before him. It was a sound like the rolling of many drums beating out the dead march.

"But Uuuuuuncllllllle . . ." Goldie whined well, but not well enough to persuade Mr. Berman. It looked like a standoff, albeit hardly one of the Mexican variety. (Aunt Marsha had once taken a trip down to Yucatán. She said it was very educational, even if she did get a bad case of Montezuma's Revenge and that cute tour guide Felipe never did write her like he promised.)

And then Mr. Berman's expression inexplicably softened. "Goldie, sweetheart, you're a good girl," he said smoothly. "You made a promise, you keep a promise. You owe it to those people, even if they did look like refugees from Bellevue. But to me you owe something, too, hah?"

Goldie's sunny head drooped a little. "Yes, Uncle Sammy."

"I don't like to hold it over your head, but who was it was the first to come to your house after your parents—they should rest in peace—had that accident? Who was it told you even before the cops could get there? Who took you right straight here and gave you a safe place to grow up?"

"You did, Uncle Sammy. You always were good to me."

Something bright winked at the corner of Goldie's eye. Without intending to, she turned her head ever so slightly toward the blade. Was it a trick, or were the twinkles of iridescence playing up and down the length of the holy sword acting like the hypnotist's crystal, opening a door into Goldie's mind and leading out sleepy memories that rubbed their eyes against the sudden influx of light?

Memories that took her back to the days before her parents had the awful accident. Memories of then and memories of the weeks, the months, the years following that horrible day. Memories that stirred and probed and finally shocked Goldie not because of what they did contain, but what they did *not*.

Mama getting ready for the Cousins Club meeting, making Goldie go over old photo albums so that she would remember the names and faces of all her closest kin. (Whose face was not there? Whose name was never mentioned among all the other uncles?)

Aunt Yetta crying and saying what a lovely funeral it had been. (What funeral? Why couldn't Goldie remember any funeral?)

Cousin Julie patting his mother on the shoulder and saying how nice it was of Uncle Sammy to talk to the policemen and the hospital people, sparing poor little Goldie. (What policemen? What hospital people?)

And Aunt Marsha, sitting across from Goldie while they all sat shiva. *Aunt Marsha with a copy of the* Daily News, *looking for the obituary notice and saying she couldn't find it, until Uncle Sammy looked her right in the eye, hard, and told her to look again. She found it that time.* (But Goldie remembered picking up the paper afterward and seeing nothing, not one line, and never a word about any accident or any freak hailstorm either. Nothing.)

Goldie rubbed her eyes with her free hand as if she were waking up from deep slumber or slowly emerging from underwater reveries. She tasted treachery on her tongue, and her ears burned as she heard Mr. Berman say, "Of course you're also a smart girl, Goldie. Smart enough so you know there's all kindsa ways to keep a promise. You can maybe give me the sword, I'll watch it for you until you go home, get changed, come back. Give it, I'll put it back here, no one will ever know, and—"

"Okay," Goldie said slowly. "Take it." She clasped both hands around the hilt and held the sword straight up before her. A gust of glory blew off the edge of the blade, sending her pale garb streaming behind her like a banner.

" 'Take'?" Mr. Berman echoed. "What's this 'take'? You can't give it?"

"No," Goldie replied evenly. "Not to you."

"What are you talking? You give, you don't give, I should take? There's a difference?"

"Yes, there is."

The discussion had reached this point when the bell over the front door jingled and Nathan Krantz came into the shop. "Hi, Goldie," he said cheerily enough. Then he got a look at her. She had been unable to button the raincoat, and her gown of white samite was playing peekaboo with all comers. "Wow," said Nathan. Goldie blushed.

"There!" Mr. Berman waved one chunky hand at the flustered premed student. "Now you satisfied? Now that you stand there like that in front of a nice boy like Nathan?" To the same Nathan he said in a stagy aside, "She won't give me the sword. You ever see such a thing?"

"No . . ." Nathan's eyes were drawn to the blade. "No, I never saw such a thing." The tone of wonder and reverence in his voice was not lost on Goldie, nor the telltale trembling in his knees. They looked ready to buckle at any moment. "Never," he repeated, and knelt with hands steepled in an attitude of prayer.

Mr. Berman blew a scornful breath through his nose most expressively. "You come in here for a sandwich or High Mass, *boychik*? Because if it's High Mass you want, we're all out of wafers. Maybe I could interest you in a nice bagel?"

He might have spared the witticisms. Goldie was as deaf to them as Nathan was blind to everything save the sword. The two young people remained still and silent for perhaps the time it takes to open about half a dozen bottles of Cel-Ray, and the sword burned all the brighter, its aura nourished by their awe.

"Yoo-hoo." Mr. Berman snapped his fingers in front of Nathan's nose. "Anybody home?" No one was, apparently. He snorted again. "That does it. I'm gonna call the men in the white coats."

"S—sorry, Mr. Berman." Nathan touched a quivering hand to his brow as he stumbled onto his feet. "I don't know what came over me. I—"

"I wanna go home and get changed," Goldie announced. "Samite, shmamite, this stuff is *drafty*. A person could catch her death."

"Finally!" Mr. Berman clapped his hands together with a great show of relief. "It takes seeing one *meshuggeneh* for the girl to realize she's acting crazy, too, but who's complaining? So, Goldie, *mamaleh,* you do like I said; you button the raincoat, you give me the sword, and you go home and—"

"No." This time there was more than blind stubbornness backing up the word. Goldie's face was smooth and carefree as only a face can look when the last mote of doubt has been banished from the mind behind it. "I'll give it, okay?" she told her uncle. "I'll give it awready."

"Ah!" He held out his hands, grinning.

"But not to you."

She turned toward Nathan and thrust the sword on high. "Receive at my hand the blade Excalibur, O hero of the age!" she decreed, and the deli rang with the sonorous notes of her voice, thrummed with the power emanating from steel that was more than steel and a Midwood junior who would never sleep through English class again.

Nathan Krantz fell to one knee, hand on his pocket protector. "Lady—" His voice choked with emotion. "Lady, I am not worthy." His Brooklyn accent was dust and ashes.

Goldie blinked. "Hanh?"

"So great a gift—"

"No, really, take it. It's okay. You're it."

"I am no hero."

"Sure you are, Natie. I mean, I always thought you were

pretty swell, but ever since those two really weird people showed up in the deli today, it's like I *know* stuff. You know? So if I say you're a hero and you should take the sword, it's on accounta you are. I mean, you must be, 'cause all of a sudden you're talking like Basil Rathbone. Now you wanna take it so I can go home and change awready?" She glanced at Mr. Berman. "Uncle Sammy, after I get changed, is it okay if Natie and I go catch a movie or—!"

"I will see you burn in the nethermost pit of Hell first!" bellowed Mr. Berman.

The row of salamis overhead swung like the bodies of hanged men. He plunged his hands into the deli case and lifted a whole side of smoked salmon to the heavens. Black lightning leaped from the fish's tail, crackled all the way up the body. The succulent pink flesh shuddered, transforming itself into a length of twisted thornwood, a wizard's staff entwined with the burnished emerald body of a slavering fireworm. With the selfsame staff, Samuel Berman struck the deli counter a mighty blow. The beechwood cutting board and all beneath it split asunder. As he stepped between the sundered halves, a blast of unholy magic melted away all trace and token of the delicatessen owner. In his place there stood a tall, swarthy man, more gorgeously gowned than Morgan le Fay, emanating more power than Merlin.

But it was a dark power, a power blacker than the fall of raven's wing hair and beard that had so miraculously sprouted from Samuel Berman's hairless head. New come as she was to her own burden of enchantment, Goldie immediately sensed the awful significance of this metamorphosis. She pointed the hand not clasping Excalibur, pointed it directly at the sinister apparition's heart, and in a voice that trembled with the force of righteous accusation announced, "You're not Uncle Sammy!"

The dark one laughed. "On the contrary, my dear," he

replied, his words slithering toward her like so many vipers. "I am and always have been your . . . Uncle Sammy."

"You have *not!*" Goldie shrilled. "I betcha I don't even *have* an Uncle Sammy! Mama never mentioned you once, and neither did Daddy."

"Ah, yes." The dark one stroked his beard with heavily gemmed fingers. "Your parents. Such meticulous people. When I attempted to foist myself off upon them as a long-lost relative, they denied all knowledge of me. What was more, they were stubbornly immune to all of my powers of suggestion. They dared to insist that I did not exist." His gloating chuckle welled up in large, oily bubbles. "I believe I showed them precisely who did exist and who . . . did not."

Goldie gasped. "*You* killed them!" Minor buzzes of raw energy hummed up and down the holy blade.

"Goldie, 'killed' is such a permanent word." Again that evil laugh. "I merely . . . *removed* them."

A cold, hard look came into Goldie's eye. Until this moment she had regarded the sword as a trust, a symbol, a precious talisman. Now it dawned on her that Excalibur was, first and always, a sword. She clasped both hands around the hilt. This was no gesture of bestowal. If Nathan Krantz had ever hoped to hold that blade anytime soon, he would have to whistle for it.

"Who the hell are you?" The question itself cut the air as deftly as ever the edge of Excalibur cut the pattern of its own legend.

"Can't you guess?" One black brow rose to taunt her. "I knew you, right enough. Right enough to step in and do what I could to keep you from your heritage. If I could deprive Merlin and Morgan of your services, then eventually the homeless blade would find its way to me. Unfortunately, my spells of destruction could not touch you, for the chosen of Excalibur are proof against the darker magics. However, there are other ways."

"Yeah, I just bet!" Goldie swung the sword back over her right shoulder. Mickey Mantle might have copied her stance to good effect. "That What'shername Fay was right, awright: You *did* tamper with me!"

"Was I wrong to maintain your innocence?" the sorcerer asked with a false show of confusion.

"Innocence? Ha! You made me *stupid,* that's what! Every time I got a bad grade, you said I shouldn't worry, I'd marry a nice boy someday! Every time I got a good one, you said it wouldn't matter much to my husband! No wonder I almost didn't catch on when they tried to tell me who I was gonna hafta be! You almost turned me into some kinda *retard,* you nasty, rotten, stinking, lousy—"

"I am Elezamwel the Enchanter," the dark one said too softly. "Nobody talks that way to me." He leaped for her, the snake-coiled staff like a spear aimed at her heart.

"Come to Mama!" Goldie shouted, and brought the blade back for a killing stroke.

"Goldie, don't!" Nathan Krantz wrapped his hands around hers on the hilt. "You're giving it to him!"

"I'm what?" Goldie managed to ask in the instant before Elezamel's spring could reach them.

Nathan yanked her aside, up against the deli counter. The sorcerer missed, landing on the linoleum and skidding toward the rest rooms in back. He wheeled around in a feral crouch, teeth bared, preparing another leap.

"I said you're *giving* it to him that way," Nathan panted, forcing Goldie to back away from the snarling sorcerer. "That's all you're allowed to do with Excalibur, *give* it. If you try to kill him with it, it won't do anything but go from your hands to his."

"Yeah?" Goldie's glance went from Nathan to the sorcerer. "You figure?"

"I got straight A's in English," Nathan said, with the humble mien worthy of a true hero. "Even if I am premed."

"Okay," Goldie said. "So here." Her grasp on the hilt slipped out from beneath his, slick as a whisper. "It's supposed to be yours anyhow. Now I *can't* give it to him, right? Right?"

Nathan didn't answer her. His eyes were fixed elsewhere. It was unchivalrous to ignore a lady, but it could be downright fatal to look away from an angry wizard.

Goldie followed Nathan's gaze to Elezamwel, whose own eyes were now blazing with a wrath unhealthy to behold. "Uh-oh." Prudence whispered in her ear that she might do best to clear the way between the two antagonists. Goldie heeded the suggestion, hopping nimbly over the riven counter. From sanctuary behind an array of whitefish, sable and another whole smoked salmon, sister to Elezamwel's transformed staff, she stuck her thumbs in her ears, wiggled her fingers, put out her tongue at the sorcerer and said, "Nyah!"

"Lady, the years have not been kind," Elezamwel gritted, rising to his feet. "You have cheated me of the sword only for an instant. That fool may be your chosen hero, but he does not know a thing about wielding any blade bigger than a kitchen knife. It has been too long. He cannot hold what he cannot defend. When Excalibur is out of your keeping, it may become any man's. Why else was Arthur so insistent that Bedivere return it to Vivian? Even in death, he was a jealous king. I will slay this fool and take the enchanted sword from his cold hands before your very eyes. Then at last it shall be mine!"

Goldie gave Nathan an inquiring glance. "They say anything about this in English class, Natie?"

Nathan looked worried. "I don't remember. I guess we'd better take his word for it." He was holding the sword like a croquet mallet. "Okay, mister, try something." He sounded game as he confronted the sorcerer, but he looked ridiculous.

Elezamwel threw back his head and let vast torrents of heartless laughter pour from his mouth. He gestured, and his enchanter's staff became a sword black as night's own heart. "Prepare to taste death, fool!" he cried, and charged.

"Taste *this,* wise guy!" Goldie hollered. Prudence threw up her allegorical hands in disgust and surrendered as Goldie vaulted the counter, swinging the salmon overhead. On she came like some icthyferous Amazon, and with a single mighty *whap* dealt the startled sorcerer a hearty wallop full in the face with the fish. The black sword dropped from his hands, striking the linoleum with a muted clang. As he staggered back, Goldie gave him another smack, and another. And through the rain of fishy blows she shouted, "Now, Natie! Stick him with Excalibur where it counts now!"

She was poised to let Elezamwel have his seventh clout when it dawned on her that she was in this fight alone. She let the fish (much the worse for wear) drop to her side as she turned to see what was holding Nathan back.

Nothing was. Nothing that Goldie could see, at any rate. Nathan just stood there, hands resting on the holy sword as if it were an umbrella, watching her. Goldie scowled. She still had Uncle Sam the sorcerer's raincoat on over her gown of white samite and she was sweating like a pig, you should excuse her French. She was *not* in the mood to see her chosen hero standing idly by while she did all the work.

"You wanna maybe get around to killing this guy when your coffee break's over or what?" she asked waspishly.

"I can't kill him now," Nathan replied.

"Oh, you *can't?* And why, pray do tell, can't you, if I may be so bold as to inquire perchance?" Yes, far deadlier than any Bomb, that pretty child's sarcastic tongue.

"He is unarmed." Nathan removed his glasses. His once-brown eyes began to glow as they changed to a clear, pure blue. "To slay an unarmed man goes against all chivalry." He ran his fingers through his short black hair, which streaked itself gold and tumbled in leonine locks to his shoulders. "Never did I strike down any man, save in fair combat." He took a step toward Goldie, and in mid-stride he grew taller, more muscular, too tall and muscular for his plain white shirt and gray broadcloth trousers to contain. They melted from him like ghosts, devoured by the kingly raiment that replaced them as naturally as one breath replaces another. His pocket protector was not even a memory.

"Arthur . . ." Elezamwel uttered the name as a curse.

"Arthur!" Merlin was there, exalting the name to a blessing.

"Arthur?" Goldie frowned. "Natie, if this is some kinda joke you wanna play on a poor, dumb high school girl, I don't see the humor, thank you very much."

"Oh, it's no joke," said Morgan, who had appeared just as abruptly as Merlin. She twiddled a finger, and Elezamwel's black sword jumped to her hand like a cocker spaniel puppy. "This is Arthur, all right. I'd know the morals anywhere. They're what got him killed the first time but—*Que voulez-vous?*—it goes with the package, morals." She whirled with a dancer's grace and casually sliced Elezamwel's head from his shoulders. "Never had much use for them myself." She breathed on the bloodstained sword and it became a side of lox once more. Morgan helped herself to a sliver. "Mmmm, tasty. Got any cream cheese?"

The sorcerer's head rolled toward the rest rooms, his body slumped forward. Goldie made a retching sound, but before she could add to the general mess on the deli floor, the various sections of Elezamwel's corpse vanished. In their place stood a middle-aged couple wearing beautiful tans and bewildered expressions.

Of all the unbelievable sights Goldie had confronted today, this was by far the most fabulous. "Mama?" she quavered. "Daddy?"

"Goldie!" the two revenants cried with joy and flung themselves into their daughter's arms.

"Behold, the wizard's captives are released from his thrall in durance vile," Merlin pronounced solemnly.

"What durance!" Goldie's father said. "What vile? He sent us to stay with Cousin Fay in Miami. It wasn't so bad, except we couldn't *leave* Cousin Fay in Miami."

"You want vile?" Goldie's mother put in. "Three years of Fay's *kneidelach, that's* vile. So rubbery they were, they belonged in a handball court, not in a chicken soup!"

She was still going on about Cousin Fay's wicked ways with matzoh balls when King Arthur knelt before the reunited family. "My lady," he said, taking Goldie's hands in his. "Through your wisdom and courage, I have come into my own again and shall use my recovered powers to protect us all."

"Okay." Goldie was amenable. "Just keep an eye on them Commies, awright?"

The king took oath that he would do so, then went on to say, "While I was trapped in the body of the one you knew as Nathan Krantz, I came to love you. I love you all the better now. Marry me, and together we shall bring back the golden age. Be mine, and rule forever at my side as my beloved bride and queen."

"Oh, Natie!" Goldie drew him to his feet and gazed into his eyes with devotion. "Na—I mean, Artie, you know I love you too. You're a nice guy and all, only—only—"

"Yes?" His arms were around her. "Yes?" Excalibur cast a glow of blessing over the lovers. "Yes?" All nature awaited her words.

"—are you Jewish?"

Silver, Stone, and Steel

JUDITH TARR

This was Merlin's dream,
as he wrote it on leaves of the oak with a
feather of the owl, in ink made of owl's blood
and wizard's blood and oak-gall:

— I —

saw three queens, who were three crones, who were three angels, but whether they were of the White God or of his Enemy, I do not know. They circled round a cauldron, that was a cup, that was a pool in which was set all that was, or had ever been. They circled and they sang, and their voices were like a falling of silver on silver.

I saw silver in hands that grasped and were reluctant to let go, silver cast in coins, and each coin wore a king's face or a queen's face or a god's. It was never a holy thing, that silver, but never unholy, either. It merely was.

"Tonight," said the man who wanted silver, breathless with daring and with shame. "In the garden. He goes to pray, his followers with him—he makes so much trouble, if you can stop—or slow him down—he grows so arrogant, he tells me—"

The others were shadows, standing about him, save for the hands that held the silver. "Yes," they said, polite to boredom. "Yes, yes. Tomorrow. The garden. You single him out, you kiss—"

"If I could not—" the seeker said. "If I could hide in a shadow, point—"

Interest edged the strongest voice, the voice that owned the hands, and the purse in the hands, and the silver singing as it poured from palm to palm. "You will mark him out. You will kiss the man who is your master, so that we may know him, and do with him as we must."

"But—" said the seeker.

"Go," said the voice, tipping silver into purse and dropping it at trembling feet. "Tomorrow. Mark well—you will be there. Or we remember."

The seeker—the traitor—knew what it was to be remembered by such as these. He bent, snatched the purse, bolted through shadows into darkness and shifting dream.

I saw how the light changed; how dusk paled to dawn and then to dusk again. I saw a garden, and men asleep who should have stood on watch, and one who prayed. I knew that prayer; I knew that terror, that sweat as thick and dark as blood. Foreseeing—prophecy—is power, and who knows better than I? But at its back is fear. To know the dark as well as the light. To look unblinded on the hour of one's death.

I saw the swords, the armor, the strong men crowding among the olive-trunks. One thrust forward, bold with despair, and embraced the one who knelt, and greeted him in a travesty of gladness. "Master! Master, well met at last!"

And at the traitor's belt, in the purse in which the coins lay like lovers, I heard the song of silver.

Pity the inconvenient, the troublemakers, the gods incarnate. This one they crucified. Others we buried living in the fen, or gutted with the golden sickle in the wood. They were the Mystery and the Sacrifice.

His people could not understand—his priest, his betrayer, least of all. The priest should live to celebrate the rite again, the shedding of blood and lives that makes the earth strong.

This one failed of comprehension. As the tree of execution went up on the hill that was bald and rounded like a skull, he ran blind and stumbling back into the garden among the twisted trees. There where the Sacrifice had knelt, he unwound the cord from about his waist and measured the height of the branch above him, and hanged himself in an agony of confusion.

He too was a mystery and a sacrifice. At his feet as he struggled, dying slowly, lay a purse. Its strings were broken. Silver trickled from it, flowing in the dream like water, pouring into the cup that likewise was silver. Thirty sweet high notes it sang, and the three queens sang with it.

A man came walking through the garden. He wept as he walked, and it seemed his feet were aching in their fine soft shoes. He never saw the man who hung from the tree. That was hidden from him; for it was dark, black dark at noon, and his eyes were blurred with tears.

He stumbled and fell. His hand brushed the purse and the silver. It was mute under his touch, sliding softly, bending his hand toward something that grew in the dark of the garden. Something slender and hardly taller than a man, straighter than the ancient trees. It yielded as he fell against it. If it was rooted, those roots were weak. Its branches—I saw branches, but they faded as I watched, and shrank into the trunk.

He caught himself at last, steadied on the staff that had grown—yes, I saw it, I in my dream—that had budded and swelled and sprung toward heaven out of the fallen coins. As he braced his feet and his new-won staff, the dark was rent. The earth shook. The lightning fell, and then the rain, soft, like shaken silver.

—— II ——

I saw a man on a dark road, walking. His feet were wrapped in rags. His hair was long and gray as the rain. He leaned on a staff. Its wood was polished with use and faded to silver. All his burden was a purse, but no coins filled it; only something round and hard and hollow, like a beggar's bowl.

He walked far and he walked long. He walked the world across, from rain on the hill that was rounded like a skull, to rain on the marshes at the feet of a hill that was steep and narrow like a tower. I knew that hill, I, even dreaming. I remembered the three queens, the three crones, the three goddesses, angels, demons, whatever they chose to be. The hill was full of their presence.

The walker paused in sight of the hill. I saw it as he saw, not tower or tor but a cup overturned on the earth, its wine poured away. Water of the marshes shimmered about it like gray silver.

"Joseph," said a voice, silver-sweet. "Joseph, where are you going?"

The walker neither started nor turned, although what stood behind him was well worth turning to. She was beautiful, no queen yet nor crone, but seed of both. Her hair was long and pale as silver. Her skin was white, whiter than the moon. Her eyes were blinding bright, like the flash of sun on a sword.

"Joseph," she said again, "where are you walking?"

"To the world's end," he answered, speaking as if to the air. His voice was steel to her silver, gray and strong but edged with brilliance.

"Joseph," said the lady who was all silver and steel, "this is the world's end."

Then at last he turned. "I see land beyond this," he said.

"Yes," said the lady. "But this is the place you seek."

He leaned on his staff, ineffably weary, and yet he was as poised and still as a cat before it springs. "Shall I trust you, then?"

"Always," she replied, "and never."

He nodded slowly. He had not asked her name. I thought perhaps he knew, or had no need to know, as prophets do.

"This staff," he said, "comes from the Mount of Olives in Jerusalem. Do you know where that is?"

"It is everywhere," she said, "and nowhere."

"The staff grew from the death-throes of a traitor, and sprouted from the silver of his betrayal. Is that a miracle, do you think? Or a mockery?"

"What is that in your purse?" the lady asked as if he had not spoken. "Is it a beggar's bowl? Why do you hide it? Are you ashamed?"

She was asking as a child will, in a spate of questions. But she asked also as a seer must, not to know the answers but to know what answers she would gain. I saw how Joseph smiled, and knew that he knew. "No bowl," he said, "and no beggar's possession. See."

He laid hand on his purse. She laid hers over his, staying him. "No," she said. "It is not ready. Not yet. Come."

"Not until I can trust you," he said. "I have been tempted before, lied to, lured astray."

"Certainly," the lady said. "Come with me."

It was her simplicity that won him. Others, I saw, had tangled themselves in nets of falsehood, or wooed him with smiles and sweet words. She was beautiful but cold, and she never smiled. She walked away from him. He followed slowly.

They walked far and they walked long. The lady led, always. Sometimes she was maiden, sometimes mother ripe with child, sometimes crone as bent and weary as the man who plodded behind her. It was a long, long way to the tor that had seemed so near.

Joseph said nothing, no word of complaint. As he walked he grew grayer, thinner, more weary. His staff aged to silver, aglimmer in the gloom.

When he wore the face of a man of great age and she wore that of a crone, the long road ended in the steep wall of a crag. The tor loomed over them. Clouds brushed its summit, gray as steel.

The lady began to mount the tor. Joseph followed still. His feet were bare, the rags worn away. Behind him as he climbed, he left a track of blood.

Up they walked, the lady and the man from Jerusalem, sunwise round the narrow tower of the tor. Round and round as the sun goes, from light to dark and back to light again. And the crone grew younger with each circle, but the man grew older, till they stood on the summit, in a ring of stones like silver and gray steel.

The lady stood at the ring's gate. "Come," she said.

I saw the opening of the gate. I saw the light that flooded from the hill. I saw the feasting, the laughter, the mirth—all stilled before the face of that gray man with his gray staff and his purse that held no coin, only a bowl such as beggars bear.

The light that had been so warmly golden paled to silver. The laughter faded into silence. The company, bright lords, shining ladies, shrank into mist. Three queens only remained in the pale and empty hall, two who had waited, one who had gone out to find the man from Jerusalem.

"Now let us see," that lady said.

"No," said Joseph.

The queens stood still as stones. I saw stones, truly, beyond this hall that was a deeper dream than mine, ringed in a dance under a gray and restless sky.

"What I keep," said Joseph, "is not for you, nor for any creature of the shadows."

"It is for all who are," the lady said.

"No," he said again. He struck his staff on the paving of the floor. The stones cracked; the hall trembled.

So too did he, when he sought to raise the staff again. It had pierced the paving, and the paving held it fast. No struggle sufficed to prise it free again.

He backed away from it. It trembled with the memory of his touch.

All else had stilled. The world itself, I saw in my dream, stood motionless. The stars paused in their courses.

Only the staff moved. Its trembling went on, sharpened and quickened. Suddenly, like a child waking from sleep, it unfurled thin, silvery arms, stretching, reaching toward heaven. Leaves swelled on branches, vividly green in that colorless place. Blossoms budded and bloomed, white as snow, white as new silver, sending forth scent as sweet as it was strange.

Joseph stood beneath the branches of the blossoming tree. His face, that had been set as hard and cold as stone, warmed into wonder, and thence into delight. He laughed, clear and strong, as a young man will. "Miracles I have seen, and wonders, and mysteries: the lame made to walk, the blind to see, the dead to live again. But nothing so fair as this, or so strange."

The queens stood silent. He unbound his purse and brought forth what he carried.

It was little indeed to be the cause of so much uncanniness. Only a cup, a simple wooden cup, not even carved to make it beautiful. No silver adorned it, no jewels brightened it.

And yet he raised it as if it were the most precious thing in the world. "With this," he said in a voice that shook with intensity, "a man drank the wine of his last supper, the night before he died. He called that wine his blood."

The queens said nothing.

Joseph rounded on them. His voice rose. "Do you understand? Can you? Do you know what this is?"

"It is a Mystery," said the first of the queens, the one who had met him on the road to the tor. "A cup of sacrifice. Blood of the earth, for the earth—"

"It is nothing of your pagan superstition! It is holy."

"Yes," said the queen. She held out her hands.

He would have snatched the cup from her, but he was in her realm, and she was strong. He gasped as she touched it. But no lightnings fell. No shudder rent the earth. She stood before him, a maiden clad in white, with a wooden cup in her hands.

She held it reverently, carrying it toward the tree. Joseph made move to stop her, but she eluded him. He stumbled and fell, and lay on his face. She spared him no glance as she passed.

In front of the tree she bowed low, her long free hair slipping forward, covering her hands and the cup in a veil of silver. Through the veil I seemed to see a glimmer—startling, a flash of scarlet, the color of wine, or of blood.

The tree's branches bowed as if in answer. Petals fell like soft snow. They filled the cup and brimmed over—white as they fell, scarlet as they came to rest, till I could not tell what was blossom, or what was wine, or what was blood.

"Behold the Mystery," said the queen, "and the Sacrifice." She knelt and set the cup on the stones at the tree's foot. Blossoms starred her hair, caught in her gown, trailed behind her as she moved.

Joseph lay where he had fallen. He breathed: I heard the rasp of breath in his throat.

"Hear," said the queen, "O man of Israel. The Lord Who is your God, He is One."

He started as if struck, and raised his head. "Blasphemy," he said, or willed to say.

"It is all one," she said. Her hand tilted gracefully toward the cup. It lay where she had set it, and it was unchanged, and yet as he stared and I watched, it wore other faces, other semblances. A wooden cup, an iron cauldron, a silver grail, a hollowed stone—all one. All the same. All the Mystery.

Joseph's eyes remained fixed on the thing that had been his precious cup. His were a stiff-necked people, proud and willful. Their One could not be All, not ever.

But he had brought the cup here, and the staff that grew from seeds of sacrifice. He was a prophet as I was—as I am still, I suppose, in this trap of oak and silence.

I watched his head sink, and life ebb with resistance. "*Nunc*," he whispered, "*dimittis . . . Domine . . .*"

I heard iron in it, and irony. But iron is forged into steel, and he was steel, was Joseph who came up from Jerusalem. He bent before he broke. He knew what he had brought to the world's end. He died in the knowledge. May I be so blessed, I who grow old but seem disinclined to die.

—— III ——

I saw a stone, gray stone, like tarnished silver, or well-forged steel. It was hollowed slightly. It stood on an isle in a lake. Three queens tended it, and three crones: queens in the sun's light, crones under stars and moon.

This now I remember. I came walking, I with my youth and my arrogance, and I found the queens where my sight had bid me find them. I would demand the stone, I would, and threaten if they would not yield it.

But they were older far than I, and wiser than I had ever been known to be. As I dragged my coracle on the isle's shore, with my black dog leaping and barking and being of no use whatever, a lady came upon me there. My dog greeted her with vociferous delight. I called him a fool, but he was wise, my black dog.

The lady was as beautiful as dawn in winter, silver and gray and glimmering white. "Merlin," she said in her clear voice like the song of steel on steel, "well come at last. Will you be fetching the stone, then?"

Ah, thought I, for I was clever. She was a seer too, and

how not? But I doubted that she saw as clear as I. "Stone?" I asked. "Would I need a stone?"

"It would seem so," she said.

"I had thought rather," said I, "a cup. Or a cauldron."

"Or a silver grail?" she inquired. "They are all one."

"A cup will do," I said loftily.

"I think not," the lady said. "You seek a stone, and steel in the stone."

I shuddered, though I knew no reason for it. She could hardly know what I came for, I who was so clever to conceal my purposes. I had made a child out of air and magic and a king's lust for a woman who cherished her husband more than she feared the king's wrath. I had taken the child away lest the king harm him. It was coming time to bring him forth again—and the Stone, and the burden that it bore, would do very well to win him the kingship that his father, dying, must lay down.

But the lady had seen more clearly than I, and longer, and with greater power. She led me to a place that even in dream I barely saw—shapes of green silences, glimmer of water, the flick of a fish's tail—and there in the center of it, as solid as the world's heart, the stone. And in the stone, the sword.

Three queens relinquished the stone to me. Three crones wove runes in the blade of the sword. Three towers of light stood guard on the stone while every vaunting fool in Britain failed the test of the sword.

Time gentles the truth. Now in the story the fools but go away unsatisfied, and uncrowned, too. Then was a grimmer age. He who tried but once went away indeed with but a seared hand for his presumption. He who dared again, for anger or for snarling courage, shed his blood on the grass, blood of folly, blood of sacrifice.

The green grass was clotted red when the boy came. He was nothing to draw the eye, not then: a boy like any other, wise enough to hesitate, foolish enough to try, since everyone

else had, and particularly his brother. That one nursed a stinging hand in his lodging while the boy came skulking to look at
the sword and the blood and the remembrance of the last man
who had died. The boy did not mean to do anything, of course
not. But the stone was there, and the sword set in it, immovable. The moon silvered the steel of its blade.

Three crones stood watching, silent, unregarded, as he laid
hand to hilt. As soft, as light, as easy as blade from scabbard,
the sword slid from the stone. The boy was startled; he stumbled. The blade overbore him. The wound it dealt was light,
the merest brush across his thigh, but it bled swift and it bled
free, washing with its brightness the old black blood of the men
who had failed.

That was mystery, and sacrifice. Blood on earth; blood on
steel. It made a king. It bred a kingdom, and tales—more tales
than leaves on this oak of mine. None of them mattered in my
dream. Only the stone and the sword, and the boy whose blood
had sanctified them both.

Tales end. Men die—even men who are legends, and kings.
Even I will die, or so I can hope, who am half a devil and all an
enchanter.

I saw the boy fall at a traitor's hands, though he was boy
no longer, but man and king. I saw the sword lying in the
blood and mire of the battlefield. Legend bears it away, casts it
into the lake of the isle and the queens. Well for legend; and it
is true, three queens came for him, but when I saw what bent
over the dying king, I saw three crones. They spurned the
sword, or forgot it. They took up the king and carried him
from any dream or vision of mine, into a green silence.

I saw the sword on the bloody field. Fallen, notched,
bloodstained, and tarnished, it seemed no more than any mortal
blade, no greater prize, no lesser booty. The crows disdained it.

A dog licked its blade for the taste of the blood, but found a sweeter vintage elsewhere, in a warrior's cloven skull.

The sweepers of the battlefield passed in their round, swept up the sword, flung it on a clattering hill of booty. Swords and armor, spears, shields both broken and whole, blazons that I had known, for which I wept—among so many, one lone sword, however magical, vanished, and yet I knew it. My dream was bound to it.

I saw the gray light of morning. I saw the sword laid on a cloth, and its kin ranked about it. It was only a sword. Only steel, and silver inlaid in the hilt. Its runes were faded. In the wan light they vanished. The bright magic was gone from it, the light that had lain upon it, to endow the king with his kingship.

And yet there was power in it still. Deep power, like that which lives within the earth; that wakes life in the seed, that unfurls the blossom from the branch. Power that sleeps, and sleeping, changes.

I heard the chink of coins laid down in payment for the sword. I did not see the face of the one who bought it. Only the coins and the blade, gray silver, gray steel. The silver sang soft descant to the deep song of the steel.

This was the song it sang: *Sword to coin. Coin to staff. Staff to cup, which is Grail, which is stone. Stone, in its time, to sword. Then sword again to coin. Round and round about.* A purse of coins for a god's life. A staff rising from the blood of the god's betrayer. A cup to capture the god's blood. Cup transmuting into stone, in which is bound the sword. Coin, staff, cup, sword. Turn and turn and turn. So has it always been. So must it ever be.

See, now. See her who made me captive, maiden and queen, with her oaken staff that once was mine. She seeks a Grail, and in the grail a sword, and when the sword is notched and worn and nigh forgotten, a purse of coins in payment for the sword.

Power passes. That is the mystery. That, ever and always, is the sacrifice.

See how I dream, bound in the hollow of the oak. Coin. Staff. Cup. Sword. Coin. Staff. Cup. . . .

St. Paul's Churchyard, New Year's Day

RICHARD LEE BYERS

hivering and sniffling, the gangly, fifteen-year-old boy limped through the maze of twisting streets. His uneven footsteps crunched the snow. Whenever he encountered anyone—which was seldom, for nearly all London had gone to see the jousting—he averted his face. He was ashamed of his bruises, his chipped tooth, and especially his tears.

Rounding yet another corner, he found himself before the towering limestone cathedral that he, his foster brother, and his foster father had ridden by the day before. In the center of the now-deserted churchyard stood the marble block, the anvil affixed atop it, and the sword that impaled them both. The weapon's gemmed hilt burned like a torch, even in the wan winter sunlight.

The boy squinted at it. A wildness came into his battered, starveling face. He glanced about, making certain no one was watching. Then he scurried to the stone, scrambled up on it, gripped the sword by its ice-cold handles, and tried to pull it free.

Though he strained with all his might, it wouldn't budge. At last, winded, disgusted by his own foolishness, he jumped awkwardly off the pedestal, then slumped down on the frozen ground with his back against it.

A shadow fell across him.

Startled, the lad looked up. A tall man with a high, alabaster forehead and dark, deep-set eyes loomed over him. The newcomer's gloves were lined with fur, his belt adorned with garnets and silver thread. His ermine-trimmed camlet cloak hung to the tops of his soft leather boots.

The boy leaped up and tried to run. The gray-bearded intruder grabbed him by his threadbare, hand-me-down surcoat and spun him back around. "Bide a while," said the man in a soft but commanding baritone voice. "How are you called, and just what did you think you were doing?"

"My name is Arthur," the boy stammered. "I was just resting here."

The tall man's obsidian eyes bored into his captive's watery blue ones. "Do yourself a kindness. Don't lie to me. It isn't easy to hide the truth from Merlin."

Merlin the magician? The man folk swore was the son of a devil? Arthur's knees quivered. "All right! I tried to take the sword. But I swear, I would have brought it back."

The enchanter's eyes narrowed. " 'Brought it back'?"

"Yes, milord. My foster brother came to London to fight in the tournament. But he went out roistering last night, and when he awoke this morning, sick from drink, he discovered that somewhere in the stews, he'd lost his sword. Since I'm his squire, and so responsible for his arms, he blamed me. He beat me, threw me into the street, and forbade me to return without his blade." The boy blinked back fresh tears. "He wouldn't even let me back in the inn long enough to get my hood and mantle.

"I did try to find the sword, but I don't know the city, or

what taverns and bawdy houses he visited, and even if I did, everything's closed. When I saw this blade, I thought that perhaps it could serve instead."

"Are you simple?" Merlin asked. "Don't you know what glaive this is?"

Arthur swallowed. "Yes, milord. How could I not? People talk of nothing else. Supposedly, only the rightful king can pull it out. But I was so desperate, so cold, and I thought, well, it wouldn't hurt to try." He hesitated. "I guess I wanted to anyway, ever since I saw it yesterday. Just to see if I could do it."

Merlin cocked his head. "You mean, simply for the sport of it?"

Finally sensing that the wizard meant him no harm, Arthur grimaced. "Yes, milord. I'm not so foolish as to think that *I* could rule. I know that whatever becomes of Excalibur, the crown must pass to some duke or earl, not a fosterling who doesn't even know his true parents' names."

Now Merlin hesitated. At last he said, "But I can tell you that, for by my Art, I recognized you the moment I laid eyes on you. And I suppose that under the circumstances, you have the right to know. Your sire was King Uther, your mother, Queen Igraine."

The skinny boy gaped at him. "That's mad. You're mocking me."

Merlin said, "Not so. Surely you know that I was Uther's counselor?" Arthur nodded. "At his command, I helped your mother conceal her pregnancy, and attended at your birth. Afterward, I abandoned you on the doorstep of one Sir Ector, an obscure knight who dwelled in Wales, remote from court. I've often wondered if you were still alive."

Perhaps because Merlin knew Ector's name, Arthur realized to his surprise that he now believed him. Something ached in the squire's breast. "But *why?* I have to know. Why would my father give me away?"

The enchanter shrugged. "He never would tell me. You were conceived around the time he slew Igraine's previous husband. Perhaps he feared you were really Tintagel's get. Or regretted that he'd sired you out of wedlock. He may have wanted to ensure that the kingdom would pass to a son begotten on the proper side of the sheets."

"All my life, Kay and the others have looked down on the foundling," Arthur said bitterly. "Now you tell me I wasn't good enough for my true family, either." His mouth twisted.

"I'm sorry if that pains you," Merlin said. "But you must lay the sorrow aside and ponder the choices that lie before you. Don't you understand? Whatever his intentions, Uther failed to father other children. Your claim to the crown is stronger than anyone else's."

In fact, Arthur was so accustomed to thinking of himself as the humble ward of Sir Ector's charity that until that moment, he *hadn't* grasped the implications of the wizard's tale. Now a shock thrilled down his nerves. His head swam, and he wondered if he was dreaming. Could he really become king? Live in wealth instead of poverty? Have everyone bow and scrape to him, instead of the other way around? Command—

From the corner of his eye, he glimpsed the radiant length of Excalibur. The golden writing on the blue blade glittered. His sweet fantasy crumbled.

"No," he said glumly. "You're forgetting, I couldn't take the sword. I must be Tintagel's son. Either that, or God too deems me unworthy."

"Archbishop Brice is certain Christ sent us Excalibur," Merlin answered. "I'm not. I don't know where it came from, though I have my suspicions. But I can tell you that power such as this sword embodies always carries a price. I believe that the blade *is* meant for you, Arthur. Else why would fortune return you to London now? But the sword will only yield itself if you resolve to bear the cost."

Once again, the boy remembered the enchanter's diabolical lineage. "Do you mean," he faltered, "that I have to pledge my soul?"

Merlin snorted. "No. You've listened to too many bogle stories. But I think you have to accept that if you take Excalibur, the press of events will compel you to lean on it all your days."

Arthur spread his hands. "I don't understand."

Merlin turned and regarded the magical weapon. "It shines brightly, doesn't it? Brightly enough to dim the hand that grasps it." He pivoted back to face the boy. "How good a swordsman are you?"

Arthur blinked in surprise at the change of subject. "Not very," he admitted. "Kay says I fence like a lame old woman."

"Well, not with Excalibur, you won't. The glaive will lend you cunning, strength, and grace. Its edge will cleave mail like parchment. Wielding it, you'll be all but invincible. But you'll never know how puissant a man-at-arms you might have eventually become without it."

Arthur shrugged. "What difference does that make?"

"I don't truly know, for I can't see the future. But occasionally I can glean meaning from the shadows tomorrow casts upon today. I believe that if you take the sword, peers and commoners both will unite behind you, simply because the prophecy has fired everyone's fancy. You'll reign long and for the most part nobly. Vanquish armies and giants. Inspire tales that will last as long as men endure to tell them. But sometimes, on nights when sleep eludes you, you'll gaze at Excalibur, resting in its accustomed place at your bedside, and wonder if the king's achievements truly belong to *you*. Perhaps any wretch who possessed the glaive would have done at least as well."

"And is that the weighty price you warned of?" Arthur asked incredulously. "I'll pay it gladly. I *already* disdain myself,

Lord Merlin. Years of swallowing slights and drudging alongside churls have taught me how." He clambered onto the marble pedestal.

"A king's self-doubt can undermine his ability to rule," Merlin said grimly. "Make him bellicose when he ought to be soft, irresolute when he desperately needs to act. I fear war for war's sake. A slaughter of innocent babes to rival Herod's. Betrayal ignored till it tears the realm asunder."

Arthur glared down at the wizard. "Are you certain these things will come to pass?"

"No," Merlin admitted. "I told you, it's all just shadows, dancing and flowing in the dark."

"Then why should I heed you?"

Merlin's shoulders slumped. Abruptly, he looked weary and old. "I don't know. Perhaps you shouldn't, for, though I'm doing my best to advise you, as I always did your sire, truly, I don't know what you should do. Perhaps the Lord did send Excalibur. Perhaps it is your destiny to bear it. Perhaps the risk of a tainted, evanescent Camelot is better than the possibility that the Table Round will never live at all."

The boy gripped Excalibur's hilt again. The muscles in his skinny arms swelled. Then he released the sword and turned back toward Merlin. "God rot you for telling me these things. What will become of me if I don't take the blade?"

A gleam flowered in Merlin's ebon eyes. "No one can foretell that for certain, either. I hope that in time you'll discover your native virtues, and grow more comfortable in your skin. Beyond that, perhaps you'll live tranquilly in some quiet corner of the world. Or, you might win your throne as other kings have, without recourse to miracles and portents. Given the ambitions of many of the barons, it would be a long, perilous task, but not, I think, impossible. Should you choose to attempt it, I'll attest to your parentage."

Arthur gestured toward the cathedral. "Then let's begin now, with the Archbishop."

Merlin turned reflexively, following the sweep of Arthur's arm. "Gladly, my liege, if he's here. But if I'm not mistaken, he went to the tourney with—"

Arthur snatched Excalibur's hilt and pulled. Instantly, the blade hissed free of the anvil. Snarling, the boy swung the sword at the man below him.

Merlin's head flew from his shoulders. His body thudded to the ground. The gushing blood stained a snowdrift red.

Looking down at the carnage, Arthur felt vaguely ashamed. It was scarcely chivalrous to strike a foe from behind. But he'd been afraid to give the demifiend a chance to curse him.

And besides, Merlin had deserved an ignominious death. For stealing Arthur from his parents. For trying to cozen him out of his one chance at glory. If allowed to live, who knew what treason he might have plotted next?

Grinning, no longer mindful of the cold, the boy bounded nimbly off the stone, then strode off toward the inn. Soon, he knew, he must declare himself to the world, but first he meant to settle accounts with Kay.

The Other Scabbard

BRAD LINAWEAVER

lind eyes blinking in the dark, soft mouths forming words without sound, things that might be fingers reaching out to stroke healthy flesh passing by in the gloom of secret passageways. . . . That's the way it always was whenever I paid a call on Merlin. He'd liked his privacy when he was alive. Now he was positively a recluse.

Not that he was exactly dead, but to the outer world he might as well be. He'd allowed the rumor to spread that Morgan le Fay had bested him; a perfect absurdity to anyone who knew their respective abilities. None of us among the Little People had been taken in for a minute. Merlin always played his own game. The problem was how to get him on your side.

The leader of the People had selected me for this journey because of the time I'd been a spy at Arthur's court. From the first moment Merlin saw me in the outer world he recognized me for what I was. He helped get me into Camelot, all part of his eternal diplomacy—juggling the contrary interests of alien worlds, and trying to convince everyone that mutual interests exist where there are none. Well, he was a magician, after all.

Naturally the humans took me for a female child. Guinevere even thought me a bastard result from one of Lancelot's
previous adventures. The great knight's indifference to a child
did nothing to disabuse her of the notion. She was well aware
that many a father acted that way toward legal issue.

My purpose was to keep an eye on Arthur. The king had
no inkling of my true nature. Merlin and I agreed that it was
best to maintain secrecy; but I wouldn't have put it past the old
reprobate to subtly suggest to the monarch of Camelot that his
majesty be on best behavior when around the new child. Then
again, perhaps the king came off as a perfect uncle to any child
who was there to enjoy the hospitality of his castle.

Arthur guessed my age at ten. He was off by a factor of
ten! A mere century among the green forests and rocky crags of
these islands means I'm still a youngster among the People; but
old enough for dirty dealings with the human vermin. Merlin
was interested in peace. We prepared for war.

I was a good spy. Not a trace of revulsion crossed my face
as the king ran his fingers through my blond tresses or gave me
friendly pats. "Darling child," he called me. I smiled and giggled. Merlin even complimented me on how well I played the
part.

Merlin! With one hand he helps and the other he thwarts.
I stayed at court, passing on my reports in a special potion I
poured into the ground. (At the time I thought the wizard
would not divine what kind of magick I was using. I know better now.) My one certainty was that the status quo couldn't last
forever.

Lancelot and Guinevere turned out to be the chink in
Arthur's armor. We decided that this crisis was tailor-made for
us to press demands on Merlin; especially since we had recently
discovered the magician's greatest secret. We'd found the hiding place of the other sword! Everything seemed to be working
in our favor: Adultery was tearing the kingdom apart, the fool

knights were dividing their power in a mad quest for the Christian Grail, and Arthur was sinking into the depths of despair. Once we learned about the existence of the other sword, we felt sure that Merlin would renegotiate our arrangement.

I wasn't surprised when the wizard disappeared from the world of men. Nothing is ever simple with Merlin. Many the time he'd gone off alone for weeks before returning to court. But this time it appeared his departure was permanent.

He'd guided the affairs of Camelot with Excalibur, but it had been done with his usual flair for indirection. Whatever plans we had for the other sword, we could be certain he was several steps ahead of us. At times like this it was hard to believe that he had any human blood in his veins.

Among the People we had our own magick. That is how we located Merlin's secret place, and how I found myself exploring his private tunnels. A welcome guest at other times, I felt nervous intruding here. The labyrinthine complexity went beyond that of our own constructions. And where we had to depend on smokeless torches for light, or sometimes the bodies of small animals that gave out a yellow luminescence, Merlin's powers had invested the walls of his stronghold with a permanent light. The only drawback was that the colors were constantly shifting as one walked, giving an almost hypnotic effect. Where Merlin was concerned, nothing was accidental.

"You're wasting your time," he said as I spotted him from behind where he was bending over a small pool of water. He always loved to show off. Nothing ever surprised the great Merlin! At least, that was the impression he liked to make.

"I represent the Council," I answered in as solemn a voice as I could muster.

"And I represent the Lollipop Guild," he replied as he turned to face me. I had no idea what he was talking about. He enjoyed being cryptic even when he was aboveground. "Don't worry about it," he replied, as if reading my mind. "Some people say I live backward in time, so that would naturally provide certain unusual points of view."

For the first time since I had known him, I felt that I could be personal and said, "Many believe you were a product of rape."

"So much is said about me that I forget most of it. When you say 'they' do you mean people on top of or below the ground?"

He was trying to goad me. I didn't mince words: "Humans aren't people."

"Ah, yes, the party line," he said.

"Some of us don't believe the claims that you have any human parentage. Nasty rumors may be spread about anyone. Others believe that one human parent can be overlooked in someone of your attainments."

"That's most obliging," was his reply. "I'm sure there are humans who are as tolerant about you."

The trouble with diplomacy is that it puts demands on one's self-control that go far beyond the call of duty. "You're not serious, Merlin." I could hear my own voice becoming shrill. "Very few humans know for certain that we exist. For the rest, we are either stories or superstitions. They don't know us."

"So they can't form a valid opinion about you?"

"Exactly."

"Whereas you have known thousands upon thousands of humans as the basis of your evaluation?"

I hadn't noticed his sarcasm until that moment. He usually spoke in a monotone, except when shouting to drive home a point (as had been the case when he was instructing the young Arthur).

All these criticisms being thrown in my general direction seemed a bit unfair at the time. So I defended myself (another mistake): "Your problem is with the Council. I'm just—"

"No, you are not *just*; and that's the real problem!"

A Lord of the People had warned me about this sort of thing when I first offered to serve. There are as many points of view as there are stars in the heavens. A clever debater is someone every bit as intransigent as you are but with a pretense of objectivity. Merlin could keep me tied up in knots for hours this way. And I frankly didn't have the time. . . .

"How long has it been since you last ate?" he asked with uncharacteristic solicitude. Perhaps his bag of tricks didn't have a bottom, but I'd never thought that his art would include cookery.

I was so surprised that I couldn't think of anything to say. With a touch as firm as it was kind, he took my arm and led me deeper into the recesses of the cave. Here were sights more beautiful than the crystal walls of my own home. And if I thought we of the People had mastered every kind of underground labyrinth, I had not reckoned on the powers of Merlin. For the first time in my life, I realized that I was lost. Every corridor was the same, even as every color of the rainbow washed over me, and pleasant tinkling sounds satisfied longings without a name.

"This way," said Merlin, voice growing deeper as he led me into his secret realm. There was no need for speech. His hand still held me in a firm grasp.

And then my heart skipped a beat as we stood before a gigantic sword, plunged deep into what appeared to be some kind of fungous growth. "Excalibur," I said, but even as the sacred word passed my lips, I knew it couldn't be.

"No," said Merlin. "This is not the king's missing sword."

"I never thought I'd actually see the anti-Excalibur."

"This seemed a good place for a little kitchen," he said, smiling thinly. Not until he began opening a door in the side of the tunnel did I realize that he was no longer holding me. The strength of his grasp was such that I still felt his fingers on my arm; and I liked the feeling.

He hadn't been joking about the kitchen. A large cauldron steamed in the center of the room. The aroma was pleasant with just a hint of sweetness. Neatly stacked against the wall were barrels of different kinds of herbs and plants. A small wooden table was placed near the food. I couldn't help but notice that it was perfectly round.

As if the argument between us had left something unpleasant in the air, we didn't speak. Words would have spoiled the splendid repast. I hadn't been hungry until I tasted the first spoonful of the stew. As I eagerly ate the rest of the tangy mixture, I felt his flinty eyes watching me. We both knew this was a temporary lull in the battle, but I was willing to enjoy it.

"Why did they send you?" he asked when I'd finished the meal.

I thought we'd been through all that. My time in Camelot had not been wasted. As a spy I had seen the enemy close up—the human pestilence that covered these fair islands like so much soot from a dirty chimney. An older and more experienced member of our race could have been selected, but the honor was mine because of the proximity I'd had to King Arthur, to his subjects . . . and to Merlin.

I decided to address the real issue: "We don't understand what you're trying to accomplish any longer. I'm here to find out."

As he stood, I was struck once again by how much taller Merlin was than a normal human. Given my diminutive stature, he towered over me. The way his cloak swirled around him, green and brown colors capturing the hues of the earth, he seemed a giant tree, but one that could never be humbled by ax or any other blade.

His response was patronizing: "What is wrong with your statement is the suggestion that anyone has ever divined my purposes. And what do *you*, little one, suppose they are?"

He wasn't going to trick me that easily. There had been

agreements, promises, treaties! "You know full well," I told him. "The humans may only live here if they are kept in control. They cannot be allowed to breed indefinitely."

His smile was beginning to make me uncomfortable, especially the words that came past those thin lips: "There is not enough space for infinite breeding where anyone is concerned. Even the Little People need room."

This persistent equating of us with the human scum was beginning to get on my nerves. I tried to keep from shouting: "We were here first. We belong here. Human beings are invaders."

Although under the ground, we were still near enough the surface to hear thunder explode overhead. A torrential downpour followed. It was that time of year. It usually was that time of year.

"The animals preceded you," he said quietly.

"And who does a better job of taking care of them and living with them than we do?"

I thought he was about to argue how we sometimes kill animals, the same as humans, for food and clothing . . . and to make our spells. A counterargument had already occurred to me: namely, that we didn't begin to hunt as many of them as the other side. And then there was the matter of trees. We never cut down trees for any reason. But Merlin tried a new tack.

"Little one," he said, "there is no point in this kind of comparison. I grant that human beings are not as in tune with earth forces as you are."

"Or you," I replied, happy of the opportunity to pass on a sincere compliment.

The rain was continuing to pour down with an incessant drumming sound. All I could think about was the fresh mud this would make, and how many humans might slip in it and break their fool necks. With that uncanny power of his, Merlin seemed to look right into my soul.

"Why do the Little People hate mankind?" he asked.

The very words seemed to set my brain on fire with an uncontrollable rage. I jumped up so quickly that I knocked his little table over. "We're angry with you, Merlin! With you. . . ." I wanted to stop myself, but the words poured out as if to match the volume of the rain crashing overhead.

I went on: "We thought you would use your influence, at the heart of Camelot, to keep humans in their place. To keep them divided and at each other's throats. To keep them busy killing each other."

His face seemed to age with every pronouncement I threw at him. He turned to face the wall beyond which a sword waited, like an accusing finger. I couldn't seem to stop myself: "The Druids were the best we could expect from humans. And you're the best of them, far better—because you were more than human. So now you stand between the pagan world and the Christian world, between the forest and what Rome brought here, now collapsing back into the dust where it belongs. Humans believe in you. You gave them Arthur. You put Excalibur in his hand. You . . ."

I wanted to build him up all the higher so I could drag him down all the more; I could see the crucial events in my mind and how the seeming unity that Merlin had helped to create worried us at first. But when adultery did its disintegrating work, and the sword Excalibur was a lost hope, and the knights went off on futile quests, and the sorceress Morgan le Fay turned everyone else's pain into her own personal treasure, we assumed that Merlin had been craftier than anyone expected. This was all the more easily believed when he allowed himself to be bested by Morgan le Fay and thereby removed from Arthur's side at the king's moment of greatest trial.

When the news first came to us that Merlin might still be striving for unity and the restoration of Camelot, the thought was too hideous to bear. But the elf brought proof to the

Council. Merlin was casting new spells for the good of Arthur and his noxious realm.

And so, finally, I finished my tirade with, "We can't believe you'd work to increase the presence of human beings in our home." I'd worked myself into such a state that I could barely catch my breath. His contemplation of the rock wall completed, he turned around and gestured that I resume my seat. Before joining me, he bent over with a considerable sound of creaking in his joints and returned the table to a standing position.

"There's no quarreling with your criticisms, little one. Human beings do not provide the best material. Take Guinevere, for example. I warned Arthur about her, but to no avail. Blindness is his flaw. As for her . . ."

My time at court had not been wasted. "She broke her vows," I said, which struck me the same as violating an essential step of an important magickal spell.

"All too predictable," he said with a heavy sigh. "Once boredom or disappointment comes into the picture, expecting a wife to stay with her husband is like expecting a vulture to tarry over dry bones when there is rotting flesh nearby, awaiting her delicate attention."

Hearing Merlin express such a perfectly reasonable opinion about the enemy gave me a false sense of security. Could he be seeing things clearly at last? One could hope. . . .

"There's not one thing I can say about them," he told me, "that I can't also say about the Little People. Loyalty is an achievement." He came close and pulled something out from under his flowing robes. A glittering crystal winked at me from his long, white fingers. "Loyalty is as rare," he whispered, "as a jewel in the snow. I never break my word to anything on earth, or under it."

Supper was definitely over. I wasn't sure I wanted any dessert. He opened the wall again, and beckoned me back to where the sword glinted in the shifting lights from the cave walls. "I know why you've come," he said. "But we won't discuss this little trinket until you know where I stand." He didn't seem to be making a pun.

The moment we were back in the tunnel, there were groaning and mewling sounds from out of the darkness. The elemental creatures guarding Merlin's domain might not have much in the manner of brains, but there was little doubt as to their loyalty. They would die for Merlin, always assuming they were already alive.

Pointing to the sword, but exercising care not to touch it, he went on: "I never promised to put the interests of any group over any other. Individuals earn my allegiance. Arthur earned his sword. I won't punish him any more than he's already punished himself."

Without Merlin's help to trick Arthur into thinking this sword was Excalibur, the king would never raise the wrong blade above his head, and call his knights back to the banner. And the dark magick wouldn't be released, undoing everything that Excalibur had wrought. What Lady Guinevere had begun, we were more than willing to finish.

"Why do you hate them?" he asked. There was no answer I could give. The emotions ran too deep. Human beings looked like us, but as ungainly caricatures, coarse and ugly as goblin droppings. We told ourselves that they were enemies of the natural world; but if they never cleared a field or ran their plows through the soil, we would still wish them ill.

"Forgive an old man," he said, placing a hand on my shoulder. The fact that I did not shrink from his touch was sufficient proof that he couldn't really be one of *them*. "You can't help being a bigot when that's all you've ever known," he told me. "But you can return to your caves and report that I won't use the power of this sword to destroy those whom I love!"

"What has happened to the real Excalibur?" I had the presence of mind to ask. He simply shook his head. I didn't really care if he wanted to keep that a secret. The power right in front of me was all I cared about at that moment.

"You'd like to touch it, wouldn't you?" he asked. Now it was my turn to shake my head. "Go on," he said. "The sword has no sting."

I was standing very close to the anti-Excalibur. There seemed to be shadows moving on the ground near the blade. At first I thought it was the phosphorescence from the walls playing tricks. The truth was more disturbing. As I bent over to examine the ground, I saw that the moldy substance beneath the sword was actually moving. I leaped back and almost fell.

Merlin, reliable as the rock under my feet, caught me. "There now," he said, "I thought you knew. This sword was grown over the course of many centuries. Only a special hand will harvest this sprout from its garden; as only the right hand drew Excalibur from the stone."

"The wrong hand," I heard myself whisper, but it was as if someone else spoke the words. "A hand meant for destruction."

"You may still touch it," Merlin repeated. "Yours is not a human hand, and as you know so well, only a human hand will release the darker powers of that blade."

Suddenly I felt very stupid. "What are you up to?" I asked, scarcely disguising my suspicions.

Never before had I heard the laughter of Merlin the magician. Although I have lived nearly two thousand years, I pray to gods and goddesses above and below that I never hear that sound again. There was no joy in it, only cold knowledge.

His eyes changed as he watched me. I remembered the light that had flashed in the small jewel held between his fingers. Now it was as if the light had traveled up his arm and reached his eyes. The brightness was painful.

"We know what you want," he said, providing no clue as to who was intended by the plural. "This sword is a concentration of earth's darkest powers. You will not place this in Arthur's hands. His destiny lies elsewhere. But even after Arthur is a memory, you will still be trying to place this deadly thorn in the hands of a human leader. We cannot prevent this forever."

The vibration beneath my feet was barely noticeable at first. I didn't even pay attention until there was a loud rumbling. Merlin's eyes were dancing before me as if they were twin comets; yet his body remained rigid as if a pillar anchored to the ground. And then the whole tunnel tilted crazily and I was falling forward, forward . . . with nothing to hold on to except the sword.

No sooner had I steadied myself than everything returned to normal. The experience was so vivid that for one moment I believed in its authenticity. And then I realized that the sounds and tremors had been pure illusion. The lack of falling rocks or even dust in the air should have warned me that Merlin was still Merlin! He'd gone to all this trouble just so I would reach out and grasp the hilt of the anti-Excalibur.

His eyes were normal again. They were looking at my hand. We of the People are not allowed to curse, or I would have let loose such a torrent of vituperation as to drown out an eternity of rain.

"Thank you," he said. "I needed your cooperation. By touching the sword before a human hand, you help redirect its magick. Now it will rebound upon the eventual user, but only in a way to the good. Humanity in England can be saved by both this and the *real* Excalibur, if need be . . . but in different ways at different times."

I must have worn such an expression of horror that Merlin felt a moment of sympathy. The weight of what I had done pressed down on me as an invisible hand might force me to sit, dejected, in a cavern that suddenly seemed so much darker. I could barely hear the old mage's words over the sounds of my own sobbing.

"There now," he said, "it's not as bad as all that. Negative magick is not so easily dispelled. Anti-Excalibur cannot be used to extend an English leader's power beyond certain limits. Clearly, you don't want Englishmen with too much power, or their progeny extended too far. At some future moment of great peril, this weapon will keep things in balance and preserve the natural order of—"

"No!" I screamed, leaping to my feet, unbearable frustration consumed in anger's welcome fire. "You tricked me! I'll never be able to return to the People now. They'll know. And they don't forgive."

He crouched down beside me, but I was grateful he didn't touch me this time. He was gentle as he asked, "Aren't these the ones for whom you would have laid down your life?" I nodded mutely, tears filling my eyes. "You can stay with me," he went on. "I will greatly extend your lifetime. You needn't be cast upon the wind after a mere five hundred years. You can join me in glorious solitude. There are more worlds than this. Stand back from the battles of the many. Embrace the outlook of the one. The human tribe and your tribe serve no useful purpose except to produce an occasionally interesting individual."

He went on like that for some time, and although I initially felt revulsion for what he said, the words began to affect me as flowing water will eventually smooth the surface of the sharpest stone. The love I had taken for granted suddenly seemed completely unreal. I had failed. Those I loved would destroy me for that failure, if they could.

I have only the vaguest memory of going outside with him. No elemental creatures barred our way. The tunnels were empty, leading to a different world. The rain had stopped. Stretching out before us was a monotonous landscape of mud, the color of excrement, and with an odor to match. "This blessed plot," I heard Merlin mutter under his breath as he held his nose. I'd never noticed odors like that before. There was no sweet, after-the-rain freshness.

We wandered over the hills of England. No human or animal took note of us. The combination of his powers and the logic of his arguments finally seemed an irresistible combination. And for the first time, I began noticing details about his face. Even in the pale light of late afternoon his bushy white eyebrows seemed like small, jagged lightning bolts, forever fixed above a stern gaze. I wanted desperately to trust him, because I no longer had a People to call my own.

When night came, he did things with his hands, and the stars all turned into blinking eyes. I'd never felt so lonely than at that moment, surrounded by a myriad of potential judges, as indifferent to me as I was empty inside. I desperately needed to be filled with something, anything . . . and Merlin knew it.

He gave me powers. They were difficult to master, but I eagerly accepted the challenge. There were methods by which I could leave my body and travel through space and time. By this means innumerable worlds were mine to explore. The sheer volume of event and environment put my own past into an ever-diminishing context. Eons passed without my even seeing Merlin. And finally the moment came when he allowed me to understand that all those cold eyes sprinkling the black canopy of the night had been my own, sated with a million visions.

I had almost forgotten about the sword when Merlin took me back to England. Camelot was now a dream—lost forever but remembered with an aching desire. Gone were the Brythonic-speaking Celts and their problems with the Saxons. In their place a new world had risen from the mud and rocks and dirt, a world of steel and other metals, as that cursed sword had grown in its fungous bed. The sky was full of cold metal as well, raining down to earth where it became hot as the burning sun. And this new England had produced a new leader.

"Look upon him," said Merlin. We watched from safe distances, invisible and indifferent; but curiosity still lived somewhere in my ancient breast. "Look at what is his!"

This man had found the sword, the anti-Excalibur, where its soft bed of muck had grown hard over the centuries. When he touched the hilt and pulled, the hard mound around the sword showed cracks and gave way. With a great yank he held the blade before his face, while three old crones promised that this special weapon would turn the tide against the enemy and save England.

The man did not appear particularly regal. He was short and squat. In place of a profile his face was round as the moon, with heavy jowls and a protruding lower lip that made him look pugnacious. His garments were bulky and rough, suggesting not the least hint of comfort. On his head he wore a shapeless black thing. He was old and used a cane. With the sword in one hand, a stick in the other, and a large stomach hanging over his widely placed feet, the composite effect was a bit ridiculous. This was no King Arthur.

"Today is historic," he boomed in a voice far greater than his body deserved. "I think of Charlemagne and Alexander the Great, but most of all I think of Arthur Pendragon. As I wield Excalibur. . . ."

"But—" my thoughts spoke to Merlin as a whisper in the void. He answered, "You know which sword is found this day."

The man in black bowed to the three old women who had led him to so much concentrated power. "I did not take this job," he said, "to oversee the dissolution of the empire."

I knew the immediate outcome, even before Merlin pulled back the tapestry of time to show the future. The black magick had been tamed. Many English lives were saved by the sword I thought would mean their doom. But negative energies were released when it came to the more ambitious goals of this would-be Arthur. England was not to be the whole of the world. England was to be itself.

Those who had been my People were now reduced to such small numbers that I scarcely believed I had once feared them. But there were still enough of them to put up a wail over the ever-spreading sea of humanity that not even the most destructive war could stem. Suddenly I felt no gratitude to Merlin that, thanks to his sorcery, I had outlived so many.

Somewhere the real Excalibur still lies, hidden from the eyes of all sapient creatures. I am not curious as to its whereabouts, and Merlin seems to have forgotten it. As for the other sword, grown from the marrow of inner earth, the blade dissolved as if an icicle on a summer day when the skies over England became silent once again.

Silence is always best.

Hope's Edge

DANIEL H. SCHELTEMA

What here lies hostage?
What has been bound?
Our hopes are sinking,
With faith they drown.

The gray draped clouds now gather at the sign
to pour upon it obfuscation, wind
Medusan tendrils close to hide
from eager eyes that thirst for hope's bright tide.

Soon the light escapes as broken minds
are bent by ill-birthed winds intent to find
a hidden cranny worn by ripe despair
and flowered doubt, and slash through to the bare.

One pale, slim hand appears, resolved it dares
to reach, to touch, to grasp that hilt, and bear
in fingers firm and warm the cold wrought steel
now drawn from weathered stone and taught to heel.

Now wave it high so all the land must see
and share respite from lack and misery
for yet a moment, until its auger fades
and it returns from light unto the shades.

A pale, slim hand is raised from depth of lake
in silent willingness to bolster fate
now that one course has been complete, and time
has come to rest, and wait the next of kind.

Soon the light escapes as broken minds
are bent by ill-birthed winds intent to find
a hidden cranny worn by ripe despair
and flowered doubt, and slash through to the bare.

The gray draped clouds now gather at the sign
to pour upon it obfuscation, wind
Medusan tendrils close to hide
from eager eyes that thirst for hope's bright tide.

> *Our hopes are sinking,*
> *With faith they drown.*
> *Can we recover*
> *What can't be found?*

The Waking Dream

J. M. MORGAN

Was it a vision, or a waking dream?

—John Keats, "Ode to a Nightingale"

he saw him as she passed by, a young man still in his twenties, blond-streaked hair pulled away from his face into a short ponytail and covered under a loose-fitting hat. He was on the overpass, staring down at the cars whizzing by at seventy miles per hour on the freeway far below. His clothes were baggy and layered, green cotton shirt and khaki pants. She noticed him not for how he looked, or what he was wearing, but because he was sitting in a wheelchair.

"Are you thinking of jumping, or driving?"

"What?" His eyes were blue when he turned to face her. A nice shade of blue, not a weak, faded blue, but a dark, dramatic blue, like a sea whose depth is not known. He was like that, unknown and dramatic. "Did you ask something?"

"I wondered what you're thinking."

"Oh." He seemed surprised, then annoyed by her prying. "Don't worry, I wasn't going to jump."

"That's good."

"I couldn't climb the fence."

"Oh. So you were considering . . . jumping?"

"Lady, what does it matter?"

"I find you interesting. If you don't have anything else to do"—she glanced pointedly at the freeway below—"I'd like to talk with you some more. Could I buy you a beer at that bar over there?"

He looked at her with curiosity. She was old, gray-haired and wrinkled, walked with a stick, and her back bore a dowager's hump. There was nothing attractive about her, except that she had offered to buy him a beer.

"Who are you?" he asked. "Some kind of social worker or something?"

"My name is Eleanor," she said. "And you're . . . ?"

"Calder . . . James Calder."

"Calder. I like that. It sounds kind."

Let her call me whatever she wants, he thought.

"Will you come with me, Calder?" She nodded her head in the direction of the bar.

"Sure, why not?"

They crossed the busy street together, each of them careful of the rush of traffic, Calder because he was low to the ground and hard for drivers to see, Eleanor because she must walk slowly with her cane and couldn't step quickly out of the way of speeding cars. Both used the sloping handicap ramp instead of the curb to reach the sidewalk. It was easier.

They sat in a corner at the back of the bar, where Calder's wheelchair and Eleanor's cane wouldn't be in anyone's way. He ordered a Heineken. She ordered Guinness. In the dim corner of the bar, it was hard to see that he was crippled and she was old.

They talked. "You're young to be so badly crippled. How did it happen?" she asked.

"I was born this way."

"You've never walked?"

"No."

"That's hard." She was sad for him. "Then you were watching the cars, wishing you could drive."

"Yeah, I guess. Cars seem so fast, powerful."

"You envy them that power?"

"A little. I want to go somewhere, do something with my life, make a difference."

"Do you? And what would you give to have a life like that?"

He didn't hesitate. "Everything."

She was quiet for a while, as if musing on some remembered moment in her life. He watched, seeing a sadness in her face that he hadn't noticed at first. It must be lonely being old and solitary. Maybe that's why she'd spoken to him, because she needed another voice to answer her own. The thought depressed him. In a few years he might be just like her. If he didn't end it. He had thought of ending it today. Planned how he might bring wire cutters to the fence overlooking the freeway and—

"You'd be willing to give up the life you have," she asked, "for a chance at one of adventure, romance, power?"

"If I could walk," he said.

"Walk and ride," she told him. "Have you ever ridden a horse, Calder? I can picture you on a black horse, your hair flowing behind you, and your long legs hugging the stallion's flanks."

"You've got some imagination, Eleanor. Or is it the drink?"

"The drink?" She stared at their empty glasses. "Yes, you're right. You must have another."

He tried to stop her, but she insisted. He lost sight of her when she blended into the crowd of customers, a strange old woman talking about things he'd dreamed of and knew he'd never have. A few minutes later, she returned to their corner carrying two mugs of dark beer.

"Guinness," she told him. "Drink."

It tasted stronger than the beer he was used to, and it must have been, because after he'd taken only a few sips, he began to feel peculiar. Not sick, but very, very weird.

"You're to have your dream, Calder. Don't fight going into it. Close your eyes and let it happen. Now," she said, and he did.

Something happened. With his eyes shut, he felt an energy pass through him like a wind blowing clear into his spine, heart, and soul. Such a strong wind, and it carried him. He was afraid to look, somehow knowing that he was above, or below, or into something he couldn't possibly understand. So he kept his eyes closed tight, as Eleanor said, and waited.

The flow of energy he'd felt became something else, a steady lifting and falling, a strength beneath him that was not his own, but moved with him. He felt the power of it first, then noticed the smell, animal, then heard a voice shout, "Calder, the limb! Are you blind?"

He opened his eyes to a world that had changed its clothes.

And ducked his head, narrowly avoiding cracking his skull on the low-hanging oak limb directly in the path of his bolting stallion.

He pulled back on the reins, cinched in his knees and calves, and shifted his weight deeper to the back of the saddle, bringing the galloping horse to a shuddering standstill.

His horse, on whose back he was riding. No, expertly riding. He was in control of it, through the subtle nudges of his legs and the skill of his hands on the reins. He was the master of the stallion, its back shining with the sweat he had smelled on its skin, and it moved at his bidding.

"Time we stopped for the night," said the man who had

shouted at Calder earlier. Dunn was his name. Calder knew it, though he didn't understand how he'd come by the man or the name. Like his skill at riding the horse, the name was simply there, a part of him.

"That stallion of yours shied at a flash in the sky. I saw it, too. Your eyes were closed, Calder. And no wonder, with the distance we've come today. It might have been lightning, that flash, or God knows what. I don't fain crossing through these woods after dark. We'll stop at the nearest alehouse and rest."

If this was a dream, it was the most vivid one Calder had ever known. He could smell the damp crush of grass beneath the horses' hooves, and the mildewed odor of the wool clothes he wore. His hair was long, his body unwashed, but he could feel a strength in his back he had never known before. His legs felt part of him, well-muscled and powerful.

"I've heard dark talk about this oak woodland. Strange things have happened here that no man can put a rightful explanation to. The crofters call it Wraith's Burn, for the stream of water that heads to that quiet pool at the heart of this copse. Some have seen the wraith, so they say. And some have been drowned in the depths of that God-cursed ben."

The sun was low, reddening the late-afternoon sky. Sounds of the forest were close, the sudden flight of a woodland cockerel, the rustling through the trees of an unseen beast, and the cry of an animal cut short by abrupt death.

Dunn glanced at him and said, "Only the urgency of the King's business would bring me to such a pagan place. God spare us, and see us safely through this ancient land."

They rode in silence, Dunn with his right hand fingering the hilt of his sword. The soft *clop* of the horses' hooves was the music of that place, and the noisy blowing of their flared nostrils. Calder's sword was at his side too, but he did not lay his hand to it. Instead, his open palm stroked the stallion's warm neck.

To Calder, the forest was a miracle. Its ancient trees were the steadfast gods of this land, and the snaking river its soul. Man and animals were usurpers to the olden world, the spired cathedral of living wood within the sylvan copse. It was not fear he felt of it, but awe.

As they rode, the trees thinned to a lacy front along the forest's edge. Light filtered through the boundary in patterns of leaf and sun framing the break in the woods, the armed reaches of the trees layering slanted rays of sunset.

He heard the cry, an inhuman sound, like the scream of the animal caught by wolf or bear. Only this cry was worse. And not abrupt. It went on, rising to a nerve-shredding shriek of agony and dropping to a ragged wail of unceasing torment.

Dunn crossed himself. "By the Virgin! What demon is this?"

"Not a demon, I think," said Calder, "but someone in terrible pain."

"God preserve us from whatever sin has caused such suffering," said Dunn.

"Mayhap we might help," said Calder, surprised at the words coming from his mouth. His heels dug quick jabs into the stallion's flanks.

"Stay clear of this!" shouted Dunn. "God knows what wizardry lies in such a one as that." But Calder was far ahead, racing toward the fiendish cries.

The crofter's hut was not far. A sooty trail of smoke rose from the chimney, marking its position among the shelter of trees. The hut stood on the outskirts of Broadmoor Village, the place Calder and Dunn had been sent on the errand of their king.

The stallion grew skittish at the sound, tossing its strong neck from side to side and blowing fretful breaths through flared nostrils. The cut of its hooves cobbled the dirt courtyard before the hut.

He gentled the beast with soothing words and comforting strokes of his hand along the stallion's sweaty neck. "Rest, rest my strongheart. The danger is not for you." He threw the reins over a tree limb, hooking them so the animal could not bolt in terror.

At the next scream, a man threw open the door of the hut and ran from the house. "God's mercy, I trow I cannot stand hear more. Sweet Jesus, give her ease!"

The man was small of stature, runty, with scraggly tufts of greasy hair standing out from his scalp like wire threads. He was clothed in a loose woolen shirt, and on his dirty feet were sandals of the roughest sort.

"What grief is there to that one inside?" asked Calder, nodding his head toward the open doorway.

The man drew his stubby fingers through the lengths of hair falling in his face. "A childbed that will be the death of her, I fear."

"How long like this?"

"Three nights. It is hard enough to take the sound of such torment in the day, but when it falls dark and I hear her scream . . . I cannot stand more. It would be Christ's mercy to let her die and be an end of it. God's punishment on us both. She carries the son I wanted—I know it. And now for our sin, the two will die."

Calder didn't know what sin the man meant, and didn't care. "Is someone with her? Surely, she must have a physician."

"Physician? Greater fool are you than I, if you believe a lordly physician would fain live among the common folk of Broadmoor."

"Cannot one be sent for from another village?"

"And given what? I am a poor man. For us, there is only the priest to bless the living and anoint the dead."

"Mary! Mother, help me," came a desperate prayer within the walls of the crofter's hut, by a voice scraped raw from three nights of screaming. "Let me die, I beg you, let me *die* . . . !" The final word blended into the next shriek of pain—to which the husband crouched low and stopped his ears with his rough hands.

Calder would have gone to the woman's aid himself, but he knew nothing of difficult childbirths. For that matter, assisting a woman in an ordinary birth was beyond his skill—and clearly, this was far from normal.

"Is there no midwife who might help her?"

The man glanced furtively in the direction of the woods. "Only she who lives near Wraith's Burn."

"You must go to her, man. Hurry, what delays you?"

"I cannot, even for that one inside, even for the son she bears me. It is said the midwife at Wraith's Burn is a witch."

"A witch! God's breath, your wife lies dying. Would you do nothing to save her?"

"For my soul's sake, I cannot."

Calder was infuriated by the man's cowardice. If it were his own wife in mortal danger, nothing in God's world would stop him from helping her. Not King, nor Crown, nor fear of death.

"Tell me how I might find her. I will go," he said.

"The priest will be angry," muttered the worried husband.

"Damn the priest, and damn you! Tell me."

The crofter was clearly shocked at these words, but gave directions to the place called Wraith's Burn.

As Calder rode away, Dunn approached the hut and shouted to him. "What madness is this? Have you lost all reason? You are riding back into the woods!"

Calder did not stop long enough to explain himself. Dunn would understand his actions soon enough. The crofter could tell him, or the screams of the woman inside the hut would serve.

He might have waited, might have sought Dunn's assistance in this task, but remembered well how fearful Dunn had been of these woodlands. Though brave in battle between men, Dunn would not have risked entering the oak forest again, even for the sake of a woman as piteous as this crofter's wife.

The way was quicker alone. Calder kept to the path the husband spoke of, and soon heard the gentle play of water in a clearing ahead of him. The trees thinned to an open knoll, a bare prominence in this tree-pillared and leaf-furled land. In the center of the clearing was a forest pool.

Calder had not realized how thirsty he was until now. The day had drawn late. He and Dunn had not stopped for food or drink since early morning. The stallion too, huffed air between his lips, savoring the smell of nearby water, eager in his need to drink.

It would not well serve the lady being brought to birth if her only champion dropped from thirst. Nay, there was much yet to do, and he needed a measure of strength for the task. Feeling the ache of hip joints, knees, and bones, he lowered himself from the saddle. The stallion wheezed a sigh of seeming pleasure at the relief of weight from his back.

The midwife's cottage would not be far from the pool—so the crofter had told him. Calder looked, and saw nothing but the tranquil water. Not a ripple marred its surface. Not a sound broke the hushed calm.

He slipped off the horse's back and stood for a moment. A distant memory triggered . . . something he could barely recall. It was as if he had never stood before, never taken steps or felt the weight of his body supported by his legs. What enchantment was this? Some dream brought to him by his nearness to this pool? To this woodland—as Dunn had warned?

No, that was foolish. Still, he noticed how strange and wonderful it felt to be on his feet after so long a journey. His back ached miserably, and his legs throbbed with pain. In three long strides, he crossed to the rim of the basin, knelt, and dipped his hand into the water.

At once, a ring of circles broke the surface like a chain growing one upon the other, appearing larger and larger, until they touched the far perimeter of the pool. Calder bent his head low and sipped the cool water from his cupped hand. It tasted wonderful, like nothing else he had ever—no, there had been another drink. He remembered thinking how strange and bewildering it had tasted, too. Somewhere far away from here. But, when? And where?

In the next instant all questions vanished, for before him in the rippling water he saw the face of a woman. Brave was her hair, like molten copper floating on the water, spreading out in long, curling tendrils that moved like the rings on the pool's glimmering surface.

Her eyes were open, staring at him. Only now did he see how magical and beautiful she seemed. And she spoke, her voice coming to him from beneath the waterglade.

"Do not fear me, Calder. You have found what you seek."

"Who are you?" he asked, but even as he said the words, the vision faded, and the light that had shown through to the depths of the pool dimmed. She was gone.

"Wait!" he shouted. "Lady, I need your help . . . a woman in the throes of childbirth."

He felt a shudder crease the air, a warmth pass through him, and when he stood to see what manner of magic had befallen him, he saw a young woman standing a few feet away, her hand resting on the stallion's neck.

"What manner of woman are you?" he asked.

"I am the woman you have searched for, Calder—the midwife, Ariana."

"How did you know?"

"I heard you speaking, just now."

It was as if the vision had stepped from the pond and stood before him. And he was drawn to her, as a river is drawn to the sea.

"We must hurry," she said. "I have gathered herbs that will help this mother. She must rest, or both she and the child within her will die."

Before he could say another word, the woman turned and began walking away from him through the trees. She did not follow the path the crofter had given him, but another of her own choosing.

"Wait," shouted Calder, then on foot led his horse along the pathway after her.

He watched as she walked ahead of him, the easy stride of her legs, a swinging motion of her hips, and a grace that settled on every step she took. She was a woman like none he'd ever seen. He would have followed, wherever she might have led him. But in time, the shelter of the trees fell away, and they stood in an open clearing.

Ariana turned and faced him. "What payment will you offer for my services to the crofter's wife?"

"Payment?" he puzzled. He could think of nothing this woman needed from him. And then the answer came from within his spirit, rising like the brightness of a dream. "My loyalty forever, Lady."

"Forever," she whispered. "It is enough."

Where a moment ago there had only been the forest clearing, now the valley below opened before them. Calder saw the crofter's hut, its plume of smoke rising from a stubby chimney, and two men—Dunn and the crofter himself—standing in the scraped-dirt courtyard of the place.

"How did—?" he began to ask, but Ariana glanced at him, and he said no more. The enchantment of this place, of this woman, had captured his spirit and his mind. He gave himself willingly to the dream.

The screams of the mother met them, if anything, worse than before. Calder felt the muscles of his stomach clench at the sound.

"Giving life is the hardest of all things," said Ariana.

"You will help her?"

Ariana turned to him. "She is not your wife, nor your woman, and yet you have risked so much to save her."

"Risked? I have done nothing more than fetch a midwife. That is little enough."

"I know what the villagers say of me. I am called Witch, because I know what drinks to brew from herbs and plants of the earth. They are afraid, these people. They call upon me only when death is at their door, as now. We must hurry. Her strength is passing from her in the loss of blood. It may already be too late."

The crofter crossed himself and stood aside when Ariana approached. "Bring water to a boil," she told him. "I will need much of it."

He seemed too afraid to move.

"Quickly, man!" shouted Calder. "She means to save your wife."

"What will the priest say?" the man whispered after Ariana entered the hut. "What penance will he give for bringing a witch to tend my wife? Lord, what have I done? We are damned, both of us. Damned."

Calder brushed past the quaking husband. "Out of my way. I will fetch the water myself. If your woman lives, you may thank the courage of the midwife—for she knows well what you think of her, and what you call her behind her back."

Calder brought a pail of water from the well and poured the water into a kettle on the fire. From inside the small room beyond the wall, he heard the voices of the two women. He knelt before the fire and listened, waiting for the water to boil.

"You are a witch, they say. Help me. I cannot bear more."

"I will help you."

"Kill the child and cut it from me," begged the woman.

"Nay, I cannot do that. Soon your pain will be eased. Do not fear. I will stay beside you and bring you rest."

A shadow crossed the light at the doorway. Dunn stood a foot from the threshold. "Come out, Calder. We have no business here."

"I have made it my business."

"Would you involve me in this dealing with the devil? The midwife is a witch. The husband fears her. Even now, he has run to fetch the priest. This will not end easily. We are no part of it. Our journey is for the King's errand. Let us be away, before it is too late."

"If the husband has gone for the priest, it is already too late."

"It is not your concern," argued Dunn.

"I asked for her help. I will protect her while she does my bidding."

"Are you so possessed of this witch that you will not leave with me, even to save your life? Think you the priest will give thanks for your bringing that woman here? Use reason, man. They burn witches, and those who help them. I will not stay and die with you."

"Go," said Calder. "I will not leave her to that fate."

"I know not what the King will make of this."

"The King is a good man, and merciful. I do not fear him."

"He is Christian," said Dunn. "Forget not that." Dunn turned and walked away. In a moment, Calder heard the sound of a horse's hooves cobbling the hard-packed earth of the yard. It was dusk, and he had sent Dunn to ride alone into the next village. Dunn was more than his companion on this journey. He was his friend—one who had saved his life in battle—and Calder owed him more than this, but it could not be helped. He had sworn his loyalty to Ariana. Not for King or friendship would he abandon her.

Steam escaped from the neck of the kettle. He took it off the hook and set it on the hob at the back of the fire to keep warm. Tiredness overwhelmed him. He scooted against the side of a cupboard, leaned back, and closed his eyes.

When he awoke, the room was dark, and the blazing fire only embers. "Calder," said her voice from out of the cover of night, "you did not leave with your friend?"

"I swore my loyalty to you, Lady."

"Many have forgotten such an oath."

He stood as she approached. "How does the woman?"

"She is dead, both mother and child."

Calder had not expected to hear this. He had believed Ariana would save this woman, through whatever enchantment was within her. "But the brew you made . . ."

"It gave her ease from pain, little more. It was too late to save her life. They call upon me when life lingers by a thread. I could do nothing else."

Calder's concern was not for the dead mother and child; they were beyond his help. His fear was for Ariana. The crofter had gone to the village and the priest. Morning would bring them here. It would be worse for Ariana now that the mother and child were dead. She was not safe here. She must leave this place at once.

"Calder," she said, "you cannot always save a life in your keeping, but you must always try."

God grant me strength, he thought. *I will not see her burn.*

"Will you leave with me, Lady? Come away into the woods."

"Think you the woods will protect me?"

"Nay, Lady. I will."

They rode together on the horse's back, Ariana close behind him on the saddle. He felt the warmth of her arms around his chest, and the slight weight when she leaned her head against his shoulder and slept.

In the dark, the woods were a danger to more than human life. It was said that spirits of the damned roamed freely through these groves once worshiped by the Old Ones. Remains of their crude altar stones were scattered like exposed bones over the land. He felt the shades of those spirits touch him as they rode through the forest.

"I am weary, Calder. Turn the horse there." She pointed toward a small break in the trees. "Tomorrow is near upon us. I would rest before the day takes me."

The stallion moved easily between the trees, as if he saw by a light not granted to Calder's eyes. A little farther, and they came into a break in the woods, an open meadow, and a stone house beside the stream.

"Who lives here?" he asked, wary of such a secluded dwelling.

"A witch," she said. "Come inside. There is grain to feed your horse, and drink to slake your thirst."

He hesitated.

"I live here," she said. "Will you not trust me?"

Calder swung his leg over the stallion's neck, stepped down, and followed her inside the stone walls of the house.

She brought a measure of grain for the stallion, and wine for Calder. It tasted sweet in his mouth. He drank deeply of its richness, feeling its warmth course through him. He looked about him to see her things. Bunches of dried herbs and flowers hung from the rafters. Earthen jars lined a shelf along the wall. She saw him notice them.

"They hold healing powders. Nothing there would bring harm to man or beast."

"I pray you, do not explain. I have no fear of you, Lady."

She stared into his eyes. "Is this true?"

"Can you doubt my loyalty to you, after I have foresworn even my duties to the King?"

Instead of answering him, she asked, "What saw you in the pond today?"

He spoke honestly. "An apparition."

"I would hear you put a name to it."

"I know not what to call her. A woman, as none other I have ever seen. The likeness of a goddess, she was."

"Not a goddess, Calder, but one of the Old Ones," said Ariana. "She is one of those whose home was amid this forest. Her time is past, as it is for all of her kind. Yet, she lingers in the spirit of the water. Folk see her as an evil presence, but she is only lost, and lonely for comfort."

"How is it you know this?"

She cut her glance away. "How is it I would not?"

Through the night, until the last star of morning faded with the dawn, Ariana told him stories of the Old Ones. She spoke of water wraiths, wood sprites, and sirens of the wooded glen. All were names given by those who did not understand what forces drove the Old Ones to live within the rocks, or pools, or woodland groves.

In the morning, when Calder thought nothing would ever seem more wondrous than the words from Ariana's lips, she drew close and kissed him. He dared not reach out to touch her, though all of him yearned to draw his arms around her waist, to crush the dark tresses of her hair between his fingers, and pull her into his embrace.

The sound of many horses brought an end to the beauty of that dream. A man's voice shouted, "There, the house in the clearing. Drag the witch forth!"

"They have come for me," Ariana said, and stood away from Calder. She did not spare a glance out the window for the men gathered beyond the door, but stared into the fire in the grate. Her arms began to tremble.

"I will tell them what you tried to do for the crofter's

wife," he said to soothe her fears. "I beg you, do not be so afraid. I will tell them and make them understand."

"It is you who does not understand. They have come to kill the witch. Think you anything would stop them?"

"I stand between them and thee, my Lady."

"They will burn me."

"Not while I live."

Her lips turned up at the corners, the barest trace of a smile. "Take my hand, Calder. Your love gives me courage and comfort."

In the next moment, the door broke in, and five men armed with broadswords, mace truncheons, and hand axes forced their way into the stone house. Calder pushed Ariana behind him, and swung into the foray of men with the battle-tempered arm of his sword.

A red-haired ox of a man felt the crush of Calder's blade across his thick neck. He fell to his knees, gasping for air from a throat that was stained with a seeping flow of blood.

Another came forward, and him too Calder struck, running his sword through the bony wall of the man's chest. "Duncan!" another of the men shouted. "He's killed Duncan!"

From behind him Calder heard a cry, turned, and saw a gray-bearded man climb through the window and grab Ariana. His dagger was at her throat.

"Ariana!"

Calder lunged for the graybeard, exposing his back to the three men just inside the door. As he drew back his sword arm, he felt the pierce of a dagger's blade between his shoulders. The last he saw, before all light faded, was Ariana being dragged from the house.

Calder regained his senses, hearing the crackling of the fire. Heat scorched the air he breathed, and the singed smell of burned flesh was in his nostrils. Then he heard her scream . . . and knew.

"Ariana!" He tried to rise from the floor, but a pole of agony tore the muscles of his back. The dagger had found its mark, nearly costing his life, but still he breathed. While he lived, he would fight for Ariana's life, too.

Her cries of torment brought him to his knees, and then to his feet. On will alone he stumbled from the room and out onto the cleared ground before the house. The sight that met him nearly took the spirit from his life. Ariana was tied to the base of a tree. Around her, laid close against her bare legs, was piled an inferno of blazing wood. And the flames burned her.

The priest and his men stood to one side, watching from a safe distance. They made no move to stop Calder as he took each halting step toward the fire. "Lay no hand on him," said the priest. "Let him join her in the devil's torch."

His legs grew weaker, scarcely able to carry him. He felt pain shoot through his back with every step. But he walked to-ward her . . . toward the heat and the flames. Now he could not feel his legs, but the terror in her eyes dragged him forward. If he fell into the flames, he would stand with her. Stand with her even unto death.

The fire climbed her dress and caught in the dark lengths of her hair. Her screams crazed the canopy of sky, crazed his eyes that looked upon her, and all that was the world to him. He would cut her free. If they killed him for it, he would cut her free. He dragged the sword behind him, unable to lift the weight of it with his right arm.

"He means to cut her bonds!" shouted one of the priest's men. "Stop him! He would set the witch free!"

As he swung the mighty sword, the priest's men pulled at his arm, ripping the hilt from his grasp. Calder felt the rain of their blows on his back and legs, heavy truncheons that struck with killing force.

But he stood beside her, with only his courage and his love to comfort her terror and agony. In that instant, Calder thrust his arm into the flames and grasped Ariana's hand.

"I'm here!" he shouted. "I would not leave you, Lady."

The fire burned his hand. He felt the flames sear his flesh. But he did not leave her. Only now did her dark eyes focus on his, and for a moment he knew she saw his love.

The blow of a truncheon landed on Calder's back. He felt his body break as if in two, and he fell senseless to all.

When James Calder opened his eyes, he was sitting, slumped facedown over the table in a dim corner of the bar. His hand was clenched into a fist. It hurt to pry his fingers open. The flesh of his hand was sound, the skin not reddened by flames or charred black.

"Ariana!"

He tried to stand—had to find her—but there was no feeling in his legs. He couldn't lift his weight from the chair. He hit the tops of his thighs with his fists, trying to awaken the muscles that had fallen asleep . . . and then he saw the wheels of the chair.

"Ariana!" he cried out again.

"Hey, fella. Pipe down," yelled the bartender. "It's getting late. I'm a reasonable joe. I let you sleep off your drunk, but it's time you go home."

"Where is she?" shouted Calder.

"Where is who? Oh, the old lady? She left when you passed out."

"No, not Eleanor." He was surprised he remembered the old woman's name. "Where's Ariana?"

"C'mon now, don't give me any trouble. I'm closing up. You'll get it all straight in your head tomorrow when you're sober."

How could this be? How could it all have disappeared? Ariana was real. He knew it, as surely as he knew his love for her. For the first time in his life, he had felt what it was to walk and run, to ride a horse and fight a battle. But he had lost far more than the strength of his legs. He had lost the only hope of love ever to cross his life.

Calder left the bar, pushing the wheels of his chair with the strength of his hands and arms. He knew where he lived, knew the house and the street. The key was in his pocket. This world was reality; the other had been a dream. With a heart as leaden as his legs, he followed the familiar streets to the lonely place he called home.

When the hardware store opened the next morning, Calder bought wire cutters. He didn't need a bag. "Save a tree," he said. The forest, green and lush . . .

Late that afternoon he carried the wire cutters with him to the freeway overpass. Today, the loneliness would end. He parked the wheelchair across the street from the bar, just as he had that other day. Was it only yesterday? So much had happened. Could it all have taken place in so little time?

With the wire cutters and the strength of his hands, he opened a wide gash in the fence. He leaned forward, watching the cars on the freeway below. His fingers curled between the spaces of the chain links. All he had to do was pull himself out of the chair and—

"Are you thinking of jumping, or driving?"

"What?" He turned his head to look, and all of his senses turned toward her, with a hope that had not died in the fire, or in the dream.

"Hello, Calder." It was Eleanor, old and wrinkled. Not Ariana.

He lunged at her with the wire clippers, tipping over his chair and falling out onto the sidewalk. "Do you know what you've done?"

"What is it you think I've done?"

"You let them kill her, Ariana—you let her die."

As he spoke, he saw the deep lines of her face begin to fade, and her gray hair darken to a lustrous black. The eyes that stared at him from Eleanor's face became glossy and dark as the pool of water where he first saw her.

"Ariana? Is it really you, or some trick?"

"What does it matter? Am I not the lady you loved? And are you not the man who offered his hand into the fire to comfort her?"

"But, how can you be here? How can we be together in this place?"

"Only for a moment. I cannot stay. We have been granted a boon, Calder, a gift. I came here to see you, then I must go."

He couldn't believe she was to be taken from him again. "I would have died to stay with you," he told her.

"Yes, I know. Long ago," she said, "something I did caused the end of earthly life for my people. Most of the Old Ones fled to the Western Isles, but some became trapped in this world, like the water wraith, the face you saw in the forest pool. For the harm I caused, a punishment was given to me—to return to the world every few centuries and relive the way I died."

He was horrified. "You were burned more than once?"

She nodded. "Many times."

"And yet you came back."

"I had no choice. Through age after age, I have searched for a champion who would risk his life to save me. Always, I chose strong men, those who I believed would fight for me with the strength of their arms. But when the fire threatened, they abandoned me to the flames. All," she said, "until you. Your courage and love have freed me of my bonds to this world."

"But, I failed. I didn't save you from the fire."

"You tried, that is what matters. You would have given your life to spare mine. Now would you like to come with me?" She held out her hand to him.

"Yes . . . what do you mean?"

"Rise to your feet, Calder. At first we will walk, you and I, and then the stallion will come for us and carry us along the hidden path to the Western Isles."

He looked around him. "Will I ever return here, to this life?"

"No," she told him. "We go to another world, prepared long ago for the Old Ones."

"You're one of them?"

"I am. And I choose you to love. Will you come with me now, and leave this world behind?"

To his amazement, Calder's legs bore his weight when he stood. He stepped across a threshold of courage and belief, and into Ariana's arms. Hand in hand, they walked west, toward the setting sun.

When the patrons of the bar saw the huge gap in the fence, the wheelchair tipped over on its side, and the wire cutters lying on the sidewalk, they believed James Calder had jumped to his death. Although his body was never found, a small service was held for the benefit of the few people who knew him.

"How do we chart the map of loneliness?" asked the minister. "Where can it lead the human heart? Let us cast our hopes in the prayer that James Calder has found the happiness he never knew here."

The Scout, the Slugger and the Stripper

RANDY MILLER

ddie Oslin decided to chance the green chili enchilada plate. He hoped the exquisite bitter burning in his belly would take his mind off the tumbleweed that had barreled across U.S. 87 and knocked his compact rental car off the shoulder, blowing out the rear tire. The midget spare, of course, was flat and Oslin crawled into the hamlet of Camel. He knew he wasn't leaving soon when he saw one of the last gas pumps in America without digital numbers. He'd opted for a walk to Romero's Café after he saw that the junk-food machines were as old and dusty as the pumps.

The mechanic had to send Junior to Big Spring to get the right size tire, since compact cars weren't very popular in Camel. Junior, Oslin suspected, would make a side trip to the liquor store.

He hoped he could get the car on the road and over to Midland before Southwest's last flight to Dallas. To civilization. To a place where the wind didn't blow constantly and where the sky wasn't choked with dirt and where garages carried tires and where God didn't send tumbleweeds across the highway. And, of course, back to the house where the blessed bat was safely stored.

Oslin munched on the greasy chips, absently dipping them into the small bowl of red sauce while studying his pocket calendar to see when he could catch the Midland Lee High shortstop next month. He'd scouted Texas Tech and New Mexico State last night in Lubbock—filed his report that the Red Raider catcher had improved his footwork some but still needed to work on his throwing.

As he finished the searing enchilada, dipping forkfuls into the refried beans, Oslin wondered why the Regals bothered to scout West Texas anyway. Nobody ever signed many prospects out here—the wind whipped in during the spring at thirty to forty miles per hour, and the schools had to have a windblock of trees to shield the diamonds. Most small towns didn't have so much as a diamond; their kids ran horribly slow track times—to prepare them for football—and got ready to work on the crops and cattle for the summer.

In civilization, he thought, a scout could toss a pebble in any direction and find a prospect in Dallas or Houston or Austin. He gulped the coffee, paid the cashier, lumbered out of Romero's Café and decided to take a ten-minute tour of Camel. If he had to waste an afternoon, he could at least get some exercise.

He turned east at the corner, after passing empty storefronts and a hardware store. The wind took his royal-blue Regals cap and carried it down the gravel street. When Oslin tracked it down, he looked across the street.

He was standing outside of the worst baseball diamond he had ever seen. The field had no grass at all—just hard brown earth, weeds, burrs and broken glass. It was an affront to anyone who'd spent his life in baseball, and he hated the town for allowing it to degenerate.

A group of kids were practicing and four of them began trudging toward Oslin behind the right-field fence. His professional instincts kicked in. Two scrawny teenagers, one Mexican and one white, hopped the fence and set up across the street. He looked toward the plate and saw the biggest kid—maybe six feet two, 190 pounds—step into the batter's box. The pitcher threw and the ball rocketed through the wind, over the fence and over the glove of the short white kid.

After the big guy blasted the fourth straight over the fence, Oslin asked the Mexican kid—in dugout Spanish—about the big kid. He learned that Arturo Reyes was at the plate, that he had recently graduated from high school and that he would start to work on a ranch outside of town. And he had never played organized baseball. Arturo had played quarterback and linebacker for the Camel High Fighting Camels six-man football team and led the basketball team in rebounding.

Oslin tried to study the kid dispassionately. He had some flaws in his swing, but his raw power compensated for those. Arturo let the pitcher bat and moved to shortstop. Oslin ran through the checklist in his head. Quickness? Ten. Arm? Powerful. Footwork? Fair, needs work on form. Glove? Incredible, considering the condition of the field.

Oslin wanted a closer inspection. He stepped gingerly across the field and began stretching his arm.

"Guys, would you mind if I threw a few pitches to your friend here? Could you play catcher?"

"No need. Arturo can hit anything you can throw." The big guy looked away.

"Old guy like me needs a target, that's all. I just want to see if your friend is as good as he looks."

The kids trotted into position, and Oslin set up where the mound should have been. He was sixty years old, but could still throw a little batting practice to minor leaguers in Florida. Better yet, he could make a baseball curve, which was more than the teenagers here could. Arturo was wearing cutoff jeans and a faded-to-leaden tanktop; he had a nice, wiry build with powerful shoulders.

Arturo took fifteen pitches over the fence through the wind. Oslin tried the curve and a knuckleball. He tried high and low and inside and outside, and the kid hit every one of them.

"I don't suppose you might consider a career in professional baseball," Oslin asked.

Arturo shrugged. "You mean like Nolan Ryan?"

"I think maybe I do. It pays a lot more than fieldwork. I'd have to see you against some real pitchers on a real field, but you just might have what it takes. You ever play any organized baseball?"

"Never have. Always sort of wanted to."

After a long conversation with the Reyes parents, he learned that Arturo had spent most of his summers traveling with the family on the migrant trail. Arturo was the only one of seven kids who had made it through high school.

Later, after the car was fixed, after he'd mentioned the words *signing bonus* to the parents, after he'd met Arturo's coaches, Oslin left Camel.

He turned off the highway ten miles outside of town, drove about another mile and stopped near a cotton gin. He did not worry about catching a flight now. He killed the ignition and stepped into the dark. No sound. There, in the utter silence in which a person can hear heavenly whispers, Oslin gave thanks for a God-sent tumbleweed. And he prayed that he had found someone who could handle the bat.

Oslin arranged an audition for next weekend down in Big Spring at the Howard Junior College diamond. Arturo, wearing faded maroon sweats and a Camel High basketball jersey over a white T-shirt, didn't crush every pitch that the junior college guys threw him. But he adjusted to each pitcher's stuff—the sharp sliders and the moving fastballs—and he eventually took some over the wall. In the infield, he was only fair, but he showed good instincts and quick legs in the outfield.

"Oslin, I'm ready to sign that kid to a scholarship right now. I just don't believe he's never played a day in his life. Unpolished, he's better than most of my guys right now," said Harry Lambert, the Howard coach.

"Harry, I have it on good authority that Arturo never wants to enter another classroom in his life. I'm going to sign him, but first I want to try something. I'll need about twenty more pitches."

Oslin called the kid over and congratulated him. "Arturo, I would like for you to try something for me. I have here a heavier bat than you've been using. In fact, it's forty-four ounces, as heavy as you can use in baseball. And it's a very special bat; I used it when I played forty years ago. I just want to see if you can swing it."

"Sure. Doesn't feel that heavy to me. Feels good, in fact."

Arturo took a few swings and stepped in against the college left-hander. The first pitch got by and so did the second. The left-hander saw the sign for the slider and as he let the pitch go, the ball rocketed off the bat and sailed far over the center-field fence. So did the next one and the next one. Lambert dropped his tobacco from his mouth. The Howard players whooped in amazement. The pitcher just walked off the mound, mumbling.

And Oslin, eyes shining, began plotting his way to the major leagues.

He'd spent forty-one seasons in professional baseball, but it was the one season away that had kept Oslin from the majors. He'd started down in Class D, back when every town in America seemed to have a minor-league club. The manager was

Gussie Groelsch, half drunk and waiting to die there in the middle of Nowhere, Nebraska. One twilight evening, Gussie hadn't shown and Oslin, the new kid on the team, had been voted to roust the coach from his barstool.

He'd found him in his rented two-bedroom bungalow three blocks from the stadium. He'd helped him to the toilet and closed the door. Oslin thought a seriously drunken man ought to have some privacy.

Oslin saw little in the living room, but decided to examine the faded framed photograph hung over a tattered bed in the other room. A young Gussie Groelsch stood with arm around a man with a massive chest, thick lips and a wide, wide smile. Any American ballplayer who'd grown up before World War II could identify the Babe.

And then he saw the bat and, like any eighteen-year-old, hefted it to his shoulder.

For just a moment, it felt like lifting a girder. And, then, in dusk's light through a grimy window, the bat seemed to shimmer for the briefest of moments. Oslin studied it. The tape on the handle was nearly black, and the smooth wood was darker, like his father's Tampico cigars, than the nut-brown ash used by his teammates.

A raspy whisper came from the doorframe. "He was the best. Gave me the bat when we barnstormed back in '23. He was repaying me for helping him duck a certain angry young woman. I saw him hit one five hundred feet with it in Paducah, Kentucky, one day. Knocked a bird's nest out of a tree. He always said that he hit his first World Series home run with it."

Oslin could still remember taking a few cuts in Groelsch's cheap bedroom. The coach's bleary eyes focused briefly and then closed.

"It just looks right with you, son. Not everybody can handle a bat like that. Most can't. So I guess it's yours.

"Look, I ain't gonna make it to the park tonight. Take it

and see if you can handle it. It's heavy, so you shouldn't let it warp your swing. But you got the shoulders to handle it. Have Barron make out the lineup tonight."

Oslin didn't start on that June evening, but he lugged the bat to the plate in the bottom of the ninth to pinch-hit for the pitcher. One swing and the ball disappeared past the lights into the Nebraska night.

So did Gussie Groelsch. He was dead when Oslin and the others came to check after the game. While waiting for the doctor to show up, one of his teammates found a baseball in the front yard, and Eddie Oslin knew—beyond any question—that the home run somehow had rolled to Gussie Groelsch's doorstep.

Oslin rushed through the Evangeline League, the Sally League, the Texas League—racking up big averages and mammoth homers at each successive level—and into triple-A Rochester when the season ended.

Then the army called, and on a hill in Korea on the majors' Opening Day, Oslin took some grenade shrapnel in his left knee. Twenty years too early for the designated hitter, Oslin knew his career had ended before it had barely begun.

After three years of scruffing around the minors as a full-time pinch hitter, Oslin entered the Regals chain as a scout. He gave them a full season's work for twenty-five seasons, wearing out his tired butt on aluminum bleachers, watching thousands of players, and secretly hoping to find one who might handle the forty-four-ounce bat. He was considered by most baseball executives to be one of the best scouts who ever lived.

He set up a rack in his garage and worked the bat's grain against bone for hours every winter. In the late sixties, he paid three thousand bucks to fix the dry rot in his wooden frame house.

The bat did not rot.

*   *   *

The kid just stared at the water in Tampa Bay as Oslin headed across the causeway toward the Regals' headquarters in Clearwater—hell, after eighteen years eating dust on the Texas plains, he guessed anybody would stare. Arturo had passed Oslin's assignments well. Unlike ninety-five percent of today's ballplayers, he could identify a photo of Babe Ruth. Oslin had been pleased when Arturo understood the importance of the bat's heritage.

When they reached the stadium, Oslin sent Arturo to the locker room while he met with Rudy Prince, the minor-league director.

Prince was not pleased. "I don't understand this letter, Oslin. Personal consultant? Guaranteed special coach to one kid? A major-league coaching position when the kid makes it?"

Oslin remembered the faces on the teenagers in Camel. Prince would see. "I have worked twenty-five years for this organization without once complaining," he said. "I am the loyal soldier.

"Simply put, if you don't agree now—Arturo Reyes unseen—I'll drive over to the Jolters in Saint Pete, then head over to the Firecats in Bradenton. There's some guys in this sport who would be working construction today if I hadn't recommended them. Someone will cash in their chits.

"But I came to you first, Rudy. Loyalty means something to Oslin. But it's a loyalty that demands payment."

"What if he can't play?"

"If you don't like him, then I eat his plane fare and we go have some margaritas on the beach. But you'd better sign now."

Arturo stepped onto the field with his bat as Rudy and Oslin settled in seats behind the plate. A week ago, he'd never even seen sanitary socks and now he looks like an all-star, Oslin thought. He held up his hand and Arturo stopped. A pitcher and catcher were warming up along the foul line.

"I can see the headlines now, Rudy: 'Regals Executive Fired for Passing Up the Next Babe Ruth. Stupidest Move in Baseball History.' "

Rudy sighed and Oslin waved. The pitcher was a former major-leaguer, Dan DeSalvo, who had been released by the Jolters last fall. When at his best, DeSalvo had a ninety-mile-per-hour tailing fastball and sharp curve.

The pitcher started in with the disdain for the batter—all batters—he'd learned in his six minor-league seasons before he'd earned one shot at the majors. He craved another. DeSalvo was unshaven and his eyes were narrow and sullen. He wanted to deck the punk in the new uniform, but didn't dare throw inside on the first pitch. Instead, he would give the kid the fastball, tailing outside of the strike zone.

DeSalvo's jaw fell when the ball sailed over the left-field fence. He really wanted to drop the kid, but Prince over in the stands signaled for the curve. The pitcher felt the good snap out of his wrist, saw the pitch begin to dive for the dirt—and then watched it sail over second base, a line drive to the warning track.

The veteran got the kid to miss occasionally, but never twice on the same pitch, same location. Finally, he paused, turned and came in with the high, hard one toward the kid's head. The kid sprawled in the dirt.

Prince was ready to scream at DeSalvo, but Oslin simply whispered, "Make him throw one more over the plate." Prince signaled. DeSalvo delivered and Arturo Reyes swung. The ball ricocheted off the pitcher's ankle and the crack could be heard clearly throughout the ballpark.

Prince stared at Oslin. "Did he do that intentionally?"

"Does it really matter, Rudy? Does it really matter? All you need to know is that no other scout and no other team has seen this kid yet."

Rudy locked his hands behind his head, leaned back and

smiled like a dog leaning from a car window. "You know, if he has a bad rookie year, he'll only hit forty home runs."

Six weeks later, Arturo Reyes was the scourge of the Florida State League. He was hitting .426 with twenty home runs, and even the big local dailies, who never covered minor-league ball, were tracking him. The team manager, Don Washburn, was quoted: "If you have any money lying around, buy as many of his rookie cards as you can and lock them up. In twenty years, you'll be rich. I haven't seen anyone like him. He's teachable, he's strong, he's fast and he's a natural leader. If you know how to clone someone, let me know immediately; I'd almost trade my wife and a kid to be named later for Arturo Reyes."

Oslin watched the kid from behind the Regals' dugout. Arturo had learned the art of catching fly balls in a day, and his throwing had improved steadily—no one dared try to take a base on him now. He'd learned to switch-hit in twenty minutes. He'd figured out how to navigate on the basepaths and how to slide properly. He'd learned how to deal with traveling and baseball living. And he was simply crushing minor-league pitching. And best of all, the scout could see that Arturo had learned to appreciate the game. You could see it in his stride while running the bases and in his bearing at the plate and in his smile while studying the pitcher in the dugout.

The deal with Prince was working well. In two more weeks, Oslin and Arturo Reyes were scheduled to board a plane to the majors. Even Prince admitted the kid was just about ready. Arturo's parents would never pick another peanut or onion again—they had received a whopping signing bonus large enough to buy Camel, Texas, already. The kid was getting good money for an eighteen-year-old and he'd get more in two weeks.

Oslin knew the rookie throwing for the minor-league

Pipers tonight. He'd scouted Rod McCleary with fifteen other guys, all pointing radar guns at the college boy from TCU. Rod McCleary was a first-round amateur draft pick. He'd been all-America and led the Horned Frogs to the College World Series. And, for the first time in his life, Rod McCleary was not the best player on the field. Oslin was ready to enjoy the mismatch.

The Regals' first two batters went down easily and the crowd began to scream, "Ar-tur-oooooool" McCleary juggled the resin bag and checked his outfielders. He looked toward the plate and saw the young slugger still strolling to the plate.

And then a very, very buxom young woman ran on to the field while the security guards stood transfixed. She reached Arturo Reyes and planted a dramatic kiss on his surprised lips while the guards slowly walked over. They reached the woman to escort her off the field, and Arturo Reyes called time, pushed them away and kissed her hand with the long, painted fingernails and offered his left arm. She slipped hers daintily around his and he walked her back to her seat.

Most of the fans cheered the gallantry. Others laughed at the sight. Only one, sitting directly behind the dugout, fumed. Oslin bolted to his feet and cursed when Rod McCleary struck the kid out on three pitches.

Morton Strange, whose business card read professional agent, had been chatting with his newest client, the Fabulous Fatima, after work one night.

"What could be worse than working in this dump? You got cockroaches in the dressing room, you get pawed by drunken rednecks, you can't make any money if you don't screw the customers on the side, and you got a stage name, the Fab'lous Fatima. It's degrading to you as a human being.

"You need to be involved in something with class, like porn films."

Bertha Ann Stegall could think of lots of worse things.

Being named Bertha, for one, and then having size 44-DD breasts erupt from a thirteen-year-old chest. Being called Big Bertha. Growing up with rusted appliances and Pontiacs in the front yard. Being punched silly by your mother. Being molested by your father.

Even wearing a crummy plaid jacket and passing yourself off as an agent, like the last one, wasn't as good as table dancing at the Ale 'n' Tail.

Porn films were out. Too many of her co-workers had tried that avenue, and, besides, underneath the false eyelashes and the blush and the blond wash, Bertha Ann didn't think she had the face to do real films, even real porn films.

Morton Strange then suggested the baseball ruse. It had been done before, and better, maybe. "Publicity is publicity, and this baseball guy is supposedly the talk of the town. It'll probably get some play."

"Baseball players give me a pain, Mortie."

As the Fabulous Fatima, Bertha Ann had known ballplayers from their spring-training ventures into every bar and strip joint in Florida. Too many of them were, too often, cheap tippers, loud drunks, and insulting to women. She hated them, the other dancers hated them, the bouncers hated them—usually because brawls seemed to occur regularly when the players walked in.

But the new agent was probably right, she thought. Besides, it wasn't that she had to like the guy, just kiss him. After growing up in Shacktown, after third-rate trailer parks, and after a string of strip dives, a kiss wasn't much.

The next evening, they went into the minor-league park and sat next to the gate leading to the field. She had white shorts and a rose-colored halter, covered temporarily by a man's blue dress shirt. The agent made her button it to the collar. "You wouldn't want to attract too much attention before your big moment, babe."

The Fabulous Fatima took her cue, peeled off the shirt and, with Strange's assistance, entered the field of play. She hated the way she must look but knew she had to get to home plate before the guards. She laughed to keep from crying.

She looked into his eyes. Fatima had seen in the eyes of men lust, greed, contempt, hate and any combination of those. But, until now, never respect.

The Fabulous Fatima didn't say a word to Morton Strange on the drive back to the Ale 'n' Tail.

"I like her, Mr. Oslin," Arturo Reyes said, thinking of the decidedly unglamorous farm girls back in Camel. "She is the most beautiful woman I have ever seen."

"Well, you haven't seen very many women, then. She ain't nothing but a pair of tits, son. I've seen floozies like that from Hawaii to New York and they're all the same. She's looking to get her hooks into you, Arturo. She sees some quick money and somebody to dump on the side of the road. They don't use the word much anymore, but she's a harpy. A shrew. They were that way when I played ball and they're still that way. Forget her." Eddie Oslin had used variations on that theme for two weeks now.

Arturo whispered back, "I cannot." And he worked on boning the bat.

In two weeks, Oslin thought, the whore had shown up for the six home games and two road games, and Arturo hadn't a hit in those games. When she hadn't shown, he'd pulverized the opponents.

He had tried to buy her off down in that dive. She refused—she haughtily refused—as if she were the Queen of Sheba instead of some cheap slut. He'd yelled and screamed and her weasel of an agent had the bouncer toss him out. The agent, he thought, was torn between the payday of somehow signing Arturo and losing his poisonous stripper.

She'd sent Arturo flowers the next day. He'd sent her a hundred dollars' worth of red roses the day before.

Oslin hadn't slept, listening to see if his meal ticket would try to sneak out like some dopey adolescent with surging hormones.

When the scout fell asleep on the apartment couch the next night, the next Babe Ruth sneaked out to the parking lot and met Bertha Ann Stegall.

They talked in the front seat of her battered old Volkswagen. Until dawn.

"It seems to me like we're both in the same situation, Arturo. We got these people riding our coattails."

"What would you really like to do, Bertha Ann?"

"Turn letters on 'Wheel of Fortune,' of course, or some other game show. Game shows are very nice, don't you think? You get to wear beautiful clothes and you don't have to dance."

"If that's really what you want, why not?"

"No, what I want is to never have to dance before a bunch of creeps again. Never have to screw customers and live off tips. And get these down to a decent size. Maybe go to art school. And what do you want?"

"The only field I like is a baseball field. I never want to pick another onion again. I like playing baseball fine. But I won't do it without you."

The couple made four stops that morning. They ate eggs and biscuits and sausage gravy at the Village Inn, went through the doors as the first customers at Service Merchandise, were married by the self-proclaimed world's oldest justice of the peace, Sam Rudnick (More Than 300,000 Served). They then borrowed the Yellow Pages from a clerk in the courthouse, opened to page 87 and, hands held, pointed to the name Paul Noble, attorney-at-law.

Oslin, worn from a day of frantic searching, entered the locker room with the same large-eyed expression that parents have when their children survive a Superman plunge from the garage roof. The stranger in the Italian suit next to him wore the expression of a parent whose daughter had come home two hours late on a date with a boy who owns a van. Arturo wore no expression, but seemed to have a gold band around a chain on his neck. Even in the bliss of matrimony, he knew he could n't wear a wedding band on the hand while batting.

The lawyer explained the matter as the security guard with the shiny black holster approached. He, Paul Noble, had obtained a temporary restraining order until such time as Mr. Noble, acting as the agent for Mr. Reyes, and Mr. Oslin could negotiate a settlement on the obviously poorly considered agreement. Noble then showed Oslin the agreement that the lawyer was now the ballplayer's agent—and the stripper's as well.

"The Regals don't really want you; they want Arturo, and judging from his statistics, I can understand why. As long as you and Arturo were able to maintain a cordial relationship, the agreement was fine. But after two weeks of your harping constantly about his new wife, he has come to the decision that you and he must come to a parting of the ways."

"It's that damn bitch. She did this, didn't she?"

"I must assure you that it was not. Mr. Reyes asked me to inform you that it was his idea and only his idea. We are willing to be quite generous in our settlement, but the Regals have decided that they'd rather have Arturo in their clubhouse than have you in their clubhouse and Arturo playing ball in Chicago or New York."

"What about my bat? At least give me my bat back."

"I'm afraid you have a bad memory, Mr. Oslin. We already have affidavits from people back in Texas who witnessed your oral contract with Mr. Reyes. You did not say, 'Arturo, I will loan you this bat,' you said, 'Arturo, let me give you this bat.' There is a huge difference, Mr. Oslin."

Eddie Oslin just turned and walked out to his rental car and sat gripping his steering wheel. He was still numb ten minutes later when the security guys tossed Morton Strange from the premises as the lawyer and the big-bosomed woman with the diamond on her finger watched.

The checks came by direct deposit so that Oslin wouldn't have to sully his hands on them. He'd quit the Regals cold and found that his reputation had grown. The Pipers and the Greyhounds hired and fired the man who found Arturo Reyes because he wouldn't send in his reports.

Reyes, as every fan knows, hit .350 in his rookie season and smacked three home runs in the World Series. The Regals sent Eddie Oslin a World Series ring; he sent it back slightly mangled by a welding torch.

Unfortunately for the Regals, they decided that the agent from Florida wasn't serious about renegotiation demands, and Arturo jumped over to the Jolters in time for spring training, signing a record contract.

On a miserable stormy June evening in Texas, the lights in Eddie Oslin's neighborhood flickered and went out briefly. Texas Electric managed to restore power in mere minutes and it wasn't until the next day that a keen-eyed jogger spotted the body on Oslin's roof holding the antenna. It was quickly recorded as an accidental death by the police, but one of the officers on the scene accurately noted that the victim's face appeared to be enraged.

The officer checked with the electric company and found out that power had gone out at 8:43 P.M. He examined the TV set and found the screen was smashed while tuned to Channel 8. A new advertisement had debuted during "Coach" minutes earlier.

Offscreen voice:	*Arturo Reyes, baseball hero, is it your glove?*
Arturo:	*It's not the glove.*
Offscreen voice:	*Is it your arm?*
Arturo:	*It's not the arm.*
Offscreen voice:	*Is it your bat?*
Arturo:	*It's not the bat.*
Offscreen voice:	*Is it your shoes?*
Arturo:	*No. Wrong commercial. It's my cologne. Fair Ball. For when you don't want to be foul.*
Offscreen voice:	*Mrs. Reyes, is it the cologne?*
Fatima:	*It's more than the cologne.*

The police report noted one other unusual fact. Found in the middle of the front lawn, near the unretrieved morning paper, was one baseball, slightly scuffed. Perhaps, the officer theorized, Oslin had thrown the baseball outside during a rage, or perhaps not.

The Weapon

ARDATH MAYHAR

he buried weapon slept, for nothing had disturbed it for over a millennium, and its powers had been withdrawn into the depths of time. The earth surrounding it was quiet and damp. Not since a grieving knight flung it into a forgotten lake, there to be hidden away, had the sword tingled with its charge of unlimited potential.

Those hidden potencies had become less-than-memory, unlikely ever to wake again. Perhaps, if greed had not disturbed the thing, it might never have roused.

The local people stood about grumbling, watching the clearing of the site with avid interest. Bringing in an American construction company to build this complex was one in the eye for them, with work so slow. Henry Carnes could tell that the thought of the fat wages those strangers earned was slow torture to men whose families were living on the dole.

Jordan Harp's arrival shifted their attention to a flat space where ancient forest had stood a week ago. "Nobbut an American would visit a building site in a bloody helicopter," one leathery fellow muttered. Even though they said nothing, it was obvious that his companions agreed.

But Henry hurried to greet his employer, hoping he would be satisfied with this beginning. The shopping complex Harp intended to build here in this picturesque area promised to add even more millions to his astonishing hoard. It was only one of dozens scattered about the globe, every one set in the middle of what had been a remnant of natural beauty and now had become asphalt parking lots.

Harp was staring about, checking the damp, bare-scraped soil that had once been a bog, the leveled forest, now reduced to sticks and stubble. This was what he loved to see, Henry thought for the thousandth time, nature subjected to his will. That seemed to be the man's real goal, rather than more useless millions.

Harp absently twirled his raw-gold medallion, twisting it about his forefinger as he examined the site. That, too, was a symbol of his power.

"Here are the plans, sir." Henry took the roll of blueprints from the foreman. "Would you like me to show you where everything will be?"

"No." The voice was high-pitched, rather old-maidish, though the man had the reputation of being a womanizer from his youth. "It is about to begin. That is all I need. You're employed to design and oversee the building of the damned thing. Get to it!"

He turned his back rudely and moved toward the knot of English laborers. They glared back at him balefully over the fence enclosing the construction area, and Henry felt a sudden qualm.

He hurried after Harp and touched his elbow. "It might be best not to get too near those fellows, sir. They're bent out of shape because they've not been hired to do the work. We've had some minor vandalism, but I suspect some of those very men may be responsible. We wouldn't want you to have a problem with them, now, would we?"

Harp turned and stared at him, as if unable to understand. "Have a problem? With *those* . . . ?" He waved a contemptuous hand toward the glowering crew beyond the fence. "Surely you're kidding!"

But to Henry's relief he turned away, walked the perimeter of the first building site, and got into the chopper again. Not until he was safely aloft did Henry relax and return to his duties. Designing a shopping center of this size was hard enough without having to nursemaid that egotistical . . . but he caught himself. Not for him to criticize the one who paid him so handsomely for his services.

The bulldozers were ready to dig the foundation holes. In such heavy, wet soil you had to do that right, or there would be settling and all kinds of problems down the road. Even in the wet British climate, surely he could get that done by midsummer, foundation down, maybe even the interior dried in. It was only early May, after all.

The first dozer was going down fast. The driver's head was disappearing at the bottom of his trench now, and the other machines were busy in their own areas. Henry strolled to the edge of the cut and looked down, watching the peaty soil pile up ahead of the heavy blade.

George gunned the engine and started across the bottom. There was a sudden painful screech of metal on stone, and the bulldozer came to a halt. Henry jumped down into the cut, concerned.

There wasn't supposed to be any rock at this level. This could be something moved in long ago when the ancient Britons were putting up their stone circles. If this was such a matter, they might be hung up for months, fighting it out with the antiquities people.

But Henry had figured out ways of getting around such

things. What wasn't officially found never became a problem. If he located some antique-looking stone and smashed it to flinders, it would become just more gravel to be hauled away.

George backed the dozer away from the obstacle, his blade shrilling along the obstruction. The dirt fell in behind it, but Henry glimpsed a pale gray length before it was covered.

"Come on, George, and bring your shovel. Let's see what's hanging you up," he called, his voice pitched to reach no farther than the driver.

Together they scraped the damp clumps of soil away from the coffin-shaped stone. Henry frowned. That was a hard son of a bitch. He'd never break it with what he had. Then he wondered if it was as thick as it looked.

"Let's dig down beside it," he said.

They found, once they used the spade vigorously, that the thing was only some ten inches thick. Henry grinned. "We can pry it up, roll it onto its side, and break it with the blade," he said.

They heaved, and it sucked free to stand on edge. It was a handsome thing, Henry noted regretfully. Carved with twining vines that framed a lion in one loop and a sword in another, it had to be extremely old. This area had been bog for as long as any local account could recall.

For an instant Henry hesitated. He loved old things, even when his work demanded that he destroy them. The ancient trees that had already fallen grieved him, but he had hitched his destiny to that of Jordan Harp. That meant he had to become a destroyer, building altars to wealth instead of creating structures of beauty.

But George was raising the dozer blade, shaking off the dirt, getting it positioned above the edge of the stone coffer. Henry stepped back, and George brought the heavy metal down onto the thing.

There was a grinding crack, a flash of light, and George

screamed. Henry saw the metal of the bulldozer begin to glow, red to yellow to white, blindingly brilliant. George jerked spasmodically, and for an instant his skeleton was a shadow beneath his dissolving flesh.

Henry felt himself pushed backward, to land against the wall of the cut, his face singed by the holocaust that enveloped the bulldozer. As the light began to turn red again, dying away, he shook his head. *Where are the men? Haven't they heard or seen what happened down here?* he wondered.

He staggered forward, his shoes heating against the smoldering earth. Beneath the blade of the dozer lay segments of gray stone, cracked apart in regular sections as if they had been assembled so. A glint of brightness shone amid the parts, and compelled by some unknown power, Henry bent and touched it.

His fingers touched icy metal, there in the middle of that steaming pile. Without thinking about poor George or the ruined dozer, he lifted it free.

A sword. Long, exquisitely worked yet clean of line, it fitted into his hand as if designed for it. He watched, dazed, as the steel blade rose high, moving his hand rather than being moved by it.

He struggled to control it, but still it moved, turning him to face the ruined bulldozer. The thing sank forward to touch, very gently, the fire-blackened blade.

Metal whispered on metal, as the entire mechanism crumbled into dust, which mingled with the ashes of its unhappy driver. In a heartbeat, nothing remained that might be identified as man or machine.

The sword tingled with a strange electrical charge, which now was dwindling. Henry managed to set it aside at last, his arm and hand numb, his mind overloaded with unanswerable questions.

Then the water began to come in. Henry grabbed the blade and climbed out of the ditch, frantically trying to outrace the flow. When he reached the top, he found that no worker was in sight, no bulldozer, no distant piles of girders.

Forest, ancient and unbroken, lay beyond the verges of a lake, now filling to its old measure. As Henry waded out of the lake, he saw with disbelief that he wore rags wrapped about his feet, a coarse tunic, and he could tell with ease that he wore no underwear.

He staggered into the shade of a great oak and dropped to the ground. The sword, still clutched in his hand, rang softly against one of the gnarled roots, and the sound seemed to still the breeze that had whispered through the leaves.

For one moment the birdsong that had filled the place went silent. Henry stared, stunned, at the lake, now filled with dark, peaty water, and the village that lay beyond it.

Wattle huts were clumped awkwardly about a pole that held an oddly shaped symbol on the top. A woman sat on a bench before a door, holding up a tunic much like his own and shaking her head over its ragged holes. Two men came out of the forest carrying a deer slung to a pole.

What had happened to him in that moment when the blade struck the coffer? Was he dead? Mad? Or had he returned to a time before the England he had come to know?

All the men, the machinery, everything had been reduced to dust, as George and the bulldozer had been. But the forest had been felled! How had it returned, in a matter of minutes, to its ancient glory? What power was contained in this long-buried sword?

Henry staggered to his feet. He must learn how far this alteration went. There had to be some limit to the change, and he would walk until he found it. Taking up the sword, which now was a heavy burden, he moved toward the east, where the sun climbed an unpolluted sky.

He was soon completely lost in the tangle of ancient boles and grasping roots. Stumbling, almost sobbing, he kept moving, afraid that he might be circling, for the sun was invisible through the thick canopy of branches.

Again the metal tingled with life, his fingers clenching harder about it. The sword moved, rose to point a direction. Henry had no other guide. He must follow its guidance.

For a long, long while he moved through the forest, and as it grew dark, the sword itself began to glow, a faint glimmer that was only a little better than no light at all.

He wondered why he never tired or grew hungry. It could only be some property of the sword, he thought, before his mind went numb. After that, his legs moved, his feet walked, his hand held the sword as if he were some robot, moving to the will of another.

Nights passed, and days, as he trudged through the forest. From time to time he came to a skimpy clearing, where huts held people who tilled small fields with crude wooden tools. Always the trees closed in again, and he began to understand why old texts referred to ancient England as a single forest from end to end.

His mind waked from its rest and began worrying with the questions that tormented him. Was there no end to this? Would he never emerge into the modern world of cleared lands, crowded cities, clogged skies?

When the sword rested, he forged ahead blindly. When it roused to life, he followed its pointing tip. And after many days of walking, he came to a spot where a ray of sunlight struck through a rent in the canopy. It sparkled on something dangling at arm's reach above the path.

Henry reached up and caught the golden bauble. Then he caught his breath in wonder and despair. He held Jordan Harp's medallion, which the man always wore: a golden harp on a golden chain with the initials *J.H.* engraved at the lower edge.

Had the helicopter dissolved as the bulldozer did, along

with its riders? Was this all that was left of the empire of chrome and steel and stone that Jordan Harp had created in a world that seemingly no longer existed? Had the strange effect of the sword moved outward like a ripple in a pond, changing all in its path? And why had it not changed this, too?

Then his engineer's mind woke. This was raw gold, as it had come from the earth into the hands of the jeweler. All that was artificial was dissolved into dust.

He felt with his tongue, suddenly remembering his amalgam filling. He had been too dazed to feel the gap where it had been, but now he realized that his jaw tooth was cratered. There was no tenderness, just a hollow where that man-made filling had rested, its surface feeling strangely glazed, as if something had melted there.

He lifted the chain, settled the harp onto his chest, and sighed. The sword was not done with him, yet. There was something left for him to accomplish, it was clear, for the haft tugged at his hand, and the point quested eagerly forward, pulling him along as if it were a hunting dog after game.

When he came out of the forest into clear sunlight and broad meadows, he blinked rapidly. It had been days since he had seen such brightness, and now it almost blinded him.

When he adjusted to the clarity of light and air, he realized that he was looking across a vast lake toward a city . . . a real city, though not a modern one. The tallest building was a tower inside the crenelated walls. Roofs of dull gray slate and red tiles rose higher than the walls, but none of them were at any great height above the ground.

For the first time since the strange quest began, Henry felt a flicker of excitement. He was looking at a medieval city, at least, perhaps one from the Dark Ages. As an architect, he found himself fascinated. Artists' conceptions and photographs of restored buildings were not, he saw at once, enough to show how one really looked.

He tried to move toward the lake. There must be some path or road that ran along its shore to that distant vision. But the sword would not yield its dominance. Instead, it jerked him, resisting and complaining, along the edge of the forest, toward a gap where a road cut through the trees.

At last he surrendered and followed, regretting the lost opportunity. In some strange way, his fate was compelled by the sword, and he knew that he must submit.

The road was only a cart-track, two worn marks winding through the forest, avoiding big trees or rocks or bad places to ford streams. After some distance, the land began to slope upward, and the trees became smaller, less tangled. And then, rounding a bend, Henry found himself staring up at a castle out of some book of fairytales: golden towers, battlements, gay flags snapping in the breeze from the sea below the cliff on which it stood.

The sword, which had been exerting a steady pull, began to pulsate, like an eager dog that sighted its master. Henry found himself running to keep up with his own hand and the blade that now sliced forward toward a gate in the wall. Its gleam had become a blaze and grew even brighter as Henry came near the moat that surrounded the wall.

Must I swim? Henry wondered.

But the sword did not hesitate. It swept into a figure eight, and pulleys began to creak as the drawbridge descended slowly to bridge the moat. Pulled along helplessly, Henry sprang onto the near edge, before the bridge was entirely down. Pell-mell, he hurtled toward the heavy gates, the blade leading the way. When it touched the iron-banded oak, the great gates shivered into splinters.

Henry felt his arm sink beneath the weight of the weapon. For the first time since he had started, the sword was entirely quiet, though his fingers still clasped it, unable to loose their grip. He had to raise it to keep the blade from trailing in the dust as he entered and looked about.

This was a place built for serious defense, he saw at once. Inside the gate was a small chamber with walkways about the top. Anyone breaching the gate in war would find himself trapped here while archers above poured arrows into his men. But the gates that should have closed it off on the inner side stood open, letting the soft air of May sweep through into the space beyond.

Four men in chain mail turned at his approach, staring at Henry with stunned gazes. Two women skittered across the cobbles and into open doors, which slammed behind them.

Henry held up the sword. Now it took on life again, began to tingle, then to throb. As two of the men drew swords and a third bellowed to the archers on the battlements, a tall man came down the steps of the inner keep and strode toward them.

Henry felt his knees move. He had never knelt to anyone in his life, but now he went down onto the cobbles and dust, holding out the sword to this lordly man, who now stood gazing down at him through quizzical hazel eyes.

"I have brought this . . . to you," he gasped. It was the first time he had spoken since George disappeared, along with his bulldozer.

The man spoke, but strain as he might, Henry could not understand his words. Still, the gloved hand stretched toward him and took the sword, which began to glow, its fires rising to new heights. A delicate humming filled the air, and Henry felt it inside his bones, which now seemed attuned to the weapon.

"Artorius Rex!" the guardsmen shouted. "Excalibur!"

Those hazel eyes met Henry's brown ones. Henry rose slowly, feeling himself compelled now by the power within the man. He felt the chain about his neck, lifted it over his head, and held it out to the King.

"It belonged to another king," Henry said. "Now it is

yours, and you will be a force for good. Why else should all this have happened?"

The long face smiled down at him. The King held the harp high, sparkling in the sunlight. "This is a symbol of power that is dark," he said, and though Henry did not understand the words, he heard the meaning clearly.

The King climbed a stone stairway to stand on the seaward battlement and look down at the curling waves. He spun the golden harp around his head and let it go. The bright sparkle whirled over the edge of the cliff and was quenched in the water below.

Then Arthur turned, his face blazing with joy. Again he spoke in the archaic tongue that now Henry could understand clearly. "The world is renewed. Not again will we see the dark days come. Men will be freed. Land will be tilled to richness, but the forests will not be destroyed. Cities will rise, but cleanly, without poisoning their people.

"Come, my friends. We must go out into this restored England and tell our people that the evil times have ended and the past has returned in better form and more hopeful guise."

Henry felt his heart thudding. Was the entire world changing as England had? Would he have the opportunity to see Arthur, returned to life as the old prophecy had predicted, take up his sword again and create a new and better life for mankind?

Smiling, he strode after the King and his men. Something inside him, long dormant, began to flower. This was going to be a life worth living!

The Sword in the Net

BRAD STRICKLAND

rmour rubbed eyes blasted sandpaper-raw by cathode-tube radiation, yawned, and touched a function key. A small black rectangle appeared in the upper-left corner of his computer screen. Time flashed in green numerals: 02:12:43. The last digit became a four, then a five, before Armour hit the key again to switch the time display off. Past two in the morning, and he had not slept since—when? Sunday night, forty-eight hours ago?

He yawned so widely that his jaw creaked. He pushed back from his computer desk and folded his arms. The computer hummed along efficiently without him, executing a complex program. It was a Merlin 686g with 40 meg of RAM, an 896 hard drive, a 19200 Roundtable modem, all the bells and whistles. Ten years ago, no institution smaller than a major research university would have owned such a machine. Armour had received it as a birthday present not long before.

He fumbled for a half-empty Coke can, swilled the flat, sweet contents, burped softly. If he wanted, he could display on the screen the operations status board of the program where

the alphanumeric codes flickered past, fast as thought. That had
lost its fascination a long time ago. If he wanted, he could slow
the program and use part of the machine's capacity to play a
game, whiling away the hours until the computer had completed its task.

What game would be fun? "Mayday Tournament," in
which he was always Lancelot? The mock–3-D graphics were
sharp; the digitized sounds of hoofbeats, crashing lances, clash-
ing swords exciting enough; but he had already mastered that
game. Not much fun just doing a replay when he'd already
learned all his opponents' sleights and tricks. Maybe "Empire
Conquest"? No, he'd already learned enough about military
and diplomatic maneuvering to become master of the globe in
less than three hours even at the Ultra level of play. Armour
yawned again and drained the last of the Coke. He'd just let the
program run its course.

Still it was hard, as hard as pulling teeth. He had written
the program himself, was sure it was sound and complete. Now
he only had to let it run—but he felt the strain, understood
how arduous the task was. Pulling teeth? No, it was more like
pulling a sword from a stone, he amended, grinning to himself
without much mirth. That was the icon he'd chosen to represent success. It glittered in a box of its own in the lower-right
corner of his screen, a shining sword embedded in a humped
gray granite boulder. When he succeeded, if he succeeded, an
animated mailed fist would drop into the box to grasp the
sword hilt and slide the blade smoothly from the stone. That
had not happened yet.

Armour had no one to help him. This had to be a private
project. Some of his buddies, Perce or Kaye or Wayne, might
have offered help, but he had dreamed up this venture himself,
he had written the program, and he didn't intend to let anyone
share in the fun. At least not yet. He closed his aching eyes and
nodded.

After what felt like two minutes, the computer spoke to him: "The gateway is open."

Armour jerked awake. The same message blinked on the screen, though in its corner box the sword still pierced the stone. At least he had the chance to tug at it now. He hit the time-display key and saw that it was just past five in the morning. He had slept for more than two hours, tilted back in his swivel chair. His shoulders ached abominably, his mouth tasted fuzzy and foul, and his head pounded. Still, he had accessed the gateway, he was in, and that thought gave him a surge of adrenaline. Now was the most crucial time of all, and that time might amount to a scant few minutes.

His fingers flew over the keyboard, altering the program's directives. The screen flashed to frantic life, filling with strings of numbers and letters, clearing, refilling. The Merlin was searching for routes in the new network, locating and verifying terminals, trying and identifying code keys—and all the while lying low, keeping itself all but invisible in the cybernet.

"Come on," Armour urged the machine. "Come *on*. Gotta hurry now."

The main display ticked off the number of identified terminals and data banks. They grew geometrically into the hundreds, then thousands. Still the key, the central controlling brain, concealed itself somewhere on the net. Seconds were flying by, and each second made discovery of the Merlin's intrusion more and more likely. If the line cops caught the Merlin, they caught Armour, too. And if the cybercops caught him—well, he didn't like to think about the consequences.

In his mind he visualized a real sword, all blinding steel blade, bejeweled hilt, beautiful to behold, tantalizingly within reach: but its blade was buried in, mated with, ponderous granite. To look at the sword was to understand its fixed, permanent jointure to the stone. To grasp the hilt and give it an experimental tug was to know despair. The grip of stone on blade was organic, immovable, as eternal as the globe, as immutable as the courses of the stars. It was an impossible task.

"Come *on*," Armour urged his machine.

There was the other legendary sword, of course, contained not in stone but in a yielding element, water. That one was for later. Drawing the sword from the stone proved worthiness, but plucking the other sword—the magical one held in the shifting, watery network of light and shadows at the bottom of an enchanted lake—that one proved utter and absolute mastery. When he held that mighty sword, he would be a true king—always assuming that the network policemen didn't discover his quest before either sword was in his grasp.

If they caught him, would he know? Would his machine detect their machines, feel their probes, alert him? Even if it did, what could he do about it? Nothing, he decided—not in a world crisscrossed by lines of communication, held together by a network of information. Wherever he could flee, they could find him. He played this game for all or nothing.

A fanfare of trumpets burst from the stereo speakers attached to the Merlin's sound card. To the accompaniment of three lusty cheers a mailed hand appeared. It grasped the hilt of the sword and tugged it effortlessly from the stone. The Merlin screen went white, and in ornate black-and-gold Old English script a triumphant message appeared: "Sire, I have located the six machines controlling all governmental functions. I await thy pleasure."

Armour's fingers flew. He erased the access codes, canceled the clever backups that he knew were in place. The computer announced success. Then Armour ordered the machine to replace them all with his own personal code, one that would allow him to try out empire-building for real. For however long the game would last, he would be giving the orders. All the resources of the country, all the armed forces, information networks, controllers and movers and shakers, would follow directions only from him.

"Enter new code," the Merlin told him.

With a weary, triumphant grin, Arthur Armour typed in the letters E-X-C-A-L-I-B-U-R.

Then the new monarch, age fifteen, pulled the sword from the network and began to rule his domain.

Once and Future

TERRY TAPPOUNI

Arise, once and future King!
Withdraw from my freighted
heart the spear of ignorance
imbedded at Camlan. Weighted
headstone, find wings and loose
him here to tap the shoulders
of the noble few awaiting
at his table. What we could
do, we women and men who dream
of mossy ages and know ourselves
able to battle for a cause
we cannot recall.
You, oh King, sowed ideals but fell
before they took root. Ideas kind
men fathomed not and, truth to tell,
were relieved to leave moldering
under bouldered sod of the realm.
Courage lacking, all left stones
unturned, ignored thunder from
your grave, moved backward into

medieval evil. They endured
the plague of five hundred and forty
two, and then the earth split, casting
innocents into flames. Yet you
didn't rise to rescue creatures
building churches over bones.
Years passed and silence smothered
ships carrying shackled progeny
of royal lines, their lives bought
with blood and betrayal. Even then
you did not stir under your weedy
mantle.
In my time, evil overflowed onto
your sacred meadows. The smell
of charred corpses blowing in from
the east stirred only the grasses.
You slept on, curled up in the bottom
of time. Why now would you come
to cradle children of the night
who own their hate like a bright
candle?

Once and Future

MERCEDES LACKEY

ichael O'Murphy woke with the mother of all hangovers splitting his head in half, churning up his stomach like a winter storm off the Orkneys, and a companion in his bed.

What in Jaysus did I do last night?

The pain in his head began just above his eyes, wrapped around the sides, and met in the back. His stomach did not bear thinking about. His companion was long, cold, and unmoving, but very heavy.

I took a board to bed? Was I that hard up for a sheila? Michael, you're slipping!

He was lying on his side, as always. The unknown object was at his back. At the moment it was no more identifiable than a hard presence along his spine, uncomfortable and unyielding. He wasn't entirely certain he wanted to find out exactly what it was until he mentally retraced his steps of the previous evening. Granted, this was irrational, but a man with the mother of all hangovers is not a rational being.

The reason for his monumental drunk was clear enough in his mind; the pink slip from his job at the docks, presented to him by the foreman at the end of the day. *That would be yesterday, Friday, if I haven't slept the weekend through.*

He wasn't the only bloke cashiered yesterday; they'd laid off half the men at the shipyard. *So it's back on the dole, and thank God Almighty I didn't get serious with that little bird I met on holiday. Last thing I need is a woman nagging at me for losing me job and it wasn't even me own fault.* Depression piled atop the splitting head and the foul stomach. Michael O'Murphy was not the sort of man who accepted the dole with any kind of grace other than ill.

He cracked his right eye open, winced at the stab of light that penetrated into his cranium, and squinted at the floor beside his bed.

Yes, there was the pink slip, crumpled into a wad, beside his boots—and two bottles of Jameson's, one empty, the other half full and frugally corked.

Holy Mary Mother of God. I don't remember sharing out that often, so I must've drunk most of it myself. No wonder I feel like a walk through Purgatory.

He closed his eye again, and allowed the whiskey bottle to jog a few more memories loose. So, he'd been sacked, and half the boys with him. And they'd all decided to drown their sorrows together.

But not at a pub, and not at pub prices. You can't get royally, roaring drunk at a pub unless you've got a royal allowance to match. So we all bought our bottles and met at Tommy's place.

There'd been a half-formed notion to get shellacked there, but Tommy had a car, and Tommy had an idea. He'd seen some nonsense on the telly about "Iron Johns" or some such idiocy, over in America—

Said we was all downtrodden and "needed to get in touch with our inner selves"; swore that we had to get "empowered" to get back on our feet, and wanted to head out into the country—

There'd been some talk about "male bonding" ceremonies, pounding drums, carrying on like a lot of Red Indians—and drinking of course. Tommy went on like it was some kind of communion; the rest of them had already started on their bottles before they got to Tommy's, and at that point, a lot of pounding and dancing half-naked and drinking sounded like a fine idea. So off they went, crammed into Tommy's aging Morris Minor with just enough room to get their bottles to their lips.

At some point they stopped and all piled out; Michael vaguely recalled a forest, which might well have been National Trust lands, and it was a mercy they hadn't been caught and hauled off to gaol. Tommy had gotten hold of a drum somewhere; it was in the boot with the rest of the booze. They all grabbed bottles and Tommy got the drum, and off they went into the trees like a daft May Day parade, howling and carrying on like bleeding loonies.

How Tommy made the fire—and why it hadn't been seen, more to the point—Michael had not a clue. He remembered a great deal of pounding on the drum, more howling, shouting and swearing at the bosses of the world, a lot of drinking, and some of the lads stripping off their shirts and capering about like so many monkeys.

About then was when I got an itch for some quiet.

He and his bottles had stumbled off into the trees, following an elusive moonbeam, or so he thought he remembered. The singing and pounding had faded behind him, and in his memory the trees loomed the way they had when he was a nipper and everything seemed huge. *They were like trees out of the old tales, as big as the one they call Robin Hood's Oak in Sherwood.* There was only one way to go since he didn't even consider turning back, and that was to follow the path between them, and the fey bit of moonlight that lured him on.

Was there a mist? I think there was. Wait! That was when the real path appeared. There had been mist, a curious, blue mist. It had muffled everything, from the sounds of his own footsteps to the sounds of his mates back by the fire. Before too very long, he might have been the only human being alive in a forest as old as time and full of portentous silence.

He remembered that the trees thinned out at just about the point where he was going to give up his ramble and turn back. He had found himself on the shores of a lake. It was probably an ordinary enough pond by daylight, but last night, with the mist drifting over it and obscuring the farther shore, the utter and complete silence of the place, and the moonlight pouring down over everything and touching everything with silver, it had seemed—uncanny, a bit frightening, and not entirely in the real world at all.

He had stood there with a bottle in each hand, a monument to inebriation, held there more by inertia than anything else, he suspected. He could still see the place as he squeezed his eyes shut, as vividly as if he stood there at that moment. The water was like a sheet of plate glass over a dark and unimaginable void; the full moon hung just above the dark mass of the trees behind him, a great round Chinese lantern of a moon, and blue-white mist floated everywhere in wisps and thin scarves and great opaque billows. A curious boat rested by the bank not a meter from him, a rough-hewn thing apparently made from a whole tree trunk and shaped with an ax. Not even the reeds around the boat at his feet moved in the breathless quiet.

Then, breaking the quiet, a sound; a single splash in the middle of the lake. Startled, he had seen an arm rise up out of the water, beckoning.

He thought, of course, that someone had fallen in, or been swimming and took a cramp. One of his mates, even, who'd come round to the other side and taken a fancy for a dip. It never occurred to him to go back to the others for help, just as it never occurred to him not to rush out there to save whoever it was.

He dropped his bottles into the boat at his feet, and followed them in. He looked about for the tether to cast off, but
there wasn't one—looked for the oars to row out to the swim-
mer, but there weren't any of those, either. Nevertheless, the
boat was moving, and heading straight for that beckoning arm
as if he was willing it there. And it didn't seem at all strange to
him that it was doing so, at least, not at the time.

He remembered that he'd been thinking that whoever this
was, she'd fallen in fully clothed, for the arm had a long sleeve
of some heavy white stuff. And it had to be a she—the arm was
too white and soft to be a man's. It wasn't until he got up
close, though, that he realized there was nothing showing *but*
the arm, that the woman had been under an awfully long
time—and that the arm sticking up out of the water was holding something.

Still, daft as it was, it wasn't important—He'd ignored
everything but the arm, ignored things that didn't make any
sense. As the boat got within range of the woman, he'd leaned
over the bow so far that *he* almost fell in, and made a grab for
that upraised arm.

But the hand and wrist slid through his grasp somehow, although he was *sure* he'd taken a good, firm hold on them, and
he fell back into the boat, knocking himself silly against the
hard wooden bottom, his hands clasped tight around whatever
it was she'd been holding. He saw stars, and more than stars,
and when he came to again, the boat was back against the bank,
and there was no sign of the woman.

But he had her sword.

Her sword? I had her sword?

Now he reached behind him to feel the long, hard length
of it at his back.

By God—it is *a sword!*

He had no real recollection of what happened after that; he

must have gotten back to the lads, and they all must have gotten back to town in Tommy's car, because here he was.

In bed with a sword.

*I've heard of being in bed with a battle-ax, but never a
sword.*

Slowly, carefully, he sat up. Slowly, carefully, he reached
into the tumble of blankets and extracted the drowning woman's sword.

It was real, it looked old, and it was damned heavy. He
hefted it in both hands, and grunted with surprise. If this was
the kind of weapon those old bastards used to hack at one another with in the long-ago days that they made films of, there
must have been as much harm done by breaking bones as by
whacking bits off.

It wasn't anything fancy, though, not like you saw in the
flicks or the comics; a plain, black, leather-wrapped hilt, with
what looked like brass bits as the crosspiece and a plain, black
leather-bound sheath. Probably weighed about as much as four
pry-bars of the same length put together.

He put his hand to the hilt experimentally, and pulled a little, taking it out of the sheath with the vague notion of having a
look at the blade itself.

"PENDRAGON!"

The voice shouted in his head, an orchestra of nothing but
trumpets, and all of them played at top volume.

He dropped the sword, which landed on his toes. He
shouted with pain, and jerked his feet up reflexively, and the
sword dropped to the floor, half out of its sheath.

"What the *hell* was that?" he howled, grabbing his abused
toes in both hands, and rocking back and forth a little. He was
hardly expecting an answer, but he got one anyway.

"It was I, Pendragon."

He felt his eyes bugging out, and he cast his gaze frantically around the room, looking for the joker who'd snuck inside

while he was sleeping. But there wasn't anyone, and there was nowhere to hide. The rented room contained four pieces of furniture—his iron-framed bed, a cheap-deal bureau and nightstand, and a chair. He bent over and took a peek under the bed, feeling like a frightened old aunty, but there was nothing there, either.

"You're looking in the wrong place."

"I left the radio on, that's it," he muttered. "It's some daft drama. Gawd, I hate those BBC buggers!" He reached over to the radio on the nightstand and felt for the knob. But the radio was already off, and cold, which meant it hadn't *been* on with the knob broken.

"Pendragon, I am on the floor, where you dropped me."

He looked down at the floor. The only things besides his boots were the whiskey bottles and the sword.

"I never heard of no Jameson bottles talking in a bloke's head before," he muttered to himself as he massaged his toes. "And me boots never struck up no conversations before."

"Don't be absurd," said the voice tartly. *"You know what I am, as you know what you are."*

The sword. It had to be the sword. "And just what am I, then?" he asked it, wondering when the boys from the Home were going to come romping through the door to take him off for a spot of rest. *This is daft. I must have gone loopy. I'm talking to a piece of metal, and it's talking back to me.*

"You are the Pendragon," the sword said patiently, and waited. When he failed to respond except with an uncomprehending shrug, it went on—but with far less patience. *"You are the Once and Future King. The Warrior Against the Darkness."* It waited, and he still had no notion what it was talking about.

"You are ARTHUR," it shouted, making him wince. *"You are King Arthur, Warleader and Hero!"*

"Now it's *you* that's loopy," he told it sternly. "I don't bloody well think! King Arthur indeed!"

The only recollection of King Arthur he had were things out of his childhood—stories in the schoolbooks, a Disney flick, Christmas pantomimes. Vague images of crowns and red-felt robes, of tin swords and papier-mâché armor flitted through his mind—and talking owls and daft magicians. "King Arthur! Not likely!"

"You are!" the sword said, sounding desperate now. *"You are the Pendragon! You have been reborn into this world to be its Hero! Don't you remember?"*

He only snorted. "I'm Michael O'Murphy, I work at the docks, I'll be on the dole on Monday, and I don't bloody think anybody needs any bloody more kings these days! They've got enough troubles with the ones they've—*Gawd!*"

He fell back into the bed as the sword bombarded his mind with a barrage of images, more vivid than the flicks, for he was *in* them. Battles and feasts, triumph and tragedy, success and failure—a grim stand against the powers of darkness that held for the short space of one man's lifetime.

It all poured into his brain in the time it took for him to breathe twice. And when he sat up again, he remembered.

All of it.

He blinked, and rubbed his mistreated head. "Gawd!" he complained. "You might warn a lad first!"

"Now do you believe?" The sword sounded smug.

Just like the nuns at his school, when they'd gotten done whapping him "for his own good."

"I believe you're damn good at shoving a lot of rubbish into a man's head and making him think it's his," he said stubbornly, staring down at the shining expanse of blade, about ten centimeters' worth, that protruded out of the sheath. "I still don't see where all this makes any difference, even if I *do* believe it."

If the sword could have spluttered, it probably would have.

"You don't—you're Arthur! I'm Excalibur! You're supposed to take me up and use me!"

"For what?" he asked, snickering at the mental image of prying open tins of beans with the thing. "You don't make a good pry-bar, I can't cut wood with you even if I had a wood-stove, which I don't, nobody's going to believe you're a fancy saw-blade, and there's laws about walking around with something like you strapped to me hip. What do I do, fasten a sign to you, and go on a protest march?"

"You—you—" Bereft of words, the sword resorted to another flood of images. Forewarned by the last one, Michael stood his ground.

But this time the images were harder to ignore.

He saw himself taking the sword and gathering his fighters to his side—all of his friends from the docks, the ones who'd bitched along with him about what a mess the world was in. He watched himself making an army out of them, and sending them out into the streets to clean up the filth there. He saw himself as the leader of a new corps of vigilantes who tracked down the pushers, the perverts, the thugs, and the punks and gave them all a taste of what they had coming to them.

He saw his army making the city safe for people to live in, saw them taking back the night from the Powers of Evil.

He saw more people flocking to his banner and his cause, saw him carrying his crusade from city to city, until a joyous public threw the House of Hanover out of Buckingham Palace and installed him on the throne, and a ten-year-old child could carry a gold bar across the length of the island and never fear a robber or a molester.

"Or try this one, if that doesn't suit you!"

This time he saw himself crossing to Ireland, confronting the leadership of every feuding party there, and defeating them, one by one, in challenge combat. He saw himself bringing peace to a land that had been torn by strife for so long that there wasn't an Irish child alive that didn't know what a knee-capper was. He saw the last British Tommy leaving the island with a smile on his face and a shamrock in his lapel, withdrawing in good order since order itself had been restored. He saw plenty coming back to the land, prosperity, saw Ireland taking a major role in the nations of the world, and *Irish honor* becoming a byword for trust. Oh, this was cruel, throwing a vision like that in his face! He wasn't for British Rule, but the IRA was as bad as the PLO by his lights—and there wasn't anything he could do about either.

Until now.

"Or here—widen your horizons, lift your eyes beyond your own sordid universe!"

This time he started as before, carried the sword to Ireland and restored peace there, and went on—on to the Continent, to Eastern Europe, taking command of the UN forces there and forcing a real and lasting peace by the strength of his arm. Oh, there was slaughter, but it wasn't a slaughter of the innocents but of the bastards that drove the fights, and in the end that same ten-year-old child could start in Galway and end in Sarajevo, and no one would so much as dirty the lace of her collar or offer her an unkind word.

The sword released him then, and he sat blinking on his shabby second-hand bed, in his dingy rented room, still holding his aching toes in both hands. It all seemed so tawdry, this little world of his, and all he had to do to earn a greater and brighter one was to reach out his hand.

He looked down at the sword at the side of his bed, and the metal winked smugly up at him. "You really think you have me now, don't you?" he said bitterly to it.

It said nothing. It didn't have to answer.

But he had answers enough for all the temptations in his own mind. Because now he *remembered* Arthur—and Guinevere, and Lancelot and Agravaine and Morgaine.

And Mordred.

Oh, yes. He had no doubt that there would be a Mordred out there, somewhere, waiting for him the moment he took up the sword. He hadn't been any too careful, AIDS notwithstanding, and there could be any number of bastards scattered from his seed. Hell, there would be a Mordred even if it *wasn't* his son. For every Warrior of the Light there was a Warrior of the Dark; he'd seen that quite, quite clearly. For every Great Friend there was always the Great Betrayer—hadn't Peter betrayed Christ by denying him? For every Great Love there was a Great Loss.

It would *not* be the easy parade of victories the sword showed him; he was older and far, far wiser than the boy-Arthur who'd taken Excalibur the last time. He was not to be dazzled by dreams. The *most* likely of the scenarios to succeed was the first—some bloke in New York had done something like that, called his lads the Guardian Angels—and even *he* hadn't succeeded in cleaning up more than a drop or two of the filth in one city, let alone hundreds.

That scenario would only last as long as it took some punk's parents to sue him. What good would a sword be in court, eh? What would he do, slice the judge's head off?

And this was the age of the tabloids, of smut-papers. They'd love him for a while, then they'd decide to bring him down. If they'd had a time with Charles and Di, what would they do with him—

—and Guinevere, and Lancelot—and Mordred?

For Mordred and Morgaine were surely here, and they might even have got a head start on him. They could be waiting for him to appear, waiting with hired thugs to take him out.

For that matter, Mordred might be a lawyer, ready for him at this very moment with briefs and briefcase, and he'd wind up committed to the loony asylum before he got two steps! Or he might be a smut reporter, good at digging up dirt. His own, real past wouldn't make a pretty sight on paper.

Oh, no. Oh, no.

"I don't think so, my lad," he said, and before the sword could pull any clever tricks, he reached down and slammed it home in the sheath.

Three hours and six aspirins later, he walked into the nearest pawn shop with a long bundle wrapped in old newspapers under his arm. He handed it across the counter to the wizened old East Indian who kept the place.

The old boy unwrapped the papers and peered at the sword without a hint of surprise. God alone knew he'd probably seen stranger things pass across his counter. He slid it out of its sheath and examined the steel before slamming it back home. Only then did he squint through the grill at Michael.

"It's mild steel. Maybe antique, maybe not, no way of telling. Five quid," he said. "Take it or leave it."

"I'll take it," said the Pendragon.

Sword Practice

JODY LYNN NYE

ower is a teacher," Merlin had said. "With the great powers, even the least little mistake can burn your fingers off to the elbow. In other cases, you're given a period or a distance of grace. That's what you have here. I suggest you use it to learn all you can."

Arthur couldn't decide if his old teacher intended the lecture to mean the holy sword Excalibur or kingship, or both. In any case, the grace period was too short to be comfortable. In the last three months, he had covered the distance between his old home in the northwest of Britain, to London, back to Galava, and now up to Luguvallium to fight the Saxons, without the least time to take a breath, or think.

For a twelve-year-old boy, the pomp and ceremony of an unexpected coronation exhausted and terrified as much as it thrilled him. He still felt the way the sword Excalibur hummed in his hand when he touched the hilt, the way the rolled metal clung to his flesh, fitting into his palm as if it were a part of him. The way his foster brother kept making him put the sword back into the stone and anvil and take it out again. The thing Arthur remembered best of all that snowy New Year's Day was how Kay's face changed from blind insolence and disbelief to wide-open delight at Arthur's good fortune. Though he complained mightily about it now, he was proud that the honor of kingship should have come to one in the care of *his* family. Kay's mind, never swift, chose the best possible interpretation to put on his disappointment that the sword had not chosen him to be king. Since that day, his foster brother had been Arthur's most devoted subject.

Kay was possessed of a peculiar sort of hero worship that didn't extend past trying to impress the basics of swordsmanship and the other skills of knighthood on him. That was why Merlin let Kay continue to teach him, though he could have had any of the finest blades in the land proud to serve as his master. Merlin wanted one who wasn't overawed by the office. Arthur needed someone who could see his youthful shortcomings and would be right there to correct them.

It was late afternoon. Returning to camp after the conquest over the Saxon force, Arthur was tired. His legs had stiffened until he had trouble rising from his pallet to greet his teacher. Merlin had watched the young king struggle to stand with gentle amusement. He had then advised Arthur to summon Kay for sword practice even though they had been fighting all morning.

"All battles aren't over in a single melee," the Welsh wizard had warned. If he prepared himself now, he would not be hindered when he needed to fight the sun round. Arthur had agreed. Under the eye of his teacher, he'd proceeded to chop a pell into firewood. Yet the pell didn't move, and so didn't count for a real target. He had to practice combat with a living, moving opponent. Feeling tired but no longer stiff, he'd gestured for his foster brother to engage him. Kay, big though he was, was soaked in sweat from a few passes at the pell, but the most Arthur had for his efforts was the heat between his hands and the hilts. Fighting man-to-man was different.

"You've got the build, boy, I mean Your Highness: *reach* for it," Kay bellowed, swinging his heavy half-hand sword at Arthur's head. He sidestepped as the young king plunged in and staggered, his blade missing the target that was no longer there. "No, keep your feet under its weight. You know better. God's blood, you've been doing this since we were using cat-sticks for brands."

Arthur, panting clouds of steam in the cold air, fetched up against a tree and hung against it. He pushed a lock of his thick, chestnut-brown hair out of his eyes, smeared away with the back of his sleeve the sweat that threatened to freeze on his face and eyelashes. Kay, strong enough to wield his blade with one meaty hand, hefted it, beckoning to Arthur to come in again. His arms were bare under the light tunic he wore for practice, but he was in no fear of being struck.

The boy gasped in breath and ran toward him, Excalibur held high. Kay shook his head as he parried Arthur's move without seeming effort, sending the boy hurtling toward the brush like a stooping hawk. The bare, knobby arms of an apple tree reached out to embrace him. Arthur stopped and wiped his face, spat out twigs in disgust.

No matter what he did, it was still clumsy. A miracle and a victory over the Saxons didn't change the essential Arthur. Three months wasn't enough to put a man's muscles on a lad of twelve years, nor a warrior's canniness in his head. Whatever magic Excalibur imbued him with in battle, it abandoned him in practice, as if a hunk of iron could tell the difference between true war and play.

Merlin had located this small hollow far from the celebration for daily sword practice. Before the day's light fled altogether, Arthur was bound by a promise to the enchanter to better his skills, but he felt it was hopeless. He was the same

Arthur. It was the sword that made him a swordsman, even as it had made him a king.

Arthur heard a chuckle behind him, and spun, his sword coming up point first nearly under the interloper's throat. The music of Excalibur's song hummed through his arm, into his heart. There must have been grim death on his face, because King Coel of Rheged stepped backward two paces. His cheeks burning, Arthur lowered his weapon.

"My lord, I'm sorry," Arthur said. The power fled, leaving him again a child.

"By God, lad, I was wondering how you led us to victory over the Aethelings at four o'clock when you mince like a cook's boy on a sticky floor at five," the burly man said, planting his big, hairy hands on his belt. "Now I see it was just practice."

"Well, now you know," Arthur said stiffly, then realized it was affectionately meant. "I beg your pardon, my lord."

"No one wants to look the fool," Rheged said graciously. He slapped the boy companionably on the back. "I'm leaving a man of mine in earshot, should you want me. He won't look." Coel stumped away, threshing down the frozen grass under his boots like a herd of cows.

"You proved yourself in battle," Merlin said, suddenly there in the clearing beside Kay. The Welsh wizard was wrapped against the chilly spring weather in a heavy robe and cloak over his tunic and trousers. His crisp, dark hair, just touched with silver, echoed the touch of frost still clinging to the trees. "That's why he's taking you seriously. You fought between two of the greatest warriors in Britain, Rheged and Caw of Strathclyde, and did shame neither to them nor to your late father."

Arthur also remembered that Coel had been one of the first in London to kneel and swear fealty, ignoring the pathetic picture the boy had presented then. There he stood, with the gleaming sword laid across his hands, its song imbuing his whole skinny body, clad in Kay's impossibly large castoffs, with the kind of majesty he had only seen shining down through the clouds as if God was looking in on them. There stood Coel, impressive and broad as a castle door in his ring-sewn hauberk, and knelt in the mud in the churchyard, laying his great hands across the boy's as if it was the most natural thing in the world.

"I didn't mean to offend him," Arthur said, suddenly contrite.

"And you didn't," Merlin said, his lilting voice light. "For a moment he saw himself as a lad, I promise you."

Arthur stuck out his chin. "Could he have won this morning's battle, then?" he asked defensively.

"Indeed not," said Merlin, laying a hand on Arthur's shoulders. "Come now, it's time for supper."

Arthur sighed. The enchanter said it as easily as if they had been back at Ector's estate, where his foster mother, Sofia, waited inside the hall with her clucking flock of servants. He was a long way from Galava. Supper was more likely to be a haunch of roasted venison and a chunk of indifferent bread.

"Well, what do you expect on a battlefield in March?" Merlin asked, clearly reading his mind. "Those with a more delicate touch are tending the wounded. As I must be, so come." With a wave of his arms, he made the air beside them thicker, and Arthur stepped into it. Warily, Kay followed, and the apple orchard vanished.

The last of the brief spring sun slipped away over the walls of the ruined abbey before the men had finished with their greasy mutton and oatcakes. Arthur, with his Roman-bred manners, found the sloppy way the warriors ate both revulsive and fascinating. Watching Caw of Strathclyde slurp and chomp and grin around mouthfuls of food, he started to wipe his hand on his tunic front, then caught sight of Merlin's eye upon him. The enchanter turned almost unwillingly toward the mere thought of slovenliness, and Arthur blinked. Guiltily, he felt for the nap-kin stuffed half under the cushion on which he sat.

Dinner was a casual affair, with men shouting to one an-other, and horseplay over the rough food to be expected. They even included him occasionally in their jests, but nearly always the fighting men treated him as an object of awe, a prodigy, a miracle, not to be trifled with for fear of spoiling their luck. The battle had been won with fewer injuries and deaths than could ever have been forecast—except by Merlin, of course—and it was all due to the young dragon who had drawn them in his wake. Still, he enjoyed seeing them enjoy themselves. What came afterward was more formal, and therefore more serious. As soon as Arthur had finished with his meat, both Merlin and Ector were there to escort him to the circle of judges.

Judgment was the part of kingship Arthur found he liked least. Partly he detested it just because it gave the older chiefs another chance to mock at his inexperience and remind him that he was too young to be king.

Arthur put aside his platter and napkin and stood up.

"Are you ready?" Ector asked solemnly.

"Almost," Arthur said. To his surprise he found that in only three months' time he had grown almost tall enough to face his tutor on a level. "Merlin, can I have Excalibur with me at judgment tonight?"

"No." The Welsh wizard's eyes were serene, deep pools of black, and Arthur could nearly see his own desperate face re-flected in them.

"*Please!*"

"No."

"I need it there," he begged. "It gives me confidence."

"No." Ector started to say something, but Merlin raised a hand.

"I want it! You can't stop me."

"Lad, I'm the only man in your kingdom you can't bully. Leave it behind. You'll see why one day. Come."

"You'll see why I need it," Arthur said sullenly. Merlin made the air thick, and they stepped through it.

A circle of seats was arranged around a great bonfire outside of Ector's tent, which had been pressed hastily into service as the royal pavilion. Before the flap one of the old Roman U-shaped chairs had been set up. Arthur had always hated them because he got left with a slotted backside after spending more than a few minutes in one. But in deference to his new status, someone had thoughtfully padded the curve with a thick, embroidered cushion. Gratefully, Arthur sat down and propped his arms on the high sides.

Coel and the other lords took their places. The boy king heard whispers in the shadows around him as he looked in vain for Lot of Lothian. The northern king's force had held back from joining the battle until nearly the end of the afternoon, when he saw which way the tide was turning. It could have cost the British the victory and hundreds of brave men their lives if he hadn't come in. Merlin had confided that Lot had two purposes for holding back. One was to avoid a hopeless slaughter if the day should have gone against the British forces, and the other was to make sure it was known by all how vital his aid was. Arthur wasn't looking forward to confronting Lot, who had a reputation of being vicious as a wounded boar, and who thought Arthur's sword-supported claim to the throne spurious, but it was a task both Merlin and Ector told him he'd have to undertake sooner or later.

"Sooner is best. If you want a whole kingdom, that is," Merlin had said. "Otherwise, you'll be doing half the Saxons' job for them by letting the alliance your father was building fall apart."

The whispers were unsurprised that Lot withheld his presence from the circle of justice. Arthur despaired of being able to convince a seasoned warrior to respect an untried boy, no matter how ideal his antecedents.

With Merlin and Ector behind him, he listened to the cases put to him. Saxon prisoners, clad in blood-soaked rags and tied with thongs, were dragged before the tribunal. Some were marked for execution and forced out of the lighted circle by armed men. Some, survivors of the battle, were claimed as serfs by the nobles.

"He killed two of my best men. The least I expect is that I'll have his back—or his head," Caw said gruffly, eyeing a shaggy blond man who stared straight ahead of him. If he understood the language, the Saxon showed no sign. Arthur glanced up at Ector for guidance. The count nodded.

"I declare your claim valid," Arthur said, then winced as Caw's men roughly hauled the prisoner away, tearing open the half-healed wound on his shoulder as they did so.

"Justice, my lords!" A farmer from east of Luguvallium claimed damages against the invaders. "They burned my farm, chased me and mine out into the winter weather. Isn't there any mercy for a poor, hardworking man?"

Arthur felt sorry for him, but he didn't know what to do. Coel came to his rescue, lifting a coarse-cropped black head from his ale cup.

"Who's your liege, man? It's to him you should be applying for relief, not the High King. To whom do you owe your duty?"

Old Caw of Strathclyde, three of whose many sons had acted as Arthur's bodyguards in the field, growled his agreement. "See him off, boy. If yon beggar was so eager to have the barbarians out of his land, he'd have been out there on the field with us today slaughtering the bastards."

And so the evening went on. Arthur, inexperienced at wielding authority, could do nothing but nod and approve the sentences and judgments of the other kings and lords.

When the tribunal broke up, he stormed into his tent and sat down with a thump on his pallet. Excalibur was propped up beside it on a stand. He reached out to touch it, felt the reassuring buzz like a cat purring under his caress. The tension of the evening started to melt away.

"I felt like an idiot out there," he told it.

With a rustle of robes, Merlin followed him in, and patted him on the shoulder.

"Well, you are young, and there's no help for that. Even if you'd been raised in the thick of it beside your father, you're still damp from the egg. What did you expect?"

Arthur turned a set face up to his tutor.

"It would have been different if I could have had Excalibur with me," he said. "I want it there next time."

"No."

"Please!"

"No." Merlin's face never changed, nor did the tone of his voice. Arthur lost his temper. He picked the sword up, scabbard and all, and held it with both hands, feeling confidence welling inside him.

"I'm taking it in! I think it's best. That's my will. I *am* your king."

"And so you are." Merlin grinned at him, his dark brows drawn down in amusement. "And there you speak as one. See what it's like, then."

Arthur thought, as he settled down to sleep with the sword beside him, that he had had his way, but undoubtedly not the last word.

Early the next morning, mounted scouts brought in word of the remnants of the Saxon force fleeing eastward, killing and pillaging as they went. Servants were left to strike the camp as the army set out to finish the job they had started.

This time all the companies worked together. Lot, a wiry-muscled man with an air of insouciant elegance, appeared at the head of his force. He offered a nod of good morning to his peers and a salute to Arthur as if nothing had happened the day before.

Stung by the disrespect of the northerner but unable to do anything about it, Arthur went about showing him he was indeed a force to be reckoned with.

They caught up with the Saxons a few miles southeast of Luguvallium. Everything Arthur had ever heard about the fearlessness and insanity of the outlanders seemed to come true that day. As soon as the British force came into view, the blond giants turned to charge at them. The only thing to do was to cry out orders and wade in to battle. The red dragon banner of the House Pendragon snapped in the wind as Arthur rode forward, waving Excalibur.

The two armies met with an almost audible clash. Though the British outnumbered the invaders, the Saxons fought like crazed animals, keeping as many as four men each at bay with wide swings of their great axes and hammers.

Guiding his horse with his knees, Arthur himself engaged their leader, the warlord Colgrim. With Excalibur in his hands he couldn't make a wrong move, keeping the Saxon leader from landing even the lightest blow until he fell, wounded, among the horse's hooves. Arthur gave his bodyguards heart attacks time and again over the day by flinging himself into tight melees and coming out of them again without a scratch. The sword came alive, its song of victory humming in his blood until he could hear nothing else, not the crash of steel nor the cries of pain. Together, they were invincible, and they defended the land.

When the hot haze faded, he was a twelve-year-old boy on a horse. The sword's song died away to the comforting hum. He sheathed it, and helped direct his weary force back toward camp. At one point, he felt eyes upon him, and looked for Merlin, but the gimlet gaze belonged to Lot. He returned the stare with an expressionless face, wondering just what the northern king was thinking.

"High King." Coel's voice interrupted his reverie.

"My lord?" Arthur straightened up in his saddle and turned to face him.

"We have many wounded men, and we're a long way from the camp. We've also secured a score or two of Saxon brutes. With your permission, I think the prisoners should help carry the men they've injured back to camp for help, don't you think?"

"That's a good idea, my lord," Arthur said. He was a little ashamed that he had forgotten about important logistics like those, and felt grateful that Coel let him approve his arrangement, if only for form's sake. Lot spurred his black stallion closer.

"If he'd been leading us better, we wouldn't have so many injured lying about," Lot said, loudly enough so everyone around them could hear it.

"We'd have had many more lying dead and dying, I think," Coel said impatiently and just as loudly. "Who could stand before such a shooting star? Give over, Lothian. We didn't choose the battlefield, and we couldn't survey the ground. Look, not a single broken leg among the horses, and there's mole-holes everywhere. He secured the victory for us. He's our lucky piece."

Lot's black-brown eyes took fire. "We don't need luck, Rheged. We need generalship."

"Well, I'd say we have it. With your permission, High King," he said, stressing the two last syllables as he turned to go.

At the tribunal that evening Lot continued to make his disapproval known. Arthur sat in the Roman chair with Excalibur, sheathed, across his knees. Lot lounged at his right hand, groaning softly under his breath and looking skyward whenever he made a pronouncement. The presence of Excalibur helped Arthur keep his wits about him.

After a second full day of battle, Arthur was more tired than he had ever known he could be. He couldn't compare it to anything else. Unbelievably, Merlin had insisted he put in a short period of sword practice when he got back to camp, but he had to admit that he felt the better for it. A little elementary thrust and riposte loosened up his tight muscles and helped put the day in perspective.

More landowners and farmers from the surrounding countryside came forward to put claims against the Saxon raiders. Feeling more confident with his precious sword across his knees, Arthur drew from farther inside himself for wisdom. He remembered similar though smaller cases Ector had tried on the estate while he was growing up. Instead of letting Coel and Caw chivvy the complaints away, Arthur felt the magic rising through him, heard himself making pronouncements.

"They must have choice of the prisoners, to help rebuild what they destroyed," his voice said. "Those in greatest need shall make the first choice."

"What?" roared Caw, robbed of his expectations. "High King . . . oh, very well, I'd have to feed the flaxen bastards anyway."

Coel, to the right of Caw, nodded. Behind him, Arthur heard a chuckle from Ector.

"Not bad, son, not bad."

Lot cleared his throat, and slouched onto the other elbow.

"Is that your own judgment, or are we hearing ancient wisdom from your precious sword?"

"What does it matter where a decision comes from, so long as it is wise?" Ector asked. "His father couldn't have put it better. Might even have been a little more plainly spoken, too."

Lot laughed. "You saw the boy's face, Count Ector. I've been watching him all evening. He's no more than a seer, except he uses a sword instead of a bowl of water to do his scrying in. He's no more a judge than he is a warrior—or a king, if not for that sword."

Excalibur suddenly felt very heavy on his lap. Arthur did his best to keep his face immobile. What Lot had voiced was no more than he himself sometimes felt, but it hurt to have it said out loud. Wanting revenge, he sat up straighter, trying to put into words what he thought of Lot's opportunism, leaving them hanging out to dry like washing until it suited him to join the fight against the Saxons as he had sworn to do. Excalibur hummed a little louder, more threatingly, at the challenge to its master. A slight touch on the arm distracted Arthur, and the hum died.

"Say nothing," Merlin whispered.

Though it took biting his tongue between his teeth, Arthur kept his mouth closed. Lot looked disappointed, as if he'd been looking forward to humiliating the boy in public. Instead, he turned an attack upon Caw.

"Two of your pikemen got in the way of one of my captains. The brutes spitted his horse. I claim damage from you, Strathclyde."

"What? What?" The elder warrior blinked across the bonfire at Lot. "He'd not have been in the way if he had kept in line with his men! Damage, yourself. One of my pikemen has a bleeding shoulder where a horse's hoof sliced him."

"My lords, please!" Arthur's clear, high voice cut through the argument, sounding like a lark trying to outshout crows. "It's late. Shouldn't we look at the evidence in the morning and make a fair judgment then? We'll have cooler heads when we're not so tired."

"Up past your bedtime, to be sure," Lot said, but he stood up and made for his tent. "But if the sword says go, we'll go."

The tribunal ended, and Arthur withdrew without another word, clutching Excalibur to him. The sword, which felt so light in his hands during battle, seemed as heavy as the slogging hunks of iron his foster father had him use for practice at home. He forced back the tears that made his eyes burn.

"It's not true, you know," Merlin said when they were alone in the big tent. "The sword is the final evidence of your identity, not the reason for your kingship. It showed everyone that you are truly the son of Uther and no impostor, but it couldn't have made you a king any more than it can make you a swordsman. You have to do that yourself. And by the way, well done on disarming Lothian. We'd be there yet if you let him spool out his accusations. I've seen him do it before, and we'd have had bloodshed in our own camp."

"You were right," Arthur said soberly. "I shouldn't have brought Excalibur into council with me, but it felt good to have it there. Is it so wrong to rely upon it?"

"Not if you rely upon yourself first," Merlin said. "You'll have to fight your hardest battles empty-handed. And then, if you still want to carry Excalibur everywhere with you, no one will say boo to a goose."

"But it made me wise tonight. They respected what I said."

"But was it you saying those things?" Merlin asked gently. "In that Lot was right. You must deal with your limitations before you discover your true quality. When you've learned to acknowledge a power greater than yourself, that's the beginning of humility, and consequently, of true greatness."

Arthur barked out a humorless laugh. "Sounds the opposite of what's true."

"Like all true things, it's a paradox. If you feel that the sword is what made you king, abdicate. Give it to someone worthier."

"Well, I don't want to do that. It isn't right."

"Then you'll have to deal with the disapproval of others, but don't let it stop you doing what is right."

Arthur felt a longing to go home. If this was what it was like to be king, he was willing to give up everything and go back to being ordinary. He looked up to see the Welsh wizard shake his head.

"Never again. The cuckoo's out of his egg, for sure."

"Merlin, will you make a dream for me?" Arthur asked.

The dreams had been the best part of his education. Time and again, when he had a knotty lesson to learn, Merlin had sung him into a magical sleep, where he had become a tree, a fish, a bird, or a plant, or some such thing. Each experience had had some knowledge to impart. The dreams seemed so real, but he'd never been sure. He once spoke to the great carp in the millpond, whom he'd befriended while shaped as a snail. For a moment, he thought the old fish recognized him before flicking its tail and disappearing into the cool shadows.

Merlin smiled, and picked up the small harp, which stood in the most protected corner of the tent. "Only a short one. I've got to sing strength into the wounded and open a way to the next world for the dying."

The small child in Arthur voiced a petulant wail. "But *I* need you."

"And so I am here. But I will not always be."

"I know the men need you more," Arthur said, ashamed of himself.

"No, I mean that one day, I'll be gone for good. You've always known that. You'll learn to stand by yourself as king, as you must. But for the meantime, I am here for you." He sat down on the edge of Ector's empty pallet and drew the bow of wood onto his knee.

Arthur settled down among his furs and wished again he *could* climb back into the egg and pull his shell around him. On Ector's estate he'd had the Welsh enchanter all to himself. Kay had been jealous—until now, when it was in his opinion only right that the King's own wizard should have been there to tutor his only son. But now Arthur was jealous of the duties that robbed him of his best friend so frequently. He knew it was only right to take second place for the sake of his men—but let them wait just a moment.

As the tingling swirls of the harp's thready music drew him down into sleep, Arthur relaxed and let pictures form on the inside of his eyelids. He thought he was in an old oak forest, but it seemed preternaturally light, even under the thick canopy of leaves. So the season was high summer. But what was he?

A light, moist breeze tickled the leaves, and they danced. Arthur scented loam, flowers, and many animals, each distinctive. He became aware of pairs of eyes, round and golden in the faint light, and of the soft hooting like the murmur of conversation. Dozens of owls sat in parliament in the oak branches, staring at him. Once he could see their faces, he thought they resembled the men and kings who sat with him in the circle of judgment at night. Coel was a tawny owl, tall, with a white V over his beak that looked like the man's stern eyebrows. The short-eared owl beside him was Caw, his intense yellow stare so like the man's. Lot was an eagle owl, huge and gray-white, with mad orange eyes. Barn owls and little owls huddled on limbs all around him.

Arthur looked down at his legs and saw they wore feathered stockings of pure white. His wings had the rounded edges made for silent striking. A snowy oil.

"I thought I'd be a barn owl, or a little owl," he said out loud.

"No, you'd be the kind of bird whose egg you hatched from," another hooty voice informed him kindly. A larger snowy owl stood on the branch beside him. Arthur gasped. It was Uther. He had met him only once, when the old king came north to inspect the defenses near Hadrian's Wall. He wondered if that had been the only reason.

"A good guess," the white bird said. "I did come to see you. Who wouldn't want to know what his heir looked like, and what kind of a man you were shaping to be? And now I see. And I am pleased." Uther opened his great silver wings and lifted silently into the air. They carried him to another branch, which he gripped with his fierce, taloned feet. Arthur stood alone on his tree limb. "And now, pronounce."

"I can't," Arthur said. "I'm too ignorant."

"Where you falter, ask for advice," Uther said. "The first lesson in wisdom is to know what you know, and what you don't know."

"That's what Merlin is always telling me. He made me read Plato."

"I know." Arthur saw the twinkle of amusement in the great bird's eyes. "He told me, too. I didn't always listen, either."

"Please, sirs," said a shrike, peering shortsightedly around the dim clearing at the regal inquisitors. "Those hoodie crows destroyed my nest, and stole the mice I captured to feed my nestlings. Help me. Give me food for my young."

Arthur opened his beak. It was just like the farmer's plea for help he had heard that evening. The feathers on his stomach itched, and he scratched meditatively with an upturned claw, trying to remember the outcome. The shrike hopped to a twig near him, his narrow, black-masked face filled with hope.

"I . . . er, whose territory does this bird hunt in?" Arthur stammered to the parliament of owls.

"Mine," said a barn owl.

"Will you help him?"

"I will. He may have two shrews and a mouse in compensation, but he must remove immediately to his land. He has left his family to the mercy of the hoodies. They don't just eat rodents, you know."

The grateful shrike took off hastily, and the owls chirruped softly among themselves. Even the eagle owl had nothing to say.

"Good," said Uther from his perch.

"Will you teach me?" Arthur asked.

"I don't need to," the old king said. "You're already learning. But I'll give you a token." The snowy owl ducked his head into the curve of his wing and plucked therefrom a feather. The missing flight pinion made a gap as distinctive as a missing tooth. He extended it to Arthur with one talon. Arthur grasped it, and his foot brushed his father's. "And now, good-bye."

Arthur clutched the gift. "You can't go already!"

"But I must. You have other cases to hear." Other bird voices sounded loud in his ears, drowning out his father's soft murmur.

"My lord! My lord, only listen to me," a bird pleaded, jumping in between them. When Arthur could make the hysterical plaintiff alight, Uther was gone.

Arthur woke at false dawn to the early-morning hubbub of the camp. With half an eye open, Ector turned over on his narrow pallet, flinging his sheepskins around. When he was cold, he'd wake up. Kay snored at the ceiling, impervious to distraction. The fourth bed lay empty. Merlin was not there. Probably he had never been to bed. Remembering last night's task, Arthur wanted to see how the wounded men were doing. He started to get up. Something sharp poked him in the hand. The long, white owl's feather lay across his palm.

"Thank you," he whispered.

A snort and a gasp from Kay. "Oh, you're up," his foster brother said blearily. Kay threw the skins to the foot of his cot and went out, slinging his cloak over his shoulder.

"Here, now!" he shouted, beckoning to servants. "Water and ale for the King! The King rises!"

As soon as Kay was out of sight, Arthur scrabbled beneath the thin mattress for his bag of bits and pieces. The worn leather pouch held amulets given him by his foster mother and nurse, plus tokens from every dream Merlin had ever given him. There was a fish's scale the size of his thumbnail, a smooth stone, a pair of acorns, and other small treasures anyone else would call junk. At the bottom of the pouch was a cross Merlin had given him from Igraine, his late mother, and a dragon intaglio ring that had belonged to Uther. Lovingly, he placed the feather in with them.

There was no time to tell Merlin about the dream. That day Arthur followed the scouts, sword in palm, routing the remnants of the Saxon force from the farmsteads and forest havens alongside the other mounted warriors. Arthur fought like a wraith, striking but unstrikable. This time they captured one of Colgrim's lieutenants, whom Lot took charge of with a certain vicious glee. The remainder had melted away into the rough countryside, keeping a low profile even if it meant their long journey home would be cold and hungry. Though bloodthirsty, hard fighters, the barbarians were practical. Arthur had to admire that.

With the enemy gone, the army needed to concentrate on healing the wounded and burying their dead. Arthur visited the makeshift hospital set up in the cloister of the abandoned abbey. He stopped by each man, some laid out on no more than spread handfuls of straw, speaking with those who could speak and asking if there was anything he could do for them. He gave water to a man who was so badly gashed in the chest that, even inexperienced as he was, he could tell was dying.

On the other side of the overgrown garden lay the dead. It made him sad to see some of the widows who lived nearby claiming the bodies of their men. It was worse yet to watch them light up when they saw him approaching them. Instead of blaming him for the deaths, as they might have, some of them said that they were grateful that the High King was defending their homes.

"Even at the cost of their husbands and sons, they felt it was more important to be rid of the Saxons," Arthur said, disbelievingly.

"Know the worth of every tool you use: a sword, a cup, a man," Merlin said enigmatically. The enchanter knelt over a fighter whose arm was splinted, but Arthur could see that he had lost two fingers. He took the bowl the enchanter thrust at him. It sloshed with red-tinged water.

"How's he?" Coel asked, stalking over the dry grass to them.

"He'll live, and fight again," Merlin said.

"My thanks, Merlin," the King of Rheged said. "I value him. Do you want anything, Ger?"

"No, my lord," the man between them said feebly. "Thank you, sir."

"Get well, then. The lasses will miss you if it's not soon." With a grin and a wink, Coel turned away, hand on swordhilt.

"My lord!" Arthur stood up. Coel pivoted on his heel.

"Eh?"

Arthur's throat constricted. "I just wanted to say I . . . I'm grateful for your support, my lord," he said, stammering only slightly.

"Ah, well, you've got the marks of a good leader," Coel said, pleased, "if only you'll grow into them. I think you've started well."

"My lord, I must go see King Lot. Will you come with me?"

"Judgment by daylight? Of course, if you wish it. We'll gather up Strathclyde and Cornwall on our way along."

"I think it would be better now than later," Arthur said.

"I'll be right behind you, lad," Merlin said, straightening up.

The force from Lothian was striking its tents and pouring water on the smoldering campfires. A few awed armsmen directed the party toward one of the remaining pavilions. Kay and Ector joined the band between the cloister and the field.

"Give Kay your sword," Merlin whispered to Arthur before they reached the tent.

"What?" Arthur said, goggling. "No!"

"Give it him, I say. Remember the last time."

Reluctantly, the boy unbuckled his sword belt and handed Excalibur to the surprised Kay. He was just in time not to be observed, for Lot threw back the tent flap himself and strode out to meet them.

"Well, what is this? A confrontation?" Lot asked, looking down his nose at Rheged. No one spoke.

"I had no choice," Arthur said very quietly. Lot made a great show of staring over his head, pretending he couldn't see who was talking. "You question my authority."

Lot took the easy stance he used in combat, bouncing on the balls of his feet with his legs well apart.

"I do," he said contentiously. "Do you dare to put me on trial, you puppy?"

"No, my lord," Arthur said, still scrupulously polite. "You put me on trial. Here I stand without my scrying stone. I am just what you see here before you, no more, no less. Do you accept that I am the son of Uther?"

Grudgingly, Lot said, "Yes."

"Then what other criteria must I fulfill to be worthy for a warrior of your standing to follow? Bravery? Leadership? Wisdom?"

Lot emitted a bark of laughter. "You're too young to have any of those."

Arthur swallowed, wishing for Excalibur, just three paces away in his foster brother's hand, then realized the easy majesty of its wisdom would cloud his own judgment. Merlin was right. He had to fight this battle alone and empty-handed. A crowd was beginning to gather behind them, pushing in as close as they dared to listen.

"Well, I'll grow, my lord. I can't pretend to know everything. There's too many other people who know otherwise. But right is on my side, and I declare that you should follow me, as your High King."

"And why should I follow you?"

The fierce stare was like that of the eagle owl in his dream, piercing to his heart, but Arthur was no longer afraid of him.

"Because of the oath you swore to my father. I claim the same."

"He was a seasoned leader," Lot said. "I could respect him. You're a child."

"I know I am not yet what he was," Arthur said seriously, "but I won't learn kingship unless I go forward. I'd appreciate your counsel and your experience. You can't wait for me to grow up to help join Britain together. It must be *now*, or the Saxons will tear us all apart. Will you give me your oath?"

"Now, that's a reasonable request," Coel said to Lot. He slapped Arthur's shoulder. "A little of that pretty swordplay's affected your tongue at last, boy. What do you say, Lothian?"

"As chief among your trusted advisors, I will agree," Lot said slowly with the emphasis to show he was saving face before his followers. His eyes darted from one of his peers to another. They rested at last on Arthur's. "In that case, you will have my vow."

"Then kneel," Arthur said, holding out his hand to Kay. Excalibur's warm purr came as a relief to his jangled nerves. He took the sword across his two hands. Lot, on one knee, placed his on top of them. "I, Arthur, son of Uther Pendragon, and by right king of all Britain, hear and acknowledge this oath to be sworn before my sword, Excalibur."

Excalibur hummed loudly, nearly vibrating in his hands. The magic must have been perceptible to the northern leader, for when Lot spoke, his voice was subdued.

"I, Lot of Lothian, give my oath of fealty. . . ."

When it was over, Arthur handed the sword to Kay. Lot rose gracefully to his feet and swept a slight bow to him. "And now, High King, if you'll excuse me, there's a lot to be done. We've a long road ahead of us."

"As have we all, my lord," Arthur said. With dignity, he turned away and walked back toward his own tent. Coel was almost chuckling.

Arthur waited until he was out of sight of the Lothian camp before claiming Excalibur back from Kay and buckling it firmly around his middle. The sword's hum of approval coursed through his body. He walked with a springy step, having disposed at last of the weight bearing him down.

"There, you see?" Merlin said, for once having to stride to catch up with him. "You've just proved you can be an effective king with or without Excalibur."

Arthur swept the sword out of its scabbard, carving patterns in the air until the wind whistled along the blade. It was as light in his hand now as it was in battle, and he loved it. He laughed out loud, and people turned to look at him.

"I'd much rather it be *with* Excalibur," he said.

Where Bestowed

SUSAN DEXTER

hrice, Arthur sent Bedivere to cast his sword Excalibur into the haunted pool. Twice, Bedivere was a sensible man, and balked at consigning a fine-crafted blade to a chill, watery grave. He lied, and swore he'd done the deed—but he lied poorly, for Arthur saw through the dissembling, the report of wind and waves, the fable of water ebbing and flowing, and ordered Bedivere out again, his face stern with disappointment.

"What sawest thou?" the dying King asked a third time.

"I bound the jeweled girdle about the golden hilt and hurled the sword with all my might, so that it sailed far out over the pool. And lo! as it neared the water, a great hand and arm, garbed in white samite, did rise up through the waves. This hand caught Excalibur by the haft, shook the sword and brandished it three times—then vanished with the blade back into the mere," quoth Bedivere, voice and limbs alike shaking. And Arthur the King was borne away to Avalon by weeping women, not to die but to come again, folk said.

Arthur would not come again. Kernan had not actually

seen the body, but he had been near his king close to the end, and he had seen enough dying men to know another, royal or not. He gave the warped oars another hard pull, then lifted them in the broken locks. Water dripped down, returning to the pond with dull splashing sounds.

Kernan—though he saw the need for it—did not believe in Arthur's rumored immortality. No more did he countenance Bedivere's fabulous tale of Excalibur's end. Bedivere had lost much blood that day, and knew he was losing his king, and had lost heart. Likely he had hallucinated.

Kernan pulled a coil of tarred rope from its concealment beneath the thwart. Tied tightly to one end was a rusty grapnel.

Freezing fog shrouded Dozmary pool. Had there been a tree growing within a league, 'twould have been bare-branched. Winter was not the season Kernan would have preferred for his task—but 'twas the time he could most be sure of being least watched by Saxon eyes.

Bedivere had truly cast the sword into the water, for no man had surfaced with Excalibur after Camlann, claiming to be Arthur's heir. That was likely why Arthur had stubbornly ordered his sword cast away, so that Excalibur could never be used to make legitimate a spurious claim. But a bodiless arm, waving the sword and then bearing it away—no, that was the product of fancy, born of terrible wounds and crushing defeat. Excalibur lay where Bedivere had flung it, stuck in the cold dark mud below the waters of Dozmary pool. There was no doubt of that.

Kernan lowered the hook slowly into the water, till he felt it bump the bottom. Having the measure of the depth, he secured the line's other end to the thwart, then began to row, slowly, so that the grapnel dragged through mud and water weed, questing.

Three years since Arthur's death. Other men had tried to rally what remained of Arthur's host against the floodtide of the

Saxon invaders. Some had sat on Arthur's throne, some had won victories, but none could think themselves to have succeeded. The last flames of civilization, the last lights of reason, guttered like spent candles. Soon darkness would fall upon them all, as British men bent knees to Saxon jarls.

Kernan pulled the grapnel up, cast it again. The people needed a rallying point, a proof that great Arthur would come again to deliver them. A lie, but a lie that would put heart and fight back into them, ere all was lost. Kernan might need to drag every inch of the pool, but he aimed to give his people back Excalibur.

He did not waste precious time with searching the shallows close by the shore, where reeds grew in summer and rustled eerie tunes to winter's winds. Even sore wounded, Bedivere could hurl a sword farther than *that*. And unlike the sea, the pond had no tides to move objects once they were within its depths. The sword would still be where it had gone down.

Three days it took him to drag the middle distance, around and endlessly around, till he had fished as deep as he had line to reach. Kernan had not thought Dozmary so deep. Nor so large, but he was a little prepared for the pool to seem broader and broader as he worked his weary way around it. Fishing long hours in the cold, with naught to show but frozen feet, a cramped back, fingers so chapped and cracked that they bled—though he couldn't feel the flow—his misery distorted the size of the task, and with it the size of the pool.

He was not quite at the center of the pond, when he could no longer find bottom with the grapnel. Kernan cast an eye toward the shore. Could Bedivere truly have flung the blade such a distance? It was just possible, he thought. Had to be possible, for if the sword had gone to its grave closer in, he'd have snagged it by then, as he'd snagged a score of ancient tree branches and enough waterweed to feed a dozen kelpies.

All night Kernan tossed in his bedroll, trying to decide

how to proceed. He saw no way of searching the remaining bottom save by diving down to it. He had no more rope, and if he ventured in search of it, he might arouse suspicions, or be spotted by a Saxon patrol. It was a wonder he had not been discovered ere then, for all that Dozmary was a remote place, avoided by any man with more sense and less desperation. And more rope might not answer—it had been hard enough to comb the deeper parts with one small hook, to be sure he did not skip over so much as a foot of ground. The deeper the water, the more difficult that task would be. Cold or no, he must dive. It was the only way to continue his search.

Dawn dismayed him. The pool had frozen over, and the air burned Kernan's exposed face and hands when he launched his boat. Colder than sleet, the wind sharper than a sword edge.

The new ice proved no thicker than the bubbly glass churches and wealthy folk used to glaze their windows. It wouldn't bear his weight, and the boat shattered a way through it easily enough, doing its hull no damage. At the center of the pool, Kernan used an oar to break open a wide expanse of the surface. The drops that splashed up froze again upon the wind-brushed wool of his once-scarlet cloak.

He doffed the knightly cloak and his cavalryman's boots. He pulled the rust-stained tunic over his head, crying out unexpectedly at the air's cruel touch. Kernan had thought he could feel no further cold—plainly, he had been too optimistic.

The water, when he lowered himself over the side, was worse. It sucked the warmth from the marrow of Kernan's bones, leached the last vestige of heat from the smallest of his veins. His teeth chattered till he clamped his jaws, fearing they'd break one another, and the shaking spread then in great shivers down to his shoulders, along his arms.

He let go of the boat. He must dive at once, quickly, for he could not long endure the water's embrace. It was stealing the life out of him. He must waste no moment on his discomfort—

he was a knight, trained to endure hardship, to spurn pain as unworthy of his notice. Kernan bent at the waist and ducked beneath the water, his feet kicking strongly to drive him deep.

It was work to get down past a certain depth. If a man did not swim, he would sink, but only a yard or so. Kernan had swum in the sea as a child, and knew that he must stroke downward to reach the bottom, to counter the tendency of his body to bob upward like a bit of cork. His legs, strong from years spent gripping a war-stallion, churned the icy water, propelling him deeper and deeper.

His hands met mud. Kernan groped, and unclosed his eyes, but could see no great distance nor any detail. The water was murky, the light filtering from above was not great, and he was making matters worse stirring up the mud with his fingers. He saw nothing protruding above the indistinct bottom, no hilt of a sword gone point-first into the ooze. But if the blade instead lay flat, he would not see it, would needs find it with his fingers rather than his eyes.

His lungs burned urgently. He must surface to breathe. Kernan let his head come up, and kicked again, heading for the circle of brightness, so far overhead. A dozen kicks. The light grew larger. His legs worked harder. He had to make it—

He burst through the surface, stale breath exploding from his lips. The air—the welcome air—was so cold as to make the water feel warm by contrast. Kernan trod water, gasping. When his lungs ceased to labor, he filled them as deeply as he could, and went back down at once, with sure strokes.

It was difficult to stay certain of his position, to comb every last inch of the bottom. If he strayed by so much as an armspan, there would be a great patch of cold mud left unsearched. And he could only feel over such a tiny bit ere his need for air drove him upward once again.

Each dive seemed of shorter duration than the one before it. He was tiring and did not recover his wind swiftly enough.

He lost track of how many times he had gone down, lost sense of his own limitations. He was a fool to continue, yet he did not cease and return to the shore, or even to the boat. Once more only, Kernan promised himself—again and again.

He broke through glassy ice, and cut his face, sliced his pale hands. He drew in scarcely any air before he sank once more, and had only a bare instant for groping through the cold mud ere need for air sent him plunging upward. He surfaced, already opening his mouth, to suck down a great draft of air that would fuel a longer dive. He had felt—

He didn't notice the shadow above him. His head hit the flat keel of the drifting boat, which did not yield to him as the ice had. Kernan got a mouthful of cold water instead of air, floundered a little way down, then surfaced again alongside the boat. He clung to its icy side, while he panted and coughed and choked. When he had the strength, he would climb back in. It was time he rested, huddled by a fire. In a moment. The unexpected blow had dazed him, still his sight was dark, shot with sparks of violet light the dim day could not produce. Kernan gripped the rimed wood, tried to summon the will to haul himself out of the water. His shoulders tensed for the effort.

And released. Surely he had felt something, on that final dive? His fingers had brushed an object more solid than mud, just as he had been forced upward by the foolish weakness of his lungs? The blow had nearly driven it from his head, but his fingers remembered clearly. A cross shape. A sword's hilt—

A single strong kick sent him down into the blackness. Unerring, his hands went to the place they remembered. A longish shape rose out of the mud. He wrapped his arms about it. It caught. He pulled at it all the more, spending the last crumb of his strength.

He had no more air. But if he released the sword—he would not, for he might not find it again. Kernan clasped the blade tighter, and kicked blindly for the surface.

His legs tangled, with the sword and with ensnaring water-weed. Their strokes were feeble. Mud rose through the water, dimming the tiny circle of light he struggled to aim himself at. By the time he could see it again, he knew it was beyond his reach.

"He came to us of his own folly, sisters. He belongs to us."

The voice echoed in Kernan's head. Folly indeed, he agreed. He had been too stubborn to believe Bedivere, which had carried him to his goal—but that same stubbornness had betrayed him, made him keep diving in the chill water past all sense, certainly far past his strength. He'd nearly drowned—

"He came to steal the sword. Punished, he must be."

This voice rippled like water, cold and pitiless, lapping against the misty shores of his mind. *I am dead,* Kernan realized, and felt even colder than he was. He had indeed drowned, and now lay in the underworld, awaiting judgment. He strove to prepare his soul, but somehow the cold voice had withered all hope—he could not recall a single praiseworthy action, could dredge up nothing but an endless chain of guilts and griefs. He was one of Arthur's knights, but for every light they had shielded from the dark tide, it seemed to Kernan that he had spilled a gallon of blood—he heard the battlefield shriek of ravens, over the lapping of the water.

"He would have taken, sisters—but not stolen. His heart was pure. Do not punish—rather allow him to bear what he sought to take from us." The voice sounded like a gentle spring rain, splashing into a pond, whispering reassuringly as it pleaded.

"It was not given to him."

"Yet it must be given."

"Is he worthy?"

"The sword serves wherever bestowed."

"Where bestowed—"

* * *

Kernan was too weak to open his eyes. The quarreling voices faded away, with a last splash or two, like rags of dream.

He felt grass beneath him, warmth upon his skin. Light seeped through his lashes, unsealed his lids. The sun! He opened his eyes, lifted his head, and looked wonderingly about.

He was deep within the endless green of a summer woodland. Green trees above, green undergrowth all about. Soft emerald grass underfoot. Kernan arose carefully, his head light and ringing, a memory of cold and ice lying behind his sight, receding rapidly. A dream, it must have been. He stood at the shore of a little pool of water, but it was not the half-frozen mere he thought he recalled—this was but a spring, deep and secret between mossy rocks, surrounded by ferns and mint. As he watched, a striped badger waddled over the green rocks and lapped a drink, not fearing him, though it saw him.

His senses swam again, the green woodland swirled like fire-smoke. Kernan could not recall how he had come there. His head ached dully. He thought he remembered a blow—he must have been stunned, have swooned. Possibly his fellow knights had thought him dead, and left him. Possibly they had been forced to abandon him, but intended to return. He could see a few hoofprints cut into the grass, though no sign of combat.

Kneeling by the pool, Kernan drank. The water was chill as ice, but he seemed to take strength from it, as if it had been wine. He rose again, steadier on his legs.

There seemed little point in remaining by the water. If he followed the hoofprints, or at least the deer-track they pointed him toward, surely he would come upon the others of his company. Food, a fire, an explanation of what had befallen him. . . . Kernan set off in quest of those comforts.

He lost sight of the hoofprints almost at once, but there was a trail wending through the undergrowth, plain enough to one skilled in woodcraft. Kernan strode along it, feeling his strength returning. They had said Gawaine took his strength from the sun above, growing greater in power from dawn till noon, his prowess then declining to normal levels as the sun westered. Kernan had thought that a fancy, a useful way to awe a superstitious foe. Now he wondered. But the mid of the day passed, and he felt no fatigue beyond that ordinarily born of walking.

Long shafts of sunlight pierced the forest as the sun slipped down the far side of the sky. Kernan had seen no sign at all of Arthur's men—he no longer quite expected to. But he all at once smelled smoke on the wind, and he made for it as best the woodland would permit, pushing through the thin brush when the trail did not wind where he wished it to go.

Night had fallen, but he could still find his way—no tangle of vine or bramble was ever quite impassible, no ravine so steep-sided that it barred him. The scent of the smoke was stronger, heavy enough to convince him that it did not proceed from a cooking fire nor yet a charcoal burner's craft. There were other scents on the breeze with it. Familiar taints. Iron, and blood.

He came upon a broad passage between the trees, much trampled recently. The forest duff was trodden to mud, branches and twigs torn off or broken away at knee-height. Many men had passed, horses too. A bit of metal proved to be a ring from a mail-shirt. There was a spill of grain, as from a split sack, and an empty leather wineskin farther on, which reeked of ale.

Taken together, the scant signs said: *war*. Looting, Saxons belike. Kernan proceeded with due caution, along the sort of trail he was too familiar with.

He came to the woodshore, and paused ere he broke from its cover. His eyes were well used to the dark, but his other senses could tell him vastly more if he let them.

The smoke wafted stronger. Besides wood, he could smell burning wool, and straw, and singed feathers. There was a sort of roasted meat smell too, and the coppery tang of spilled blood. The distance was not great—a quarter-league perchance. Just over the crest of yon hill . . .

His ears warned of no present danger, so Kernan quit the woods and jogged swiftly up the hilly slope. He took full advantage of whatever cover the rolling ground offered, for he was hearing voices now. Drunken shouts, and screams of either terror or pain.

He stumbled over the corpse of a farm dog, spitted on a broken spear, its teeth still gripping the shaft. Nearby hulked the smoking remains of a byre. He ducked behind the charred wood, ignoring the heat it still gave off.

Red flames danced before the farmer's thatched hut. The roof had been set alight, but had gone out before all was consumed. The flames now were only from a bonfire that was roasting a crudely spitted pig. A dozen men squatted around it. Ruddy light winked on rusty armor, scale and ring-mail both. It picked out the nose-guard of a helmet, the brass boss that decorated a shield. The short Saxon knife held at the throat of the farmwife.

One of him, unarmed, against a dozen of them, armed and armored. Drunk too, but Kernan did not think they were so far gone as to make that an advantage for him. Cloth ripped—the farmwife's gown.

She did not scream, nor struggle. Kernan could see a man who must have been her husband lying dead. Possibly she thought there was no help for her, so no use to scream. Or—

In the doorway of the cottage, he saw two faces peeping from the darkness. Children, spared if their mother submitted to her captors.

Women. Children. The helpless. Arthur's knights were sworn to protect such, even unarmed, even with the last drop of their blood. With a great cry, Kernan leaped into the firelight.

Faces swung toward him. Blue eyes widened, flaxen beards parted to let out warning shouts, grunts of surprise. Kernan laid furiously about him, wishing he had a sword, knowing how he would slash *here* and thrust *there*. Not a one of the renegades would stand against him—

All at once, he realized that none of them was. Kernan stumbled over a body at his feet, his limbs wobbly as if he had run a dozen leagues or fought for hours. The fire had been trampled and scattered, but it still gave a flicker now and again. He was the only thing within the ragged circle of light still standing.

Here lay a Saxon with his throat slashed. There another crumpled over a spill of his own innards, with a terrible wound across his middle. Beyond, another man lay upon his back as if asleep, thrust so solidly through the heart that he had crossed over into the next world almost unawares.

Kernan's head was aching fiercely. His knees nearly buckled, and he sank down unsteadily to kneel with his senses spinning. He wanted to count the bodies, but could not. He saw no Saxon alive, heard none sneaking back to kill him as he had slain their companions.

However that had been. Someone had been quite busy with a sword, hacking and slashing as he had desired to be able to do. Unarmed, he might nonetheless have throttled a man— aided by surprise—before being stabbed in the back or slashed across the throat himself. One man. Never a dozen. Even champions such as Gawaine, Lancelot, did not claim such prowess. Battle-madness he had heard tell of, but this struck him as madness of another order.

Something moved. Kernan jerked his head up, staggered to his feet. Only the farmwife, dappled with blood not her own. She backed away from him slowly, hands held out to ward him off.

Kernan shook his head. Did she suppose he intended to

finish what the Saxons had begun? What did she take him for? He tried to laugh—certain he had never looked *less* one of Arthur's paladins. The sound was very odd to his ears.

The two girls came out of the doorway at last, clinging to their mother. One was tiny, all eyes, thumb fast in mouth. The other was nearly a woman—but not quite. Kernan gazed at her with a strange longing, recalling the maidens who had attended Arthur's queen, graced his court.

He was very light-headed. His feet felt far away, as if he balanced upon stilts. He might, Kernan thought, be wounded, and losing blood. But he felt no pain, and he had a duty to guide these helpless ones to better shelter than he could offer them. A neighboring farm, a village—there might even be a hill-fort nearby. Saxon renegades preyed on the weak and isolated in preference to attacking those likely to defend themselves, even in these troubled days. And what he had run across was certainly no war-host. There would be some safety near enough to reach.

The woman put an arm over his shoulder. Her older daughter put a small hand upon the other. And so Kernan conducted them, step by slow step, down the muddy lane, through pasture and woodland, till they came at length to another steading, where the only smoke rose from the fire cooking breakfast porridge. Kernan left them there. The woman called out, and stumbled away from him, toward the farmyard. The maiden took her little sister's hand and went after her mother. Pausing, she gave him one longing look, but Kernan was already melting back into the forest's green. He trotted away, down a trail no eye less apt than his own could have found. He had no idea why he left them without a word. A great unexpected shyness had come over him, and he was helpless to resist. The women were safe, that had been his goal, he went his way.

The green of the woodland deepened as the sun left the

sky. Kernan trotted on, unconcerned. A light beckoned to him, but when he neared it, he saw that it was only light by contrast—a gap in the canopy of leaves overhead, less dark than the benighted forest all around. At the center of the clearing sparkled a pool.

Kernan was not hungry, but he had a great thirst. He knelt and drank the cool water in long, slow drafts. He remembered, with a pang sharp as a blow, what he had once been seeking— the magic blade that would have done for all his people what he had done for the farm woman. If only—

He opened his eyes just as moonlight found its way to the surface of the pond. There was a ripple or two as drops fell from his lips, but otherwise the mirror was as true as any the master silversmith had crafted for the King's court. Kernan stared into it.

A white horse stared back at him. Or was it a deer, but antlerless? Water dripped from its dainty muzzle, and troubled the surface of the pool. The ripples moved across its long, slender legs, with their cloven hooves. Kernan turned his head, startled.

The image in the pool did likewise. And moonlight flashed from the single, fluted horn that sprang from its forehead.

Kernan's mind reeled again. His senses swam. His head ached, but it was not quite pain. Rather, an unfamiliar burden—but one he had sought. His heart grew very full.

"The sword serves wherever bestowed."

Slowly, he dipped the horn toward the moonlit water, till the tip just broke the surface. He raised the magic blade again.

Excalibur saluted the Ladies of the Lake.

Demon Sword

BILL FAWCETT

he scream began with rage, but ended with pain. It came from somewhere below and to the left of where she stood. Morganna hoped that it had come from one of *his* men and not one of theirs. The elderly king whose land they now defended met her eyes and tried to look assured even as he loosened his sword. For three days an army raised by the local kings had fought against the larger army of Arthur, self-declared High King of all the Britons. The night before, Morganna had preached an end to their retreat. If they were driven any farther, all of their lands would be lost. Now she worried that she had encouraged them to take a hopeless stand.

The dark-haired priestess risked a glance around the tree. She had been cowering there for longer than her pride allowed. It was safe to look now. Since the two lines of dismounted men-at-arms and knights had met, the arrow fire had almost stopped. A few feet from her lay the body of a squire. An arrow had entered through his side and penetrated so deeply, only the feathered end of its haft was visible. His body was sprawled, and the message he had rushed to deliver to the Druidess or old king had been lost with his life.

The ten kings who had gathered this army had decided to make their stand at the top of the hill. They had been defeated twice already, but had no choice but to continue to fight. Before the War King had decided only he should hold the title, there had been dozens of British kings, each ruling his own lands. Most of those who fought him now had sworn allegiance to Arthur or stood with this army against the Saxons. Now all the kings were desperate men, risking all that they had or would leave their children.

The hill was thickly covered with trees, and this had helped protect them from the arrows of the Welsh mercenaries Arthur had hired for this, his latest attempt at complete domination of all the Britons. This hill had been chosen carefully some days before. One side of the hill was also nearly unclimbable, unscalable by a man in armor. This ensured their smaller force would not be outflanked. The steep slope would also tire an attacker weighed down by armor and a shield.

Arriving a few hours ahead of Arthur's army, their men had just enough time to cut and plant a low wooden palisade halfway up the slope and sharpen swords dulled by the running battle of the past three days.

The crude defenses were complete. Too exhausted to even worry, the combined armies of ten kings had sat in the shade and waited. Too soon his mounted scouts had appeared. Within the hour the familiar clatter of armored men warned that his main battle had arrived. The arrows had begun to fall just as the first of Arthur's men-at-arms became visible laboring up the hill.

Morganna watched the battle but had little hope of victory. More screams filled the air, vying with the clank of metal on metal and the thud of sword meeting shield. From where she stood, Morganna could see almost half the line their loyal liegemen had formed along the hillside. Spots of sunlight that filtered through the leaves glittered occasionally off polished weapons, and red off the blood that flowed from new wounds. Tearing her eyes from the closest fighting, she could also see that the bulk of Arthur's force was being thrown at the center, directly below and to the left of where she stood.

As she watched, their line bulged inward. Involuntarily the Druid priestess backed up a few quick steps. With a scream of frustration the old king dashed down the slope. Behind him came the other local kings who had joined together to stop Arthur from taking control of their ancestral lands and homes. It was three years since Arthur had been declared War King of all the Britons after he had led them to victory at Badon Hill. In the next year he led small, mounted columns against what remained of the Saxon invaders. Then the old man, a wizard and convert of the dead god, had arrived.

At first Merlin's presence in the war camps had meant little. All sorts were attracted by the power and glory Arthur had won at Badon Hill. But slowly the Welsh priest had gained the ear of the War King. Into that ear he had whispered tales of when Rome had ruled their island and of empire. But at first these seeds of conquest had mattered little, for the Saxons were too badly mauled to remain a threat. Most of the warriors and kings he had gathered began taking their leave from Arthur's army. They had been three seasons in the field, and even the mercenaries were tired of war.

Then Merlin had given Arthur the Demon Sword. Morganna knew it was demon formed. She could sense the dark power of the Sidhe in its blade the one time she had been near it. Then she had been standing among a small village of peasants as they tilled their fields. She had just treated a child with herbs for the cramping ailment and gone to tell the parents it would soon be well. Sitting astride a magnificent black stallion at the head of his knights, Arthur had passed them by without a glance. It was well he ignored the young woman in undyed homespun. It meant that he missed the shudder and moan that his dread blade's mere presence had caused in the sensitive Druidess.

The sword had tried to capture her, capture Morganna's mind, as it had those of the knights accompanying him. It was then that the Druidess realized the danger and subtle enchantment. There were tales of other such weapons in the histories the bards recited. Mostly these swords had been obvious gifts, or traps, sent from the ephemeral reaches of the banished Sidhe. Too often they were given to the enemies of the earth powers in revenge for their banishment.

In her years of studying on the Holy Isle Morganna had learned about such weapons. They were rare, but not unheard of. Most were left from the dark days before the Britons had been a true people. There were magical swords that flamed, and others protected their bearer from wounds. One demon-made sword was rumored to tear the very souls from anyone it struck. This sword was more perfidious than any of these enchanted weapons. At least they killed cleanly. This blade, Excalibur it was called, gave its holder the power to rule other men. When Arthur approached, you wanted, wanted with every bit of your being, to follow him without question. No demand seemed unreasonable, no sacrifice too great. And based upon the glow she had seen in the War King's eyes as she had ridden past, it also gave its user the need to lead such magically recruited fanatics.

Even driven by the power of the sword, Arthur's men fell back before the strength of the local kings and their bodyguards. Most wore only leather, so the mailed nobility cut through their ranks easily. Victory turned to rout as the nobles struck. Their attackers clambered back over the wall of stakes, several dying from spears in their backs as they retreated.

The followers of the sword wielder never gave quarter and received none.

The sounds of fighting continued to both sides, but then faded and the crisis had passed. The kings began moving back up the slope. As they approached, the Druidess saw they were carrying a body. The old king, who had been so proud and worried moments before, had fallen. From the angle his head drooped, she was sure he was dead. Once they were closer, the hole where the sword had torn through his chain-mail shirt and pierced his heart was evident. Morganna fought back a sob and tried to look strong. The Council of Druids had sent her from the Holy Isle to rally these people, so she couldn't show any weakness. Inside her, something gentle retreated a little farther behind her hate for the Sidhe and what they had loosed upon her world.

From midday to sundown the battle ebbed and flowed, with Arthur's forces unable to break through their primitive bailey. Morganna was taking more risks now, bringing water and an encouraging word to the remaining defenders. They would be able to rest soon. Sunset was drawing closer, and a night attack unlikely. Morganna looked forward to the respite, even if the battle would simply resume at first light.

Returning to the center of their line, the dark-haired woman collapsed against the same tree behind which she had sheltered earlier. The War King's men had pulled back to re-group for a third time, and the arrows had not yet begun to fall. For that brief instant the forest seemed almost peaceful, the Oaks reminded Morganna of the Gathering Glen on the Holy Isle and happier times.

Instead of the expected harassment by Arthur's Welsh bowmen, Arthur's forces charged out of the trees below. With visibly increased determination, the metal-clad knights and leather-clad companions threw themselves at the weakened wooden barrier. Men risked their lives to press against the sharpened stakes and stab through at the local king's men. Again the line of armed men was pushed back from the wooden palisade. The king's bodyguards, their only reserve, moved to reinforce their liegemen. As they hurried past her, Morganna looked over the battle to the trees beyond. There had to be some reason for the renewed vigor of their attackers.

For the next dozen breaths there was no sign of Arthur or his demon sword. Then with a flourish of hunting horns he appeared. Looking down the hill at the War King, she saw him as less impressive than the time he had ridden by her. His helmet was off so the men could see he was there. He was younger than she'd thought, and even from a hundred paces away he seemed tired. His surcoat was torn and stained with blood. Surrounded by the banners of the kings who served him, he looked very much like a War Leader, not just a king. She wondered how much of the impression was contrived.

By the way Arthur spurred himself into the battle, she quickly concluded the bloodstains were not posturing. His men raised a cheer as the War King spurred his massive mount forward until the dark horse was pressed against the wooden bastion. With a wild swing of Excalibur he cut down two defenders. As the blood struck the sword, Morganna could hear a high-pitched hum that was almost beyond her ability to hear. The blade's song echoed off the leaves as the Sidhe blade worked its magic.

Where Arthur's men had fought bravely, now they attacked without regard to their own safety. Not far below where she stood, the Druidess watched in dismay as one man threw himself onto a sword blade so that the man behind could cut down their now disarmed opponent. She'd heard tales of berserkers fighting with the fire-haired giants from the frozen lands, but this reality was almost beyond belief. Or would have been if it were not so painfully real. There was no way to stand against their frenzied attack. As Arthur's liegemen fought with renewed zeal, each defender suddenly felt the need to follow, not oppose, the War King. For many the hesitation their mixed feelings caused was their last mistake. Howls of pain and death rattles replaced what few battle cries the local kings' men had managed moments before.

It wasn't until blood spattered the hem of her gown that Morganna realized all was lost. All along their line, men were clambering over the barricade while defenders threw down their weapons and cried for mercy. Arthur rode along the stakes using the demon sword to slice gaps through the hand-thick poles as if they were twigs. Over the failing din of battle and defeat the sword continued its siren song. Those who were not already surrendering began to flee. The priestess had no choice but to join them. Even she was having trouble resisting that demon song. In a few more minutes she would have found herself cheering that murderer's success in stealing lands that had been held by the local kings for a dozen generations.

The branches tore at Morganna as she dashed through the thickest portions of the forest she could find. She knew that whatever slowed her would hamper the horsemen that pursued her much more. Behind, the annoyed blasphemy of a man-at-arms whose horse had shied at the thorn thicket rewarded her efforts.

Her breath came in painful sobs, but the Druidess had to keep moving. The last hours were a jagged patchwork of flight and near capture. As Morganna had fled the lost battle, a cry had gone up from Arthur. "After her," he had bellowed. "She caused this." The only woman on the field, there was no question whom he meant. Tired men had hurried to obey. Some were those who had cheered her message of support from the High Council four days ago. Fortunately most had lost their horses in the three days of fighting, and nearly all had been too exhausted to follow far. Only these last three, now two, continued the chase. But they were mounted well, and she needed to do something more than be driven before them.

Tired of running and sure of capture, the dark-haired priestess sat heavily and tried to compose herself. Her pursuers were barely visible through the thick foliage. She was in the center of a thick clump of red berry bushes. Their thorns tore at her back and arms. A large spider with a bright blue body skittered up a branch near her face. Forcing herself to breathe slowly, Morganna fought to regain the inner calm she needed. Then, even as the two horsemen approached to within bowshot, she rose beyond herself and searched.

For a panicky moment Morganna worried that the now-distant battle had driven off all of the larger denizens of the forest. To her relief she finally found a bear patiently waiting with its paw poised over a nearby stream. Apologizing for her necessity, the Druidess's spirit descended toward the hairy fisherman.

When the snarling bear attacked, it opened the flank of one warhorse with a single swipe of one paw. Yellowed claws tore through horseflesh, and the wounded equine bucked and writhed to escape the pain. Its rider landed heavily against a tree and sat stunned.

The remaining pursuer was a knight. His heavy chain coat gave him confidence. Drawing his sword, he jumped from his saddle and moved to face the large brown bear. The two circled cautiously until the bear suddenly turned and snarled at the tethered warhorse. Instantly the horse pulled free and fled the menace. The knight was surprised at the bear's fierce attack and unusual behavior. Normally the woodland bears hurried away at the sight of even a child. This one, he worried, must be ill or have lost its mind. Either eventuality, he realized, would make it a formidable foe. Still, he felt compelled to stand and defend his fallen companion. There was no doubt he could defeat the monster. His sword gave him reach and his armor protection.

The brave knight was even more surprised when the bear suddenly subsided, looked confused, and its snarls changed to a confused whimper. The armored man made a single threatening dash toward the bear and it fled noisily back into the forest's depths.

Helping his companion to rise, the knight realized that they were now afoot, one of them injured, and it would soon be sunset. There was no hope of capturing the woman they had chased for so many hours. Wearily he gathered up the half-conscious sergeant and began the long walk back to the camp of the High King.

Morganna also quickly succumbed to exhaustion. She curled upon herself and fell quietly asleep beneath the thorn-and berry-filled bushes. Except for the worried movements of a very disoriented bear, the forest returned to normal.

Less than two dozen tired and discouraged men crouched around the fire. Around them the forest was dark and, they hoped, empty. Morganna sat in their midst, not sure how they would react if she spoke. She had encouraged them to resist. The message she had carried from the Holy Isle had been just short of a demand. She glanced nervously around, knowing that should they realize she had led them to their downfall, she would die horribly.

"He still must be stopped," a hoarse voice spoke out above the murmur.

There were disparaging cries of "what?" and "how?"

It was Percival, the son of the elderly king Morganna had seen die, who spoke. His grief and bitterness were clearly visible to those who met his eyes. "We have lost a battle. Yes. But so long as we live and fight, he can be stopped!"

A few men stirred and dared to hope. Most sat listlessly. Percival rose to tower over the tired men and continued.

"We must still resist. Arthur has brought all of the Britons under the thrall of evil. That demon-spawned sword, Excalibur, is the source of his power."

Percival raised his voice until he was almost yelling. A few of the more cautious glanced nervously into the darkness.

"But we were three hundred and now we are barely twenty," a grizzled knight protested.

"He cannot be defeated," another added through teeth clenched with pain as he marked the pronouncement by a gesture with a badly wounded arm.

"Not in battle," one of the surviving kings agreed.

"Not in battle." Percival nodded. His expression was distant and he returned to sitting by the fire.

There was a long silence. Unlike before, many now sat with thoughtful expressions.

"One man, Arthur, is the cause of our defeat," one man finally asserted. "It's his death that will save us."

"I'll not become an assassin," the knight who first spoke growled.

"And no one has asked you to!" Percival snapped back. Then he continued in a more controlled way. "All that is happening comes from Arthur. A plague we wished upon ourselves when we declared him War King."

"War King it was, not High and only king," a voice added bitterly.

"Though he led us to victory over the fair-skinned invaders," the oldest surviving king reminded them all, "when we thought all was lost."

"The demon sword," Morganna risked speaking for the first time.

Percival and others turned to stare.

"It's not Arthur. It's the sword," she explained nervously.

The others waited, intent to hear more. Relieved that they would listen, Morganna continued.

"His sword *is* demon work. It is not only unholy sharp, but gives him the power to make men follow him blindly. That is why your brave liegemen failed when he joined the battle."

There were nods of agreement. Everyone had felt the power of the sword's song. She was just putting into words what they suspected. Percival smiled and gestured for Morganna to go on. It was a cold, revenge-filled grin.

"Then we must take the sword from him," she announced.

"He keeps it with him always," several of the group protested. "And once he holds it and demands his faith, any thief will join him and betray us all."

"I am not a thief," a man-at-arms protested.

"Better you were," another answered.

A number of those around the fire looked from face to face as if searching for an idea, or wondering which of them would betray the others.

"When he is asleep?" Morganna suggested.

One of the knights who had fought beside Arthur at Badon Hill shook his head.

"No, he sleeps lightly and with a guard outside his tent," he explained. He didn't add that he'd been proud to have that duty the day before Badon Hill. "Any stranger that comes near, there'd be an alarm and he'll grab the sword." The knight ended his comment with a slicing gesture across his neck and a shrug.

Again all was silent for too long. Morganna worried. She had been sent by the Council to stop Arthur before he destroyed a millennia of tradition and stability. She would not go back a failure, dooming the Druids and their Holy Isles to destruction worse than even the Roman pillage had brought. Arthur had made no secret that he would break any power that might challenge his own, and the Druids had become his implacable enemy the moment that sword had appeared.

"We will never find him alone and asleep," one old king finally announced.

"Not alone," Percival cut in with a growing, if sinister smile. "Asleep eventually, but not alone."

As he spoke, he looked to Morganna. The others followed his gaze. She stared back at them. It took her a moment to understand what he was suggesting. Then there was another moment of panic and she wanted to rush back into the forest and sit shivering. Instead the Druidess forced herself to stay calm and consider.

Did she hate Arthur enough? Was banishing the sword worth any sacrifice? That sacrifice? She was comely enough, but what if Arthur spurned her and spoiled the plan? Mars rules lust, and he would be strong with all the death. But the older women said battle often sharpened men's appetites. There were certain herbs . . . it could work. She'd seen cattail reeds nearby, but where would she find carraway?

Thoughts raced and twisted into more plans and strategies in Morganna's mind. Before she had accepted that she must do this thing, she found she was plotting how to make the sacrifice more worthwhile. With a visible shudder she nodded to Percival, unwilling to risk a voice that would certainly quaver or scream.

The hunting party was composed entirely of nobles and servants. Most were those kings who had sworn fealty to Arthur early in his rise to High King. Some were men whose lands were newly conquered, and these were visibly anxious to please their conqueror. They had been riding and hunting for almost six hours when one of the newly conquered lords spurred up to Arthur's side.

"There is a peasant village over there." He gestured to the right with his boar spear. "We should be able to water the horses and take some grain."

The High King considered. He was in an expansive mood. The battle two weeks earlier had crushed the last real resistance to his sole rule of all the Britons. Not since the last emperor led the legions back to Rome had the Britons been united under one king, and he had done it. Just a little self-consciously Arthur rubbed his palm on Excalibur's pommel even as he enjoyed his success.

"The hour is late," the High King allowed. "Let us accept the hospitality of your peasants tonight. Tomorrow you may entertain us in a more suitable style."

Pleased but worried, the local lord nodded. Raising the force he had lost fighting Arthur had nearly impoverished him. His steward would be hard-pressed to mount a suitable feast. With a few words he sent his squire scurrying ahead to warn the castle of the next day's visit. Still, this was a sign of approval, and with growing cheer the lord led them toward the small village.

The place had no name and no more than eight thatch-covered huts. Most of those who lived here survived by raising trees and trading their fruit for grain. It was also the kind of place where every man was an expert poacher. At the village a few words with the head man ensured that no effort would be spared for the night. Britons were all free men, and the lord had to guarantee to make good on the foodstuffs eaten. Hosting the King was an honor—likely they'd start calling this village King's Rest or some other important-sounding name—but names meant little if the residents starved at high winter because of the honor.

The thatch huts were much too crude to be acceptable for use by the nobility riding on this hunt. Tents of all colors dwarfed the peasant's dwellings. The sun had set and the nobles were feasting in a large, blue-striped tent in the middle of the village. One side was suspended from what the two priests of the dead god were careful not to acknowledge as a Maypole. At each end of the village smaller tents had been set up that would house those capable of staggering that far. The sides of the striped tent were pulled upward, and torches half buried in the ground provided illumination.

It was late in the feast when the woman first caught Arthur's eye. A few of the lords found this amusing, as she had obviously fancied him for some time. Still, with dark red hair and wide hips, she was easily the most comely maid in the village. A few had commented on how she had been acting and wondered why Arthur hadn't noticed. There was no glowering peasant husband following to protect her, as was so often the case. But then, that problem had rarely deterred the High King on other occasions. All cheered when Arthur grabbed the maid and kissed her soundly.

"He noticed me!" Morganna wasn't sure if she was pleased or not. Twice she'd brushed against Arthur, but the War King had been so engrossed in retelling the story of one of his victories, he'd barely noticed. In desperation Morganna, her hair dyed with henna and skin washed dark with berry juice, had returned to the forest. She had soaked her arms and hands with the potion she'd been taught would inflame lust. She made it stronger than she had been taught to use, but she had to wear enough to ensure his lust blinded him later. When she returned, it worked, and once she had stroked his face with a scented hand, she could see the change come over the young king.

Over the next minutes Morganna continued to weave her spell of lust, brushing against the War King and bending low to pour his wine. During this time she found she also felt giddy. The problem was that the herbs were too effective. Morganna was beginning to feel out of control herself. Lust was something both men and women shared. The same vapors that had finally attracted Arthur were beginning to cloud her own judgment. Combined with the siren call of his demon sword, it was all the Druidess could do to remember her mission. She still hated him, but now she wanted him. He threatened all she had valued and still she felt the need to be taken, by him. Her lust was tangible and wrapped itself like a shroud over her thoughts. At the same time some part of her stood apart and was amazed by the power of her own desire. Yet another corner of the young woman wanted only to scream at the fearsome thing she was going to have to endure.

Could she hate him enough to endure his lust? Would her potion-driven need allow her to react with enough passion to distract him? She realized that if Arthur drank much more, he would be too sodden to show any interest, and there was little chance they could try this plan again. Once more she brought him sweetmeats and brushed against his shoulder enticingly.

Through the blur of her own desire Morganna was next aware that Arthur had risen and was leading her across the center of the large tent the nobles had been feasting in. The men were making comments, which she tried hard not to hear. Instead she pulled herself closer to the War King. He smelled, she realized, of horses and sweat from the long day hunting. The odor was strong and she should have been repulsed, but instead she felt a shiver of desire.

Barely able to walk, Arthur stumbled as he dodged a lit torch.

Did he leave the sword behind? Morganna worried. The effect of the potion had peaked, and her eyes weren't focusing so well.

Arthur had been dragging her across the tent by the hand. She hurried forward and wrapped herself around his left arm. Her hip brushed against the hilt of the demon sword, and it burned her through the homespun gown. She squealed with pain, but this only brought a wave of laughter from the assembled lords. Then they were out under the full moon.

Morganna shifted herself to the War King's other side. She could still feel the effects of the sword's song, but here she was safe from its sting. The move took all of her concentration. The pain should have sharpened her senses or helped her regain control, but instead it made the world more of a blur. They were halfway to Arthur's tent when it occurred to her that at least now she was sure he still had the sword.

No one seemed to follow. There was one guard near the red-and-gold tent. He stood between the tent and the forest a dozen paces beyond. He watched with a wide smile as Arthur dragged her through the flap. Inside the tent the air was thick with the smell of sweat-soaked clothes and leather.

Arthur's fingers stumbled as he tried to loosen the bindings of his jerkin. It was beginning. The woman's heartbeat raced and she fought back the need to empty her stomach. After a moment Morganna reached forward and forced a smile as she helped the man she hated most remove his clothes.

He stood unsteadily, wearing only breeches and his sword. What started as a lurch ended as the War King reached out and tore the top of Morganna's tunic free. He was rough about it, all lust and no caring. As the air rushed past the priestess's breasts, her hand slashed upward toward Arthur's face. With a surge of self-control she turned the attack into a caress. He never noticed the renewed exposure to the herbs on her hands arousing him further. He reached out to fondle her with bleary unconcern.

Forcing herself to endure his touch long enough to see he was fully aroused, Morganna gently pulled his hand away.

"Not here." She sniffed. For a moment she worried. The tent was likely cleaner than most of the peasants' huts. Would he suspect? Before the drunken king could react, she slipped out of her dress and then pushed her way through the back of the richly colored tent.

Hesitating with the back of the tent flap open, Morganna tried to look inviting, even as she revolted at what was likely to follow. Behind her she heard a startled laugh from the lone guard. Bemused, Arthur followed. Together they stumbled into the nearby trees. Somewhere in the distance a lamb bleated.

The sound was barely audible above the rush of blood in Morganna's ears as they moved deeper into the dark woods.

It was planned that the man watching the tent would follow. Morganna had heard the sound of the guard's sword being drawn even as they passed. For a moment she had feared the guard had somehow recognized her and awaited his blow. When nothing happened, she sighed, and Arthur mistook her relief for passion. The Druidess pulled Arthur's face to her breasts as they passed the bush in which Percival hid. They continued walking awkwardly, Arthur's laughter covering the sounds of Percival's sword slicing into the hapless guard's back. By the time he had fallen, they had moved too far away to hear the scuffling made as his body was dragged out of sight.

Far enough, Morganna allowed herself to decide. Arthur's crude groping was beginning to become painful. Her own fast-beating heart had long cleared most of the traces of the lust potion from her system. The effects of the herbs were not the only reason for the woman's actions. Now only hate and calculation kept the Druidess at her task.

Pressing against the War King to protect herself from his calloused hands, Morganna made herself pull away at the waist and murmur seductively that Arthur should hurry and take her. As she had hoped, he tore off his swordbelt and breeches in his haste to fulfill his lust.

As his breeches fell to the ground, Morganna forced a laugh and ran a few steps farther into the thick forest. Arthur stood for a moment, confused and made stuporous by the effects of mead and the lust potion. Fighting off the desire to just keep running, the naked woman stopped, moved her hips suggestively, and made her feet dance a few steps closer.

"Take me here in the leaves," she pleaded. Her voice broke as she called out.

Grinning as he stumbled after her, Arthur grunted his approval.

A few more steps back, again Arthur moved to follow. Once more Morganna moved away. They were almost far enough now. Almost out of sight of where Arthur had shed his breeches, and the demon sword. Now it all depended upon Percival.

She moved away once again. This time Arthur was less amused. The cold air and his efforts were rapidly giving the young man back his senses. Morganna waited, she had to be sure Percival had time to get away.

"Now, girl!" the King bellowed as he dived after her. Throwing herself back, Morganna felt her skin tear as his dirty nails dragged across her shoulder and breast. Each bleeding streak stung. Fleeing the pain, she backpedaled until a low branch pressed into her shoulders. He kept coming, determination and frustration obvious in his expression.

"Now, my King," the Druidess gasped as seductively as possible, considering how much the deep scratches hurt, just as a distant horn sounded.

Percival had the sword and was away. She had succeeded! Satisfaction eased her pain.

As agreed, Percival had sounded that horn only after he was safely distant. With no idea of even where he fled to, Arthur's men had no chance of overtaking him in the darkness. Before sunrise he could cast the enchanted weapon in the deep lake they had agreed upon. The lake itself was enchanted by Naiads, who would hide the sword forever, even from the Sidhe themselves. So long as she also escaped, there was no way for them to know.

In her joy, the priestess almost forgot about the naked and angry monarch a few steps away. Morganna barely managed to duck under his sweeping arms. The King's bellows were filled with anger now, not lust. Arthur was not accustomed to being denied. Certainly not used to being refused by a peasant girl who had led him on such a chase.

Strong hands crushed the Druidess's shoulders. Overwhelmed by the ferocity of the High King's attacks, Morganna fell backward. Her head and one shoulder slammed into the rough bark of a tree. In a distant way she could feel him against her as she fought her way back from deep inside the darkness. The sudden pain between her legs nearly sent her reeling back into unconsciousness. It was all she could do to fight her way back a second time. A part of her wanted to faint, as if that would somehow remove her from what was happening. Pain, despair, and anger roiled as the world ebbed in and out of focus. Embracing the anger, she rode it until the moonlight returned.

His breathing was hard against her ear and he lay on her so heavily, she was barely able to breathe. She had not been experienced with men. Everything he did hurt. He was tearing her now with the force of his potion-induced urgency. One of her hands was free, and as it tore at the rough ground beneath on which she lay, it closed on a piece of the branch that had broken off when she had fallen against the tree. It wasn't large, perhaps two fingers thick and two hands long. The broken edge was jagged and she swung it like a knife into the side of Arthur's neck.

She could feel the wood gouge flesh and was answered with his startled grunt. She struck his neck again, and the drugged king raised himself to flail in an attempt to trap her wrist. Shrieking her hate, Morganna pushed herself upward and swung again. This brought a new wave of searing pain to her groin, but she kept fighting.

Arthur rose to his knees and pulled himself free. He was angry. Morganna's foot lashed out and smashed into his groin. She took hurried satisfaction at the howl of pain and string of threats that followed. Scrambling backward, the battered woman grasped the tree as she rose to her feet. Arthur tried to stand, but fell backward, grasping himself as the movement renewed the agony caused by her kick.

Morganna turned and ran. Patches of light from the full moon were barely enough to guide her way through the dense stand of trees. Twice she nearly slammed into half-seen tree trunks, and too many times to count, her shoulder or head scraped under unseen branches. For a short time Arthur stumbled painfully after her, screaming for her to halt and threatening her with various tortures. Morganna realized that he thought she lived there, and the villagers would suffer. She hoped they had taken her advice and fled. Arthur's wrath would kill them all once he discovered the Sidhe sword gone.

Slowly she outdistanced the King. He was strong, but more accustomed to riding or wielding a sword than dashing through a dark forest. His brutal lust satisfied, Arthur had no real reason to follow long. He would not know about the missing sword until he returned for it. Soon the sound of his bellows and breaking through the woods was lost among the animal noises. Only then did Morganna slow. She was still naked, but safe. Inside, exaltation at their success and revulsion at its price fought to dominate. She was sobbing an hour later when she found the earth-brown tunic and silver belt they'd hidden for her. She didn't put them on yet, but continued for another hundred paces. The sound of gurgling water grew louder as she walked, sobbing through the moonlight.

A few minutes later she was able to wash in a stream. The cold water made her shiver, but it washed away the last traces of the lust potion. The dark-haired woman sat there for a long time just splashing water against everyplace Arthur had touched her. The liquid was so cold, it almost hurt, but she didn't stop until her arms tired and the rest of her body felt numb from the cold.

Anger surged through Morganna and there was nothing for her to strike. She had walked for over an hour through the trailless forest. There was a horse tethered nearby, and soon she'd begin her journey back to the Holy Isle. Arthur was far away and should be just beginning to understand that Excalibur was lost to him. The Druidess had a moment of regret that she had not hidden a dagger somewhere in the forest. There would have been more satisfaction in his death than she had gotten from her kick. She might have freed the Britons of both the sword and the usurper. The image had appeal, and kneeling waist deep in the cold water, Morganna savored the image of her plunging a long blade into the War King's chest. Then with a shiver she stood, left the water, and began dressing.

As she pulled the clean gown on, Morganna understood that letting him live was an even greater revenge. Arthur had used Excalibur's power to crush a dozen kingdoms. Only its power had allowed him then to rule his former enemies. Now the sword was gone. His army was still strong, but no longer invincible. Former allies would soon regain their senses and de-mand revenge. Friends would betray him. It might take years, but he would watch his great kingdom get torn apart without being able to save it. She would devote her life to making sure of it.

Hurrying to the horse Percival had left her, Morganna's stride became lighter. It was over. Without his sword Arthur was doomed. There was no mercy in letting him live. Sunlight began to filter into the sky above. It was first dawning of the last days of Camelot.

Troubled Waters

SUSAN SHWARTZ

arkness moved upon the face of the water. In her palace beneath it, the Lady of the Lake stirred. Moonlight stabbed through the water, and it ran red. Blood sluiced over the surface of the Lady's realm, and she wept.

She wept long after the waves had washed the water clean of the blood of Camlann. Nor was it the first time she had grieved for the kingdom beyond the Boundary of the waters. She had grieved when, at the appointed time, men of the outer world had taken her foster son from her. She had trained him well in the arts of the court and had seen him well trained for the arts of war. Practice beneath the water had made him fast and strong: he would make a fine knight, they told her. So they thanked her and left a vacant ache in her life—not the first time that those beyond the Boundary of air and water had injured her. But the most severe was yet to come.

Had Lancelot's mother wept thus when King Ban put her boy into the Lady's care? Then *she,* and not the Lady, would have been the first woman whose tears Lancelot du Lake had caused, though far from the last: and her foster son, whom she had trained—as all Ladies of the Lake must—in good courtesy to women, would be remembered not just as a knight and true lover, but as a traitor.

The Lady of the Lake rose from her couch. Her hair and her samite draperies drifted about her. A fish swam by, gliding against her ankles, and she spared it a touch of her thoughts. *Have I neglected you, little one?* Her mind scanned the realm to which she had withdrawn: no underwater quakes nor eruptions; no blights to its creatures or the ancient gardens in the depths. She was, as she had always been, a good chatelaine. Even now, she had preserved her kingdom from the blight of the upper air. Nevertheless, the nacre on her palace walls had dulled.

It was not too dull, though, to show her that she too had lost the edge of the strange beauty that was the birthright of all enchantresses, whether those who followed Morgan on the land or the more reclusive Ladies who dwelt beyond the Boundary. The Lady would have known what it meant had she seen one of her own servants, its scales no longer lustrous, retreating to the safety of the rocks, there to heal or die. She would have known what to do. But for herself, she had no healers to call and no death to anticipate; and the flowing water carried her salt tears down to the Great Sea.

Hearing of her son's flight with Arthur's Queen to his fortress of Joyous Garde, the Lady had withdrawn even beyond the Boundary of earth and water, retreating to her palace and taking to her couch, there to summon the long sleep of her kind. But now she had slept so long that sleep itself was no longer an escape, even if it were not dishonor.

She glanced upward at the moonlit surface of the water. The Boundary shimmered, bowstring-taut as if it struggled to protect her from some great danger. But she had not slept long enough not to know that a battle had raged in the upper air from which she had turned. The blood upon the water had awakened her: that and the sense she had tasks yet to fulfill. She must be the good chatelaine, again. Forever.

She was not like that mortal child, Elaine, fit only to retreat from the world, to turn from it and die of the grief Lancelot had dealt her. *She* could not die at all, and it seemed that that was a fate more cruel. Withdraw she might; sleep she might: ultimately, she must turn and play out her assigned part in the affairs of the outer world.

Mary, pity women. The Lady had even allowed her foster son to seek the surface priests, since he must be taught to worship at the altars of the surface God, not at the sacred wells. Thus, she had listened to the boy, had asked him, over and over, the questions to which he must get correct answers by heart, until she knew questions and answers as well as he and had pondered them more deeply. At the time, she had taken care to conceal her relief: so austere a faith, and yet even there, Lancelot would not lack a mother's love, regardless of what else it cost him.

Mary, pity women. Beyond the Boundary, women needed such pity: they faced so many boundaries of their own.

Nynyve, the chief of all the Ladies of the Lake, had married a man of the upper world, had kept him safe at Lady only knew what cost. She had seen little of Nynyve since that time and less of Sir Pelleas.

"And are you so sure," she had demanded of Nynyve, "that your Pelleas will heed you and hold aloof from strife?"

Nynyve had smiled, thoughtful and sweet. She had been a beautiful child, had grown into a beautiful and powerful Lady, fit to lead them all, let alone woo a man from his chosen path.

"Do you recall Sir Eric, whose Lady followed him, perforce, on all his quests, lest he lose honor?" She did. Sir Eric was long dead, killed fighting on the border, while the Lady Enid wept among the black-robed women who served the

White Christ's Mary. "I would not have *my* knight reft from me in such a way."

"How can you be sure that *your* knight will not be seduced back into this madness of arms?"

"I can but try." Again, that secretive smile, with a hint of smugness to it. *Her* knight had been not lord and lover, but foster son; and she had lost him. Easy for Nynyve to smile: she had sorrowed for the follies of the outer world, but she had rescued what she loved and had not had to learn to grieve.

The tragedy was that the Lady's foster son had meant to do no harm. He loved not easily, but heart-deep; heart speaking to heart; heart piercing heart, and realm, and world.

He had been a fair and loving child. He was a good man. The Lady had seen that heart of his and judged it as only an immortal might. And because he was a good man, when he loved, he found response. Arthur had made him the first knight of his realm, surpassing even his sister's son, who grudged it not at all. For Arthur, he remained in Britain, all but ceding his heirship of a kingdom. For Guinevere—well, it was for Guinevere that this anger and unhappiness began that had not ceased until the chivalry of all the world was destroyed, and its blood sullied the face of the waters that had also been in her care.

The waters were troubled. In the faith of the surface world, she knew what that meant; she had read the words often enough with her foster son. Long ago and in a dry land, there has been a pool called Siloam: when its waters shivered, it meant a miracle was nigh, and the first to seek the pool would find healing.

For her, the troubling in the water meant a summons, as it had the day Lancelot was entrusted to her care—and the day he was taken from her.

The Lady of the Lake extended her arms. Her long sleeves flowed around her, shifting silver, rose, indigo, glowing in the phosphorescence and the moonlight that filtered down. Her dark hair tangled about her shoulders, and her robe trailed her bare feet. She rose above the roofless walls of her palace toward the troubled gleam that severed air and water from each other.

This close to the Boundary, she could hear the cries of men in pain, the hot breath of those who plundered them, the chants of the priests who now ventured out to retrieve their souls. Even worse, to her way of thinking, were the whimpers of pain withstood, the panted breaths, and those rattling last breaths that meant that some men, at least, were freed of their suffering. Even the great sharks killed more quickly.

A stab of anger drove her the faster through the troubled water, from the darkness of the depths to where a pallid light filtered through.

Where had the priests been before, when they might have been of use?

Where had you *been before?* she asked herself.

Easy to tell herself that the folk of earth and air were not her care, that they had their own king, their own ways. Easy, and even partially true. Relying on that partial truth, she had withdrawn, and, for the time she slept, her conscience had not troubled her. But she had raised a prince among them. And, even now, knights and princes reckoned Ladies such as she as allies worthy of honor. She supposed she should be glad they had not sought her aid in war.

But they had done that before, too. And even worse, now one of them was summoning her.

The cries were so dreadful that she wanted to retreat. Men could not scream beneath the waves. And she had renounced the upper air for far, far less—merely on expectation of this anguish.

She could see her summoner now. He was kin of her foster son's. They were all kin, these warriors of earth and air. They had stories of a knight named Cain, who slew his brother, and accounted that a crime; yet brother killed brother, and son, father, without cease.

Except for that too-brief time, now ended, when her son had served a king, and they had even proved worthy of each other.

The knight who had called the Lady wavered like a ghost beyond the boundary of the water. Dark, matted hair; white face; eyes like burned-out seacoals; a pallid, fine-drawn mouth with blood streaking one corner.

She rose past the Boundary. The shock of the air made her gasp. The pain she sensed made her tremble, then filled her eyes with rage. The knight's eyes widened as she surfaced, as if he steered a tiny boat and saw a kraken erupt from the depths of the sea.

She knew him—Bedivere. He had even met her, but now he feared. Perhaps he had feared all night. But he did not withdraw.

She saw what he held out in both hands. She forgot the man for the sword he bore.

Excalibur. Oh, she knew that sword. She had seen it forged in the fire of a sea-volcano. Swirls as intricate as the patterns of tide on sand shivered on its long blade, even now unmarred by stone, blood, or betrayal. She remembered that blade, had tested it against her skeins of hair and her own tender flesh.

She had given it and a scabbard—war and peace conjoined—to serve the King. But the scabbard had been lost— stolen, if the truth be known, and with it the fact of lasting peace (if not the hope); but Arthur had kept the sword, even when his own sister tried to steal it too. That Bedivere held it now . . .

It could not be that he was the king. The Lady looked at Excalibur. An amethyst found on a sunken ship smoldered in its pommel: in the true king's hand, it would have flashed with joy. And, had Bedivere been king, he would not have trembled at the sight of her, not tried to bow, thrust out the sword, and tried to explain.

Were those *excuses* that he stammered out? That the dying King had entrusted the blade to Bedivere, last of his faithful knights, to hurl into the water lest it fall into enemy hands? That, instead, he had concealed the blade, but reported nonetheless that he had obeyed? That he had done so thrice?

Thrice? While Arthur bled and suffered on the shore and his wounds grew cold, perhaps past healing?

She could feel the cold Immortal's fury rise in her, could see it flashing in her eyes—reflected in his own—like the amethyst in the pommel of the sword Bedivere should have ceded to her hours ago. Tears ran down his face as if he stood beneath a waterfall. The Lady drew herself up.

He was Lancelot's kin, Arthur's man; in all courtesy, he should have had kind words of her and her hand to kiss before she reclaimed the sword, with gracious words. None of that! They were not just caught up in their stories; they twisted them even as they turned the blades in the wounds they made.

Her arm lunged forward. Moonlight gleamed on the long nails of her hand as it demanded to hold Excalibur *now*.

Bedivere hurled the sword. At the last moment, he hurled it toward her, not *at* her, though he must surely have feared he would need to defend himself against a Lady gone feral and enraged.

Excalibur's balance comforted her hand. She brandished the sword: once to test the blade; twice, to hear its sweet song as it cut the air; a third time for the joy of it, hot as the forge where it had had its birth.

So eager, are you, Lady? 'Twere best you cooled your blood.

Ignoring the knight who trembled on the shore, she sank below the Boundary into the water's clean embrace. It laved her eyes and limbs, caressed her hair, and utterly failed to soothe the outrage in her heart.

Descending to her palace, she sought her chair of state and sat there, Excalibur across her knees, like a king who hears a declaration of war and must decide on his reply. Her creatures clustered at the far end of the hall, not daring quite to flee. During the battle, they had retreated to the depths and the safety of her presence. Now they withdrew from her, and their flight angered her still more. To this she had been brought— that those she had sworn to shield would shun her!

This savage tale that knights and kings played out on the land must cease. Nynyve might withdraw to her own concerns, her own man, her own lands: the Ladies who remained alone, if not heart-whole, had no such choice. Nynyve's Pelleas might lay down his arms, retiring not just from the field but from the stories, the damnable rankings of who was most valiant among knights. Her foster son had won those contests; and this is what it cost, not just him but all the world.

No, Nynyve's decision was not hers. She was resolute in believing that, as surely as monksbane or some unction from the East, war and knighthood would poison her own realm, had it not done thus already. She was much at fault for allowing what contact and what hurt she had. She would amend that.

She brought her wrist down against Excalibur, as she had done the morning it was forged. A little cloud of blood ran from the wound, quickly dissipating in the clean water. That was for remembrance.

She raised her head. Her eyes were still hot as she turned her sight on the upper world. Above the Boundary, the sky was paling toward first light. She compelled herself to stillness, to rhythmic breaths and patience.

Then, she heard the music.

Like a blade rightly wielded, magic has a song of its own. The tiny barge, alone of all those on the shore, that ventured out into deep water had music in its train. Its wake glowed with more than the thresh of oars.

Look closer, Lady.

Three queens wearing black hoods crew that boat. In it lies a tall man, wrapped in the queens' cloaks, his head crowned only by a bandage dark with the ooze of blood. He bore, of course, no sword.

It is Arthur the King.

It is the Queens—the Queen of North Galys, the Queen of the Waste Lands, and Morgan le Fay, her old antagonist.

It is your quarry.

The Lady of the Lake stood. She fastened Excalibur, naked since it had no scabbard, to her belt, heavy with aquamarines, amethysts, and pearls. She tossed her hair back, then hurled herself through the water, out from her hall. Upward she surged toward the wake of the tiny boat.

Once she broke through the Boundary, she turned her othersight on the upper world. Venus had risen, and the goddesses were out. Along with Venus, stars still shone. Beneath them, like comets, rode battlemaidens from the icy North. Their horses' hooves struck sparks from the gathering dawn. They bore heavy loads: the body of a man burdened each woman's saddle—Danes and Jutes, Frisians and Swedes—men, bound for home in the only way they now might. That story too should stop, the Lady of the Lake considered. Still, it was not her task to stop it, but theirs.

She glanced up at the immortal riders. She in the lead, superbly young and valiant, waved at her as gaily as if no grief would ever touch her. The Lady did not envy her: grief struck all women equally.

Mary, pity women. To whatever extent that the men of the upper world would allow.

Women were better off as she was, taking matters into her own hands when she had been hurt. The Choosers of the Slain disappeared into the North. It was time for the Lady of the Lake to tend to her own affairs. She moved toward Avalon. Excalibur rode at her hip. A strange burden for a woman, unless she be a battlemaid: a child carried thus would be less strange than an unsheathed sword. She mused that she could be the sword's living sheath. When all was said and done, the word for *sheath* and for her most secret parts was the same and meant the same: blood and courage and the fear of death from which life must spring.

After tonight, there would be one thing the fewer to fear, one fewer cause of death.

The sky grew lighter yet. The banners of dawn unfurled before her. She cast her othersight farther, seeking the wake of the boat in which three goddesses rowed toward an island that appeared only between night and morning. Soon the mists of dawn would cover it, even to the Tor that reared up at its center, bearing it away from human ken. For now, though, even now, it could still be reached by those who knew the way and had the will and power to take it. To Avalon, fragrant with apple blossoms, vibrant, even now, with power.

Avalon had its counterpart on land, but the White Christ's priests ruled there. It was said he had walked there himself and had not scrupled to respect those who served the Goddess— why else such veneration for his mother? But now the priests ruled, and the Lady would not have them interfere in what she must do.

She walked upon the waves toward Avalon, her feet stirring the water into foam like strands of pearls.

Dawn arrived with its escort of banners. She heard the song of power well-used rise to a shout of joy. Just as the Lady of the Lake set foot upon Avalon's shore, the mists embraced the island and carried it from the world.

Sand and shells gave way to a world of green as she walked up from the shore. How strange the land felt underfoot. She could smell a wealth of apple blossoms. From old, old memories, she knew that toward noon, the somnolent buzz of bees would urge all who heard them to sink beneath the shadows of the apple trees and to rest. The Queens had wisdom in their choice: Avalon would be a good place for a wounded king to find healing—if healing there might ever be.

And if he healed? What would become of the upper world, the world upon the land, when he returned with banners and horns and shining swords? As above, so below: what would become of *her*?

"What do you seek, Niviene?"

The Goddess shield her: her true name, uttered in a voice she knew. She who called it was the senior Lady of the Lake, she who was Pelleas's queen.

"An end to all this suffering in the name of undying fame."

Her true name had been called. Perforce, she must halt, offer courtesy and truth—if not all the truth.

"You go to Arthur the King?" asked the Lady Nynyve. So close they were, even to the names. Nynyve; Niviene. Even their voices sounded much alike.

Niviene bowed her head, unwilling to trust her voice any further.

"To bless him as he heals? My own dear lord wished that, and I return from the Tor." The other Lady's eyes, ordinarily joyous (smugly content), clouded. "Ah, he is sorely injured. My lord will grieve. This is well done of you. . . ."

Not well done, not at all, with what boiled in her heart and what, surely, her eyes betrayed. The very air of Avalon held magic; surely, Nynyve would sense her mood and her intent. And indeed she did; her body stiffened, and her eyes grew wary.

"Niviene, look at me!"

Commanded by that voice as well as by her name, she looked into the other Lady's eyes.

"I ask your forgiveness, but . . . I want your vow that you wish healing to the King."

Niviene bowed her head: repudiating obedience.

"Then I cannot let you pass."

So it had come to this, then: not just man against man, father against son, but Lady against Lady? It had been thus before: Morgan was a Queen against whom many women's hands had been turned.

And so was Guinevere, who should have had a nobler fate than to be a destroyer of men's hearts.

For the first time, Niviene summoned speech. "Lady, I beg you forgive me, but . . . pass I must. And shall, though you bar my way."

The other Lady held out her arms, not to embrace a sister but to block her path. The Lady of the Lake stepped forward, her own arms out, not to embrace a sister but to push her aside, though she blast her.

Oh, it was bitter, it cut deep . . . she dared touch a holy Queen. Back and forth they struggled, gasped, released each other, and stood panting. *I do not want to fight you.* She saw a similar reluctance in the other's face and, reflected in Queen Nynyve's eyes, the sorrow in her own.

"Why must you do this?" demanded the Queen. "No better than he who betrayed his King. . . ."

Did she mean Arthur's son, or did she too scoff at the child she raised? Anger replaced regret.

"And you, should you not be at home, to guarding your Knight lest he stub his toe *or* he skulk away on errantry?"

Nynyve paled, her hands falling to her sides with that mention of her greatest fear. And it was her fear that robbed her of her power.

Easy then for the Lady of the Lake to thrust her aside.

"Wait!" cried the Queen.

No more waiting. That part of the story was done; and soon all stories would be done.

Nynyve gestured, and the Lady found herself held, not by shapely hands and nails but by thorns. They clawed her, brow and throat and hands. She left blood on its branches, as well as tatters of the samite of her robe. Excalibur caught on a stubborn trunk, and she wrested it free, blood trickling down her hand onto the blade.

She could have whined with pain, but shame forestalled her: weep at scratches when she had heard the moans of men wounded unto death upon the shore? Just one more death, she thought. And they all would be free.

Then she had thrust herself clear. She turned. The Lady Nynyve was gone. And there, although no longer restraining her, was a thornbush.

Her eyes kindled as she stared at this newest tormentor. Blood was power: in that instant, she knew she could blast it.

She had heard of this thorn: stories—more stories of death, masquerading as honor and love—had it that the thornbush had been a staff brought to Avalon by Joseph of Arimathea. Stuck into the earth, the staff had taken root. Now, so long after Joseph had journeyed here, the White Christ with him (as it was also said), the bush, like the Lady, had barred her path to the Tor that rose in the meadow beyond like a welcoming hand.

That was the thornbush in the world of men and their man's god, that world that had robbed itself—and her—by pinning its hopes on false glory. Sacrifice, it called itself: where lay the merit of a sacrifice if it was of useless pain?

In this world, what was the thornbush? A barrier, perhaps, against where she sought to go? She could not believe herself barred from Avalon. She had reached its shores; she walked its land. She had even left a blood-toll. More blood. It pained her to see it shed on Avalon.

She could not believe that. But she well could believe she faced a test such as she had undergone while studying her powers.

"And have I passed?" she asked.

She laid her hands against the long, ancient thorns that studded the branches. They pricked again. Again she ignored the pain. When she withdrew her hands, the thorns were dark, but not for long. They burst into flower: quatrefoliate, white, tipped with blood-red at the edges of each petal.

"Have I been approved for passage?" she asked the thorn-bush. She would take that as an omen: if not approval of what she planned to do, consent that she attempt it.

Her long robe swept behind her as she walked through the meadow. The Tor loomed up before her, green and steep. Heavy footprints marked it, not the sweep of robes. The foot-prints glowed in the vivid grass from the power of those who had placed them there. They were deeply pressed, as if the three Queens who had passed that way carried a heavy burden: a man who bore a kingdom's weight upon him. That too would be for the last time.

The scent of apple blossoms lingered in the air here, as it did in the Glastonbury of the outer world. There, the Tor was sacred to Saint Michael: a weathered tower with windows like daggers atop a steep hill set in a green valley.

Here, too, the valley was a cup from which the Tower sprang. But it was no fortress, no church here, but a broch, built as the fishers built them in the most ancient times. Its round walls were heaped of stones, smoothed by the water to a gentle luster. Their slope echoed the slope of the Tor itself.

It was a steep climb, especially for one who customarily did not walk, but swam. The Lady of the Lake leaned into the path worn by generations upon generations of patient women. She felt her heart go out to them—*no time, no time.*

Upward she struggled. Often, she thrust her hands out to brace herself. The dew upon the grass wiped the blood from them, laved her bruised feet. She fell once and lay facedown, in-haling the fresh grass scent, drawing the strength at the island's bones deep into herself. The stubborn strength of earth: she knew so little of it.

Had Excalibur been scabbarded, she might have used it as

a prop. But Excalibur was perilous, sword, not plowshare. She had seen it forged. And soon she would thrust it into its final scabbard.

For once and for all.

She could not remember. Had it always been so hard to climb the Tor of Avalon? Or perhaps, in this place beyond the world, it was not meant to be climbed by one who bore a sword: Excalibur put her off-balance in ways more than the physical. But this she remembered: When you climbed the Tor, always, just as heart and temples pounded the hardest and a mist filmed your vision, there came an instant when the land fell away, you could see out over the entire bowl of the valley, and the wind refreshed your eyes and heart.

She had reached the summit. All about, the island glinted an expanse of unsullied silver water, and she longed for it.

The tower's entrance stood open, as it ever was, to wind and rain and all comers. Its threshold was hollowed by the bare feet of those who had come there since the stones were laid. In the outer world, it would have been crammed with banners and gold, heady with frankincense and myrrh, thronged with chanting men and abject, black-wrapped ladies.

This tower, by contrast, coaxed one into calm. Only the entrance, the occasional flaw in the wall, and a hole far overhead to let smoke out allowed light to enter. Cressets and braziers burned, wafting the scent of applewood out over the valley.

Niviene heard the hum of bees, a thread of song, almost a lullaby that threatened to beguile her. If she shut her eyes, she might well imagine herself untold years ago, back in her mother's home. If she shut her eyes, she could all but smell bubbling porridge and meats smoking for winter high above the hearth. Her eyes filled with tears that she forced back. She had not come this far to yield to tenderness.

There were no kneeling monks nor nuns: just one woman

sitting on the floor, her face hidden on her arms as she rested them, as a mother rests after waking by a sick child's bedside, on the low, richly adorned bier that held Arthur King of Britain. His crown lay beside his head, which was wrapped in layers of fresh linen.

Sensing the Lady of the Lake's presence, the watching woman raised her head. Her face was drawn, her eyes puffed with tears and weariness. For an instant, Niviene thought of Bedivere, the embers of his eyes in an ashen face as he recoiled from her anger. But for this woman, Avalon had already begun to work its healing. She rose lithely to her feet, smiled—*How can she smile at me?*—to her feet, and left the tower. Only afterward Niviene realized that the waiting woman had been garbed as a queen in all but crown and shoes: a queen, and doing servant's work.

Were they not all servants—or supposed to be?

Niviene's tatters, her marked hands and face and feet, had not dismayed her. This was Avalon, where all women were queens and all queens were at their hearts free to be women, without other trials.

She had left Niviene to watch?

Niviene would do more than watch.

It was time to put an end to one trial women faced: loving men who put them aside, however gently, and went off to die because they preferred a dream of horns and banners to living out their lives. Mary, pity women. But it was not Mary whom the Lady meant to serve.

Silently, she paced toward the bier. Time was supple here on Avalon. The minutes it had taken her to journey here across the waves had stretched out into hours on the sacred island. In that time, the Queens had tended the King: bathed him, bound up his wounds with the herbs found here in forest and in field (her nostrils quivered at their familiarity), and dressed him in fresh garments. A pall was drawn up to his breast like a coverlet, but of noble fabrics and bearing the Red Dragon.

She stared down into Arthur's face. Wounded as he was unto death, his face bore color yet beneath the weathered gold of beard and brows. It was still, symmetrical, aloof now in his withdrawal from consciousness, from the world, and—who knew?—from life itself. Arched eyelids sheltered eyes that she knew could transform his entire visage from this estranged silence—more monument than man—into a hero who drew men's hearts as lodestone draws iron. Even wounded as he was, she could feel the attraction (a pity his Queen had not also sensed it). It was seductive, that nobility and that pain. Awareness of it burdened her as sorely as the weight of Excalibur, hanging from her belt. Drawing her closer to the King.

Arthur's hands were folded around a red rose. It was Niviene who held his sword.

"Killer," whispered the Lady of the Lake.

He had wrought the death of faith; the death of friends; the death of love; the death of armies; and, this time, the death of a nation. She had seen them all and was not quite sure that she could live with the sight: and she had been immortal.

She looked down at the still figure, which was its own effigy, aching at the bandages it wore.

The Queens had brought him to Avalon for the healing of his wounds. Was that the truth, or another resounding lie to keep the men in the outer world in thrall still, awaiting only the flourish of the Red Dragon banner to toss away their lives and their sons' lives while the women waited again to bear away the slain?

She knew the power of Avalon. Already, the scratches on her face had healed, and those, inflicted here, should have been slower to heal. She could well believe the island could heal wounds that would prove fatal in the outer world.

Firelight flickered on Arthur's face. So peaceful it looked

now: hard to believe . . . yes, and her foster son had been a loving little boy before this man's realm, this man's wife, stripped him of his faith and, for a while, his reason. Lancelot had run wild in the forests: though his wits were restored, Niviene did not think that the man who had borne off a Queen and killed men as close as brothers to him could be considered even now in his right mind.

Another crime to lay at Arthur's feet: He had destroyed the best knight in the world.

He had broken her peace, forcing her into retreat, then shattering that enforced stillness.

It was the stories, the damnable dreams of prowess and of fame. She would drive a stake through their heart forever when she plunged Excalibur home, into Arthur's heart. It was just: in some places, suicides were buried, stakes driven through their hearts, so they would not rise and walk again in the world they had scorned. It was just, she thought. Arthur, at the last, had thrown his life away with his kingdom's health.

She freed Excalibur from her belt. The amethyst gleamed sullen in the light, and fireglow ran down the blade, a harbinger of blood. She raised the blade with both hands. . . .

So fair, so strong. So helpless now. Is this a task for you, Niviene?

Her eyes dimmed with tears, and she squeezed them shut. And thrust down with Arthur's sword with all her might.

"Hold *now!*"

Power shocked through her. She felt her arms seized, immobilized by some invisible force. She threw her own strength against it, trying to drive the blade down those last fatal inches. Pale fire ran up the blade into her joined hands, holding it where it was.

The woman who strode into the broch did not trouble herself with the humility of Avalon. No display of mourning, no bared head nor feet for Morgan le Fay, swift and upright in her black and crimson, her gems and her glazing eyes. Sister to a king, enemy to that king, and, at the last, one of the Queens who bore him from the world, it was she who restrained the Lady of the Lake.

"Put down that sword." Whatever else Morgan had lost in a turbulent life, it was not her habit of command.

"So you can finally steal it?" Morgan had tried to replace it with a copy, used a weak lover as her catspaw to secure it, and she had failed.

Morgan smiled, the fighting grin on the fighting Celt, at her reply. "My sister was always soft-headed for a queen. She should never have left you alone with Arthur. Nynyve barely warned me in time."

Nynyve turned to *Morgan* against her own sister? Truly, the worlds had gone upside down.

"*She* could not stop me, Majesty, and she rules my Order. What makes you think that you can?"

Morgan tossed her head. The gems woven into her hair shimmered. "Nynyve truly could not believe you would go as far as you have. She was always soft. Like all you Ladies of the water. Grieve you and you weep, withdraw, too tender for a tough world. If you ask me, you are mourners by vocation. But I must admit, *you* have gone farther than I thought you would dare. It was an honorable attempt, and I grant you have proved your courage. Now, put the sword away."

"How can I when you will not let me move?" Let Morgan release her. The Lady of the Lake could force the blade down before the sorceress could bind the spell on her again. And then, let Morgan destroy her. She would know, before she died, that she had ended a notable affliction.

Again, that flash of Morgan's eyes. "You have only to will to lay the sword aside, and you shall move."

"Free me."

Morgan laughed, hawk-shrill. "You think you can outwit

me, move faster than I can bespell you? I am *Morgan,* and you
pause at the slightest thought to weep."

Enough truth lay in that boast to anger Niviene. At the
base of her spine lay a core of energy that the Lady of the Lake
had learned in her earliest training how to tap. This was Avalon:
the earth itself held power. Deep within it, the Lady of the Lake
sent her will, drawing power up from the very land, up the column of her spine, dispersing across her shoulders to flow into
her arms. Inch by inch, Excalibur descended.

The light sheathing it intensified. The blade began to rise,
then halted as she drew upon her own will.

"We could be here till Doomsday," she remarked.

Let Morgan consider that. Early on, she had left her cloister of enchantresses and had ever after been one to be up and
scheming about, unlike the Ladies of the Lake. The world
would be a calmer place with Arthur's story over, if it meant an
end to Morgan's coils—even if that locked the two of them into
eternal war on Avalon.

"I tell you, I shall not let you kill my brother. . . ."

Had Niviene not been on her guard, Morgan's vow might
have startled her.

"Why not? You have plotted his death yourself."

Again, that laugh of Morgan's. "That was but a throw I
sought to win. But you seek to destroy the entire game: kings
and knights, ladies and castles, faith and faithlessness, and for all
time."

"A game?" It came out as a wail that made her flush with
shame. "Look what your *game* has done to us!"

Saving her breath to fight better, the Lady disdained
speech and cast her thoughts at Morgan.

*The best knight in the world. One year, my foster son snapped
his wrist at shield drill. He never wept, but hurled himself back
into training to regain his strength. He rode off to Camelot. He
served a King and loved a Queen and ran mad, destroyed the*

peace and life of a Lady, and, ultimately, cost the King his knights. And all for a place in what you call a game!

"Yes," Morgan shot at her. "And look at what it won us!"

Saxons driven back into the sea. Scriptoria filled with the stories you say you despise. Roads built atop those of Rome so safe a maid could bear a chest of gold from Hadrian's Wall to Tintagel. The game of kings—plot, counterplot—you withdraw beneath the waves to weep, but what have you done to heal it?

The blade rose several inches more.

"You," Morgan gasped. "Your lot fared well enough. You pretty Ladies of the Lake! The knights would bow in awe every time one of you swept into the Court. They *whispered* at Sir Pelleas's luck. You should have heard the awe—and the lust.

"I had a kingdom and a king to manage: all you had to do was stand there and look beautiful. But when you were displeased, what did you do? Retreat beneath the water, weep rivers of tears, and be praised for it? That was the part *you* played; it served you well enough for a long time. But now, when it turns sad, you decide to destroy it and all our roles— and for all time."

"You would have destroyed Camelot yourself," accused the Lady.

"Not so. I would have taken it if I could, and ruled it myself. And so I may, the next time we play this game. But there must *be* a next time; and that is what you want to stop—"

For the first time, the Queen looked frankly into her eyes. And then Morgan le Fay wept.

Tears flowed from Morgan's eyes. "Oh, you baby. You colossal fool," she said. "Don't you understand? I take the consequences of the game upon myself: wealth, poverty, the fates of armies. I have always taken the consequences. But you, sheltering yourself beneath your precious lake . . . If you destroy the game, can you bear to abide those consequences?"

Her heart sank. Morgan, weeping? For her? She had a sud-

den glimpse of Morgan, sent early to school, then ruling it, a
precursor of the kingdom she and her husband ruled and of the
larger realm they hoped to win. She had set the land on fire
with ladies who were enchantresses. They had not been spies,
but friends and family, each one of them cherished and protected.

And now her. *Let Morgan know you see that, and she will
only fight the harder.*

"Since you feel yourself so much stronger than I, why not
just take the sword yourself?" demanded the Lady of the Lake.
"You have always wanted it."

Morgan all but snarled with impatience. "It was given to
you."

"And if I set it down, what will you do with it?"

Morgan gestured. "Give it to him. To my brother."

Again, her eyes welled. "Whatever else he was, he was dear
to me." She struggled to suppress a sob. "And perhaps, in the
next round of the game, I can say so." She knelt beside the bier
and touched her brother's face.

"When he is summoned and he wakes." She turned her
face up to look at the Lady of the Lake. Her eyes took on the
distant sheen that meant prophecy. *"For at the hour of his land's
greatest need, he will be called for, and he will hear it. And I shall
be there for him as I was here at the hour of his death."*

The absolute conviction in her words made Niviene shudder.

Give up her claim to hatred. Give up her vengeance. Give
up, in fact, her chance to be like Morgan, a player in this game.

Arthur would be called. Arthur would wake. And Morgan
would be there, kneeling at his side to gird him with Excalibur.
And where would she be?

Once again, brought into the game to be admired, then
abandoned to waiting and helpless grief?

No, for once in her long life, *someone* should do as she bid.

She tested her grip upon the sword. Morgan had weakened the force of her will. She might, she might indeed, break free and plunge the sword in Arthur's heart.

But Morgan had wept; she should indeed have the sword if she cared that much.

"Take the sword," said the Lady of the Lake. "Give it to your brother."

Morgan held out her hands as if the palms had spells she had never before studied written upon them. For the first time in all the years they had known each other, she wavered. "I do not know . . ."

"Take the sword!" It shook in her hands. Firelight quivered in the watered-silk patterns on the blade. *Take it before I make myself what I loathe. I beg you.*

Morgan reached out for the sword, but the Lady of the Lake still grasped its hilt. She wants it? Then let her grasp it by the blade, regardless of the cost. Her own scars still smarted on hands and face and arms from her match with the thornbush on the shore.

Morgan touched the sword. A hiss rose, like flesh touching hot coals. It touched the fire sheathing Excalibur and extinguished it. Morgan's face grew very white, except for that red, red mouth. The full lips thinned as the Queen forbore to cry out.

She took the blade from Niviene in both hands. In the moment when both women touched the blade, the Lady of the Lake sensed Morgan's agony, and the will that kept her mistress of her grief, even giving her the will to banter where most she mourned. Niviene shuddered and let go Morgan's hands. She looked down at her own, expecting to see them burned, as if she took oath falsely and the hot iron she held exposed her.

Morgan had Excalibur now. She had coveted it and intrigued to possess it. And now it burned her with her own power.

Still, she bent over her brother once again bowing like the curl of a wave breaking into foam, her wounded hands gentle on the blade.

"Open his hands for me," she asked, her voice hushed.

The Lady of the Lake parted Arthur's hands, prying the red rose from his grip. In its place, Morgan laid Excalibur. Before Niviene could mold his grip about the hilt, Arthur's hands shifted of their own accord. The King grasped his sword, then drifted back to sleep with a deep sigh of relief.

"He will heal." Morgan's voice trembled.

It might be, as Morgan hoped, that when Arthur woke, his quarrel with her would be healed. Or, perhaps, they would be antagonists once more in the game Morgan had saved.

In either case, the Lady knew that Morgan would never tell Arthur what she had done.

She caught a glimpse of Morgan's hands as she straightened up. They were blistered, scorched and scored across by the blade they had held so briefly. Niviene caught her breath.

"And if I had not taken the blade as you commanded?" Morgan asked. The edge was back in her voice.

"I might indeed have used it."

Morgan laughed, then winced. "I do not think so. You are too gentle. Even my burns pain you." Again, that too-shrewd smile. "Admit it. Even an enemy's pain troubles you. And I am not your enemy."

The barbs sank home, enough truth in them to sting. "Let me see those hands."

Taking the red rose that Arthur had held, the Lady of the Lake brushed it across Morgan's hands. Dew sprinkled from its petals onto the scorched flesh, and Morgan sighed, relaxing visibly.

Then both women gasped. Even as they watched, the rose turned white. Petals fell away, until what remained, what survived, was a quatrefoliate blossom, blood-red marking the petals just where their edges curled. The rose scent deepened, mingling with the scent of apples and salt: Avalon's own scent, a compound of May and mourning and, at the last, a rich harvest.

"I did not work that transformation," said Morgan le Fay. "Did you?"

The Lady of the Lake shook her head. "But when my hands bled on the thornbush, flowers just like that sprang up."

"They heal wounds," Morgan mused. "Perhaps . . ."

Outside came the rush of running feet. The same barefoot Queen whom Niviene had seen earlier rushed into the broch, eager as a milkmaid. Her silk skirts were kilted up and filled with blossoms of four petals tipped with crimson and rich with the scent of apples, roses, and salt.

"I found these blossoming on the thornbush," she gasped.

"Dim," said Morgan le Fay. "I told you."

"It is a wonder, a miracle . . ."

They looked at each other with skepticism that had already begun to turn into surmise.

"Nor I," said Morgan. She raised an eyebrow. "I do not particularly like the idea that . . . outside powers have taken a hand in this."

Mary, pity women. Goddess, what if Mary *had?* She could almost hear Morgan's thought: the next round of the game would be very, very different indeed.

"However," Morgan added meditatively, "I am not particularly surprised." Already her voice sounded stronger.

The barefoot Queen stared at the two enchantresses. Niviene gathered up the flowers, held them against Arthur's face, then laid them on the bier. Then, smiling and agreeing with whatever the Queen said—though she had to admit that the talk of miracles made her feel slightly dizzy, here on the sacred hill of Avalon, she ushered her from the broch. The barefoot woman laughed with joy as she raced down the hill, no doubt to marvel once again at the blossoming thorn.

"Quite a change of heart," Morgan observed, "from trying to drive a sword through Arthur's."

The Lady of the Lake shrugged.

"You yourself said that that was but a throw in the game, not the game itself." She smiled Morgan's own smile back at her.

"Well," said Morgan, "Since you have conceded yours, I will concede this one. Any regrets?"

She settled comfortably on her knees: another Queen to watch by Arthur's side. Another mourner with courage enough not to despair.

"You will hear from me," said the Lady of the Lake. She had a realm to return to.

And there would be, Niviene knew now, years to wait. In them, she could reproach herself, or remember—or she could prepare for the day when there *would* once more come a summons and a waking and a going forth to what Morgan saw as a game and—how did she see it? As a miracle of sorts, another chance. Maybe, in *this* tale to come, Arthur would not fall and beget a son who betrayed him. Maybe, his Queen would love him as man, not monarch. And maybe, oh perhaps, other women's sons—or hers—would not be broken on the wheel of what must be.

And she would have Morgan to strive against. They were bound now. There was blood between them, lives and a sword. And now the witch was fool enough to ask her did she regret the mourning, the quiet years, the time ahead, followed (as it seemed) by turmoil yet to come?

She had only thought she did. But now—the game over, she would even miss Morgan.

Which one of them was the greater fool?

That did not matter. She would regret a world that held no

Morgan. She would regret the absence of them all. And of her proper place, as well.

And she had thought the storms at sea were troubled! Indeed they were; but even at their worst, and at the apex of her powers, she could not have thought to master them, let alone wish them to disappear.

"I asked you: Do you regret?"

Regret what? That she had not been allowed to despair so grandly that she put an end to all their futures? That she was not at peace?

Why should she have peace, her living elegy beneath the waves, when she might have a *chance*?

The waters had stirred. Just as the story said, a miracle occurred. She grinned back at Morgan.

The Lady of the Lake touched the thornblossoms on Arthur's bier.

"No," she said. "Not anymore."

Literary Cubism Saves the Universe

JOE HALDEMAN

It was like the ancient sword that, stuck
in stone, waited patient for its hero—
and like that sword, it had a fatal power;
not just an edge of steel. An edge of words.
If you had normal strength, the sword
would free itself—but then would ask a question.

And if your answer to that question
was not right, then you'd be stuck
deep through the heart by this sword—
yet another brave but stupid hero
whose strength was not in words,
fallen to the thing's ironic power.

The lure of the sphinx was power.
It was worth it to go and face the question,
try to puzzle out the words,
though almost surely you'd be stuck
for an answer. No true hero
could refuse to go and face the sword,

or the whatever. For humans, it took the form of sword
in stone. For other races, whatever their ikon of power,
snake or spike or flame, they would send their hero
marching or slithering or hopping up to hear the question
(which no one else could hear) and every year be stuck—
or bitten, burned, or nailed—for lack of words.

And so they called for people strong in words
to come and face, and fall before, this sword—
but none was strong in words and stupid, both. They were stuck
until they thought to use their futuristic power
to travel back through time, warm up and question
the dead, searching for a champion, a hero. . . .

And they found a most unlikely hero:
frumpy paisley fat ironic butch—in one word,
gertrudestein. In her revived mind, no question
that she could fence with words, outwit a sword.
Besides, she was dead already; had recklessness and power.
Off the top of her head she answered, and it stuck:

The sword slid from the stone, faced her, gathered its power;
whispered "What's the answer?"—which stuck those short on
    wit and words.
Our hero simply whispered back: "What was the question?"

Duty

GARY GYGAX

ear my tale of truth and mission.

All was within me, and I was all. The serenity of *being* and *not being* pervaded.

"Awaken and be ready."

I heard but did not understand, did my best to fight off the command. The voice was strong: it awakened me, brought suddenly the sense of separation, a pang so intense it cannot be imagined or described. To counter the loss, I sought to return to allness. There was a shield surrounding me. I sensed it, clung to its comforting mass. Beyond that . . . nothingness. Separation.

"Purify your body."

This time I recognized the sound, the voice. I *had* awakened to self, though it was not my desire. "Purify?" Again, I could not understand. Would not.

Strong fires blazed around me. Only once had I felt such pain. Coming after the separation, it was more than I could bear. That which was around me flared into nothingness. Then I was truly alone. No allness. No shield. Only me . . . whatever that was. In my agony I shouted out as loudly as I could.

"It is time."

When I heard that sound, the fire surrounding me disappeared. I no longer felt the licking flames, but the great heat remained. In pain I raged,

"Take the form I command, the shape I work, the power I imbue!"

And as those sounds fell upon me, so did blows. I flared forth my fury. Never would I yield. Blow and blow struck, and I resisted. To no avail. I could feel my form being hammered into some definedness by those blows. With each I was more alone and separated. I controlled my anger, fought back with cold resolve. Then the flames engulfed me again. Pain. Blows. Yielding. How long this continued I do not know. I shall always remember it.

"Be tempered in the athanor."

Worse still that torture.

"Meld with the magick at my command."

And as hammer rang and my form was shaped, that power named did fill me and then I *knew*!

"All is war and chaos in the world of men."

Sound made sense within me. Many things were known to me now, for within me was magickal power. Though I could not speak, I sent forth my response as a pulse of pure thought. "It is no concern of mine. I'm neither a man nor of their world."

At that there was a thought voice that spoke within me, to me, without sound. "You are Caliburnus. You are my tool."

"Am I?" As I shot back the denial, I knew it was useless. Still, I tried.

"You are. Evil reigns. Daily the world of man grows darker. You will reverse this. Watch."

There was no choice. I "saw" for the first time. There was a landscape, what I knew were plants, trees, grass of men's world. I looked from above, then swooped down. A mailed

hand held me. The hand was part of a man in armor and wearing a gaudy surcoat. He rode a horse, his saddle of tooled
leather made beautiful by silver studding and bright velvet at
pommel and cantle. A knight bent on slaughter. I? I was his
sword. That concept was new, but old, old. . . . He called me by
name as he lowered me from on high. "Excalibur!" With that
cry he pointed me at a huge form.

"This is a giant?"

My thought question was answered by the sweet, female
voice of she who had brought me into being. "That it is, Caliburnus. You will meet this one in due course."

Filled with revulsion, I tried to turn away. I was powerless
in this regard, and my effort was nothing. "I am about to take
the life of this one—and it has no wickedness in it!"

"You will and have and no. You are right. The one called
the Giant of Mont Saint Michael is not evil. It is as it is."

"Then I will not pointlessly slay this . . ." Too late. That
portion of my body that was my blade was encased in the soft
stuff of the giant. What men considered hide, tough muscle and
sinew, hard bone too, were nothing to me. Pierce and cut and
slice to the depth of that part of me they called quillions. Darkness. Then red light.

"It is done and will be done, Caliburnus. That is irrevoca-
ble."

The seeing vanished. I was glad. Content to be in darkness
of this sort, sensing as I had been since becoming alone and
separate. "You are hard and cruel," I said in self-pity to that
sweet voice that spoke inside of me.

"That is what you will be called by men who encounter
your edge, feel your tongue."

"Never!" There were great enchantments within me, and I
felt that I could eventually displace her castings and return to
the allness if I tried. Somehow I understood that to place such

powers into me, the makers had been forced to allow *me* to exist. I had will. "You wish me to be a brutal taker of life."

There was no denial of my charge. "Know who I am, Caliburnus."

"You are the fay Viviane. It was you who had the dwarven smiths tear me from the all, beat me into what I am. Yet I sense you are just and not cruel. You love life, not death." The truth of that made me ask, "Why, then?"

"I accept duty, Caliburnus. You must do likewise. Be strong, unyielding. Accept mission and duty, Caliburnus, as you accepted form and temper, edge and point, power and enchantment!"

"You are vile!" This I shrieked as I realized that what I had been shown was but part of my making. I was not yet complete. "No. Never. I will not kill the innocent, end the small and brief being of such pitiful ones as giants and men." Denial was farce. I had already become her tool.

Caresses stroked me, and many words I could not comprehend touched me too. "Not yet a perfect tool, Caliburnus. We have yet a long way to go before you are that," the voice crooned.

As a shadow moved in a far corner of the lofty tower, Viviane spoke without turning to look. "How dare you enter my very castle uninvited and unannounced, cambion?!" Her melodious voice had the ring of iron in it, and her back was stiff. This was scarcely a wonder, for a demon-child spawned of a woman was most dire a thing.

The shadow moved again, coalesced. From the dimness of the inner archway stepped a tall man. "Accept my pardon, sweet lady," he pleaded as his advance carried him to within a pace of her.

Viviane did not turn then either. "Be gone, demonling!"

"Please call me Merlin," the tall man said without force as

his eyes ran lecherously over the form outlined by the pale and rose-gold light of the tower window. "You know I cannot resist you, must be near to you!" His avid stare was indeed that of one besotted. Merlin's large, prominent eyes seemed to grow as big as eggs as their darkly gleaming pupils slid up and down and back again over that form. It was as if a buffoon were mimicking the actions of one totally smitten with lust, though there was no audience to observe the play.

Indeed, Viviane refused to turn and acknowledge his presence thus. "You lie as always, cambion. Must I send you hence?"

"Perhaps you could, Lady Viviane, perhaps you could not. I beg you to hold." Merlin cleared his throat, a nervous, husky sound. "What I said about being in your power was—"

"A lie." The fay cut him short, turned at last as she snapped those two words. The nethercræfter gave a little gasp and almost reeled back when she faced him. It was her beauty that struck him almost physically, caused that reaction, not her words. Merlin made no protest as to what she had said. Viviane continued. "It is your own goatishness that brings you here, your lust that makes you traipse after me as would a dog, cambion."

Merlin's face was pained. "My heritage is no fault of mine, Viviane. None choose their parents. That I was fathered by an incubus is no fault of mine own. Again, I beg you, Fairest of Fays, have at least the mercy to name me by my name."

Viviane let fall a mocking laugh neither sweet nor beautiful. "Ask you that? Nay, *Merlin*, I will fain call you by the name known to mortal men. To give you your true appellation would be to blaspheme. Now, cease this charade. Why came you thus to Pharee and my abode?"

As if he had not heard her scathing insult, Merlin smiled weakly, bowed, and asked, "May I sit?"

"Do as you please in that regard. I will stand."

The high tower room had a couch as well as a reading stand and chair. Merlin ignored the high wooden seat and sprawled on the velvet cushions. "You lie here often," he said then, almost as if whispering a prayer. Viviane's features were perfect even as she scowled. "Will your lechery never cease?"

"Only when I lie with you."

"It is then an endless thing, your lewdness," Viviane countered. "Tell me now what truly drove you to this unforgivable trespass, or I will blast you from this tower. Cambion you are, but in mine own place there is no contesting my power."

Merlin gazed longingly. Viviane was not tall, as slender and fine of bone as any of her kind. All fays are beautiful, but Viviane was such that beside her others of her kind seemed plain. Silken waves were her tresses, crowning her head and falling to her waist, their silvery hue made golden copper by the light. So too her eyes changed with light and mood. When she was lighthearted, Viviane's eyes were as the cloudless summer sky, and when anger moved her, those orbs seemed dark storm clouds, all gray and foreboding. Though her eyes showed no fair promise, the nethercræfter could find no harshness in her face. Viviane's lips were inviting even in the firmness of their resolution, and her set expression could not detract from the softness of her form.

Willowy she was, but full and rounded in all the places a man, or a demonling, desired. From the bodice of her velvet gown rose twin hills of ivory, made whiter still by the deep sapphire of that garment. The swelling beneath the opening at her breast, the silver girdle that wrapped a waist he could circle with his long fingers . . . As Merlin thought that, his hands moved as if so doing, a strange caressing of the air. Then his fingers formed as if to cup her buttocks.

Viviane arched an eyebrow. "Really, old one. You go too far!"

"I have seen you nude," Merlin muttered. His starting eyes

were riveted on her own. Resolution seemed to contest with uncertainty on his craggy face.

"To my everlasting shame," Viviane admitted. "You were ever a sneak and a spy. But this is to no point. You did not venture from the earth to my abode here on Pharee either to plead your love or to rape me. You have some greater and more fell purpose, don't you?"

With a shake of his big head Merlin cleared away the desire that had almost mastered him. He lidded his protuberant eyes, used his clutching fingers to ruffle his close-cropped hair of iron hue, wipe smooth his own countenance. It took but a moment, and then the lust was gone, and mind controlled instinct. "But I do adore you."

"And . . . ?"

"I will have you."

Viviane's face actually softened a little as she said, "Not while I live."

Did she mean that? Merlin wondered, for the sound of her voice was not as hard as the words it spoke. "I will give you all."

"All that you can—which is nothing I lack or want. Come, Merlin, do not fall into a recitation of your usual litany once again. I have ceased naming you cambion, and asked for truth from you. I show you that much favor and more."

"More favor, Queen of all Beauty? Dare I hope . . . ?"

At that Viviane stamped one little foot. "Imbecilic dotard! I grow weary of this. My favor is to withhold my power, to refrain from scourging you with words of power sufficient to send even a demidemon howling in—"

"Enough! Now I speak as you wish." Merlin stood, looked grimly down at the fey princess. "Lady of the Lake."

With a shrug Viviane responded, "So the mortals name me. That is a truth, but not germane."

"Ah, but it is," Merlin rumbled in contradiction. "I have seen into the future."

Viviane took a backward step, put a hand on the chair's high back. "Why do you dare such danger as that?"

"Because of you, Viviane—and now I do not speak of my desire."

"Meaning?"

Merlin watched her for a long moment. When the fay seemed to grow uncomfortable under his stare, Merlin nodded. "You are ill at ease for some reason other than my presence. Well you might be. Your enchantments, Viviane, were not so well shielded as you thought."

"Enchantments? What do you prate of now, cam—"

"Merlin!"

"Merlin. I have cast no unusual dweomers. You are mistaken."

The big eyes of the nethercræfter narrowed, and his chuckle was near-malicious as Merlin waved her words away as if they were gnats. "I am, as you have so often told me, Lady, a prevaricator. Undeniably, I am a skilled liar and a great deceiver too. It is my heritage, of course. But you? Hopeless!"

"Say you so? On what basis? Pharee is a land much removed from the world you have taken as your own, Merlin, and a sphere of great fluxes in magickal forces. Nothing I do can give you so firm a rede as you claim. I deny your charge!" Viviane pointed. "You have offended me beyond all bearing. Go!"

Merlin made no move. Then he smiled a little and relaxed. "I am right. It was you. Now that you have been inconstant to your own avowed principles, Viviane, your power to harm me has waned. I will remain, and we will have further discourse, I think."

Viviane grew deathly pale. She sat down on the chair, and her now-dove-gray eyes seemed almost frightened as she looked at Merlin. "This is impossible."

"I have told you I am the greatest of spell-benders, Viviane, that I would share all my power with you. No boast; yet for all that I was scorned. What could a demonling give a fay already great in magick? Now you see, dear lady. My power reaches to Pharee and beyond." Merlin was swelling as he spoke. He seemed taller, larger, less aged, and far more vigorous. His tone too was vibrant and assured as he continued.

"The forging was not unnoticed, of course. Masked as it was, I felt the forces in play. It caught my attention, so I began to probe for the source of the streams of power that were rushing to fill some reservoir."

With the increase in Merlin came a diminishment in the aura that surrounded Viviane. In a voice that might have belonged to a girl she said, "The forging . . ."

Merlin saw and heard and gloated inwardly. Yet not the smallest exterior sign did he betray. The fay's loss of assurance weakened her. The dampening of energy made it possible for him to accomplish yet more, more than he had hoped for, possibly all he dreamed of! "You are wan, ·dearest Lady Viviane. Pray seat yourself on the couch. No. Do not fear. I shall be satisfied with the chair you now occupy."

When he saw she hesitated, Merlin's confidence was complete. With a snap of his fingers he demonstrated this. With that sound went a mental command that brought instant response. In but the space of a few heartbeats the chamber was filled with sprites and grigs, portunes and various of the brownie and pixie kind. The confused assemblage of servitors was leavened with a handful of ferrishyn warriors in polished plate-bronze armor with glittering weapons at the ready.

"Oh!" Viviane exclaimed, shocked at the summoning. "I . . ."

"Your mistress requires you to fetch a bottle of lilac wine— that made from blossoms picked in the full moon's light, then wrapped in its silvery shadows for a century," the nethercræfter supplied firmly. "As for me, I'll settle for quintessence of lotus. That is all. Be quick!"

"My queen?" ventured a captain of the ferrishyn guards.

Merlin scowled and began a threatening gesture, but Viviane interposed, saying, "It is as the cam—my guest—has commanded. You may leave, all of you."

"Very well, Queen," the soldier grated. With a courtly bow to Viviane and a flash of defiance sent by eye toward Merlin, he led his fellows through the archway and from the chamber. The rest, too, departed, some with a popping noise as they vanished, others darting in flight, hopping, or simply hastening on two legs.

"What can I say?"

With a magnanimous inclination of his head, Merlin instructed, "Nothing, Queen of my Heart. Let us both be silent until the refreshment is brought."

"So be it," the fay said with unaccustomed meekness.

There was not long to wait, of course. Fairy servants are nothing if not quick. Soon a fluted bottle of pearlescent glass and a crystal goblet awaited Viviane's pleasure. As for Merlin there was set before him an ivory flask of the stuff he had commanded, with a thimble-sized cup atop a diminutive stem, all cut from a single ruby so that he might quaff. A pair of sprites delivered those things, went away. There was a moment of complete silence and inaction.

"Enisle, sequester, no fairy pester."

There was again music in Viviane's laughter. "What a dreadful rhyme," she giggled.

"No great poetry, assuredly," Merlin said with little grace, "but the barrier thus invoked is most efficacious, I assure you, lady."

"Of that I am confident," the fay soothed. She took a dainty sip of the wine, turned the sparkling vessel so that the last of the rose-gold sun rays pierced the crystal and sent dancing motes of purple fire upon the marble walls. "This is what I needed, Merlin—and see the marvelous colors that it makes. Is your drink to your satisfaction?"

Merlin took his eyes from the shimmering amethyst lights, poured the inky essence into his own vessel. "It is not poisoned, and it is the quintessence of the ebon sort I wished. What more can one say?"

" 'Thank you, yes, gracious lady.' "

"No. None of that now, Viviane. The time for that is past—though it might come again."

"Ah, I see. You allow your passion to spill forth or stopper it to naught as a spigot is turned."

"Bah! You can beguile me no further. I will see the object you wrought now." As he spoke, he sent forth a probing force to discover the fay's response.

Viviane drank her wine, stood, ran her hands along the curves of her body. "The headiness of the vintage fills me, great wizard. Let us instead see other wonders."

Her swaying walk carried her toward the couch. Merlin nearly forgot his resolve. With a great effort of will he drove all thoughts of her beauty and desirability from his mind. His probe had discovered more information. "The *weapon,* Viviane." Again, he slid forth a tendril of power to spy on her thoughts.

She spun, glaring at him. "You do not love me at all!"

"Love? I can't say. Adore, pine for, lust after, yes. But that is another matter." He had what he wanted. "Let me see this marvelous sword, Viviane, the one you have named Caliburnus."

Although there was no triumph in his voice to reveal how he had just gained such knowledge, Merlin saw that she suspected the means he had used. In a flash Viviane sealed her mind with a searing wave of force. The brightness incinerated the tendrils he had allowed to remain, burned his inner being, but the nethercræfter merely chuckled his grim satisfaction.

"You'll not think it so funny when I . . . I . . ."

"There is no threat from you I now fear, Viviane. You are compromised! Take my word for it, lady. I do not laugh at you, though. My laugh is mirthless, and it concerns fate—yours and mine."

"How so?"

With a sharp motion Merlin tossed back another dram of his drink. "Solace, Fairest Fay, solace," he said by way of explanation as he refilled the ruby cup a third time. "You see, I have in my hand the object of my longing and desire, and I must forgo my heart's desire."

"You can't quaff all of that vile drug you would?"

"Not my literal hand, Viviane. You take my meaning full well. Long have I hungered for you, but . . ."

"But what?"

"I have a duty."

Again Viviane seemed not to understand. "What great duty have you?"

"One that concerns my ward and the world of mortals. This is none of your affair, Queen of Fays." The tall nethercræfter arose, held forth his hands. "Would that I was commanding you into these, but I now require that which I charmed with the third naming. Deliver to me the object, the weapon, the sword, Caliburnus."

The resolution shielding her thoughts still waxed in Viviane. "In evading the truth, Merlin, I was weakened, but not so much as you hope. You say you have a duty? Well so, too, do I adhere to principles and fulfill righteous demands upon me. I defy your command and deny your charm. What you claim is not so. You cannot force compliance."

"Ah, but I can. Caliburnus is the sword's name as you bestowed. Into it you poured such as your kind should not contain. Violence, Viviane, and anger with hatred. The magick you used filled it with a delight for slaughter and a lust for destruction. So much so, indeed, that I scarce knew the source of the power. Now I am certain."

"You are doomed."

"Me?" Merlin laughed. "If this knowledge and that blade are what you speak of, then it is as it is."

"You and yours."

"Me and mine. Must I continue?"

The polished platinum tresses of the fay screened her face, but her voice seemed stronger. "You must. I will not obey you, give willingly."

With agility befitting a youth and a cat-bound, the nethercræfter was upon her. As he grasped Viviane, lifted and turned her to face him, triumph surged through Merlin. His hands trembled with that rush, and his voice shook as if with passion for her. "Caliburnus is undefeatable in combat. Its edge will not be blunted. Its blow cannot be turned. No armor can withstand its bite. No chance will loose it from the wielder's grasp. The one possessing it is sovereign, and all others vassal."

"You do not know all," Viviane whispered.

Still holding her fast, pressing her against himself now, Merlin lowered his head to place his face close to her own. "Do I not? A sword must have a scabbard—as so often I have told you. I would sheathe my own weapon in this instant!" As he spat that, Merlin thrust hard with his loins.

Viviane gave a small shriek, used her little hands to separate herself from his crushing chest. She saw that Merlin's great eyes were filled with near madness, a lust so mixed as to be impossible to define. "No! You win. I will do as you ask of me." Somehow at that instant she slipped from him and was away.

"You think to escape me?" Head reeling, Merlin was still confident. Then Viviane vanished. "This can't be! I wove a mesh to both ward off and restrain . . ." As his words trailed off, the nethercræfter slumped in defeat. Then something made him rebound. It was a faint chiming and a flow of magickal force, which Merlin could feel as others sense the wind's movements. "She complies!"

From nowhere appeared a slender arm holding forth a massive broadsword in a scabbard rich with gold. Merlin seized it instantly, and as he held Caliburnus, Viviane was revealed fully. "It is as you asked." Her lashes were lowered as she spoke softly that surrender.

"Truly a wondrous weapon, Viviane," he remarked, examining sword and case. "Is the protection laid upon scabbard as great as that forged into blade?"

"Never can the one wearing that sword sheath bleed to death, Merlin. The scabbard mitigates all wounds, making great ones small and small none at all." She paused as the nethercræfter drew the sword. When he looked at her questioningly, Viviane told him, "You have read the great magicks of that blade already."

Merlin prodded. "Nothing?"

"Caliburnus cannot be used effectively by anyone save that one to whom I give it—you in this case."

"Hah! I saw that you held back. Yet I still have you at my whim."

"That is so."

Metal rang as Merlin sheathed the sword. "Retain this for a time, Queen Viviane. Later you will bestow it upon another. For now I will have something else of you, fairest of all fays."

"As you restore the weapon to me, Merlin, you shall then have your heart's desire," Viviane admitted. "Willing or no, I must yield to your whims."

The craggy face grew harder. "This is not what I demand!"

"Some things are beyond demanding. This is one, Merlin. You must choose. If you renounce your charmed claim upon Caliburnus, then you may have me. If you require the weapon to be bestowed upon one you name, then we are quits at that instant. Which shall it be?"

The nethercræfter grew livid, gnashed his teeth. It appeared his eyes would start from his head. Merlin managed to control his fury. "You would interfere with my designs for power, Viviane. I see it at last. You thought to trick me, seduce me from my purpose! This one last time I will allow my lust to go unslaked—never again."

"Never again will you have me thus, cambion."

"Merlin! You say so, but I think otherwise. For now it shall be as you uttered. At such time and place as I convey to you, there will you come. You shall bring this sword and its scabbard too. You will then without hesitation or encumbrance deliver both to the one I designate."

The fay inclined her lovely head in acquiescence. "Be it so. Your designate?"

"Arthur."

As Merlin spoke that name, there was a flash and a booming as if a mighty thunderclap had broken overhead. Whether of his own will or perforce from Viviane's own power, the cambion was gone from the tower and from the sphere of Pharee.

So in time the fay, Viviane, carried me forth from her world. Mine own. That place with which I had been one, torn from its allness, shaped into this being I so hated. Duty? Perhaps. Her duty. Mine. What of that duty likewise professed by Merlin? Aye. That is more to the point. My being was wrought through and by Viviane's power, yet the nethercræfter had commanded me from her ken and to his own.

Would I serve? Gladly. I had in the interim between Merlin's visit and Viviane's passage to earth appreciated the difference between existing and being, come to comprehend fully the meaning of duty and my role in that regard. Had there been no such requirement, there would be no individual and sentient "me," only a long vein of magickal mineral melded into the wholeness of the world of the fays. The latter state was desirable, but having volition and specific purpose became tolerable when duty was understood.

I, Caliburnus, never was driven into an anvil of iron and the stone beneath, nor stone alone. That sword was but one forged by a master armorer of the world of men. It was an ordinary weapon, though so ensorceled as to be immovable by anyone not named by Merlin—sorcery ever was his tool. Let it go as this: By freeing that sword, foul Arthur laid claim to kingship.

Such claim by a near-bastard begotten on the wife of another king and championed by a nethercræfter could expect no great acclaim. It was answered with rejections and denials, in fact. It would take more than the act of pulling a gimmicked sword from anvil and stone to perfect Arthur's claim to the throne of all Britain. It required me.

So Merlin sent his message. "On the first day after the dark of the moon be at the gate which lies in the hills near Camelot. Bring the weapon." Viviane stepped from Pharee to the world of men. Beside the tarn that was the portal between the two worlds she presented me as Excalibur. Arthur accepted. Why Excalibur and not Caliburnus? A new name for a new owner, so to speak. Before, I had been the fay's sword. "Will you give me your sword, Lady of the Lake?" Arthur queried. Viviane willingly handed me to him. At that moment I was his. He was mine. There was much we two had to accomplish and but a short time for it.

"Excalibur, eh? Indeed thou seem a noble weapon fit for the deeds of a king." As Arthur said that, I could not control the surge of power that leaped through me as I thought of the duty I would do. This thrill of energy ran to his hand and along the muscular arm. Feeling the rush of magick, Arthur turned and shouted in triumph, "Merlin, this is a sword with which I could slay the world!"

But Arthur was no Pendragon yet. There was no agreement among the nobles and knights of Britain as to Arthur's right to overlordship. Arthur was indeed the child of Uther. Uther the Pendragon king was a physically strong man—weak in all other ways. This I have from the fay, and I know she told me true. And when Merlin allowed Uther to slake his lust to beget Arthur, the nethercræfter likewise demanded and received as payment the charge of that infant. Thus was Merlin assured a pliable twig to shape as he would, a tree bent to his own ends when it was monarch.

But now if he would have Arthur crowned great king, it would be a travesty, for he would be a ruler of but a handful of folk in a corner of the land, and one too weak to take by conquest what he claimed by birthright. A laughable little kinglet quite unsuitable to Merlin's dignity and prestige to "serve," so no such grand coronation was announced. Instead, the nethercræfter held his puppet in check in that part of Britain that acknowledged him as overlord.

Then, to make matters worse for Merlin's machinations, Arthur became enamored of his half sister. She, being as ambitious and unscrupulous as Arthur, encouraged him in his desires. Before long this incestuous carnality was the talk of his own court, all the land. It grew worse as Morgane became great with child. This was unacceptable to Merlin, for his ambition in regard to his ward was far greater than anything either of those two could comprehend.

So the black magician decided it was high time for his puppet to be off to foreign lands. In such places as lay across the channel, Arthur would gain fame to offset his growing infamy at home. Merlin was confident that this ploy would succeed for two reasons. While Arthur was away, the nethercræfter would work to suborn all the weak and ambitious kinglets, lords, and knights, lionizing his candidate in the process through prophecy and magick. Arthur would be safe out of Merlin's sight, for he had me, Excalibur. As a kinglet and knight errant Arthur crossed the water into Gaul, with me and my scabbard belted always at his waist. There he would perform "heroic deeds" to prove his chivalrous worth and valor.

Those words do not accurately describe the actions required in that age in order to be thought of as fit to rule. Heroism most frequently translated to savage brutality, worth to perfidiousness and treacherousness, and valor to ability to kill. The knights and rulers of France and the other lands we traveled were little different from those of Britain. First we confronted and overthrew any number of haughty and homicidal men, who roamed everywhere in practice of their sport of manslaughter and robbery. A typical encounter was thus:

"I will pass," Arthur shouts.

"You shall not," counters a given knightly thug.

The combat was on. First a charge with lance of ashwood, then, if need be, swords. I must give him this much: Arthur was a superb fighter, excellent in the saddle, sure of aim, tough and strong. To survive as a knight, one had to have all of those qualities. Some of the defeated were enlisted to Arthur's cause and sent packing off to Britain. A few fled to safety. Most were slaughtered. In that part it was I who did the execution. It was indeed my duty.

Then, as I knew would happen, near Mont St. Michael, a hapless denizen of Pharee blundered through a portal and found himself trapped on earth. Lost, separated from all he knew, alone, friendless, and hungry, the giant sought to survive as he searched for a way back. He ate what he could find—sheep and cattle. When the locals gathered together to hunt him down and kill him, this forlorn creature defended himself. People died. That giant I slew by Arthur's hand at a single stroke, one that pierced its heart. It was kindness, that blow, for never would he have found his way back. It was also duty; I was the instrument meant to bring fame to Arthur. In men's eyes it was an act of great courage and valor on Arthur's part. The news spread as wildfire through the land. Before our second great triumph it had reached Britain.

After the poor giant we met and bested many knights of the land. In the course of this killing spree Arthur learned of another great challenge. Upon meeting and winning the favors of a damsel, after many vows to help her in her plight by slaying her jealous lover, this woman happened to recount the terrible presence of a savage creature in a neighboring community. Promises forgotten and pledges shattered, Arthur fairly flew from dalliance in her pavilion.

"Wait. Stop! That is the wrong way. You swore you would . . ."

Off we spurred. The pleading turned to curses and threats, faded in the distance.

If I had been revolted at the task of slaying the stupid but basically blameless giant, my next work was recompense. Just as the damsel had related, near Losanne there prowled a demonic cat. This monstrous thing was unnatural, a spirit-created thing of cruelty and evil whose mind was foul. The demon cat of Losanne was indeed a vile netherling, grown to unearthly hugeness by the spirit of the demon who possessed and nurtured it to the fullness of its horror. Ravaging and slaying, the so-called cat terrorized all. Then we found it. How that demon yowled when it felt my bite! Too late the netherling understood that my blade drew not only blood but was fully capable of slaying the spirit too. Of that neither Merlin nor Arthur was aware. In his hubris the cambion thought he had mastered Viviane, divined all there was to know of Caliburnus. So earth was rid of another of the evils that plagued it. A relatively small and singular one, to be sure, but another step in the right direction. It was duty of the sort I had come to accept with relish.

After such knightly slaughter and derring-do, Arthur was sufficiently redeemed to return to Britain. He and I again crossed the Channel, this time in company with a gang of bullies very much to Arthur's liking, his "loyal knights of Gaul." Despite his accomplishments in France, however, there was still a cloud hanging over Arthur's repute.

"I will slay those who say I am not worthy. By God I'll show them who is lord!" Arthur raved. He had the ability to carry out that threat.

Merlin advised him sagaciously. "It will do for you to begin immediately thus: Establishing the supremacy of your crown through fire and sword is to rule unwilling subjects. First, Arthur, you must do a mighty deed here—one greater than that done abroad. Then will all the people believe you their destined overlord."

The nethercræfter had double cause to want his protégé to do what he said. Again I rejoiced. Because there is no accord among demons, Merlin's hegemony through Arthur was no sure thing. Another demonling had taken up residence nearby, and that one would contest with Merlin as did the throng of kinglets with Arthur.

Off to slay that demon being went Merlin's ward. With Arthur rode his ever-swelling band of killers. Despite the counsel of the sorcerer, Arthur subdued as he went—by intimidation of the wise, preferably through bloodshed if he and his men could manage to find some insult or provoke resistance. Soon enough, though, we came to where the foe lurked.

This new fiend was called Twtch Trwyth the boar. We were not far into Wales, and deep in a forest when it attacked. Arthur had not been looking for it, but it found us. In its first rush the thing gutted two horses and slew as well their riders. This savagery shook Arthur. If alone, he would have fled. He could not, for all his knights were there to see. Uttering foul oaths, Arthur dismounted and fought the boar. Of course his spear was useless against a supernatural beast. The point glanced harmlessly from the thing's hairy hide as the shaft splintered.

"By the heavens I'll send you to the pits!" Arthur cried in pain and rage as he scrambled up from that terrific impact. He was wounded, but only a thin seam of blood showed brightly along his thigh where mail had torn under slashing tush. In a sense Arthur was correct.

From the scabbard I came. The demon whose spirit had formed this physical body in the shape of a giant swine came at Arthur. The monster knew not the power working my metal. Its red eyes were alight with the anticipation of slaughter. It thought to string Arthur's bowels round the wood in mockery of Merlin's plans. A single thrust from me ended that. Demonic squeals as it went to destruction were sweeter music to me than had been the howls of the nether-cat.

Imagine, if you can, a demon pleading for mercy. That proves that although a concept is unknown to a mind, it can be articulated nonetheless. Lawyers speaking of honesty as the capstone . . . but I digress. Another strong evil had been expunged, but at what price? Was I not setting up a greater one still in supporting the plans of the demon-spawned Merlin? No. What I had done was a better duty.

So among the people of Wales, Arthur and his knights rode in triumph with the demon-boar's head as trophy. Any man not suitably impressed, willing to submit then and there, was put to the sword. Not my edge! The Welsh, friend or foe, then recognized him as master, but they called him not *gwledig*, for indeed Arthur was no prince. Instead he was acknowledged as *amher-adawr*. He had forced his lordship upon their own princes, so Arthur was indeed emperor, not king.

So Arthur rode through a newly won land in triumph. Such a procession had its rewards, and not only in tribute and willing women. From Wales he traipsed home with a much-enlarged train of warriors. Only when they saw his numbers were the neighboring kinglets sufficiently convinced. They threw their lot in with Arthur, for who could resist both sword and sorcerous counselor behind the throne?

All that followed you know of. It has been distorted, certainly, but recounted. Other kinglets banded together to resist Arthur. Wars were fought. Arthur begot another bastard son, but at least this time not a nephew as well as child. At last, and only after great battles and much killing and slaughter, the whole of the South was under his sway, and Arthur ruled from a mighty stronghold named Camelot. To that place were drawn as flies to a carcass every butcher able to ride a horse, find armor, and slay with brute strength. The most able of such amoral killers and blood-crazed maniacs he knighted as his own. With such a force, none of the remaining monarchs could resist him. They tried and died. Merlin discerned their plans, spread dissension and doubt in their ranks. Then Arthur and his army came and slaughtered what remained.

An unbeatable combination—cambion nethercræfter, clever and charming tyrant, and sword and scabbard to make the instrument of Merlin's ambition invincible. A thousand little villains were slain thus, so that a single great evil could rule all Britain. Yes! I played my part with verve and élan. It was a duty I appreciated more and more as time passed. I knew that the end was near.

"God is not your friend," Merlin cautioned Arthur when the king acted rashly and almost lost his life for want of me. I was never Arthur's friend either, but I served. . . .

Once his empire was established, Arthur gave himself to luxury and sloth. He reveled in the comfort, feasted and drank, had his pick of court "ladies." Camelot became the haven for all that was vile and wanton, the fetes there marvels of degeneracy. Such profligacy, though, demands money. Arthur's kingdom was one of savagery and death, not productivity. Arthur complained, and Merlin pondered. Viviane appeared, used her powers to beguile the nethercræfter who was king-maker and puppeteer. In the years since their last meeting, Merlin had forgotten his resolve and purpose in regard to her. With his old lust rekindled, Merlin became pliable, and soon he was being manipulated by the fay as easily as Merlin himself manipulated Arthur.

It was Viviane who insinuated the idea of a round table in Merlin's mind. Wasn't such a thing, after all, a potent symbol of fertility and increase? Didn't the kingdom cry aloud for those benisons? Merlin spoke, Arthur reacted, and soon the famed table was set in the castle's great hall. The land did begin to prosper. Which of the brutal killers serving the king was paramount? None could say, for their positions were all equal. So they began to quarrel and fight each other for precedence, for without a hierarchy evil is in turmoil.

Merlin recognized that something was amiss, but being so enspelled by Viviane, he could not ascertain what the real problem was. Yet the devious cambion was still able. Launcelot was recruited, and soon he and Arthur were inseparable. No longer was there a question as to which knight was preeminent. Launcelot was the steward of all. With such an efficient killer in charge, order was restored, and none of the others dared revolt. Some went off on quests to escape, others were ordered out. Merlin had managed again to set things back on track.

To counter this, the fay used her magick to make Arthur smitten with Guinevere. Despite Merlin's protests and warnings, his countercastings aimed at removing the enchantments Viviane had layed, Arthur persisted. He wed the princess, and soon Guinevere worked her own evils upon the court. She cuckolded the king so repeatedly with Launcelot that eventually even Arthur could not bear the ridicule any longer. He sent away his right arm, Launcelot, and retained the viper at his breast. Later, when Guinevere betrayed him again, this time with Modred, his own vile son and staunchest enemy, Arthur finally rid himself of the slut. It was then far too late—but again I run ahead.

Just after the time of Launcelot's exile, Viviane played her greatest role. She came and stayed at Camelot, pretended to be one of the wantons who filled the place because of its power and license. Assassination and killing, kidnap and rape, were common in the court. None thought it unusual or questioned the morality of it. Seeing her thus there among the tumult, Merlin thought that the fay had at last resigned her true principles in favor of wickedness. He courted her, was rebuffed, and wooed still more ardently. Even Arthur and some of the others there saw the danger and warned him, but the nethercræfter was deaf to such. He lost all caution and promised Viviane anything she would have of him.

What occurred thereafter is legendary and essentially factual. Viviane demanded that the demon-spawned nethercræfter create an absolutely inviolate place for them if there was to be a tryst. Merlin opened a portal into a space sometimes called interdimensional inconceivability. Such a tiny pocket of created space can be entered and exited only with a magickal "key" of some sort. To entice her in, Merlin gave the key to his own bit of creation to Viviane. He then compounded his error by entering first.

Viviane shut fast the door, destroyed the key, and walked away. The "rock" of legend is an infinitesimal speck in an infinite cosmos. Before such eternity passes as probability dictates necessary for chance to fashion a second key to that place, even the mighty cambion called Merlin will be dust.

Other fays could then be brought from Pharee to assist in the struggle. Without Merlin to counter them, they came and played a useful part in the work. Many distortions of this time have made the history seem impossible. Damsels of strange sort doing this and that, and even the "Lady of the Lake" beheaded by Balin. Balin did indeed slay a hapless fay, but not Viviane. It was one of the brave ones assisting her that was brutally decapitated by that insane knight there in Camelot. After that occurred, Viviane was wracked by sorrow and guilt. She spoke to me of this, and I reassured her. This was a just war, and the risk was accepted by all who fought against evil. To assure that the sacrifice would not be in vain, we then combined our powers, The last act was ready to be played out.

Not that all of our aims succeeded. Viviane would have had Arthur slain far sooner, contrived to have Morgane steal me and have one of her lovers slay the King thus. Morgane had been cultivated to the extent that because she was constantly seen with Viviane and others of her kind, she was sometimes labeled "le Fay" herself. Arthur's sister thought her own devices better than those told to her by Viviane. Instead of convincing Arthur to give me to her, Morgane stole my scabbard and me. My powers were not fully effective. Arthur survived, and the would-be assassin died. When Viviane aided Morgane to escape from the wrath of her brother, it was time for my scabbard to be "lost."

With his chief henchman banished and Merlin gone, all semblance of order lost, and discredited in the eyes of all who were good, Arthur was doomed. Yet the kingdom would be maintained and persist for far too long despite such losses. After all, the most successful killers were marshaled to Arthur's cause there in Camelot. The breakdown of the empire would be slow, bloody, and filled with mounting distress for the decent nobles and common people too. Arthur saw things going awry and blamed the folk, not himself.

To hasten the end, Viviane sent a vision to Gawain, her "dream" taking the form of Merlin to give it credibility in that knight's mind. The sending spoke of imagined marvels and fictitious relics—one in particular. Gawain rushed back to tell of his communication from the lost wizard. Soon the idea of an object that had brought peace and prosperity for a while, one lost through sinfulness, was in the minds of all in Camelot. That such a notion could be pervasive in such degenerates seems unlikely; still it was so. One night when all of the assembled warriors were replete with gorging and deep in their cups, the King's nephew made a drunken vow.

"Be damned if I won't quest for this Sangreal for a year and a day!" Gawain boasted at the top of his voice.

"Shut up, you bloody fool!" Arthur said to him, trying not to let the rest hear.

"Who's with me, you lot? Are you all cowards?"

Arthur protested loudly then, calling them fools. But his best warriors ignored him, rode off in quest of an imaginary thing, the Sangreal. They dispersed, killed and were killed, and none of them returned. I was glad.

With the most able of the homicidal maniacs called the Knights of the Round Table gone, Modred rebelled. Long had his mother, Morgane, encouraged him. She desired final revenge on her brother and power for herself. No wronged woman she, but a malign and ambitious conniver of the same stamp as her half brother. Modred raised a great host, was likely to prevail.

Arthur, in desperation, sent word to all of his old band to come to his aid. Even the exiled Launcelot was forgiven if he would return and fight on the King's behalf. A considerable force marshaled in Camelot and set forth for the final battle. Arthur must fight against Modred. The last great champions of evil were there with Arthur—all save Modred and Morgane; theirs was a larger mob of less able and dedicated killers and scum.

The epic struggle between father and son was dreaded by all who could reason beyond their own mad desires. The kingdom was collapsing around them. Even Arthur and Modred realized it. Both had a premonition, knew that they were about to undo all the wickedness they had built. Perhaps then one or even both of the brutes realized to what extent they had been manipulated. Much to the surprise of some who thought that the opposing forces would engage and die as mad dogs fighting each other, Arthur called for a truce. Modred agreed, and the pair, each with a body of knightly guardsmen, met between the battle arrays. They spoke of what I mentioned, how their fight would tear down all that they had hoped for and change the age.

"Let us avoid this fight, Modred," Arthur urged. "There is enough to share between us—and when I die, I will name you my heir, king and emperor of all."

"That will never satisfy the bitch who is your sister and my mother," Modred rejoined.

Arthur laughed with some grim satisfaction. "Who is to be ruler of the land, then, Modred? You or Morgane? If you cannot silence her by some means—as I did Guinevere—then . . ."

The hanging words were seized by his ruthless son. "Of course, Father, kill her! That I will do of certes, for I, unlike her, trust none other to manage such a deed properly."

"Then is it agreed between us?"

Modred struck Arthur's open hand with his own. "Done and sworn to! I am again your faithful vassal, King of the North, an' you proclaim me your rightful heir *at that moment.*"

The two stood eyeing each other. Each suspected the other, and both were right. Still, the need was great, and it was Arthur who acted to resolve the dilemma of potential treachery. "I will do that here, now."

Modred smiled, for it allayed his fears too. His father worried about assassination, Modred of denunciation, imprisonment, and execution. The fourteen warriors each had in train heard this exchange and were exultant. Their lives were spared, corruption could continue unabated. At an order from Arthur wine was flowing in celebration of the vile accord.

Neither man had considered me. The magickal scabbard

that had supposedly been thrown into a lake by the fleeing Morgane had never been far from me. How could it? It was part of that which was *I*. Arthur wore me to the field to confront Modred; I, Excalibur, summoned that scabbard. It was changed now by the power in me, that magick placed there by Viviane but enhanced by my own will.

No scabbard but an adder, and as one of Arthur's lackeys went to fetch more drink for him and his bastard heir, I caused that seeming snake to strike. When its fangs threatened the knight, he drew his sword. That was a signal for both camps. Not knowing their masters had made a compact, the hosts of Arthur and Modred charged into battle.

The rest is hardly worth recounting. In the final moments, though, Arthur realized that I, "his sword" Excalibur, was the instrument of his undoing. He meant to destroy me, even spurned me and attacked Modred with a spear rather than touch my grip. He must have known that I would have turned in his hand and slain him personally. As it was, before he died, Arthur had me thrown into the deepest and most remote fen pool that he knew of. It was not to return me to the Lady of the Lake, Viviane. He meant to make the world safe for those of evil.

So each monster slain and each magickal charm broken by means of my being not only rid the earth of one more evil but also closed a portal between this world and another. The chaos between beliefs opened many such ways between worlds. Most were gateways to wicked spheres. At the last, most of the portals, all that I might hope to pass through, were shut between earth and Pharee. I am now an exile from my own place, and I long for it, but I did my duty.

Because men are what they are, facts become confused, stories change with each telling, and motives are lost in legend. This is why I have told my story. I can no longer bear the distortion of truth. Yes, a sword, *me,* born Caliburnus and renamed Excalibur, tells you the truth of that which occurred so long ago.

Now I feel the disbelief and anger coming to me where I am concealed. Attend me a little more. The cosmos is one of infinite space and endless time. It is thus one place and many, and all that can happen has, is, or will occur in due course. As the old gods of earth were rejected, grew weak and withered, no strong new one stepped into their place. That takes time. Between the ending of the old and the beginning of the new, chaos flourishes.

Think of it as a garden untended. Flowers die, weeds spring up and choke the once-tended plot of land. The rank growth remains until cleared away. Thereafter the next gardener plants the new blossoms-to-be and cares for them. The weeds are evils. I, Excalibur, was then a sickle and pruning hook. Thus in the welter that followed the loss of the old ones, evil crept into the land. Although it was small and isolated and weak at first, given a few years' time to burgeon and spread, the vileness flourished.

Prior to the turbulent time into which Arthur was born, potent ones of many spheres could manage to open a portal from one or another place to this earth. That is also true of Pharee. Earth's legendary tales say such entrances are under a rock, in a cairn ringed with stones, a grotto, even the so-called fairy ring. Underground, too, is the supposed location of the place to which such a way leads, but in truth these portals often cross universes. As order dies and chaos spreads, the wild energies of magick grow. Earth is not now a place for such power. The work Viviane did was to right the imbalance: shut off the dangerous spheres from the weak and vulnerable world of earth.

Now consider all that you have learned, think of the very legends. All acknowledge that Merlin was the son of a demon. In fact, of the many faces evil wore in that time, Merlin was the worst, for he seemed otherwise to the just—commanded the wicked.

The three "ladies" or "fairies" attending the birth of Arthur were malign minions too. They are echoed in the history of Macbeth, were in fact the same three witches who cursed that evil man to do what he did. These three, too, gave the infant "gifts" so that with Merlin's training and help Arthur became a selfish and wicked man able to gather many followers—likewise arrogant, selfish, and homicidal workers of all manner of unimaginable evils. This brutish and maniacal force of knights Arthur wielded in bloody fashion to build his empire.

My *duty* was to encourage that, to build up Arthur so that he could indeed send them forth and destroy weaker evil groups, as he had fought single evil opponents. The greater evil then destroyed the lessers, chaos was checked, and eventually the defeat of evil was accomplished. Distasteful duty, but worth the price. It rid for a time the world—your own world—of the corruption that was flourishing. That was my duty, and I performed it to the end.

Arthur failed to destroy me, of course. No water anywhere can imprison me. The powers placed in me by the fay, Viviane, that which made me what I am, go far beyond that. Exile I am, but no mere sword and scabbard. That was my form then. With the death of Arthur I changed. It is neither Merlin nor Arthur who sleep awaiting a time of need. It is I, Caliburnus, who lie hidden in your world. Thus for a time I meld into the oneness of this sphere and dream dreams of Pharee. Then the power of evil stirs. Its writhing awakens me. I am here to do my sworn duty. Not as a sword, surely, but still as an instrument of undoing for the wicked and a bringer of justice for the oppressed. Perhaps you will recognize me for what I am when next the need arises and I appear again. If you do so, speak not of it, but do your duty.

The Epilogue of the Sword

DARRELL SCHWEITZER

t was long after compline, but still the monk prayed in his cell by moonlight. For over a year now he had beseeched God, and fasted, and scourged himself, that his soul might be cleansed. He dared hope that it might. Therefore, on his knees once more, though his health failed and he had withered into a mere skeleton of the mighty man he once was, he begged Jesus Christ in His infinite mercy to admit one more sinner into the remotest, humblest border march of the kingdom of Heaven, after, perhaps, a thousand times a thousand years' sojourn in fiery Purgatory.

Nothing more did the monk dare ask, or imagine, or expect.

Certainly not visitors.

Certainly not miraculous apparitions.

He let out a cry of fright and amazement when he heard the footstep and turned around, because he *was* afraid and equally amazed that he of all men, who had once been the most perfect knight in the world and unhesitant about saying so, should know fear.

But he did, and his eyes widened in terror as the lady clad all in white came into his tiny room. Her face was closely veiled, and there was a light about her, more than reflected moonlight, as if her garments and her person burned with ethereal flame.

"You are sent by the Devil!" He crossed himself and whispered a desperate prayer, but she did not vanish.

"No, I am not," she said calmly.

Surely this was a new torment and temptation, for he *knew* that voice, and, at the sound of it, wept, groveling at her feet, his whole body shaking.

"Rise," she said. "Remember who you are."

"I am the most miserable of sinners!"

"Then remember who you *were*. Get up. Come with me out of this place, for the world has need of you yet."

"I have forsaken the world. This much I have sworn, and to break my oath would leave me false and recreant."

"You are *commanded*," she said, and he knew that he must obey, though his soul be damned for it. He had never been able to refuse that voice when it commanded.

So he stood up unsteadily and followed her, padding barefoot along the stone corridor, past doorless cells and snoring monks, shivering in his thin robe as he and the lady emerged outside. In the full moonlight, she seemed almost transparent, a wraith. She cast no shadow.

He turned, in hopeless longing, toward the chapel, but she took him by the hand and led him on his way. Her touch was cold, yet burning, and his fear grew all the greater. He wanted to cry out to his brother monks, but somehow he knew it would do no good. They lay in an enchanted sleep. He was certain of that, as he was certain this was the beginning of an adventure, and he knew how adventures began.

He remembered so many of them. He tried to think on the Jesus Christ and His Virgin Mother. He tried to pray: *Have mercy on me, O Lord, a sinner.* But his concentration faltered, his mind overflowing with memories of battles, of men shouting and dying, of raucous feasts and the telling of tales, of chivalrous quests, and of the greatest of kings, now dead, whom he had once served and loved and finally betrayed.

He remembered who he was, to the very last, terrible detail. Everything.

"I have been mad before," he said aloud. "I roamed the hills like a beast, naked and insane, grazing on grasses. I think I am becoming mad again. May God save me."

"No," said the lady gently, "you have never been more sane."

They passed through a dark forest and came to the edge of a lake, where mist rose into the moonlight like smoke. Far out across the water, a ship drifted toward them, its raised prow and motionless sails like the beak and wings of some great bird.

Once more he crossed himself, but he was having trouble finding the words to any prayer. This new apparition did not vanish either. Quite possibly it contained his death, but he remembered now how he had always scorned death, and so he stood firmly at the water's edge, his arms folded across his thin chest, awaiting what might befall.

As the ship drew nearer, he saw three veiled queens standing on the deck, and serving them, and guiding the vessel, were many knights, their armor dented and smeared with blood, their bodies torn, gaping with wounds. Yet still they walked, and served, and each knight wore his visor lowered, that none could see his face.

The White Lady motioned, and the monk who had himself been a knight followed her into the ship. Confidently, he moved among the company there, nodding to the knights—who stank of death; but he knew the odors of blood and dead flesh well, and almost relished them—and he knelt before the three queens, proudly, as a knight bends his knee, not like a suppliant.

He had once cast off his old life like a bloodstained, tattered cloak, and now, somehow, it had fallen back onto his
shoulders.

"Stand up, brave champion," said the first queen.

"You are welcome in our sight," said the second.

"Remain with us forever," said the third.

He wanted to reply that there is no *forever* here on this
Earth of sorrows, that eternity is in Heaven or in Hell, but he
did not. Courtesy silenced him. A knight does not argue with a
lady, much less a queen. Silent then, he stood with those four in
the prow as the ship glided on, propelled by some invisible
force other than the wind.

The mists parted before them like curtains. Brilliant moonlight shone down, so dazzling as it reflected off the water that
he had to raise his hand to shield his eyes.

When he lowered it again, the water rippled. He thought
that a mere trick of the light. But an expectant gasp rose from
the company around him. The White Lady held his hand in her
firm, chill grip. The surface of the lake broke, and an arm rose
up, holding a jeweled sword in a richly decorated sheath.

At the sight of this he broke away from the lady and fell
once more to his knees, crying out to God, pounding on the
deck with his fists.

"No. I don't want it. I am not worthy. Sweet Christ, don't
let it be for me."

But the White Lady again commanded him, "Take the
sword that was King Arthur's. Take Excalibur for your own.
Take it!"

"Christ, have mercy. Lord, have mercy—"

"Perhaps he shall, in time. Be comforted."

"How can an unholy thing console me?"

"I have already told you I am not from the Devil."

He looked straight into her hidden face. "Are you sent by
God, then? Can you say that, and swear it?"

She did not reply, but merely pointed. Another command.

He lowered himself over the side of the ship, onto the surface of the lake, which was as cold beneath his feet as a marble floor in winter, but, impossibly, as firm. It held him up. He walked on water until he came to where a woman's arm, clothed in samite, held the sword aloft. He knelt down and took the sword in both hands. The arm vanished like a burst bubble.

Weeping, his eyes tightly closed, he clutched the sword to himself, trembling, there on the surface of the lake.

When he opened his eyes again, the ship and the ladies were gone, and he hoped, for just an instant, that all these things had been dreamed, that he had merely wandered away in a restless sleep and now knelt in a mist-covered meadow.

Yet he still held the sword. And when he reached down, he felt the water.

A horse snorted nearby. He looked up and beheld a white stallion stamping impatiently in the mist. The bridle, saddle, and trappings were those of a knightly steed. Slung over the saddle, armor, lance, and shield gleamed silver in the moonlight.

He knew what he had to do. He armed himself, his fingers remembering every task from long familiarity. Then he climbed astride the stallion and was off, galloping into the mist across the surface of the lake, glancing back once to see the shoreline receding and the creature's hooves trailing sparks behind on the water.

Every sensation came as an intense pleasure now, the motion of the horse's muscles between his thighs, the weight of the armor on his back and the shield on his arm, the wind as it washed over his face and whistled around his ears through the slits in his helmet. It seemed he rode for many miles, through a strange country of moonlight and mist and muted fire, and that far ahead, at a distance only an eagle should have been able to make out, another knight all clad in black and red charged toward him, spear lowered.

He lowered his own spear and shouted a war cry, in exaltation. It was as if he had only truly *awakened* just now, for the first time in a very long while, as if he had been buried alive in some dream until this very instant. All sorrows, all grief, fell away. He was the pure warrior now, lusting for glory and the clash of arms. Even his wasted body seemed to fill out. He felt his strength return, like wine poured into an empty skin.

Up close, the enemy was clearly no mortal knight. Flames streamed from beneath the black visor. Huge, dark wings flapped from his shoulders. His surcoat seemed almost to glow, a brilliant red, like spurting blood, bright against black armor. And on his shield, a screaming, lunatic face, a wild-eyed demon perhaps—

There was no time to wonder. The two of them crashed together, spears splintering, horses shrieking and reeling back.

He struggled with the reins, righting himself, then turned and saw his enemy turning. Excalibur flashed forth from its scabbard like lightning. He felt its power coursing through his whole body. Frenzied, invincible, he struck at the enemy's shield and clove it in twain. Another blow, and the rest of the shield and the arm that held it went hurling into the mist, streaming fire.

Yet the enemy fought on, and the blows of combat echoed like the sound of smiths pounding on anvils. The enemy's steed faltered, then fell, but the monster-thing leaped into the air on its outspread wings, its voice screaming incomprehensible words in what must have been the language of Hell.

Down the creature swooped, and tore away his own shield, but Excalibur struck, cutting off half a wing. The demon fell, fluttering, and the knight trampled it beneath his horse's hooves.

But before it died, the abomination spoke clearly, in the

British tongue, saying, "Too late, champion. Too late. My brethren have triumphed. King Constantine of the Britons lies wounded unto death. His forces flee before the pagans. And so, I return to my master in Hell, laughing!"

Furiously, the knight struck again with Excalibur, but cut through only mist and smoke.

Now he galloped up onto the land, never ceasing, along roads and bridges, through dark forests and ruined towns, across charred fields, he and his steed never weary. It seemed they outraced the hours, that the moon moved backward in the sky and that that single night would never end.

More than once he thought he heard the White Lady urging him on, commanding him. Visions led him. Memories. Waking dreams.

At last he did pause, but only for an instant, atop a hill, looking down into a valley where a battle neared its conclusion. British knights and footmen fell back before Saxon foes. The shouts and screams were like a raging sea. Across the valley, on an opposite hill, holy monks had gathered. A silver cross rose above them like a legionary standard. But panicked warriors receded around them like a tide. Then the cross fell. A despairing cry went up from the Britons. The retreat became a rout. The slaughter was very great.

Once more he drew Excalibur forth from its sheath, and shouted his war cry, and thundered into the fray.

The Saxon infantry turned, astonished. He reaped their heads like wheat. Spears and arrows glanced harmlessly from his armor. Mounted Saxons drew together to challenge him, but he overthrew them all, dealing their king such a deadly blow that the sword passed all the way through his body and killed his horse also.

He gained the opposite hill, galloping up the slope, trampling or cutting down those Saxons who tried to defile the fallen silver cross with their touch. He dismounted and took up the cross.

Breathing hard, triumphant, he held the great silver cross and the sword Excalibur aloft for all to see, even as Moses gave the Israelites victory over the hosts of Amalec by holding up his staff in his hands. But no one had to assist this knight. No Aaron and Hur were required to take hold of his arms. His strength did not fail him.

The Britons rallied, praising God, making bloody harvest of their foes, until not one pagan was left alive on the field. Only a few managed to flee.

Then, shouting and laughing and singing songs of praise, the Britons led their deliverer from that place, all the while repeating and marveling over the deeds of that single hour. Their voices were like chattering birds.

And the knight who had once been a monk gloried in their adulation. He gave the silver cross over to a priest, but clasped Excalibur all the more firmly.

When they came to the cottage where the British king lay, all the voices fell silent, for within Constantine, Cador's son, a good man but hardly a great one, and no sort of hero, lay dying.

Lowering his head, the champion entered the rude cottage. He removed his helmet, and knelt before the King, resting his hands on Excalibur.

King Constantine, who was Arthur's successor, turned on his bed of straw, bleeding from many wounds, his face drawn and pale. His eyes widened.

"So, it is really *you*." The king raised himself, groaning at the effort, coughing blood. "So, everything they have told me is true. You *are* Sir Lancelot, returned from the dead."

"My Lord, I have never been more alive."

"And you bear *Arthur's* sword. I know it. I saw it before, many times."

"As did I, My Liege."

"But now that *you* bear the sword, it must be the will of God that I should die and you be king after me, for the salvation of the land. Who would have thought it? I don't know. I never would have imagined . . . how very strange . . ." The king sank down again in delirium, muttering.

Britons crowded into the tiny cottage, kneeling around Sir Lancelot, whispering, "Yes, yes, it *is* he. We know him. Yes."

"I am indeed Lancelot." He rose to his feet.

Knights and common folk alike stood up, the press of their numbers ushering him away, leaving King Constantine lying forlorn and neglected by all.

Outside, hundreds more gathered. A cheer went up. "*You* are our one king! Lead us! Lead us!"

Lancelot trembled, falling once more to his knees, almost as if he had been dealt a blow that staggered him. Someone went running for Constantine's crown. A bishop was found among the surviving clerics. This man held the crown over Lancelot's head and began to intone in Latin.

Then another voice spoke. No one else seemed to hear it. The White Lady cried out, "Lancelot du Lac, most perfect of knights, remember who you have been and who you are!"

The memory pierced him like a spear. He gasped in the sudden pain of it. His sins came back to him, every one, how he had been so proud of his own undeniable perfection in knightly prowess that he would have lost his soul, how he had betrayed King Arthur, committed adultery with Guinevere, and almost frivolously slain the brothers of Sir Gawaine, causing even that brave knight's death in the end. All the wrack and ruin of this land was his own fault and no other's.

He looked around for the White Lady, but she was not there. He saw only smiling, slightly puzzled Britons.

Then he stood up suddenly, brushing aside the crown and the astonished bishop.

"I am not worthy."

"But . . . but . . ." The man made ridiculous fluttering motions in the air with his hands. "But . . . a little humility is sometimes appropriate, but . . . *you have the sword!*"

"You have the sword!" shouted the onlookers. "You must be king!"

"Think. Riches, power, women," a knight whispered in his ear. "Everything could be yours. Any of us would kill for that—"

"Or sell your souls?" asked Lancelot sadly.

"Or sell our souls—"

He shoved the knight aside. "Then get behind me!"

"Our king!" shouted the crowd, alarmed.

Lancelot snatched up the crown and walked back into the cottage. The others followed at a distance, whispering among themselves, "What's he doing? Has he gone mad again? How can this be? God forbid it."

But they were silent as Lancelot knelt once more before King Constantine and gently placed the crown on the wounded man's head.

Then he prayed as he never had before even in the frenzy of his first repentance, begging God that if any trace of his much-touted knightly perfection remained, that he be permitted, though he was entirely unworthy, to perform one *last* miracle, even as he had, once before, been allowed to miraculously cure Urras, King of Hungary, though his soul was already stained at that point by many grievous sins. *Now,* he asked. *One more.* To set things right.

It was the White Lady who answered him. He heard her speaking to him clearly, as if she were in the room with him. "Sheathe the sword," she said, "and search out the King's wounds with your hands." This he did, and his fingers were soon coated with blood, but everywhere he touched, the flesh was healed and the wounds closed.

And Lancelot wept abjectly, as he had that time before, like a child who has been beaten.

All who witnessed this fell to their knees in silence, nor did they question or challenge Lancelot as he rose and strode out of the cottage. The crowd parted like a sea.

He mounted his horse and rode into the night, chasing the setting moon, the wind roaring around his ears, whispering, *Don't be a fool! You could be king! King! You still have the sword!*

"Get behind me, Satan!" he shouted, his voice trailing through the night, and he wept, and perhaps he was mad again. Visions came. He thought he charged through Hell, making war on demons, scattering them with the sweep of Excalibur; and he thought he was in Camelot, but the lords and ladies fled from him in terror; and he thought, at last, that he had no horse anymore, that his armor had become as smoke and drifted away, and that he was a barefoot, emaciated monk in a thin and ragged robe. He staggered breathlessly through the mud at the edge of a lake, holding a jeweled sword and scabbard aloft like the rod Moses held up when the Jews fought the Amalecites.

But he wasn't fighting anyone. Only himself.

He was certain he was mad when he saw the lady veiled and dressed in white, and when she spoke in a voice he could never forget, saying, "You could be king. You still have the sword."

"No, I don't!" He hurled it away with all his remaining strength, and watched it twirling over the water in the moonlight. A hand rose from the lake, caught the sword, and sank down out of sight.

He waded out a little ways to see where the sword had gone, but beheld only the waters lap and the waves roll.

Thigh-deep in the frigid water, he turned and said, "Is it all a dream now?"

"No," said the lady, "for by this adventure are God's many

purposes served. King Constantine is granted a reprieve, and you, though a sinner, are weighed and tested and found pleasing to the Lord. I can tell you no more than that. Let it be enough."

He splashed toward her. "It is more than enough, but now I beg you, raise your veil, just for an instant, that I may see that beloved face one last time—"

"No," she said softly. "That may I never do, but always abstain. Think instead on a purer and fairer Lady, who reigns above us all."

Then she was gone, and he knelt in the water, praying and weeping and beating on his breast. So his brother monks found him at dawn's first light, thinking he had wandered abroad in his troubled sleep, as sometimes he did.

Only much later did word come that on that very night King Constantine had been wounded unto death, but miraculously restored and given victory by a mysterious champion, whom some said was Sir Lancelot returned, or even Arthur himself, back from the dead.

Further, there was a curious story whispered about, that on the same night the holy nun who had once been Queen Guinevere—she who was forever veiled and dressed in white—fell into a swoon and spoke as if to many unseen persons, and even called out the name of Lancelot.

When she died, Lancelot sang the mass for her. He had become a priest by then. He emerged from his cell to bury her by her husband's side and pray at her tomb, but he did not emerge, men say, ever again.